DYING FOR
CHRISTMAS

DYING FOR
CHRISTMAS

TAMMY COHEN

PEGASUS CRIME

NEW YORK LONDON

DYING FOR CHRISTMAS

Pegasus Books Ltd
148 West 37th Street, 13th Fl.
New York, NY 10018

American copyright © 2016 by Tammy Cohen

First Pegasus Books hardcover edition November 2016

ISBN: 978-1-68177-261-5

10 9 8 7 6 5 4 3 2 1

Printed in the United States of America
Distributed by W. W. Norton & Company, Inc.

Once again, for my amazing mum,
Elizabeth Gaynor Cohen

PART ONE

PART ONE

ONE

Chances are, by the time you finish reading this, I'll already be dead.

Three interesting things about me. Well, I'm twenty-nine years old, I'm phobic about buttons. Oh yes, and I'm dying. Not as in I've got two years to live, but hey, here's a list of things I want to cram into the time I have left. No, I'm dying right here and now.

In a sense, you are reading a snuff book.

So, why did I go along with it? That's a tricky one, that question of motivation. Maybe it's because I was caught up in the Christmas spirit and feeling kindly disposed. He told me I was beautiful.

Also, it didn't hurt that he was handsome. He looked a bit like that guy from *Silver Linings Playbook*, the one who always plays nut jobs. Maybe that should have given me a bit of a clue.

Oh well, you live and learn.

Except in my case only one of those is true.

I was in the café of a department store on Oxford Street. I'd been Christmas shopping for four hours by then. Normally

I avoided in-store cafés – so claustrophic, and always someone with a buggy blocking the way, and someone else in the world's biggest wheelchair. But it was sleeting outside and I had all these bags.

I managed to find a table which, considering it was Christmas Eve, was no mean feat. I set my cappuccino down and tried to fit all my bags around me. One had to go on the table itself. It contained a toy I'd bought for one of my nephews. When I placed it on the table, it lowed like a cow. By that point I was well into that stage of Christmas shopping where you look at your purchases and know beyond any doubt that not one of them is right and the only solution is to buy more.

So I was already feeling harassed when he approached.

'Can I sit here?'

I shrugged without looking up.

'Sorry. It's just so packed in here. Seems like you'd have to sell a kidney or something to get a table.'

Then I did look up.

First impressions: blue, blue eyes.

Slightly too close together, but that was almost a relief because without that his face would have been so film-star perfect no one could ever have taken him seriously. Strong, straight nose. Brown wavy hair swept back from his face. Dimple in one cheek, near the mouth. Chin slightly cleft, just so it lent that edge of masculinity.

Men who look like that don't exist in my life. Not in 3D form anyway.

I stared down at my cappuccino like it might be trying to tell me something and wished I'd brought a book. His presence across the tiny table was an elephant sitting on my chest.

'You've been Christmas shopping I see.'

No shit, Sherlock.

Except I didn't actually say that. What I actually said was: 'Yeah, well, I put it off as long as I could.'

And that's when he said it. 'You know, you're very beautiful.'

Like I said: hand, meet putty.

There was an awkward silence. I took a sip of cappuccino and then couldn't swallow it in case the noise deafened us both.

'I'm sorry if I keep staring at you,' he said, and my eyes flicked up to find his boring right into me. 'It's just you remind me of someone.'

I focused on him, forcing myself to hold his gaze by pressing my nails into the palm of my left hand under the table. It's a distraction technique. It distracted me from thinking about the awkwardness of this whole situation, and the fact that as someone technically in a relationship, I shouldn't really have been encouraging this conversation. Or noticing the colour of his eyes.

'Really?' I said. 'I hardly ever remind people of other people. Although someone did once say I looked like Daisy the kitchen maid in *Downton Abbey*, but I think that was because I was wearing an apron at the time, and he thought it was funny.'

I ramble when I'm nervous.

He smiled, and the dimple in his cheek was like a cave inviting me in.

'You remind me of my wife,' he said, and he stirred the spoon around in the glass mug in front of him, releasing clouds of something green and herbal into the clear water. 'Actually, I haven't seen her in months so she's probably my soon-to-be ex-wife. She looks just like you. In fact, when I saw you earlier walking along Oxford Street, I thought for a mad moment you really were her. That's why I followed you.'

'You followed me into the shop?'

He was beaming, as if he'd done something clever.

'Through the Glove and Scarf department? And Toys and . . .' My face suddenly blazed, recalling my prolonged foray into Lingerie.

'Yep,' he agreed. 'It was just so uncanny, you see. And then when you came in here and sat down, I thought, "Here's my chance."'

I nodded calmly. As though strange men were forever following me into department stores off the street.

'I hope you don't mind. I'm not some crazed axe-murderer, I promise.'

If there was a noise then, like a snort in my ear, I instantly blocked it out.

'You look like you're shopping for an army.' He indicated the bags all around our feet.

'Oh, just family,' I said, conveniently leaving out Travis.

Not that my family is particularly good at presents.

Last Christmas, my parents bought me six sessions with a therapist. My mother had even mocked up a proper gift voucher on the computer: *This voucher entitles the bearer to six sessions with Sonia Rubenstein.* It was tucked inside a card that had a glitter snowglobe on the front with tiny children throwing snowballs trapped inside.

'It's not that we think there's something wrong with you,' Mum said, scanning my face anxiously as I examined the voucher. 'We just want you to be the best you can be.'

'But what if this is my best me?'

My dad laughed then as if I'd made a joke. 'Then God help us,' he said.

I'd told myself I wouldn't go on principle, but of course I did. And when the six sessions were up, I booked six more, and more after that. What, turn down the chance to talk about myself for fifty-five minutes a week? I'd have to be nuts.

The stranger across the table was saying something.

'How about you?' he repeated. 'Any significant others?'

Travis' face came into my head and again I blotted him out.

'More like a few insignificant ones.'

'Come on. Don't tell me someone as lovely as you has no one special. There must be someone, surely? Someone to buy Christmas presents for that don't come in a last-minute job lot from John Lewis?'

I thought about Travis and how in our first year together he'd bought me a £5.99 bottle of Sauvignon Blanc on his way over on Christmas Day and given it to me wrapped in a corner-shop plastic bag with the price sticker still on.

'I know you don't really approve of Christmas,' he'd said, and I'd hidden the cashmere jumper I'd bought him behind the sofa.

'No,' I lied to the stranger. 'No one special.'

In one of the bags by my feet was another stocking filler I'd bought for my thirteen-year-old niece, Grace – a little figure that expands in water. *Grow Your Own Boyfriend*, said the packaging. Well, that little figure could have been me, except I was a *Grow Your Own Victim*, handmade for him. I might as well have been gift-wrapped with a bow.

The man with the blue, blue eyes gazed at me across the table, and then stuck out his hand. His left hand. I noticed the gold band on the fourth finger and wondered why he still wore it.

'Amazing the things we find hard to let go of,' he said, and I was mortified he'd noticed that I'd noticed. 'I'm Dominic.' His fingers closed around mine. 'Dominic Lacey.'

Now there was a sound in my ear like someone breathing, or an insect's wings buzzing. My fingers burned where they touched his.

'Jessica Gold.'

'*Gold.* That's nice. It suits you.'

I should have asked him why. There's nothing golden about me. Usually I have lots of dark hair, not quite black but very dark brown, and already I've found a few threads of grey nestling in there like cuckoos in the nest, pretending to be like the others but not like the others at all. My skin is sallow, especially in winter, and when I'm tired, fat purple shadows underline my eyes.

'Talk me through the presents,' he said. 'Who's the wok for?'

'How did you know...?' Oh, yes, you followed me. 'The wok's for my brother James – he likes to think of himself as a serious chef. He makes complicated dishes for his kids and then gets offended when they only want to eat cheese sandwiches.'

'What about you, Jessica? Are you an adventurous eater?'

I hesitated. Should I tell him that I only really eat bland beige food? Cheese, potatoes, white bread, Cheerios, pasta, digestive biscuits. Should I tell him how Sonia Rubenstein's eyes had brightened when she found this out and how she'd scribbled frantically on her notepad with her big black pen?

Instead I shrugged. 'Not particularly.'

'And is James your only sibling?'

'He's the oldest. There's Jonathan too. My middle brother. My parents had a thing about Js.'

They'd wanted a matching set, you see – my parents. They'd wanted a triple deck of bright, outgoing, confident J-named kids. Instead they got two of those. And then me. An anomaly in the family. An outlier.

'And they've both got children?' He looked pointedly at the bags of toys.

'Yep, James has two and Jonathan has one. It's good, it means the pressure's off me.'

Unbidden there came a memory of Travis and I staring down at a white plastic stick with a blue line creeping across a small rectangular window. I remembered the sudden, treacherous flowering of hope that died practically as it was born when Travis said, 'Oh shit.' And then later, 'Thank god backstreet abortions are a thing of the past.'

Sometimes if I let my guard down I can hear a baby crying.

'I'm guessing you've got a job,' he said, 'to pay for this lot.'

'I work for a TV company,' I said. 'I'm an archivist. I catalogue old documents and recordings.'

I store dead things.

'And what about you?' I asked, remembering belatedly the basic rules of social interaction.

'I buy and sell liquidated stock. If a company goes bankrupt, I buy up their stock and hope to sell it on before I've even cleared it out, so I don't have to pay storage.'

'Sounds interesting,' I said. It sounded a little grubby. Making a profit out of other people's despair.

'I give them a fair price,' he said, as if my thoughts were flashing across my forehead in neon lights. 'And if I didn't do it, someone else would.'

'Is it lucrative?'

'I do all right. I'm comfortable, as they say.'

I wished I was comfortable. I was too hot in the over-heated café. I wished I'd washed my hair that morning, or worn some make-up or smarter clothes. The temperature had just dropped below zero for the first time this winter and consequently I was hopelessly overdressed. Beneath my thick cable-knit jumper I was wearing a long-sleeved T-shirt that had come in a tiny pouch from a Japanese clothing chain and boasted heat-conserving technology. My jeans were clammy around my legs.

'We're being glared at,' I said, noticing the queue of people standing by the cash till.

'But I want to go on talking to you,' he said, and his eyes were a sky you could fall into and float there. 'How about we go for a drink somewhere?'

'It's Christmas Eve. All the pubs will be packed, and I've got all these bags.'

'But I haven't found out enough about you. I want to hear more, and about how you got that little scar.' He reached out and touched my wrist, and a bolt of electricity shot up my arm through my veins.

I shrugged without speaking, in case I opened my mouth and my thumping heart flip-flopped right out on to the table. He kept his hand on my wrist like a cuff.

'My car is right here – in the underground car park. I don't live far away. Will you come round? Just for a festive glass of wine? I don't normally invite strange women round, but you seem so familiar, like I've known you for ever. And anyway, it *is* Christmas.'

He examined my face, his attention like a warm flannel dabbing at the crumbs of uncertainty until they were picked off one by one.

'You can text someone if it makes you feel safer, to tell them where you're going.'

'Oh, I'm sure that's not necessary,' I said.

A woman's laugh whooshed past my ear like a Frisbee, leaving the air vibrating. I tuned it out.

What on earth was I thinking? What would possess an educated young woman, well versed in the perils of stranger danger – a young woman *with a long-term boyfriend* – to get in a car with a man she'd only just met? And if you have to ask, you're probably too clear-headed, too normal, not lonely enough, to understand.

I didn't think he was going to be my boyfriend and this

was going to be the start of a beautiful romance. I knew men like him didn't fall in love with women like me. What I was after was an experience, a memory I could store in tissue paper and take out every now and then in years to come when no one was around. The next day Travis and I would go to my parents' house for Christmas dinner. His own parents usually spend the winter months at their house in Florida, so we tend to go to my family unless Travis is working which, as a junior doctor, isn't unusual. My brothers would also come for lunch, bringing their efficient, multi-tasking wives and their Renaissance children, whose timetables are bursting with ballet and gym and Kumon Maths. James and Jonathan would both, separately, give me the quizzical look they've been giving me since child-hood, the look that says, 'Who are you? And *where* did you come from?'

'Why does she have to be so weird?' they used to ask my parents as we were growing up, as if weirdness was an eccentric jacket I'd perversely chosen to wear.

And that's how it happened. I pulled on my parka with the fur around the hood, and gathered up my bags, though he insisted on carrying the one with the wok, and I followed him out of the shop much as he must have followed me in.

I suppressed my qualms and shut out my mother's voice in my head asking what I thought I was doing. I focused on his broad shoulders in the navy-blue wool coat with the velvet lapels, and his brown hair curling slightly over the collar.

It was the 24th of December. I'd spent all year trapped inside myself with only me for company. I wanted a break.

I wanted to be someone else for a bit, with someone else's life.

You're a long time dead, I told myself.

Funny, that thought isn't so comforting now.

TWO

The car was black and quite low to the ground. I couldn't tell you the make or model, but it had leather seats and a musky smell like whisky. When we'd loaded the shopping bags on to the back seat and belted ourselves in, he looked at me and a smile cracked his face right open.

'I'm very, very glad you didn't listen to your mother when she told you not to get into cars with strange men,' he said. 'You are a very enlightened person, Jessica Gold.'

And for that moment, I believed him. 'Where exactly do you live?'

Once I'd asked, I realized I should have asked sooner. Isn't it the sort of thing you're supposed to want to know, where you're going? Sonia Rubenstein thought that could be the root of my problem (until I went to see her I hadn't even known I had a problem). She said, 'Don't you ever get tired of reacting to events instead of driving them?' And, 'Don't you think the journey would be easier if you had an end point in mind?' That's the thing about Sonia Rubenstein, she asks a lot of leading questions.

'It's not far,' he said. 'Wapping.'

Disappointment slid down my throat like a bad oyster.

Until that moment I hadn't been aware of building any fantasy about him, but hearing that he lived in the once-industrial, now gentrified East End rather than somewhere like Hampstead or Notting Hill left me unreasonably deflated. For the first time I started to entertain doubts.

'Don't worry,' he said, glancing at my face. 'I'll give you a lift home later. Wherever that is.'

'Aberdeen,' I said.

'Ha! You're funny, Jessica Gold. I like that. Where do you live really?'

'Wood Green,' I said.

Dominic arched his eyebrows over those ridiculously blue eyes.

'It's rented,' I told him. 'It's a stopgap.'

I wouldn't tell him that the 'stopgap' had so far lasted for two years with no possibility of change.

'I won't be able to stay long,' I told him. 'I'm supposed to be having a drink with some people later.'

Some people. A different person might be able to call them 'friends', although more accurately they were friends of Travis.

There was an exclamation then. An explosion of sound in my head, rather than just a voice. I cursed myself for letting my guard down because that's when they get in, crawling under the wire, messing with my head, until I manage to tune them out.

Everyone has secrets, don't they?

'Any plans for tomorrow?' I asked him, shaking the sound off. 'What do you normally do for Christmas?'

'Oh, I used to do the whole family thing.'

By this time we were driving through the City and though it couldn't have been much more than four o'clock, the streets were filling up with smartly dressed office workers rushing to get home. Above street level many of the windows were already in darkness.

'And now?'

'Now I do what I want. It's very liberating.'

'I can imagine. No, actually, scratch that. I can't imagine it at all.'

'I thoroughly recommend it. You should try it some time.'

All through this exchange, I was wondering if the vibrations of my heart thudding against my ribcage were travelling from my seat through to his.

As we got out of the hub of the City, the crowds thinned out and the streets took on a semi-deserted air. The shabby Christmas illuminations strung across the roads wobbled in the cold wind, throwing half-hearted light on the pavements. Many of the shops had already closed, their metal shutters resolutely unfestive. We stopped at a red light, and I noticed that an artificial Christmas tree outside a convenience store had been chained to the metal framework of the shop awning – someone had wedged a polystyrene burger box and a lager can in between the plastic branches.

'Some people are scum,' observed Dominic.

Something cold prickled on the back of my neck.

'Do you know,' I said, making a show of pulling my phone out of my handbag, 'I think I will send a text. Just in case my body ends up in a shallow grave somewhere.'

I laughed then, a silly artificial giggle.

Who's laughing now?

I typed a message into the phone. *Gone to Wapping with man I met out shopping. His name is Dominic Lacey.*

Then I pressed Delete, instead of Send.

Who would I have sent it to? My parents? My brothers? Travis? No, I wrote it so he'd know there was someone who would worry if I didn't come home. I wanted him to see I was someone who mattered.

'Sensible girl, Jessica Gold.' Dominic smiled and I was sure he knew exactly what I'd just done.

By this point we were negotiating the backstreets of Wapping lined with newbuild flats with mean windows set into garish yellow brick, where the only hint of festivity was the odd flicker of a Christmas-tree light. The Thames wasn't visible yet but I could feel its presence, black and brooding between the buildings on the right, the voices of its dead screaming out through the gaps. Unease rose up in goosebumps on my skin.

'Not far now,' said Dominic. When he turned to me, the street light cut right across him so it looked like he had only half a face.

And then we were driving down a road flanked by industrial warehouses that were considered cutting edge when they were first turned into flats back in the 1980s, but now seem oppressive, all dark brick and steel girders. Nearing the end, Dominic suddenly swung sharply to the right, while at the same time pressing something on top of the driver's-side sunshade. A door slid open and the car dipped steeply down into a small underground car park full of pillars. He squeezed into a seemingly impossible space towards the back.

His was the only car.

'Most of the people who own these places only use them during the week,' he explained. 'This place is a graveyard at weekends and holidays.'

We got out of the car and I felt alarmed when Dominic started gathering up my bags.

'Not worth risking it,' he replied, lifting out the carrier with the wok. 'This place is locked but you can't be too careful.'

Waiting for the lift, I was frozen with a kind of nauseous anticipation. Too late, I wondered what exactly I expected to happen here. I remembered the feel of his hand on my wrist, my skin burning where he touched it.

'We're right at the top,' he said when the lift arrived. He pressed a button to the sixth floor.

The lift seemed to take for ever, probably because I was holding my breath.

Suddenly his hand was on my face, gently stroking my cheek.

'Relax,' he said. 'No need to look so alarmed.'

His thumb traced the line of my nose and I wondered if he could see the fine hairs that grew there. I wanted him to kiss me, but at the same time I thought I'd die if he did.

When the lift stopped and he moved away my face still bore the imprint of his hand.

THREE

The flat I share with Travis is in Wood Green. If you're not familiar with London you might imagine somewhere verdant and leafy. You'd be wrong. The place is dominated by a gigantic monolithic shopping centre and overrun with fast-food outlets. If you are what you eat, the people of Wood Green are giant walking fried chicken wings.

We live on the top floor of a Victorian terrace in the shadow of Wood Green Shopping City. That flat sees direct sunlight only between 11.30 and 3 p.m. at certain times of the year. And then only if you sit in a particular area of the living room where the television is. Downstairs is occupied by a family from Poland who have screeching rows at all hours of the night and boil meat all day long so that the whole house smells constantly of simmering fat. In a shed in the garden live three Romanians who must sleep in shifts on the two bare mattresses I've glimpsed through their open door. In the face of such ugliness, it's little wonder that what Travis and I share now is less of a relationship than a holding pattern.

I was thinking about that as Dominic opened the only door on the sixth floor, a huge, chunky, metal thing with creaking hinges, and led me inside what would once have been a warehouse space, but was now the biggest open-plan apartment I've ever seen. I'm looking around it now – a vast football stadium of wood floors and exposed brick punctuated by thick steel columns painted electric blue. The far wall is studded with full-length windows, two of them leading out on to a long and narrow industrial-style balcony made from metal is actually red, but appeared grey in the twilight of that winter's late afternoon. And there, just beyond the windows, was the black void that was the River Thames. From the doorway I could make out the buildings on the other side and, in the distance, the spike of the Shard thrusting up into the dark sky. Would Travis and I have been happier, I wondered, if we'd lived somewhere like this?

'Wow,' I said, because I had to say something.

'Nice, isn't it?' said Dominic, looking around. 'I had it all redone when I moved in here a couple of years back. Stripped and gutted.'

'It's lovely.'

But it wasn't lovely. There was something intimidating about the unbroken expanse of space, the unnatural clusters of furniture – an L-shaped sofa floating by the windows on the far left, a long zinc dining table lost in the middle, a free-standing kitchen to my right, its high-gloss cupboards reflecting the light back from the row of spots strung on thick wire above. On closer inspection, one bank of the kitchen was set against a low dividing wall that didn't quite meet the ceiling, with a space behind the partition that I assumed must lead to the bedrooms.

'Come and see,' said Dominic, setting the shopping bags

down by the door. He took my hand to lead me across that forbidding expanse of floorboards.

'A lot of trees must have died for this,' I said to distract myself from how his fingers felt wrapped around mine.

He looked down and smiled.

'Yes, but their sacrifice was worthwhile. I had this put in when I moved in, complete with under-floor heating. It's solid concrete below that. You can't imagine how cold it used to be.'

As we crossed the floor, my eyes focused on the one homely spot in that whole industrial space – a Christmas tree, at least ten feet tall, with a heap of beautifully wrapped presents underneath. Dominic let go of my hand in order to unlock one of the wide glass doors that led on to the metal balcony. Immediately a freezing wind flew off the river into my face, pecking at my nose, cheeks, eyeballs even. I gasped, but not just at the cold, at the whole sheer spectacle.

'Funny to think that a hundred years ago this place would have been used for storing and loading tea or tobacco,' said Dominic. 'They'd just have tipped the stuff out of here on to barges, and away they'd go.'

A pleasure boat came past, rocking from side to side on the choppy water, its doors firmly closed to the early evening chill. Inside, tourists in brightly coloured ski jackets held up iPhones to the windows to film their journey. What would they see, when they played it back, I wondered? A couple on a balcony, dwarfed by the building behind them. Would they imagine us to be married? Husband and wife?

'Just down there is Execution Dock,' Dominic said,

pointing away from the bridge to where the river disappeared round a bend to the left. 'It's where they used to hang people accused of piracy. Apparently on hanging day the whole river would be awash with boats crammed with people craning to see.'

'Oh,' I said, suddenly aware of the voices clamouring to be heard over the roaring of the wind.

'To make the spectacle more entertaining, they used a short rope which didn't kill them instantly but left them to suffocate slowly, which made their arms and legs spasm so it looked like they were dancing. Afterwards they were covered in tar and their bodies were displayed in iron cages along the river as an example. One of them, Captain Kidd, was left in his cage for over twenty years. Can you imagine? The woman who lives on the first floor during the week insists it must have been hung right under our building here. She swears she can hear him crying on still nights. Come on. Let's go in, you look frozen.'

We went back inside and left the clamouring voices swinging in the wind.

'A drink,' he said, when he'd taken my coat and handbag. 'There's some champagne in the fridge if you fancy it?'

He moved off to the kitchen and I sat down on the huge, charcoal-grey L-shaped sofa and was immediately swallowed up by its soft, yielding cushions. My whole body was alert to Dominic's movements around the apartment. My mind was racing, the blood rushing in my ears, loud as the wind above the Thames itself.

I sat back and tried to focus on the painting on the exposed-brick wall directly in front of the sofa. The painting had to be at least ten foot by eight. It was all done in shades of orange, pink and yellow with a weird lumpy texture, so that it looked more or less like someone had vomited over a canvas. The picture depicted the head and torso of a naked woman merging with the back half of a puma or similar wild cat. The woman's back was arched, pushing out her very pronounced breasts, on which the artist had detailed every blue vein and even the tiny bumps on her impressive areolae. Her luxuriant honey-blonde hair flowed out behind her, matching up with the end of the cat's tail. Her face too was markedly feline, with striking green eyes ringed with yellow; a disturbing, unblinking stare.

'Hideous, isn't it?'

Dominic handed me a glass of champagne and dropped down on to the sofa beside me.

'It's . . . well . . . it's very . . . big!'

He laughed, and I was acutely aware of the heat from his body just a few inches from mine.

'It's an abomination. But I needed something big enough to fill the space, and it's someone I know.'

'The artist?'

'No, the artist was me, and I've never claimed to be Picasso. I mean the model.'

'Oh.' I gazed back again at those green, catlike eyes and a shiver fluttered through me on butterfly wings. 'A friend?'

'My wife.'

My hand froze in the act of bringing the glass down from my lips. 'That's funny. I thought you said I reminded you of your wife.'

He turned to face me then, and the dimple was a gaping

hole in his face that a person could fall into and never be seen again.

'Did I?' he said.

FOUR

It was expensive champagne but I might as well have been drinking paint stripper. There could be lots of reasons I'd reminded him of his wife. He'd never actually said the resemblance was physical, had he? Maybe it was more of a general impression, some kind of aura we both shared.

'You know, I ought to be getting home,' I said in a voice scraped from the back of my throat. 'I'm having drinks with friends. But please don't worry about giving me a lift.'

'Don't be silly, Jessica Gold,' he said, brushing his fingertips over my cheek so gently I fancied I could feel the individual whorls. 'You've only just got here.'

I turned my eyes back to the painting as if it might yet reveal hidden depths.

'Where is she?' I asked, nodding towards the figure.

'Natalie? Oh, off fucking some brainless cock, I expect.' His tone was light but his fingers froze on my face. 'I haven't seen her for months.'

Even at this stage, even while the alarm klaxon was shrieking inside my head and my heart was beating out a rhythm that said, 'Where is my bag? Where is my bag?' I was still wondering what it would be like to kiss him.

'Do you think it's fair to say you struggle with boundaries?' Sonia Rubenstein once asked me. 'What I mean is, do you find it hard to draw the line between what's appropriate and inappropriate?'

Sonia always wore black, but she accessorized it with a selection of brightly coloured silk scarves that she wore looped several times around her neck. I liked to imagine her opening a special drawer in her bedroom in the flat above her Hampstead consulting room, and picking out a scarf like she was selecting a bloom at an upmarket florist.

'I really do need to go,' I said again, putting down the champagne flute with unnecessary firmness on a thick-glass coffee table and rising to my feet. 'If you'll just tell me what you did with my bag . . .'

Dominic Lacey remained leaning back on the sofa and looking up at me with amusement.

'Come back and sit down. We've only just started chatting.'

'Yes, but I'm late. I really shouldn't have come.'

'So why did you?'

His arm was now lying along the back of the sofa, his fingers drumming slowly, and I focused on his wedding ring rising and falling because I was too scared of what I'd find in his eyes, or rather what he might find in mine.

'A moment of Christmas madness,' I said. 'I wasn't thinking things through. They'll be trying to get hold of me. In fact, I must check my phone.'

'Ah yes. In case they've replied to that text you sent them.'

I looked at him then. Just the most fleeting of glances.

Enough to see the smile on his lips. Enough to know he knew there was no one looking for me.

'I'll just go and find it.' I set out across the vast ocean of floorboards. 'You put it somewhere behind here, didn't you?'

Though he remained on the sofa, I was aware of his eyes tracking me. When I arrived at the kitchen, with its half-wall leading to god knows where, I hesitated. I followed the partition around, coming out into a square, dark hallway with three closed doors leading off it.

Two of them must be bedrooms, I guessed, with the other the bathroom. And yet, there's always that fear, with unknown houses, that you might find something completely unexpected behind a closed door – a sauna or a darkroom or a temperature-controlled room for storing dead butterflies. One of my school friends once showed me her parents' 'sex dungeon' in a windowless dressing room off their bedroom. I remember looking at the swing seat, covered in fake fur, and wondering how they washed it. If they washed it. The thing is, you never really know, when it comes to other people, what secret rooms they keep, and my hand, on the first doorknob, was unsteady, my breath too fast and too loud.

It was a bathroom, that first room. Compact, compared to the open-plan vastness of the living areas, but still big enough for a free-standing claw-foot bath. The back wall of the bathroom was entirely mirrored, and my own reflection – pale and wild-eyed – shocked me.

'You are lovely.' He'd appeared without warning and his eyes in the mirror seemed to be defying me to contradict him. 'You know, I feel so comfortable with you, although we've only just met. Do you feel that too? That we've known each other for years, rather than just hours?'

I nodded, not quite trusting myself to speak.

He put out a hand and pulled me towards him. I watched us in the mirror. When he pressed his lips to mine, I closed my eyes automatically. It felt so completely different to Travis' absent-minded peck. He took his lips away abruptly and I was taken aback to feel his tongue probing the inner corner of my closed eyelid like the tip of a damp sponge.

He must have felt me stiffen because he said, 'You don't need to worry, you know, Jessica. I'm not about to take advantage of you. I don't actually do sex.'

That made me open my eyes.

'I don't like losing control.'

Then he smiled as if he had just divulged an endearing character quirk, like being scared of spiders or only ever wearing navy. 'Don't worry,' he said again. 'I get my pleasure in other ways.'

I felt the capillaries in my face explode in unison and didn't need the mirror to know that my cheeks were flaming.

'Gosh,' I said, using that word for the first time in my life. 'I can't imagine. Do you knit? Or make exact-scale models of famous landmarks out of matchsticks?'

'Funny girl, Jessica Gold.'

Only now when he said my name, it no longer sounded like a caress.

'Anyway,' I said, glancing at my non-existent watch. 'My bag? I've got to go.'

'Come on, sweetheart,' he said, very softly. 'We both know that's not going to happen.'

And there it was. The thing that had lurked beneath the perfect glass surface of our encounter. The thing I'd been trying not to face. The thing my mother always warned me against.

And it was all my own fault.

FIVE

When I was fourteen, a girl from my school disappeared. She was gone for two days and there was a massive fuss. Girls clung together in the corridors weeping, boys gathered in groups and muttered darkly about vigilante gangs. Her parents appeared on television with red-raw rings around their eyes, talking about how loved she was, how popular, how her smile could light up a room. Even after she was found shacked up with a twenty-six-year-old bus driver she described as her fiancé, a certain glamour still clung to her.

For months I dreamed of something similar happening to me. Not being abducted or ravaged, but just having people worry about me, and say lovely things about me. I'd imagine my two brothers on the telly, shoulders shaking with emotion, talking about me and how much they missed me. I imagined how contrite they'd feel about how they'd treated me over the years. How everyone would suddenly realize what a jewel they'd lost.

And now it was happening to me.

And I realized what a tit my fourteen-year-old self had been.

Dominic and I were back sitting on that charcoal sofa,

38

facing the odious painting. I found myself looking at Natalie's face in a different light now, examining her green eyes for clues. Did she look frightened? Was she trying to say something? How had she got away?

I tried to summon her up in my mind, fashioning her into a rope that I could wind around my thoughts. But she was too slippery. Sliding away through the gaps in my mind.

Dominic had positioned himself on the other arm of the L-shaped sofa. The intensity of his stare was unnerving. His eyes ran over me as if he was inventorying me.

When I first started seeing Sonia Rubenstein I'd been suffering from panic attacks – once I was carried out of Leicester Square Tube on a stretcher, hyperventilating with a tightness across the chest like cheese wire – and she'd tried to teach me techniques to corral my thoughts if they were getting out of control. Like I was to put one hand on my stomach and one on my chest, and breathe in and out from my belly, keeping my chest still. Or I could repeat over and over, 'My heart will stop racing. I'm not going to die.' 'You control your fear,' she said to me. 'It doesn't control you.'

I forced myself to breathe from my stomach, and repeated in my head, 'I'm not going to die.' But there was only one person listening, and she didn't believe it.

SIX

Kim was wrapping presents. All around her was a sea of plastic bags that she was slowly working her way through, trying to remember what she'd bought for whom, and feeling the usual creeping desolation, knowing that despite the mountains of stuff and the hundreds of pounds she'd spent, none of it was enough. Give it a few hours and someone would be crying because they didn't get what they really wanted, and someone else would have decided that the thing they thought they really wanted wasn't what they wanted after all, and everyone would be reaching that danger point where you could feel Christmas slipping away, together with all the hopes and expectations you'd pinned on to it over the year.

Downstairs, the television was on full blast. She could hear the sound of that film they seemed to show every Christmas. That grown man dressed up as a Christmas elf. Every now and then there was a shriek of laughter from Rory, followed by an echoing giggle from Katy who, at three years younger, couldn't really understand the joke and took her cue entirely from her brother.

Listening to them, Kim's heart contracted with love.

And guilt.

The bedroom door creaked open.

'Don't come in . . .'

Sean stood in the doorway, his arms folded, surveying the devastation.

'God, how much did this lot cost then?'

She shrugged. 'It's Christmas.'

'Oh, nice of you to remember.'

She turned back to her wrapping.

Sean remained in the doorway. His presence was like a black hole sucking all the joy from the room.

'I do mean it, you know, Kim? I'm not just saying it.'

Kim folded paper around a plastic toy that had cost over ten pounds. And what did you get for it? Another thing to break after a few days, leaving behind a pile of oddly shaped plastic bits that lurked in corners and under sofa cushions. The gift wrap ripped over a sharp edge and Kim cursed herself for getting the cheap stuff.

'We've been through this,' she said, trying to sellotape over the tear. 'I have to work. It's my job. You knew that when you married a police officer.'

'Then you get a new job. Or . . .'

'Or?'

'Or get a new family.'

'So, just to be clear, you're holding me prisoner here.'

By spelling out the situation in all its ridiculousness, I was giving him one last chance to make it not true. One last chance for it to be a joke, or a misunderstanding.

Dominic nodded enthusiastically, as if I was a child

41

who'd just grasped some complicated mathematical concept. 'Exactly!'

'But why?'

'Because, like many people, Christmas is my very worst time of year. It has so many memories, doesn't it? It comes so loaded with expectation. I just don't want to be alone. We outsiders must stick together. More champagne?'

He had brought the bottle over and was topping up our glasses, even though mine was still half full.

'So you want me here for . . . company?'

He nodded again and reached out to touch my knee. 'Exactly right. Company. And other things.'

I didn't like that. Those 'other things'.

'But people will be looking for me. I'm due to spend the day at my parents' house tomorrow. They'll get the police involved.'

'I expect they will.'

'Someone will have seen us,' I pressed on. 'In the café. Someone will have seen us. There'll be CCTV footage.'

'There's a chance there might be footage,' he said, as if he was considering my argument carefully. 'If we were sitting in the right place, which we weren't. Anyway, it was a last-minute change of plan, you said, to come into the West End instead of shopping locally like you'd originally intended. I imagine that will . . . confuse things. True, they will probably trace your bank-card payments. But that will take a while, and then they'll have to find out where you went afterwards. Did you see how many people there were on Oxford Street when we walked to the car? Good luck trying to find us in that!' He paused. 'Anyway, if you're worrying about missing Christmas, please don't, we have plenty of festive cheer right here.'

He indicated the tree with the beautifully wrapped presents piled up underneath.

'So, you want me to stay here for the whole of Christmas Day?'

The thought of twenty-four hours in that apartment with him was like a pair of freezing hands squeezing my chest. Now Dominic was laughing, as if I'd made a deliberate joke.

'Not Christmas Day, of course not.'

Hope surged briefly.

'What I mean is, not *just* Christmas Day. You'll be my guest over the twelve days of Christmas – from now until January sixth. Did you know, by the way, that day is called Epiphany? Don't you think that's neat?'

'Twelve days?'

'Well, technically, it's thirteen as the twelve days don't actually start till tomorrow. Don't worry. We'll find plenty to do to amuse ourselves. I have so much to tell you. That's the thing about Christmas, isn't it, you give yourself to other people, like a gift? The actual gifts are just a bonus. Have you noticed there are twelve presents under the tree? One for every day. And we have New Year to look forward to, all those resolutions to be made. The days will just fly by.'

Now Dominic had moved up the sofa so close to me that I was breathing in the warm breath that he'd just breathed out.

'I want us to get to know each other, Jessica.'

I watched his hand stroking my thigh as if it was a wasp about to sting.

'I want us to . . . unwrap ourselves for one another. Doesn't every human being long for that above all else – to be fully known?'

I wondered if he could hear the bile that had just come shooting up, swilling around in my mouth. I wondered if he could feel my leg muscles shrinking from his touch. My eyes darted wildly around the apartment, canvassing for escape routes. Not the windows, all of which gave on to the black void of the Thames. And as far as I could tell there was just the one door in and out, wide and industrial and solid. If I could just find my bag with my phone . . .

'I'll just pop to the loo.' I'd never to my knowledge used 'pop' as a verb before.

'Sure,' he called, as I made my way across the floor on trembling legs. 'Help yourself.'

Once in the inner hallway, my fingers closed around the knob of the door closest to the bathroom, even as my heart threatened to punch its way clear out of my chest. I turned it, hoping against hope there would be no noise.

There was no noise.

And no movement.

The door was locked. Likewise the one next to it.

In the furthest top corner of the hallway the red light of an alarm sensor winked.

In contrast to the other two rooms, the bathroom door had no lock. After I pulled the door shut, I slumped against it, shaking. I needed the toilet but it was on the other side of the room, beyond the distance where you could sit down and hold the door closed. I glanced around the room in a futile search for a cupboard where there might be hidden razor blades or nail scissors or mega-strength sleeping pills I could add to his champagne when he wasn't looking. There was another alarm sensor in here too. I couldn't remember ever seeing one in a bathroom before.

There were footsteps in the hallway outside.

'Is everything OK, Jessica?'

Could he tell I was just the other side of the door, two inches of wood separating his breath from mine, crouching on trembling legs that threatened to give way? I prayed he wouldn't try the handle, wouldn't try to push his way in.

Springing across the room, I pushed the steel button for the flush, catching my breath at the sudden explosion of water shooting through the bowl. I ran the tap in the sink, trying to avoid looking into my own frightened eyes in the mirror.

He was waiting outside the door.

'You look scared, sweetheart. You're not scared of me, are you?'

I shrugged instead of answering straight away. 'The situation is quite challenging,' I replied eventually.

I turned it round so that I wasn't commenting on him. I was commenting on the situation – not what he was doing but how it was making me feel, just as I'd learned in therapy. Sonia Rubenstein would have been proud.

On our way back through the living area of the apartment, Dominic paused and plunged a hand deep into the pocket of his jeans. He withdrew a huge bunch of keys, all with a different-coloured fob. 'Purple, I think,' he said. He walked over to the massive metal front door and turned that key. 'There,' he said, with a smile that cracked his face open like a coconut. 'Now we're safely locked away from the rest of the world. And you know what would make it even cosier?'

I shook my head.

'If we get rid of our phones as well.'

Now I saw he'd laid out two phones on the dining-room table – one black, that must be his, and my own white one, in its pink leather case. Without stopping to think I lunged forward to grab it.

The pain came out of nowhere, a sharp stinging on my scalp that pulled me up short. I tried to turn my head, crying out when I realized he had a hank of my hair wound around his fist.

'I don't think so,' he said.

With his free hand, he reached out and picked up the phones, then, still pulling me by the hair, he led the way over to the windows. At the glass door, he finally let go. While I rubbed my sore scalp, he turned the handle and, before I knew what was happening, he'd taken both phones and hurled them towards the river. The darkness swallowed them one after the other. Closing and locking the door in one fluid movement, Dominic turned back to me and smiled.

'Where are my manners? Let's eat. You must be starving.'

'I'm not hungry.'

The thought of food made me nauseous. I was hardly able to breathe, let alone chew and swallow.

But his face had tightened, like it was threaded through with invisible wire and someone was pulling on it. Hard.

'Do you want to hurt my feelings?'

I shook my head. He swung open the door of the huge American-style fridge-freezer, and I felt hope drain away through my veins and arteries right down to the polished wood floor. The shelves were packed with plastic boxes, all labelled. I caught sight of 'Lasagne' and 'Thai Green Curry (chicken)' as well as the 'Beef Stew' he eventually brought out.

'Did you cook all that?'

'Do I look like the kind of man who spends his life in the kitchen?' His tone was calm but his face remained unsmiling.

So he'd bought it in, all this pre-prepared food. He must have been planning this for a while.

The thought was a punch to my stomach. He'd bought in the food, locked the relevant doors, and then gone looking for a victim.

Me.

And if it was planned, he already knew what was going to happen next. And how it would end.

SEVEN

We sat down at the long dining table that delineates the end of the living-room space from the beginning of the kitchen space.

This flat is all about the space.

The shallow white bowl he put in front of me was huge – the kind you might buy on aesthetic grounds and never use once you find they don't actually fit in the dishwasher. The brown gloop nestled on a bed of rice, glistening with fat where it caught the light. The lumps of beef half submerged in gravy the consistency of mud.

'Dig in,' he said.

He was watching me intently with those close-together eyes, so I picked up my fork and scooped some rice with a bit of brown sauce.

'Delicious, isn't it? I get pre-prepared food delivered from the same company every week. I can't bear cooking. People who dwell too much on food make me sick.'

I dipped my fork again into the rice and brought it up to my mouth which was still coated with the dregs of the last mouthful.

'You're not eating the beef.'

'I don't eat meat.'

Dominic put his fork down in his dish and slowly ran his tongue around his gums.

'Then we have a problem, Jessica Gold.'

I swallowed down a clot of rice.

'It's no problem,' I said.

When it happened, it was so quick, I didn't even notice him moving. One moment he was sitting there opposite me, staring with his head to one side as though listening to what I was saying, and the next he'd leaned forward and picked up the biggest lump of meat from my plate with his fingers and rammed it past my teeth, clamping his hand over my lips so that I couldn't spit it out. I was choking, the meat lodged in my mouth, big as a boiled egg.

'I'd chew it if I were you,' he said as my eyes streamed.

I pressed my teeth into the beef, feeling that stringy texture at once so familiar and so alien.

'What is it about meat that offends you?' His hand stayed pressed to my mouth. 'Is it the idea that you're chewing on something that was once living that you don't like? Is it biting into a mouthful of tissue, fat, skin? Let me guess. You had a pet you loved once – a cat maybe, you seem like the cat type. Do you think about that cat when you're chewing on meat, I wonder? Do you imagine you're sinking your teeth into its flesh?'

I began to retch, with a violence that shocked me, although nothing came out but a trail of thin bile. He moved his hand away, looking with disgust at the traces of yellow liquid on his fingers. After washing his hands at the sink, he sat back down opposite me and sighed.

'It's like you're deliberately trying to spoil things,' he said. 'Now, will you please just eat.'

It wasn't a question.

By then the retching had died down, but still I could feel the strings of flesh caught between my teeth.

I remembered Sonia Rubenstein, and how at one session she'd been asking me about my fear of buttons. It's a real phobia. Even writing the word just now gave me the heebie-jeebies. Nasty, threatening things. I'd been talking about how it affected my life. How I couldn't stand to touch Travis when he was wearing a shirt, how if I came into a room and found a button on the carpet, unattached, I screamed and couldn't go back in there until it was gone. About how once we went to dinner at the house of one of Travis' old friends and they'd put up a decorative clock made entirely out of buttons of different sizes and I'd had to position myself facing the other way so I wouldn't have to look at it. Sonia Rubenstein listened to me, while her fingers played with the end of her orange or pink or emerald-green scarf, and didn't laugh, and at the end she said, 'You know, sometimes you just have to fake it to make it.'

Sometimes she talks like an American self-help manual. She went on to explain that when you don't have any choice, you have to just adopt a different mindset. So I'd adopt the mindset of Travis. I'd imagine myself walking into the room with his step. Imagine how I would feel, with my eyes gliding right over the front of a jacket or a coat without even wondering how big they were (the small ones are scarier) or how many there were. 'By thinking yourself into someone else's skin,' Sonia said, 'you'll learn to control your fear.'

So that's what I did now. Because I could do nothing else. I imagined myself into the skin of someone who ate meat. A habitual carnivore like one of my brothers. Someone who was so used to eating meat that a plate of stew sitting there right in front of them wouldn't even register, and when they put it in their mouth it would taste of nothing in particular.

I dug into the stew, pulled out a steaming forkful and shovelled it into my mouth. I chewed without thinking. Because if I thought about what I was eating, I wouldn't be able to swallow it, and if I didn't swallow it, something would happen.

All the time I was eating, Dominic was watching me. 'Much better,' he said.

When I'd finished and put down my fork, my stomach was protesting as if the cow I'd just eaten had got loose in there and was bucking around. Dominic still had half his food left.

'See how hungry you were, after all that fuss?' he said.

I nodded.

Suddenly he stood up and picked up his plate and scraped the rest of his food on to my empty dish.

'You wolfed that down so quickly, I couldn't live with myself if I didn't let you have more. It is Christmas, after all.'

In. Out. In – just the slightest of pauses – out. In. Out.

Kim thought she could watch her daughter breathing all night and not get tired of it. Sometimes when she looked at her children sleeping, she felt like her heart would explode with love.

At five, Katy was no longer the chubby toddler she'd once been, but she still had the plump pink lips of babyhood. Kim lowered her face so it was just a few centimetres from her daughter's and she could feel her hot breath on her cheek. She inhaled deeply, taking in the smell of toothpaste and bathtime and that other scent that was uniquely Katy's.

If only they could always be asleep, none of this would be happening.

Instantly she berated herself for the thought. What sort of mother was she?

The sort that was about to lose her children.

Though she was objectively aware of Sean's ultimatum, and knew he wasn't the type to deliver empty threats, still she would not allow herself to believe it. He wouldn't take them away from her. Not when she was just doing her job. He would see sense. It wasn't her fault she had to work tomorrow. 'Crime doesn't stop just because it's bloody Christmas,' she'd yelled at him earlier. 'Burglars and rapists don't just decide to give themselves the day off.'

But her face had burned with guilt.

Tearing herself away from Katy's bedside, she crossed the landing and nudged open the door of Rory's room. He'd insisted he was staying up all night, so he could prove Father Christmas was actually his mum and dad, but he'd been exhausted by eight and asleep by nine thirty. Now he lay splayed out on his bed, one pyjama-clad leg clear of the covers, his hair damp around his rosy cheeks. He'd never been able to stand being too hot. Even as a baby, he'd wriggled free from his blankets. She and Sean would find him in the morning on his tummy with his bottom in the air, arms spread wide and the bedcovers in a twisted heap at the bottom of the cot. 'How did we get this lucky?' Sean had whispered once as they stood side by side looking down on their sleeping son.

It was never, ever a question of not loving them enough. If only she could be sure they knew that. No matter how difficult she'd found the rest of it – the questions (*Why this? Why that? But why?*), the dull games, the picture books, the messy mealtimes, the naps, the arguments, the endless repetition that makes up a young child's life – her love had never wavered. Not for a second.

In the final judgement that would count for something.

EIGHT

'Poor Jessica Gold.'

Dominic was standing at the door of the bathroom, watching me hunched over the toilet on my hands and knees.

'Has all the excitement been too much for you?'

He strode across the slate-tiled floor and crouched behind me stroking my back. Despite everything, I had the strangest urge to arch into his caress like a cat. Already I craved comfort. I'd just thrown up so violently I thought it possible my liver and kidneys had come up along with everything else and now I felt empty and weak. I was shaking all over, so the warmth of his hand on my back felt like the sun after a long, harsh winter.

'We can't have you peaking too early, sweetheart. Not when this is just the beginning of our adventure.' He was cooing in my ear like a woodpigeon. 'I bet you're tired out.'

I nodded, almost too weak to move my own head.

'Then we must get you to bed.'

Relief washed through me. He would unlock the door to one of those other two rooms. And there would be a bed that I could fall into. Maybe even another bathroom with a lock on the door.

I ignored the tinkling laughter that drifted down around me like snowflakes.

Dominic helped me up off the floor with one hand under my elbow. Now the image of a bed was in my mind, it was all I could think of. I imagined my bed at home, with the kingsize duvet and the fake-fur throw that I needed to keep me properly warm and which Travis made a huge deal of if it encroached over even so much as his little toe. I imagined how it would be to crawl into that familiar nest where everything was safe. If only I could be back there, I'd never again complain about the sponge earplugs I had to wear to cut out Travis' snoring ('I don't snore, I have a sinus disorder'), or the way the mattress dipped slightly on my side, or next door's baby crying through the paper-thin walls. I was still trembling and felt colder than I'd ever been in my life. My teeth were properly chattering.

In the inner hallway, Dominic paused to withdraw that same bunch of keys with the multicoloured fobs from the front pocket of his jeans. His other hand was still supporting me like a courteous Southern gentleman seeing a lady home after a date.

The first key he tried – green – didn't work.

'Wrong one,' he said crossly under his breath. Clearly that was the key to the other room. His bedroom, I'd already labelled it in my mind.

'Ah, here we go.'

He pushed open the door with a kind of coyness, as if he was a normal man showing his new date around his flat.

Inside there was a smallish bedroom dominated by a huge iron-framed bed, behind which was a high window covered up by a Venetian blind. To the left of the bed was a dressing table, its surface completely clear, with three drawers underneath and a plain mirror on top. To the right of the bed was a door, slightly ajar, and my heart leapt when I saw it did indeed lead into an ensuite bathroom.

At the foot of the bed was a kennel.

'I didn't realize you had a dog.'

Dominic threw back his head and laughed.

Then I saw the thick chain coiled loosely at the entrance to the large wooden kennel, attached at one end to the iron frame of the bed and at the other to a thick metal cuff. Too small for a dog's neck.

Dominic's hand tightened under my elbow and I could feel his breath, moist in my ear.

'You'll be snug as a bug in a rug in there,' he said, indicating the small archway that led into the kennel. 'I've put in a blanket, and a bowl of water.'

I sagged as if my bones had turned instantly to liquid.

'Please,' I begged him. 'Please let me go home now. I've had a lovely day' – again that tinkle of laughter around me – 'but I need to see my family and my boyfriend.'

He stiffened then, and I could feel the tension in his body passing through his hand on my elbow into mine.

'Boyfriend?' His voice was soft as lambswool. 'Are you lying to me, Jessica? Are you telling porky pies?'

'I *have* got a boyfriend. I live with him. I don't know why I didn't tell you earlier. He'll be going out of his head with worry.'

Travis in truth isn't the kind of man who goes out of his head with anything. Travis is very much in his head at all times.

Now Dominic was shaking his head sorrowfully. 'Oh dear, Jessica Gold. Just when I thought we were getting somewhere. What did I tell you I most wanted? What was my single greatest reason for bringing you here, huh?'

I tried to remember. 'Because you're lonely?' I ventured.

Instantly I knew it was the wrong answer. He took his hand away from under my arm so abruptly I staggered backwards.

'To be known,' I yelled, suddenly remembering. 'You want to be fully known.'

'It's not a pub quiz, Jessica. You're not down your local Wetherspoon's now.' But his voice had lost a little of its hardness. 'I have to say I'm disappointed in you. I felt we'd reached an understanding. Now we're going to have to start all over again. From scratch. Why would you lie about something like that?'

He seemed so genuinely hurt I almost felt guilty.

In the end, the only thing I could come up with was the truth. 'I didn't want to put you off.'

Clearly it was a good thing to say because his hand resumed its hold on my elbow.

'I suppose I can see why you might think that, but you know your lies have really set us back, Jessica.' He paused. 'So, I'm afraid I have no option but to punish you. It certainly isn't how I'd planned for things to go this evening, not with it being Christmas Eve and your first night, but you leave me no choice.'

I asked him what he meant by punish. My trembling had returned with a vengeance. I knew he could feel it because his voice was almost kind when he said, 'I'm going to have to remove the blanket. It's a privilege, you see. It's not a right.'

No blanket. So was I to sleep on the hard floor of the kennel? In chains?

This time my legs did give way under me. He just about kept me upright.

'I know it's hard, sweetheart, but I don't have a choice.'

But now my attention was overtaken by something else, something far more pressing. My system, rarified by ten years of vegetable and dairy matter, was rebelling against the meat that had somehow survived the earlier purging in the bathroom. I froze as some long-dormant part of my gut groaned into action.

'I need the toilet,' I said in a high-pitched voice.

His hand tightened around my arm like a vice.

'I really, really need the toilet.' I was almost shouting now.

He steered me from the doorway around the kennel towards the ensuite. Only when we were inside the grey and black bathroom did I notice that he was still there.

'I need . . .'

'I know. You need the toilet. Which is here. Go ahead.'

I turned so I was facing him. 'You're not really going to . . .'

'Please don't tell me what I can and can't be or do, Jessica.' That edge was back in his voice, rough enough to cut yourself on. 'You lied. You set us back and now you've lost all your privileges. If you want the toilet badly enough, you'll go. Fully known, remember? That means no secrets, no hiding, no private places.'

Just then my stomach made a noise like it was tearing itself loose from the rest of me and I lunged for the toilet, yanking my jeans down just in time.

'God, that's *disgusting*,' said my own voice in my head. I kept my eyes fixed on the grey floor tiles at my feet, but even without looking I could tell he was staring at me.

And smiling.

NINE

In the dog kennel was a tartan wool blanket. At least there was when I first looked in there. By the time I actually crawled inside, feeling hollowed out like a butternut squash, the blanket had vanished, leaving only the bowl on the wooden floor. There was just about enough room for me to sit upright in the centre of the space where the gable cut across, but even there the top of my head was grazing the roof.

'Give me your leg,' Dominic commanded from outside the arch.

I was silent.

'Your leg. Stick it out through the opening.'

So weakened was I that I'd forgotten about the chain and the metal cuff. I began to beg.

'Don't plead, Jessica. It isn't attractive. I've told you, privileges must be earned. Now, your leg.'

I stuck my right ankle out of the archway and heard the sound of a key turning in a lock. I felt Dominic's fingers on the bare skin under my jeans.

'You might want to take these off,' he suggested.

'No!' The word shot out of me like a bullet.

I heard him chuckling. 'OK. I just thought you might be more comfortable. These jeans seem a little restrictive. Don't you understand about blood circulation? We can't have you clotting up. Not on my watch.'

That seemed to tickle him for some reason. I told him I was fine.

'OK, sweetie. Just for tonight, though, while you're getting used to things.'

Sitting just inside the kennel I couldn't see his face, only my leg attached by a thick chain to the metal cuff which was itself attached to the heavy frame of the bed.

Then I laughed. I couldn't help it. And once I started laughing, I couldn't stop. When I'd got up that morning and put those clothes on – the jumper, the jeans, the thick stripy socks – I'd thought the most interesting thing that could possibly happen that day would be if I bought myself some knickers from the lingerie section. Yet here I was, still wearing those same clothes, sitting in a dog kennel and chained to a stranger's bed.

'That's enough, Jessica,' he said after a while in a flat voice I hadn't heard before.

Laughter is a nervous thing with me. I used to do it whenever I was called in to see the head teacher at school, which was quite often. Every time she kicked off with a 'it saddens me to see you here again, Jessica' or a 'how disappointing when I thought we'd turned over a new leaf' or even just a wordless sigh, I'd start to giggle, and wouldn't be able to stop.

I even did it once when Travis and I were held up at gunpoint. We were in a bank in Madrid, standing facing the wall at the end furthest from the door, leaning against a counter and arguing about whether it was better to transfer money from the UK or withdraw it straight from a cash-point, when all of a sudden I became aware that the rest of the room had fallen silent. I turned slowly round and found that all the other customers were kneeling with their hands on their heads and expressions of terror on their faces, and that there was a man a few feet away with a gun pointing at my head. His eyes were bloodshot and unfocused, and the hand holding the gun was shaking. Slowly I turned back to Travis. And then I started laughing. 'Shut up!' Travis urged. But I couldn't work out how. Luckily for me, the bank teller nearest to us thrust a black bin bag with notes in it at the gunman and he legged it out of the door. Afterwards Travis had looked at me like I'd done it on purpose. 'You could have got us both killed,' he said.

I was remembering that hold-up and Travis' outrage when Dominic suddenly yanked the chain around my ankle, dragging me through the archway before I even had a chance to register what was happening.

'Do you think this is a game, Jessica?' His face was inches from mine. 'Am I a figure of fun to you?'

There was a glint of metal in his hand. The long blade of a flick knife.

I shook my head, all trace of laughter evaporated away. There was a searing pain in my ankle where the sharp edge of the metal cuff had cut into the skin. Looking down, I saw a trickle of blood disappearing into my stripy sock.

'Now go to sleep, Jessica Gold.' He snapped the knife

shut and slid it into the pocket of his jeans. 'Tomorrow, as they say, is the first day of the rest of your life.'

I crawled back into the kennel and curled up, my right leg with the cuff on it slightly straighter than the left. The next day I'd behave differently, I promised myself. I'd do everything he said and win back my blanket.

That's how quickly he broke me.

'Really? Is that all you've got?' This time, the voice in my head was both mine and not mine, cutting through the fug of self-pity I'd wrapped myself in. 'Toughen up, *Jessica.*' And now I imagined it was *her.* Cat Woman. Natalie. Spitting out my name like a term of abuse.

TEN

They woke her up at 6.30. This was a big improvement on the previous year where Katy was in their bed at five, shaking her awake, desperate to open her presents.

'Katy wanted to wake you up but I didn't let her,' said Rory, and despite her grogginess, Kim felt her heart swell at the pride on his face. He'd grown so much in the last year but underneath the new swagger and slimmed-down physique, he was still the solemn, round-faced baby with the huge brown eyes that followed her around the room as if attached by invisible strings.

She allowed herself to be led out of bed, aware that Sean was watching her, though making no attempt to follow. In the kitchen, she put the kettle on while the kids bounced around from sofa to kitchen chair to floor and back again, never losing sight of the stockings stuffed with presents by the fireplace.

A vat of coffee and she'd feel human again.

'Now, Mummy? Can we? Can we?'

Katy had flung her arms around Kim's legs and was looking up at her beseechingly.

'You're the best Mummy ever. I love you to the moon and back.'

Kim gazed down at her daughter, trying to commit her to memory. The small pointed chin, the curly brown hair that, even at the age of five, she already resented, the over-brimming energy of her.

If only she could pickle this moment and put it in a jar.

While the children tore open their presents, Sean wandered in and wordlessly took the coffee she held out to him. He wouldn't go through with it, she realized. Not now he could see how happy they all were. She stood beside him and hooked her arm around his waist. He flinched momentarily with surprise, but then put his arm around her shoulders and pulled her to him. They watched their children with wonder.

When the frenzied opening was over, leaving Katy and Rory half spent with adrenalin, surrounded by a sea of debris, Kim broke away from Sean and headed out of the living room.

'Wait. Where are you going?'

'To have a shower and get dressed. I'm due in the office in an hour.'

'You're still going then?' His voice was flat, like someone had ironed all the emotion out of it.

'Of course I'm going. They're expecting me.'

She held back from explaining yet again how important it was that she show willing. Sean knew how long she'd dreamed of making Detective Sergeant. She'd passed her OSPRE exam back in March but the selection process was painfully slow and ultimately Robertson's recommendation

was what would count with the promotion board.
Sean's silence followed her up the stairs like a shadow.

It's time I dealt with it. The elephant in the room.

Travis. The boyfriend that, like St Peter, I'd denied.

The truth is, the path of true love was not running smooth for Travis and me. In fact I was starting to wonder if it hadn't just detoured around us altogether. We'd met at university, where he was studying medicine and I was studying social awkwardness and a catastrophic inability to cope with deadlines. He was part of a group who came to visit my flatmate in our halls of residence, and when it got to the end of the evening and we were the only ones not either partnered off or being sick in the toilet, we drifted together by default.

Travis likes to consider himself as someone who thinks outside the box, unswayed by appearances or conventions or passing trends. In that respect I played to his self-image. I was quirky ('weird', my brothers would have said). I didn't dress up to go out or have girlie nights in or pluck my eyebrows. For three years after graduating, I had a series of badly paid, obscure jobs which supported us both in a shared house while Travis was still racking up debt doing his interminable course. Because I wasn't an obvious choice, I think Travis felt I made him appear more interesting, like he had hidden depths. He thought he'd 'discovered' me like an obscure Indie band.

For my part I liked having a boyfriend. I liked having someone to go to the cinema with at weekends. I liked how people I met would instantly relax when I used the phrase 'my boyfriend' as if I'd passed some basic first hurdle. I liked that I was suddenly less of an outsider at home.

There was affection too, of course. We'd watch *University Challenge* with me sitting at the end of the sofa with my feet in his lap, yelling out answers and whooping on the rare occasions we got one right. We did the crossword together (cryptic) and I tried not to mind if he got the clue that had been on the tip of my tongue. I loved Travis' extravagantly curled upper lip with the perfect teardrop between it and his long, very thin nose. I loved the way his pale grey eyes were rendered practically colourless behind his severe black-framed glasses and how he looked as he bent over his textbooks, twiddling his lanky dirty-blond hair around his finger.

But loving bits about each other isn't the same as loving each other, is it?

In the last couple of years, since Travis started earning a proper salary as a junior doctor, he's become more critical. 'Are you really wearing that?' he'd asked the week before when we were invited to one of his medic friends' houses for dinner and I appeared wearing my usual jeans and baggy top. He'd started socializing more, going straight out after a long shift, texting me to tell me not to count him in for dinner as he'd grab something out. He'd always been accepting of my eccentricities, but recently he's begun snapping at me when he sees me making what he calls my 'gormless face' which means I was listening to something that he couldn't hear.

'Snap out of it,' he'll say, clicking his fingers so close to my face, my cheek will be buzzing. 'Just think about something else.'

He thought the voices that sometimes crowded my head were an indulgence on my part – something I could curtail with a bit of will-power.

When we sit down together in the evening these days, and it's not often, conversation is no longer an easy flow, but more something that has to be worked on. We stocked up on Scandinavian box sets so we don't have to talk. We stopped making plans beyond the following weekend because of the tacit fear that we might not still be together by May Bank Holiday, or the summer. Worse, though, was the fear that we *would* be together, that things weren't quite bad enough to justify splitting up, that we'd carry on coexisting ad infinitum in this limbo that wasn't quite loveless but wasn't love *full* either.

Towards the end of last year, I'd presented him with that little plastic stick with the blue line in the windows like a nervous beau proffering a ring box to his beloved, and he'd taken one look and then made that comment about backstreet abortions, and that had been that. Two weeks later I'd had the procedure – that's what we called it, so we didn't have to think about what it actually was. He took two days off work. On the first day he made a fuss of me, but by the evening I could see him getting restless, and the next day he got up at seven to go to the hospital. 'You don't mind, do you?' he said. 'There's something important I have to do.' We've never talked about it again. And I never told him that sometimes I wake in the night with a fluttering inside me like a phantom baby moving around.

So that was the context in which I started up a conversation with a strange man in a department-store café.

When the sound of heavy chain links clinking against each other woke me in the early morning of Christmas Day, catapulting me right back to reality, Travis was on my mind.

I lay very still, my teeth chattering with cold, trying not to make a noise, and imagined him lying in our double bed, the plump duvet pulled up around him. I imagined myself slipping in beside him and curling myself around him for warmth, but it was too painful and I had to stop myself thinking about it. I wondered if he'd have called the police yet and decided probably not.

Not after the airport thing.

Around a year ago I'd gone to work as usual and something odd had happened between leaving the office to come home again, and actually getting home. I'd been having episodes where voices exploded in my head, too many to control, leaving me spent and shaken with a gap in my memory of five minutes or ten. A couple of times it had been an hour or more. But this was different. I left work at the usual time, just after six. I remembered walking out of the building, but then nothing. Until I called Travis at just after midnight.

From Luton airport.

All I know is, one minute I was patting my pockets down as usual to make sure I still had my Oyster card, and the next I was sitting in a padded chair at Luton airport departures hall and six hours had passed. 'But you must have some recollection of what happened?' Travis had stood in front of me rattling his car keys, still wearing his innies, as he calls his pyjama bottoms, and looking very cross. Travis just couldn't get his head around these 'lapses', as he'd taken to labelling them, as if they were some kind of character flaw.

It hadn't happened since, at least on that scale, but he still brought it up from time to time.

So no, on balance I thought he probably hadn't called the police.

Today was another matter. Today we were due at my parents' house at 12.30 p.m. My mum would have made blinis with smoked salmon and cream cheese sprinkled with dill for us to wash down with champagne and orange juice. As usual, we'd be the first to arrive – my brothers being given papal dispensation to come and go as they choose on account of their having reproduced.

When Travis woke up and I wasn't there, he'd be worried. I imagined him putting on his glasses to squint at the phone in that way he does first thing in the morning, frowning as if he couldn't quite trust his own eyes yet. It was now, I decided, he'd feel the first creeping sense of dread. Maybe he'd call the police then, prefacing his call with an apology. 'I hope this isn't wasting your time, but . . .' Or maybe he'd decide to wait and go to my parents' anyway, thinking I might have turned up there. I'm not a child – I could just be at a friend's house sleeping off a heavy night. Except that I don't have any friends like that.

That scenario seemed most likely. Travis would get in our old Golf, forgetting as usual that the central locking only works from the passenger-door side, and he'd make his way up to my parents' house, marshalling his righteous anger in case he found me sitting at their kitchen table, right as rain, while at the same time preparing to flip into worry mode in case there was no sign of me. Travis likes to cover every angle.

I was now convinced Travis would delay calling the police until he'd arrived at my parents' house. I might turn up there after all, and anyway where else was he going to spend Christmas Day?

Today was Christmas Day. I struggled to believe it.

I'm nearly thirty but this would be the first Christmas Day I'd ever spent away from my family. A tear rolled down my cheek as I thought of my brothers arriving and my niece and nephews and the sisters-in-law I'd never really made enough of an effort to get to know. I imagined the hurried exchange of information as they discovered for the first time I was missing – 'How long?' 'But where?' – and the creeping urgency as they all agreed such behaviour was completely out of character. I thought of how my mum's hand would shake and my father would fetch some paper to make a list – something practical to keep his thoughts from racing. I imagined them sitting down to dinner while they waited for the police to arrive, just to keep things normal for the kids, and trying to behave like there was nothing really wrong. I imagined my eighteen-month-old nephew George sitting at the table in his clip-on canvas chair, looking from face to face with his huge brown eyes and knowing there was something wrong but not what it was. Would he ask for me, I wondered? 'Where Jeska?' he might say. The thought was a fish barb in my flesh. Without thinking I brought my knees up to my chest. The sudden pain on my ankle was intense, and the noise of the chain clanking grated in the air.

I held my breath.

'I'm guessing you're awake. Merry Christmas, sweetheart.'

The voice came from nearby. The bed, I assumed. I tried to picture it from the very rushed impression I'd got last night. Big and iron-framed, covered with a heavy old-fashioned eiderdown.

I heard the creak of bedsprings. Seconds later, there was a tugging on my ankle. And then there he was, squatting in the doorway of the kennel, his head slightly cocked, beaming at me as if I was an honoured guest.

'Did you sleep all right?'

Dominic seemed in a very good mood as he busied himself around the kitchen making breakfast. I was sitting on a high stool at the central island that divided the cooking area from the space where the dining table was, watching his hands as they opened up cupboards and drawers. Were there sharp knives in there? I wondered. Or other things I could use as a weapon? As he rifled through kitchen implements, my unquiet mind made nonsensical leaps. I could grate him to death. Or batter him senseless with a plastic spatula.

Nothing seemed like it could possibly be real. Not the winter sun streaming in through the plate-glass windows, nor the medley of Elvis Christmas songs he had blaring from the speakers in the top corners of the room, nor the *Keep Calm and Carry On* apron he was wearing over his black shirt and dark jeans, nor the needles stabbing at the inside of my chest.

'I'm making you pancakes, princess. How does that sound? Dripping with maple syrup.'

How it sounded was disgusting. My stomach still felt weighted down with whatever remnants of last night's meat hadn't found their way into the toilet. While the batter was resting in a large glass bowl, thick and pasty, Dominic reached into his pocket and withdrew the set of keys with the different-coloured fobs. Isolating the orange one, he unlocked a drawer and withdrew a gleaming chrome kitchen knife. He didn't look at me, but he held it up as if, checking for cleanliness so it glinted under the down-lighters. I watched him pull a heaped bowl towards him and begin chopping up fruit. Crisp green apples, fresh oranges, juicy strawberries from the fridge. My digestive tract cried out with longing.

'Actually, just the fruit salad would be perfect.'

The hand holding the knife froze.

'The fruit salad is for me. I've made you pancakes. I told you.'

I used to have a teacher at school everyone was terrified of, even though she never raised her voice. In fact the quieter she was, the more afraid we were. I can still hear her now: 'Have you anything to say, Jessica?' Hardly more than a whisper.

Dominic was like that.

The pile of pancakes, when it arrived, was towering. We were sitting at the dining table now. Dominic was opposite me with his bowl of fruit salad.

'*Bon appétit!*' he said, raising his glass of Buck's Fizz.

I lifted up my own glass, but kept my eyes down. Even so, I felt his gaze burning through me and the force of his expectancy as I cut into the first pancake. Afterwards, he smiled at me like I was a dog who'd learned a new trick.

'You know, Jessica, I love looking after you. I love feeding you up and watching over you when you sleep. It hasn't even been twenty-four hours since we met and yet already I can't imagine life without you.'

Eight years I've been with Travis and he's never said anything like that. Travis is all about the passive. 'You make me happy,' he might say. Or, 'I feel good when I'm around you.' Sonia Rubenstein had once advised me to frame complaints in terms of how something made me feel so that it didn't come across to the other person as a threat. So instead of telling my mother she's an interfering old bag, I should say, 'Your concern for my well-being sometimes makes me feel undermined.' It occurred to me now that Travis has done that all the time. Framing the world in terms of how it affects him. Framing *me* in terms of how I affect him.

If circumstances had been different I might have enjoyed the novelty of being for once the subject instead of always the object.

But they weren't. And I didn't.

ELEVEN

'So she's been missing since yesterday afternoon, as far as you're concerned?'

Kim saw the twitch around the man's mouth at that last phrase. He didn't like the idea that his version of events might not be the only version.

'She said she was going to do some last-minute Christmas shopping. In Wood Green, just down the road from where we live. I was out and wasn't home until after six. Like I said, at first I didn't really worry about it, but when it got to the time we were supposed to be meeting friends and she still wasn't back, I started to get worried.'

'But you didn't call the police then? In fact, you went out to meet your friends.'

'I thought she might turn up there. She is twenty-nine years old. She's not a child.'

'Though she is childlike in some ways.'

The mother had been hovering the whole time, hungry to join in. Kim recognized that expression – the need to be doing something, anything, even if it was just talking.

'In what way childlike, Mrs Gold?'

'She's not as ... worldly as other young women of her age. She is a bit of a ...'

'Misfit.'

That was one of the brothers. Kim had forgotten which was which as soon as they'd introduced themselves. It didn't help that they looked so similar, both swarthy, muscular types with prematurely receding hair and dark probing eyes. She'd practically had to wipe the testosterone off after she'd shaken their hands.

'Not "misfit". That's not the right word at all.' The mother again, her green eyes flashing. She was sitting on a chair at the end of the wooden table that dominated the kitchen. Her legs, in their black tights, looked thin enough to snap. 'She's her own person. She doesn't follow the crowd.'

'How do you mean?' Kim wanted to know.

'Well, she's not really one for going out clubbing or parties. And she has these episodes where she, well, hears voices.'

Kim paused then, her biro poised over the notepad in which she'd been scribbling, before saying, 'Mrs Gold, does Jessica have mental health issues?'

'God, no, nothing like that.'

It was the first time the father had really spoken. He was in the seat to the left of his wife. Dark like his sons, but less solid.

'She's not schizophrenic or anything. It was more like she used to have imaginary friends. Lots of kids do. It doesn't mean there's anything wrong with them. She's fine now – she's got a great job, she lives with her boyfriend.'

A child came skidding in from the living room. A boy of about six. Kim did what every parent does, plotting him on a scale of her own children. Older than Katy, younger than Rory.

'Aren't you finished yet? When can we open our presents? You said "soon" ages ago!'

'We just need to finish speaking to these two kind police officers who are going to find Auntie Jessica.'

Whichever brother that was, he had a completely different voice when he addressed his child. Soft and rich. He'd used the same voice when speaking to his daughter earlier as she'd let them in – a striking girl of about twelve or thirteen with a Smartphone wedged into the pocket of her skinny jeans.

'Silly Auntie Jessica. She got lost again, didn't she?'

The child trooped disconsolately back out again, shoulders exaggeratedly stooped.

'Again?'

From her vantage point leaning back against the fridge, Kim surveyed the faces around the table, her eyebrows arched.

It was the boyfriend, Travis, who spoke. 'She wandered off once before, about a year ago. That's why I didn't call the police straight away.'

'What do you mean, wandered off?'

'She sometimes goes into these trances and afterwards she can't remember anything about them. They're usually over really quickly, but around this time last year she called me after midnight to go and pick her up from Luton airport – and she had no idea how she got there.'

Kim glanced at Martin, but her colleague was staring at the opposite wall, giving nothing away.

'Did she go to the doctor?'

'See?' The father again, directing himself to Travis. 'I told you she should have gone to the doctor – it could be something serious, epilepsy or something.'

'She wouldn't go. What can I do, she's a grown woman.'

Travis Riley looked agitated, but not beside himself. Tall and thin, there was a boyish air about him still, although he had to be around thirty. The severe black glasses only served to further emphasize the youthfulness of his angular face. But there was something attractive about him, nonetheless, a quality of earnestness, a smile that came out of nowhere and transformed his face.

'There's another thing.' The mother was looking straight ahead, not meeting anyone's eyes. 'She's been self-harming.'

Travis didn't like that. 'Don't!'

Kim imagined how she'd feel if Katy was grown up and she had to say that about her. The thought was a rip in the tissue of her heart.

'What do you mean, self-harming?' One of the brothers now.

'I've seen cuts on her wrists and arms. Bruises too.'

'Why didn't you tell us?'

'She won't talk about it. You know what she's like.'

'It's private.' Travis again. 'She never admitted it and anyway, it only happened a couple of times. She'd be mortified if she thought you all knew.'

Kim sighed inside herself. This put a whole new slant on things. A girl with a history of undiagnosed mental illness had disappeared. It happened depressingly often. Perhaps she'd run away or walked into a wood or a park with a length of rope. They saw it all the time.

Yet there was the television-archive job. Jessica must be pretty together to hold that down. And Travis didn't seem to be the type who'd hang around with anyone too off-the-rails. A junior doctor, he'd said. Ambitious, she thought.

She could sense her partner's interest waning. When this had been the uncharacteristic disappearance of a young woman working in television, he'd been all fired up, but now that there was this added element he would be less enthusiastic. Martin was eight years younger than Kim and so fixated on climbing through the ranks, he only wanted the glory jobs. He wasn't interested in the grubby, tangled ones. She'd hoped that would count against him when it came to them both going for promotion. She was definitely a better, more thorough officer. But he didn't have kids. He didn't have to take days off when there was an inset day at school or drop everything to race home when they got sick and needed picking up.

'The thing is,' Travis told them, 'because she was out shopping, we don't know exactly when she went missing.'

'Why does that matter?' One of the brothers. Jeremy. 'She didn't come home last night. She didn't show up this morning. It's Christmas Day. Who goes missing on Christmas Day? It's totally out of character. Something must have happened to her.'

'I do understand your concern,' Martin said, in his mild, toneless voice. 'But in the case of someone Jessica's age, we don't normally treat it as a missing-person inquiry until they've been gone a full twenty-four hours, and that's what we can't yet ascertain.'

'But,' Kim chimed in before the family could erupt, 'in Jessica's case, we would consider her to be particularly vulnerable, so we'll get moving on it straight away.'

She felt Martin stiffen beside her, but didn't look at him.

'Now, we'll need a recent photograph, so that we can put it on the system.'

TWELVE

Dominic and I faced each other across the dinner table. We were both wearing paper crowns we'd got from crackers. Mine was pink and his was blue. It matched his eyes. So did mine.

In between us was the carcass of a huge turkey that, pre-basted, pre-roasted, had required just forty-five minutes in the oven. For the last twenty minutes it had been joined by foil containers of Brussels sprouts with chestnuts and honey-glazed carrots and mounds of roast potatoes. Also cranberry sauce, bread sauce, apple sauce and gravy.

Now those empty foil cartons were littered around the table and my distended stomach was proof of where they had all ended up. My lips were greasy with turkey fat.

All through that endless first day of Christmas, we had been locked away together listening to festive music and playing Scrabble and Monopoly. Playing games with Dominic was exhausting. If I did badly he'd accuse me of not trying. Too well and he became mean. He quizzed me about how my family spent Christmas Day and when he heard we play charades, he insisted on a game, just the two of us. 'It'll be fun,' he said, the dimple in his cheek winking as he spoke. 'Just like being at home.' He threw back his head and laughed. 'I'm James Stewart. *It's A Wonderful Life.*' When he grew tired of games, we watched DVDs using one of the white walls as a screen and projecting the images from a computer. *White Christmas, The Wizard of Oz.* All the classics. When I asked if he had a proper TV, hoping I might catch a glimpse of the news and find out if anyone was searching for me, he gave me the look I was coming to recognize as his Disappointed Look.

'Now why would you want to let the outside world in?' he asked. 'Aren't I enough for you?'

I had to sit on the floor after that. And though before I'd been on the comfortable sofa, I actually preferred it on the bare boards because his finger wasn't running up and down my arm. Like a cockroach.

After a while he got up from the table and headed over to the Christmas tree.

'It's time,' he said, and I could sense the excitement basking like a shark under the calm surface of his voice.

When he came back, he was carrying a small package, holding it carefully as if it was made of the most delicate glass.

'But I haven't got you anything,' I said.

'Don't worry, sweetheart.' He was magnanimous now and I felt a pathetic twinge of gratitude that his earlier anger had gone. 'You're all the presents I need.'

Like all the gifts under the tree, this was beautifully wrapped. First there was a gossamer ribbon, so sheer that when I undid the bow, it slid open like it was made from air. Then there was a white-silk ribbon threaded through with gold. I had to pick at the knot for a while before it would untie, my fingers stiff with tension.

Finally the ribbon fell away to reveal the paper – thick and white and encrusted with silver glitter in the shape of snowflakes. I rubbed my finger over the raised granules, wanting to delay opening the present.

But Dominic was like an impatient little boy. 'Come on,' he urged. 'Get it open!'

I slid a finger under the tape and opened up the paper. Inside was a small round silver box, about three inches in diameter, with on the lid a fairy made from what looked like solid silver. It was satisfyingly heavy and quite attractive in its own way. There was a name engraved on the side and a date: *Dominic Lacey 29/7/77*.

I looked up at him and smiled, suddenly giddy with relief that it wasn't anything more awful. 'It's beautiful.'

'It *is* nice, isn't it?'

I basked in the beam of his approval.

'Open it! Open the lid!'

Gently, I raised up the silver fairy by the tips of her silver wings. Inside, the little box was lined with purple velvet.

And nestled on the velvet were five tiny teeth.

Dominic's eyes scanned my face, but the truth was I didn't know how to react. The silver box had clearly been a christening gift of some kind. And as soon as I saw the teeth, I realized the significance of the fairy on the lid. There was nothing untoward about it. The grown man, keeping his baby teeth all these years.

'Are these yours?' I asked, because he was waiting for me to say something.

'Of course they're mine, Jessica,' he snapped. 'Why would I keep a box full of someone else's teeth? Do you think I'm some kind of weirdo?'

I fell silent.

'Pick them up,' he said.

I picked out the tiny nuggets of enamel and held them in the palm of my left hand where they formed a kind of circle like a mini Stonehenge. In the split second before I slammed down the shutters in my head, I heard a baby crying.

'It was a christening gift.' He indicated the box. He sat back against the cushions of the huge sofa. 'I don't know who it was from. Maybe my aunt, may she rest in peace. My mother is the one who would have kept the box, and collected each tooth when it fell out.'

I allowed myself a smile. It's the kind of thing my mother might have done. 'I bet she's also got a lock of your hair somewhere.'

He nodded, gazing into the far distance as if lost in nostalgia. 'And my foreskin.'

I wasn't sure I'd properly heard.

'My foreskin. After I was circumcised Mummy kept that too. Much later I found a box labelled *Dominic's foreskin* although there was nothing in there, just a hard, yellow gnarly thing. Same with the umbilical cord stump. That was stored in a Ziploc bag in a wooden box. It was just a black nub by then, like a raisin.'

I felt sickened, although it occurs to me now that, as an archivist, I should have appreciated Dominic's mother's actions. 'She must have loved you very much.'

Dominic laughed as if I'd said something very funny. 'Oh, she did. Yes, she really did. Only it's a weird thing, isn't it?'

'What's weird?'

'Love.'

'Is it?'

'When I was little, I slept in Mummy's bed.'

'Well, that's not weird, I . . .'

'And when I got older, she slept in mine.'

I looked away then, not wanting to see his expression. My stomach was pulling and twisting inside me and making a noise, and I felt stodgy and bloated from all the food. Dominic leaned forward and I had a horrible lurching feeling that he was going to kiss me, but instead he took the silver box from my hands. He held it on his palm and stroked a finger around the rim of the lid.

'One time I woke up,' he said, as I watched his finger going around, 'and she was lying on top of me, pressing every part of her body into mine – arms against arms, legs against legs, cheek against cheek. "I love you so much," she told me. She didn't seem to notice that she was crushing me half to death – she was what you'd call a larger lady, my mother. "I want you to wear me all over you, like skin."'

That's when it all came rushing to the surface. Before I knew it, my mouth was full of lumps of undigested turkey. Jumping to my feet, I ran for the bathroom. I made it just in time.

As soon as she turned her key in the lock, she knew they'd gone. There was no muted sound of the television coming from the living room, no buzz of tension in the air of the hallway, that exquisite sense of breath being held for fear of waking sleeping children. Just emptiness.

Kim crept up the stairs anyway, out of sheer force of habit. The first door on the right had a big red heart on it made out of crushed tissue paper and a ceramic plaque with *Katy* spelled out in flowery letters. Kim felt a jolt of hope when she saw it was ajar – Katy always insisted it was kept ajar at night and the landing light left on. She liked to hear other people in the house. But when Kim nudged it open, the flowery curtains were apart, the white princess bed with its netted canopy, empty. There were a few items of clothing strewn over the carpet as if someone had packed in a hurry. Kim's heart turned over at the sight of a flowery T-shirt, heartbreakingly small. No sign of any of this morning's Christmas presents or the old battered panda Katy had had since birth.

Kim picked up the T-shirt from the floor and sat on the edge of the bed with it pressed to her nose. Was this how Jessica Gold's mother felt? she wondered. This chasm opening up inside you where your organs should be? At least she knew where Katy was. That was something.

Wasn't it?

THIRTEEN

The sun streamed in through the bank of windows, and even without being able to see the river itself I could sense it through the ripples of light reflecting on the walls, like LED lights on the ceilings of the clubs I'd occasionally let myself be dragged to at university, only to spend the hours bobbing awkwardly on the edge of the dance floor, nursing a lukewarm drink in a plastic cup, my cheeks aching from the effort of trying to smile. From my stool by the kitchen island, I fought back a wild impulse to hurl myself across the room on to the sun-splashed floorboards. After almost two days here I craved light.

Dominic glanced up from slathering butter on to a pile of warm croissants and saw me looking.

'Maybe we can go outside today.'

My spirits leapt. 'Where would we go?' I tried to keep my voice neutral, not wanting to betray the extent of my longing.

The dimple appeared again. Funny how quickly I'd come to dread seeing it.

'*Silly* Jessica Gold, you didn't think I meant out of the building, did you? And spoil this lovely intimacy we're building up? No, I just meant out on to the balcony. To get some sunlight on your skin. You're looking a bit pale, sweetheart. But first, brekkie.'

He put the plate of croissants down in front of me and I pulled one apart. Its insides were translucent in places with grease. I counted the croissants. Five.

I started eating.

I continued eating, even when he handcuffed my left wrist to the retro school-style radiator near to the dining table while he went to the bathroom. Dominic's desire to be fully known did not extend to matters of his own personal hygiene. So while it was OK for him to watch me on the toilet, when it came to his own calls of nature he would excuse himself with a coy prudishness.

I wanted to go outside so intensely it hurt. So I ate my way right through the wall of revulsion that rose up to greet those croissants and didn't stop until all that was left on the plate was a smear of grease and a few claggy crumbs.

Dominic seemed pleased.

'Greedy guts! You're going to be a tubby little thing by the time this is all over.'

A flare of hope. So at some point, it would be over?

He withdrew from his pocket his bunch of keys. He was wearing different clothes today. Black, slim-fitting moleskin trousers and a black cashmere jumper. I wondered when he'd transferred the keys from yesterday's jeans.

The key that opened the doors to the balcony had a pink fob. When the heavy metal frame swung open the gust of cold air blowing in was shocking after all those hours cooped up in the heat of that flat. I followed Dominic outside where there was a glass-topped table on a wrought-iron stand and two matching chairs. The river, sparkling in the sunlight, was the most beautiful thing I'd ever seen.

There were cars, small as toys, proceeding over Tower Bridge in the distance, the moving speck of a pedestrian on the opposite bank, evidence of life going on. There were boats dotted all over the surface of the water. I wondered what would happen if I shouted for help down to the motorboat that passed almost underneath us, its five occupants huddled in their high-visibility jackets. But deep inside I knew the wind would just blow my own voice back in my face.

'Usually there's a lot more to look at.' Dominic was feeling expansive that morning. 'Over there' – he indicated the low converted warehouses on the opposite bank of the river, with the cranes behind them – 'is normally a hive of activity, but I guess everyone's holed up at home, it being Boxing Day. You know, I still can't get over us being here together, like this. Bank holidays can be so lonely without the right person to share them with. Aren't we lucky to have found each other?'

I nodded, not able to speak.

Turning my head away from the bridge in the other direction, I remembered what he'd said before about Execution Dock and, of course, as soon as I'd let that memory back in, the voices were there, but the wind was blowing against them, and they struggled to be heard.

What if I jumped?

The thought blew into my mind with the wind and once it was in there, it refused to leave. I pictured myself taking that deep breath, gathering momentum, letting go. I allowed myself to imagine the freedom of falling, dropping further and further away from Dominic and this flat. I could feel the warmth of the sun on my face as I fell.

'You're cold.'

I heard the strangest thing then, a child's voice almost echoing his. 'I'm cold,' it said. I looked around but there was no one else there. Dominic took my hand and rubbed it between both of his as if trying to start a fire. His fingers disappeared up the sleeve of my jumper, the skin of my arm turning icy where he touched it.

'Goose-bumps Jessica.' He was so close to me, his breath was warm and damp in my ear. 'We must get you into a hot bath.'

He turned to open the door, and as he did so a pleasure cruiser passed underneath us. Without thinking, I raised my arm in a desperate sweep. A child in a yellow anorak was standing between two adults leaning against the rail and looking right up at me. I could almost see the colour of his eyes and the stripes on his gloves. He lifted his arm at the elbow and waved solemnly as the boat disappeared from view.

I expected to go into the main bathroom where there is a large free-standing bath, but instead Dominic led the way through to the ensuite in the bedroom, where there is only a large walk-in shower – more of a wet room really, with mosaic-tiled walls and floor and several shower nozzles at different heights. The controls are at one end, which is where Dominic stood. His expression, I noticed now, was hard and set.

'Take off your clothes,' he ordered.

Immediately I froze. By that stage I'd been sleeping in my clothes for two nights and they were rank, particularly bearing in mind the quantities of rich food I'd been consuming. The smell, whenever I lifted my arm, was of overripe fruit. Curiously, I wasn't so scared of what he'd do to me – from what I'd learned about Dominic so far, he was more interested in the power than the flesh, but being stripped bare in front of him still seemed obscene.

'Chop-chop, Jessica. We haven't got all day.'

I didn't point out that technically that's exactly what we did have.

Slowly, I pulled my jumper over my head, and rolled down my jeans. Dominic's expression didn't change. I was wearing a pair of black featureless knickers.

'And the rest.'

He sounded almost bored.

I swallowed a lump the size of Brazil and slowly unclipped my T-shirt bra, then, with one hand covering my chest, I attempted to wriggle out of my knickers.

'What the fuck is that?'

Dominic was pointing to my stomach. For a moment I was flushed through with embarrassment until I looked down and saw a large patch of pink raised skin, about the size of a side-plate. He appeared quite disgusted by the rash.

'In the shower,' he said.

I stepped in and he slid the glass doors together, leaving himself just enough room to operate the controls.

'Arms by your side. Your skin will never get back to normal if you keep it covered up.'

The freezing water hit my body like a car smashing into a wall. I screamed as powerful jets blasted my head, shoulders, arms, thighs, calves – but the glass doors allowed no escape.

'I was going to let you have a nice hot bath,' Dominic shouted over the noise of the shower. 'And then you had to spoil things. What were you thinking, waving to that boat? Did you really think I wouldn't notice?'

He twisted the knob that regulated the shower pressure so the jets slowed to a trickle before coming back on bruisingly hard.

'You're just throwing my love back in my face.'

Afterwards, when I sat shivering on the bathroom floor with my arms wrapped around my knees and my hair dripping freezing water down my back, he brought a fluffy white towel and wrapped it around me as gently as if I was a baby bird that had fallen too early from the nest.

'What are we going to do with you, sweetheart?' he purred in my ear as he patted me dry. '*Silly* Jessica Gold.'

Kim had arrived at work half an hour early that morning, prompting a few raised eyebrows, but people had swiftly looked away as soon as they caught sight of her blotchy face and puffy pink-tinged eyes. Most mornings she came rushing in, out of breath after dropping the kids off at breakfast club (as press officer for an IT company Sean was in work by eight-thirty). Even if she was on a later shift, there'd be something to hold her up – a doctor's appointment about Rory's asthma, a forgotten lunch box to drop off, a supermarket trip that took longer than she thought, the endless round of cleaning, shopping, cooking that seemed to engulf whole days – so that she'd arrive flustered and already on the back foot. Sean did what he could, but his hours were rigid, and his job more precarious than hers, so she was the one who called into work pretending to be sick when one of the kids was running a temperature and couldn't go to school. Anyway, Sean had always been less fazed by it all, more able to compartmentalize the kids' stuff from the house stuff from the work stuff, while with her it all blurred into one big jumbled mess.

At home she was always cutting corners to get on with the next thing she had to do, and getting frustrated with the kids when they noticed. 'You missed out a page!' Katy would cry when Kim was reading her a favourite book for the tenth time in a row. While Rory would give her that look when she started gathering their things together in the park. 'We can't go now – we just got here.'

And all the time she was watching her mostly male colleagues putting in the hours, showing willing, staying late, moving up. She knew she was good at her job, better than many of them. Was it wrong to be ambitious?

Sean thought so. 'Where's our family life?' he asked her. 'Where's our quality time together, just the four of us?' And the perennial complaint: 'Why can't you get a job with normal hours?'

'You didn't need to come in today, you know.' The boss was staring at her and Kim knew her tear-stained face wouldn't go unnoticed. 'I told you, either Christmas Day or Boxing Day. You didn't have to do both.'

'It's no problem. Sean's taken the kids to his parents' today.'

She didn't tell him she didn't know if they'd ever be coming back.

The same as she hadn't told Sean she had a choice about working the day before.

'I want you to go back over to see the Gold family,' the boss said.

'She still hasn't turned up?'

'No. I've asked for her bank records to be checked, and her mobile phone. But everything's taking much longer than it should because it's Boxing Day. And while we're waiting, I'd like you to act as FLO for the Golds, seeing as you've already established a relationship with them.'

She didn't relish the idea of being Family Liaison. She'd done the training and had taken that role several times in the past, but now that she was free to put in long hours, Kim wanted to stay at the station so her superiors could see how hard she was working – how much more deserving she was of promotion than Martin. But she knew better than to protest. Detective Superintendent Paul Robertson, with his large square face that went straight down on to his shoulders without any obvious sign of a neck, was not the kind of boss who encouraged a lively debate once he'd told you to do something.

'The boyfriend is still with them, apparently. Sounds very cosy, doesn't it? What was your take on him?'

She frowned, remembering Travis Riley's sudden trans-formative smile, and the petulance in his voice when he'd talked about having to pick his girlfriend up from Luton airport that time.

'He seemed nice enough. Concerned, but not weeping and wailing, not like Sheridan.'

Gary Sheridan had done a televised appeal when his wife disappeared, sobbing uncontrollably throughout. She was found two days later in the chest freezer in his disabled grandmother's garage.

Don't take anything for granted, that's what they were always being told. People are rarely who they seem.

FOURTEEN

Now I knew the rash was there, I couldn't stop touching it. I was wearing clothes that Dominic had given me. Skin-tight leggings in an electric blue, and a silk tunic that was designed to be clingy, but billowed around my narrow frame. I assumed they used to belong to her, his wife, and horrified myself by actually caring how they fitted.

I kept pressing my fingers to the place I knew the rash to be, feeling how the skin was bumpy under the thin silk. Dominic had seemed displeased when I first got dressed in the clothes he'd given me.

'There's something not right,' he'd said.

Then he'd rummaged around in a cupboard in the ensuite bathroom and brought out a bulging make-up bag. I'm not a great expert on make-up – I've basically stuck to the same things I first wore as a student, brown eyeliner, mascara, a neutral-coloured lip gloss, that's if I wear make-up at all. But even I knew that the stuff in this black cube-shaped patent-leather bag was expensive. Like take-out-a-mortgage kind of expensive. There was a little pot of cream in there that I knew would have cost more than the entire contents of my bathroom cabinet put together.

He lowered the lid of the toilet and got me to sit down, and then set about applying make-up to my face. I'm one of those people who would rather stick needles in my eye than stop at a make-up counter of a department store and have one of the Orange Women, as Travis calls them, make me over. I tense up just getting my hair washed at the salon, which is why I only go once a year. Somehow the delicate touch of Dominic's fingers on my eyelids and lips, skin fluttering against skin, was almost worse than the shower had been. Violently intimate.

I held my breath for fear of breathing in his.

When he was finished, he surveyed his work approvingly. 'Better. *Much* better. Take a look.'

The woman in the mirror had shimmering eyelids and black-lined eyes with perfect flicks at the corners. Her lashes looked a centimetre longer than normal and perfectly curled, and her lips were deep wine-red.

'Here,' he said, twisting my hair up behind my head and securing it with a tortoiseshell clip. 'See how easy it is to become someone else?'

He was suddenly back again to his most charming self, as he'd been on that first day in the café, as if I was a new person he needed to woo all over again.

He led me into the living room and settled me on to the sofa, once again acting as if I was a date he was trying to impress.

'I've got a little present for someone,' he sang, heading towards the tree.

When he came back he was carrying a large, oddly shaped present, as beautifully wrapped as the one he had given me the day before. He held it with the utmost care as if it was more precious than gold.

As he laid it in my lap, it was surprisingly light. I glanced up at him.

'Go on, silly. Open it.'

I slowly undid the wrapping – the two ribbons, then the thick glitter-encrusted paper, taking care as I slid open the tape, so that the paper would remain intact.

It was a child's plastic stool. Purple. About a foot tall. I put it down on the floor in front of me and for a few seconds we both regarded it in silence.

'It's a stool,' I said.

'Not just a stool. Tell me, Jessica Gold, what's your earliest memory?'

The question threw me. But he was expecting an answer. I tried to peel back the layers of memory methodically like an onion. Finally an image flittered across my mind and I grabbed it before it disappeared.

'I'm with my two older brothers. I'm about three. We're inside. I think it's snowing outside or raining heavily. Anyway we can't go outdoors and my mum is trying to entertain us. She's produced three big cardboard boxes. The kind you get kitchen appliances in. Maybe we've just moved into our house?' I glance at him for validation, as if he might be able to confirm the exact chronology of my memory. 'So we each have a box, my brothers and I. And these boxes are our homes. And I'm sitting inside mine and I'm feeling really happy and safe and . . . well, that's it, really.'

He had been listening to me with an unnerving intensity.

Not so much hearing the words as devouring them. His eyes were damp. He reached out for my hand.

'This is exactly what I was after, Jessica – both of us laying ourselves open, letting ourselves be known.'

'So this stool is tied in with your childhood?'

He nodded. 'Just like your box, Jessica. My earliest memory is of sitting on this stool, watching my father.'

Something unfurled slightly inside me then. I hadn't been aware how rigidly I'd been clenching my muscles against whatever he was about to say. And after all, surely it was merely a benign memory. Perhaps a father pottering in his tool shed while his small son looked on, keeping up a stream of questions, or maybe outside fixing his bike.

'He had this friend. Well, she was our next-door neighbour, really. She was called Mrs Meadowbank. Big name for such a tiny woman. My mother used to say if anyone looked at her she'd snap. Anyway, my dad used to set my stool up in his bedroom. I was so little, my feet didn't even touch the floor, I remember that. And I would watch him and Mrs Meadowbank fucking.'

It was one of those times where you know you've heard something perfectly well, but it's so different to the thing you were expecting to hear that your brain won't let you process it.

'Fuck-ing.' He helpfully enunciated each syllable crisply. 'My earliest memory is of sitting on this stool watching my father tie Mrs Meadowbank's wrists and ankles to the bedposts with blue twine – the kind you use for a washing line – and fucking her. She had a body like a boy's. I can still see it now. And he was on top of her going at it. Of course I had no idea what they were doing. He was a very fit man, my dad. Maybe I thought he was doing press-ups. On top of Mrs Meadowbank. Funny how little kids' minds work, isn't it? But then it got so I wasn't a little kid any more but I was still on that stool watching them. I remember a time when I'd grown enough for my feet to be resting on the floor, and later for my knees to be right up under my chin.'

I almost gagged on the horror of it. 'But surely you'd have said something to your mother? You were too young to know what to do.'

He laughed – a sound that was like a slap.

That time I made it as far as the kitchen sink before everything came up in one unstoppable torrent. Lumps of croissant blocked the plug-hole, leaving the sink half full of foul-smelling yellow-coloured liquid.

I felt Dominic's hand on my back. 'That's right,' he said softly. 'Let it all out, sweetheart. Think of this whole thing as a purging. Afterwards we're going to feel so light and cleansed. I can't wait.'

Some foolish spark of hope ignited then when he said 'afterwards', like the thinnest sliver of moonlight through a gap in a blackout curtain.

The atmosphere at the Golds' house was very different from the day before. Then there had been worry but it was more of the cerebral kind (well, let's see, when did she last do something like this) not the kind that eats into your gut so you can't eat or even breathe properly. Travis, who was anyway one of those pale-skinned types, looked bleached out like an overexposed photograph. The parents, Edward and Liz, were noticeably quieter than they had been the last time Kim met them. Though the brothers were still there, she was relieved to find the small children gone. She didn't know how she would have coped with seeing children today. She was working hard to keep her mind off her own kids, but she knew that just one grubby cuddly toy clutched to a child's chest, or one cry of 'Mummy' would have brought her to her knees.

Liz Gold brought out a selection of photographs to be used in a media appeal. 'They're none of them very good,' she apologized. 'It's what happens now everything is digital. We have all these pictures on the computer that we never look at. And the one time you do want to get some of them off there, of course the printer is playing up.'

Kim had seen a snapshot of Jessica the day before, but this was the first time she'd had a chance to study her properly. Not conventionally attractive. Lots of thick dark hair, probably too much, so it overpowered her small, fine-boned face (if Kim had hair like that, she'd layer it or something, take some of the weight out), dark eyes with thick, unruly black eyebrows; surprisingly full lips. In one of the photos she was sitting at a table – the one in the Golds' dining room – leaning back and looking at someone just out of shot as if listening intently. In another, she was on a sofa, not the one in this house, with a puppy on her lap.

'How cute,' she said without thinking. Then, to Travis: 'You have a dog?'

'Not any more,' he said, not meeting her eyes.

They hadn't always been in agreement then, Travis and Jessica. Kim recognized the signs.

101

'I need all of you to tell me everything you can about Jessica – who her friends are, where she hangs out, what she likes, what she hates. Everything.'

Kim didn't miss the look that passed between the brothers then, the faintest shrug that said, 'How the fuck would I know?'

FIFTEEN

On the third day, when I woke up in the morning, I had a metallic taste in my mouth and my stomach was straining horribly as if something was alive in there and trying to get out. When I put my hand to my forehead, it felt hot and clammy.

At that moment there came a tug on the metal cuff around my ankle. I froze. Dominic's face appeared framed by the archway. He didn't appear to be in a good mood.

'Day Three in the Big Brother Household,' he said dryly, unlocking the shackle. 'And let's try to make a bit more of an effort, shall we, Jessica? I'm getting rather fed up of this all being so one-sided. I feel like I'm the one doing all the giving here, and you just take, take, take.'

I didn't know what to say.

'I suppose you'll be wanting the toilet, will you?'

He made it sound like I was asking for a bath in ass's milk.

I nodded. He'd been accompanying me to the toilet since I arrived, and I'd got used to focusing my eyes on a point straight ahead and imagining myself to be alone. Sometimes, during the really embarrassing moments, I recited song lyrics to myself in my head, trying to distract myself from what I was doing.

Usually Dominic looked on with a kind of paternalistic pride, but today he was angry. 'I shouldn't indulge you in all these toilet breaks,' he said as I stared fixedly at the tile straight ahead. 'You should be more disciplined about it. Your trouble, Jessica, is that you've allowed yourself to become spiritually flabby.'

'Spiritually flabby'. Those were his very words.

'Take off your clothes,' he said as I flushed the toilet. 'Don't flatter yourself, Jessica.' He'd clearly seen the sudden fear that passed over me. 'I just want to see you.'

I took off yesterday's blue leggings, peeling them down like a wetsuit. I took off the silk tunic. The bra.

'Not like that. Hands by your sides.'

Dominic perched on the lip of the bath and assessed me like he was buying me at auction. 'That rash is still there. I've got to tell you, Jessica, it's not attractive. I can't help feeling your personal hygiene is to blame. And you're getting chubby.'

I looked down at my stomach where it rolled over the waistband of my knickers. Natalie's knickers, I should say.

'No food for you today, I'm afraid.'

As if I'd been gorging willingly on the piles of pancakes and the foil containers of cannelloni and zabaglioni we'd had from the fridge yesterday.

'It's for your own good,' he told me, handcuffing me once more to the radiator before going off to find me more clothes. He reappeared with a red lycra frock and red tights. He removed the handcuffs and made me get dressed, which seemed somehow to restore his good humour.

'You look very festive, sweetheart. You know, I'm thinking I might quite like to paint you.'

I shot a glance at the hideous half-Natalie, half-cat painting on the wall.

'Nothing like that. Don't worry. I just feel I'd like to commit you to paper, just how you look now, in that red dress.'

He started singing that dreadful 'Lady in Red' song in a soft voice, and for one awful moment I thought he would ask me to dance. Instead he disappeared again to fetch his paints. It was the first time since I'd got there that I was left alone without being shackled to the radiator. Without pausing to think, I dashed across the room to the heavy front door, but even before I'd got there, I remembered how he'd locked it from the inside with the purple key. When I pulled on the handle, it failed to budge.

'I hope you're behaving yourself,' he called from the inner hallway.

I wondered if he was in the other room. The one behind the door that was always locked. Frantic, I crossed the floor to the kitchen and started pulling on handles, but apart from a drawer with tea-towels and napkins, the others were locked.

Hearing him approach, still humming that song, I ran back to the radiator where I'd been standing before.

'You sound a bit puffed out, Jessica,' he said as he placed an A3 sketchbook and a large leather holdall carefully on the dining table.

I held my breath, but he didn't say anything more. First

he pulled out a box of pencils. Then the paints, acrylics from the look of them, and a large wooden palette. Finally he withdrew a leather-bound folder. When he opened it up there was a variety of paint brushes, displayed in order of size. He said something to me then. I watched his mouth moving. But I couldn't hear a thing over the sound of a woman's voice screaming inside my head.

The area Travis Riley and Jessica Gold lived in was what estate agents might call up-and-coming, but what Kim would call a shit hole. They'd tried hard with the flat, that much was obvious. They'd covered the laminate flooring with colourful rugs and the furniture was eclectic and might even be described as shabby chic. There was a Christmas tree in the corner of the living room. Small, but real and tastefully decorated with baubles and candy cones.

'We're saving for a deposit on a place of our own,' Travis explained, twiddling a lock of his hair around his finger. 'Fat fucking chance. We'll be drawing our pensions and still saving, the rate things are going up in London. If there are any pensions left by then.'

He sounded bitter, Kim decided. Evidently he felt he was owed something better after so many years studying medicine. Kim knew he'd left the Gold family house the night before, saying he needed to be at home in case Jessica turned up. Probably wanted to get away from the atmosphere as well. She didn't blame him.

At least he looked like he'd slept, which is more than could be said for her. Last night when she'd finally let herself into her silent house, she'd tried Sean's mobile at five-minute intervals without joy, then finally, in desperation, rang his parents' landline.

'I'm afraid he doesn't want to talk to you just yet, love,' his mother told her. 'Give him a little bit of time.'

'Well, can I talk to the kids?'

There was a sharp intake of breath then, on the other end of the line. 'It's eleven o'clock, love. Surely you remember what time they go to bed?'

She'd drunk the glass of brandy they'd put out for Santa that was still on the mantelpiece. And then she'd drunk what was left in the bottle. But still she'd tossed and turned, lying rigidly on her side of the kingsize mattress, as if there was a wall down the centre. In the end, she'd gone into Rory's bedroom, and curled up under his Arsenal duvet and fallen asleep with her nose buried in his pyjama top.

'Have you traced her bank cards?' Travis wanted to know.

'We have a few purchases that put her in Oxford Street on the afternoon of the twenty-fourth. Nothing after four twenty-three.'

'Oxford Street?' Travis said it as if it was somewhere obscure and remote. 'But she said she was going locally. What about her phone records?'

'Nothing since the morning, when she made a call to her parents. And we tried locating her phone using its internal GPS but she appears to have switched off her mobile settings.'

Travis tutted. 'I've told her not to do that, but she insists it drains the battery to leave them on. You think she'd learn, wouldn't you, after she left her phone in the back of a cab, and another time in the library? But there's no telling Jessica anything. She appears to be listening, but then she goes and does exactly what she wants. And she still hasn't set up that synching thing on her new laptop, even though I keep nagging her.'

He sounded annoyed. Kim remembered Gary Sheridan and his crocodile tears at the press conference about his wife's disappearance.

Travis Riley didn't look the type. But if there was one thing Kim had learned since becoming a police officer, it was that there wasn't a type.

The new painting was propped up against the wall, underneath the half-cat, half-Natalie picture. It wasn't bad once you got past the fact that the face was just a blur of colour, all features deliberately smudged together, mouth bleeding into eyes and nose.

The hours spent posing on the sofa in my red dress and tights had passed almost pleasantly. Afterwards I was hungry – all the enforced eating of the last couple of days meant my stomach was accustomed to food – but Dominic didn't offer me anything to eat. Instead, I watched as he selected from the plastic cartons in the fridge. My heart twanged a little when he chose macaroni cheese – something vegetarian at last. He heated it in the microwave and transferred it to a big white dish, and ate it methodically, staring into my eyes.

And now we were on the sofa, and I could tell by the tension thrumming in the air that it was present time again, and I was suddenly glad I hadn't eaten because my guts were doing weird things and I was dreading what he was going to produce next.

'You look so lovely.' His fingertip traced the outline of my lips as if he still had a paintbrush in his hand, and I wondered if he could sense how my whole body stiffened. 'You deserve another present, I think.'

My hand was still resting on my rash-covered stomach, so I felt it heave through my fingers. All through the night before I'd lain awake in the kennel, mind churning with thoughts of yesterday's gift, that little purple plastic stool, and the little boy who'd sat there and watched god knows what.

'This present is a little different.' Dominic's excitement caused an unpleasant prickling at the back of my neck.

'I'm going to tell you the context of it beforehand, set the scene for you, and then give it to you after. You'll understand why. Can you wait that long?'

I nodded.

'Did you ever have a pet, Jessica?'

The question threw me. I thought about Winston and something tight and painful wrapped itself around my heart. 'I have a dog,' I said. 'I *had* a dog,' I corrected myself.

Winston had been my fault. I was never one of those children who fantasize about having a dog. I liked dogs from a theoretical point of view but didn't really see myself as having Dog Person Genes. Then I saw a programme on the television about rescue dogs and something clicked into place in my head, or heart, or wherever such things live, and that was it, I needed to have one. I didn't question whether my sudden conversion was connected to that thin blue line in the pregnancy-test window, but it became an obsession I couldn't shake off.

Travis was completely against the idea because a) we lived in a top-floor flat with no garden; b) we were out at work all day; and c) he couldn't stand the smell of wet dog. I agreed with every one of his reservations. Yet still I yearned for a dog with every fibre of my being.

A dog would sort out my life.

A dog would give me someone to love.

One Saturday afternoon I happened to go past a pet shop – a pet shop in the East End that was miles out of the way of anywhere I actually wanted to be. And there was the most gorgeous little black and white ball of fluff. I didn't know then that you're not supposed to buy puppies from pet shops as they've probably been puppy-farmed in Romania. I came back in a cab with Winston on my lap and enough pet supplies to fill up our entire flat.

I took a week off work to settle him in, and by the end I knew it was a mistake. Winston cried when we went out of the room. He weed on the rugs and chewed up Travis' copies of the *BMJ*. He repeatedly woke us up barking in the night so that we sat unspeaking at breakfast, our eyes lost in black shadows. Travis' 'I told you so' was written into every heavy step he took picking his way around the debris of our living room, every faint, disbelieving shake of his head.

When I went back to work, partings were pitiful, even though I hired a dog nanny to come in at lunchtimes and take Winston out. I returned home dreading the devastation I'd find. Yet, I loved that dog. When he slept, exhausted, on my chest as I lay on the sofa in the evenings and I felt his little heart beating against mine, I thought I might die from love for him.

Travis found someone at work to take him. Someone whose husband worked from home and who had a garden and didn't mind their rugs getting dirty.

'You know it's for the best,' he said as he loaded Winston's basket and bowls and his toys into the car. His favourite toy of all was the remnant of a red spotty lead he'd chewed right through. He used to carry that scrap of lead around from room to room as proudly as a lion with its kill. Travis was too mortified to pack that in the bag for the new owners so it stayed in our flat.

Travis made an effort to be extra nice when he got home from dropping Winston off. He'd gone shopping on the way back and he cooked cauliflower cheese with baked potatoes. But then later that night as we were getting ready for bed, he said, 'Won't it be lovely not to be woken up in the middle of the night.'

And I wanted to kill him.

Dominic was watching as all this passed through my mind, as if he could suck the thoughts out through my skull and read them like a book.

'I knew you would be a dog person.'

'Cat person. You guessed cat person before.'

He ignored my interruption. 'There's nothing like it, is there – the devotion you get from a pet? No conditions, no qualifications, no "I'll love you as long as you do X, or are Y, or give me Z."'

'Did you have a dog?'

'I had a bird. A canary. Does that surprise you?'

I said it didn't.

But of course it did. Who has a canary as a pet? Wasn't

that the same as a budgie? What was the point of them –
they didn't even talk, did they? They certainly couldn't lie on
your chest as you watched the telly.

'There's a funny story about it.'

My heart dropped inside my chest.

'When I was about five, my mother got pregnant. Yes,
Daddy must have taken a breather from porking Mrs
Meadowbank long enough to sire another child. I think by
that stage I was already starting to exhibit what the
authorities called "challenging behaviour" and my parents
were keen not to make it worse. They were concerned with
appearances, my mum and dad. I bet that surprises you.
Someone, a health visitor maybe, told them that to prevent
any jealousy it helps to smooth the way if the oldest child is
given a present, supposedly from the as-yet-unborn baby.
They asked me what I wanted more than anything, and I
said a pet, meaning cat or dog, though I knew Mummy
would sooner eat her own fat arm than have something in
the house that moulted and brought in dirt and mud. So
one day I came home from school and there was this canary
sitting in a cage on the kitchen table.'

I smiled, but only because he seemed to be expecting it.

'While Mummy was pregnant things were almost normal
in our house. Mummy went back to her own bed. Mrs
Meadowbank stayed in her own house. And I grew to love
that canary. Guess what I called him?'

I had no idea.

'Go on,' he said. 'Guess.'

'Bertie?' I said. 'Buzzy? Buddy the budgie.'

He roared with laughter. 'I called him Dominic.'

'You called your canary after yourself?'

'Yes! That bird was mine, you see. Did you know, Jessica, in the old days servants who accompanied their masters or mistresses to other houses used to be known by their employer's name, not their own? So were plantation slaves. Maybe if you'd called your dog Jessica, things might have turned out very differently.'

I had a sudden flash then of Sonia Rubenstein, leaning forward eagerly in her chair, peering out over the top of one of her brightly coloured scarves, drinking in the significance of what he'd just said.

'So what happened?'

'Well, my parents and this health worker kept laying it on thick about how the bird was a present from the baby and wasn't it kind of the baby. They were thrilled at how well I'd bonded with the bird. They thought that would make me even better disposed to the baby when it came.'

'And did it?'

'All in good time, sweetheart.' Dominic looked irritated. 'When my sister was born, I was horrified. You'd have thought I might be glad there was someone else in our dysfunctional family, but I wasn't. I'd been so used to being the centre of my parents' attention – for better or for worse – that I couldn't get used to this needy little creature who was suddenly the focus of the whole household. For years I'd been smothered in love and now it was like they didn't even bother to find out where I was half the time. It was Annabel this and Annabel that, and is Annabel hot, does Annabel need changing? She even slept in the bed with them and if I tried to get in, they'd say there wasn't room. I remember one night I started screaming about how I hated the new baby and I wished they'd take her back where they got her from. You know, how kids can get.'

I thought of my own brothers to whom I remained a constant conundrum and had been, as a child, a constant disappointment.

'My parents were trying to calm me down. "But Annabel loves you," my mother said.' Dominic put on a creepy high-pitched voice for this bit and I wondered how much of it he could really remember. He'd been so young after all. ' "Remember, she's the one who brought your canary?" They wouldn't call him by his name, Dominic. They said it was weird.

'So, can you guess what happened next, Jessica? What might an angry little boy do with the present his enemy had given him?'

He was looking at me, expecting an answer.

'Set it free?'

He looked at me with disappointment in his eyes. 'I couldn't set him free, Jessica. That would have been cruel. He wouldn't have survived a single night out there in the wild. I took him out of his cage, and held him gently in both my hands, so I could feel his little heart right through his soft furry chest. And then I snapped his neck.'

He's lying, I told myself. Children that young don't do things like that, let alone remember them so vividly. Still, my stomach rolled over.

'That was my first experience of loss. I cried for days. I told Mummy and Daddy what I'd done so they'd know I didn't owe the baby anything, but they insisted on blaming next door's cat. They knew it wasn't true, but that's what they always said. "Remember when your canary was killed by the cat from next door?" It drove me crazy.

'After a while they forgot about Dominic, but I never did. Each man kills the thing he loves. Who said that, Jessica? You must have that stashed away somewhere in your archive of a brain?'

'Oscar Wilde.'

'There. I knew you'd know it. It was a tough lesson to learn at five years old.'

He's lying. I repeated it mentally until it took on a rhythm of its own. He's lying, he's lying, he's lying.

'Anyway, listen to me, getting all maudlin when we're supposed to be being festive. Let me bring you your third present. I bet you thought I'd forgotten it.'

He sprang to his feet and crossed to the tree. For the first time, I looked closely at the perfectly arranged decorations. They were beautiful. Round baubles made from coloured glass winking as the flashing fairy lights caught them.

Dominic selected a package from the pile. I wondered how he knew which was which. There didn't seem to be any markings on that expensive paper.

The present was rectangular, around half the size of a shoebox. I took it from him.

'That's right, Jessica, get it all off.'

As before, watching me unwrap the layers of ribbon and paper seemed to get him quite excited and I thought he looked almost disappointed when I was left holding just the plain cardboard box that had been inside.

'Open it. Aren't you dying to see what's in there?'

My first thought was, a dead budgie.

So it was a pleasant relief when I opened it to find an assortment of little paint pots and what looked at first glance to be individually wrapped brushes.

'Art stuff?'

I'd come to dread the sound of his laugh, which now ripped from his throat.

'Not quite, Jessica. I want to show you something.'

He was wearing a white linen shirt today, loose over the top of a pair of faded jeans, and he lifted it up, revealing a flat lightly tanned stomach. There was a line of hair that started at his belly button and disappeared beneath the waistband of his jeans. I tried to swallow but couldn't.

With one hand holding up his shirt, he used the other to push his jeans down at one side. There, nestling in beside one perfectly smooth hip bone, was a tattoo. Of a small, brightly coloured bird.

I looked more closely at the box in my hands.

The little bottles weren't paints, they were inks. Those individually wrapped brushes? Sterile tattoo needles.

SIXTEEN

One of the other archivists got a tattoo a few months ago. She's a strange person. Most of us there are. She's forty-two and had been having an affair with a married man for fifteen years. He's much older than her and had been promising to leave his wife all that time, but never got around to it. Fifteen years of waiting. I expect most people find that unfathomable, but I sympathized. Sometimes I feel like I've spent my whole life waiting for something. For my real life to start. Waiting is something I'm good at.

One morning she came into work and there was something different about her. She was buzzing with energy. At first I thought it must have finally happened – at last he'd left his wife. But it turned out she'd had a tattoo done on her shoulder. She showed it to me in the toilets, shyly pulling down the back of her cardigan to reveal a butterfly emerging from the strap of her vest top.

'I've wanted one for years,' she confided. 'But Paul hates them. He thinks they're common.'

Within a week, she'd finished the affair.

So I knew tattoos were powerful things.

All the time I was remembering this, Dominic was jabbing

at me with the needle. He'd had the template prepared already – a tiny bird just like his. And of course it was to go in exactly the same place, resting on my hip. He had to shave a bit of my pubic hair first. I don't think he liked that. Judging by that horrible painting I imagined Natalie was probably one of those women who get the whole lot whipped off.

After shaving it, Dominic had made a big deal of dabbing the designated area with an alcohol wipe. 'Don't worry, I've thought of everything, Jessica. It's perfectly safe. Your health is important to me.' He glanced at me then as if checking that I'd got a private joke. He seemed eager for me to acknowledge how considerate he'd been, so I held back from asking how having me sleep in a dog kennel in the cold, and eat fatty food until it clogged up my veins, fitted in with this concern for my well-being.

In truth I couldn't have said anything. My voice was frozen in my throat by the sight of those needles and that neat row of little rainbow-coloured bottles.

I was about to be branded, like a sheep or a cow, tied to this man for ever by these matching patches of decorated skin.

'Please don't,' I said, before I could stop myself.

He looked at me and smiled.

And then began the pushing of the needle into skin. 'You have to penetrate just the right amount,' Dominic explained. 'Through the second layer of skin but not so far in that there's blood all over the place. If you listen carefully, you'll hear a popping sound as it goes through each layer.'

I didn't want to hear the popping sound. I didn't want to

see the beads of blood that mixed with the black ink that formed the outline. I didn't want to see the picture taking shape on my flesh.

'There,' Dominic said at last. 'Don't you want to look, sweetheart?'

I shook my head, and to my chagrin a hot tear squeezed itself out of my eye and trickled down my cheek.

Instantly he was on his feet. He held me close and crooned in my ear, 'Poor Jessica Gold. Poor old thing.'

When he stepped back, the look he gave me was so tender I couldn't help myself from blurting out, 'Are you ever going to let me go home?'

As soon as I'd said it, I wished it unsaid.

'But, sweetheart,' he replied, and his voice was soft as the flesh on the inside of a wrist, 'this *is* your home now.'

If you'd never been on the panel at a press appeal before, they could be pretty intimidating. Kim had only done it a couple of times, and her role was only ever to sit next to the family to give moral support, but even so she found herself overwhelmed all over again by the sheer quantity of microphones and cameras flashing in her face.

Nestled in between DSI Robertson and Edward Gold behind a table groaning with terrifying audio-visual equipment, Kim felt horribly exposed. She knew it was shallow to think about her appearance at a time like this, but she was regretting choosing today to try to disguise the shadows under her eyes with the new concealer she'd rashly bought the last time she went shopping, scrunching up the receipt as soon as she'd got it so Sean would never know how much it had cost. The sales woman had assured her it was meant to be much lighter than her skin tone, but now Kim was worrying that it would show up white under the flashlights, giving her that unfortunate look skiers sometimes have when they've tanned around their goggles.

Next to Edward Gold sat his wife Liz, looking curiously shrunken since the last time Kim had seen her, as if someone had opened a valve and let some of the air out of her. And at the far end was Travis Riley, his pale eyes anxious behind those black-framed glasses.

They'd already talked about the facts – how long Jessica had been missing, where she'd last been seen, the bank cards that put her in Oxford Street on Christmas Eve afternoon. Now it was time for the Golds to make their appeal. This part always made Kim feel uncomfortable. She was well aware that the family would be judged on how much emotion they showed. Too much and it could be deemed all a show. Too little and they were hiding something. When did people start judging real life like *The X Factor?*

Liz Gold was going to do the talking for the family, they'd already decided that much. Well, she'd already decided it. At least she looked the part, Kim thought, wryly. Her green eyes were sunk in dark shadows and her brown hair had a lank, unwashed look, the grey coming through at the parting like mould. She'd put on lipstick though, Kim couldn't help noticing. That might go against her.

'Jessica is a quiet, home-loving girl,' Mrs Gold was saying. 'This disappearance is so out of character. Someone must know where she is and what's happened to her. We just want to know our daughter is safe.'

Kim appalled herself by nodding with approval when Liz Gold's voice wobbled on the last word.

Next up was Travis Riley. He was wearing a black polo-necked jumper and Kim frowned when he flicked his hair out of his eyes before speaking. That might alienate people – it was amazing the things the great British public took against.

'We love and miss Jessica very much,' he said, reading from a prepared statement. 'If anyone has any information about her whereabouts, please, *please* get in touch with the police.'

From her position at the table, Kim could see that Travis' hand, the one that held the written statement, was trembling, but she knew the cameras would focus on his face, and the wooden manner in which he was reading.

Could he have something to do with it all? Kim's gut feeling was no, but they were digging around anyway, tracing his movements since Christmas Eve. They'd already checked his phone records – lots of calls and texts to Jessica's number asking where the fuck she was, but nothing suspicious.

Reporters had been briefed that the family weren't taking any questions, but still some shouted out, desperate for more. 'The ed wants more colour,' these reporters were constantly telling her, meaning personal stuff. The little details that bring the dead and missing to life.

'Mrs Gold, can you tell us about the self-harming? Do you think Jessica might have done something to herself?'

Kim briefly closed her eyes. How on earth had that got out so quickly? The family were already on their feet, getting ready to leave, but Liz Gold stopped, blinking into the sea of flashlights.

'No,' she said, and an angry red flush worked its way up over her throat and face. 'She would never—'

Kim quickly took hold of her elbow and steered her away, leaving the rest of the sentence hanging in the air.

That night, Dominic let me sleep across the foot of the huge bed. I was still shackled by the ankle, the chain much shorter than before, but the feeling of having a soft mattress underneath me was indescribable. I was so grateful I cried.

Later, when my eyes became accustomed to the dark I peered over the satin eiderdown at Dominic. He had a disconcerting way of sleeping without making any noise at all, no heavy rhythmic breathing, nothing to tell you if he was unconscious or staring straight at you, his close-together eyes shining in the darkness like a cat's. Now his face was turned away, his chest gently rising and falling. The size of the bed meant that even though I was lying horizontally across the bottom, his feet still weren't against mine, although if I reached out a hand I'm sure I could have touched him. Making sure not to move the ankle connected to the chain, I raised myself up a bit more and looked around to see if there was anything I could use as a weapon, but there was nothing. The bare dressing table with its closed drawers was out of reach. The dull ache in my empty gut had intensified and I put a hand over my stomach, wincing when I touched the skin still raw from that afternoon's tattoo.

I began to think about my family and wondered what all this would be doing to them. My parents have always worried about me more than my brothers. Once, when I was about thirteen and nosing around in the loft looking for my old diaries, I came across a notebook in which my mum had listed, in her spiky, almost illegible handwriting, all my odd behaviour as a child, observations painstakingly dated and recorded. *10.30–11.20 a.m., March 2nd 1987: Stared into space. 3.15, September 9th 1988: Had conversation in the garden with someone who wasn't there.* She was mortified when I confronted her with it. 'I just didn't want to be . . . remiss,' she said. 'You can't imagine what it is to be a parent, how much you want your children's lives to be as easy as they can be, for them not to struggle.'

I wondered if the crisis would have prompted my mum to take up Buddhism again. I pictured her in that shrine she made in the corner of the room that used to be my oldest brother's, chanting for my safe return. James had been furious when he'd come home and found it there. 'Why *my* room?' he'd said petulantly. 'Why not one of the others?'

It seemed important suddenly that they realize I'd ended up here out of naivety, as could happen to anyone, rather than out of some inherent personal weirdness.

Lying across the bed, too nervous to move, I nevertheless relished the softness of the mattress under me, such a relief after the hard wooden floor of the dog kennel that had dug into my hip bones. I wondered what had prompted this sudden generosity, and then it hit me.

Sleeping on the bed was my reward for being broken.

SEVENTEEN

Sonia Rubenstein had a way of looking at you as if she was at a gallery and you were a particularly fascinating painting. Kim found herself considering what she was about to say before opening her mouth, for fear of giving herself away. Though what she was afraid of giving away, she couldn't have said.

'I appreciate your reservations, Ms Rubenstein,' said Kim, stumbling as usual over the pronunciation of that word *Ms*. 'However, you'll appreciate our priority is to find Jessica, so you need to tell us anything she might have said that could give us some insight into her state of mind before she disappeared.'

The psychotherapist smiled, her red-lipsticked mouth matching exactly the hue of the silk scarf loosely knotted around her neck.

'Sonia, please. Of course I want to help in any way I can, Detective Harper. But you must understand I also take patient confidentiality very seriously. If Jessica turns out to have just ... taken a breather from her life, shall we say ... I don't want her to feel I compromised her in any way.'

Though Kim was a few feet away from Martin, she could feel impatience pouring off him like sweat.

'And do you think that's likely, Sonia? That Jessica would have taken off for a breather, as you say, without telling anyone?'

The psychotherapist's smile remained fixed on her face as if it had been thrown there and stuck, like not-quite-cooked spaghetti against a wall.

'It would be uncharacteristic for her to act in that way,' she said eventually. 'But I wouldn't rule it out. Jessica is a highly unusual person. I wouldn't want to risk predicting her behaviour.'

'Unusual in what sense?' Martin was itching to get the diagnosis they'd come for and be off, she could tell.

'She doesn't think in the same way other people do. She's highly intelligent but sometimes you'll talk to her and it's like she's not even there, as if she's gone into another world altogether. She sometimes struggles to fit in.'

'We understand she's said in the past that she hears voices?'

This evidently wasn't news to Sonia Rubenstein.

'Yes, Mrs Gold mentioned that to me when she booked our sessions. She said that there was, how shall I put it, a childhood history of internal voices. However, Jessica never mentioned that to me. She said she had episodes where the outside world disappeared, but she never talked about voices.'

'And you didn't think to ask her?'

Kim wished Martin wouldn't sound so adversarial. It was just going to put the woman off.

'I wouldn't lead the sessions in that way, no. If Jessica had wanted to talk about voices in her head, she had plenty of opportunity to do so, but she didn't.'

'And I suppose she didn't mention self-harming either?' Martin pressed.

Now the psychotherapist did look shocked. 'No. Never. Who told you that?'

'Jessica Gold's mother saw cuts and bruises on her arms,' he insisted.

Sonia took a moment to digest that information before she spoke. 'That really does surprise me. I would not have imagined Jessica was in that mind-frame at all.'

'And she never gave you any indication of being suicidal?'

'Suicidal? Not at all.'

From the corner of her eye, Kim saw Martin frown. She decided to step in before he had the chance to pursue that vein of questioning any further.

'Ms Rubenstein, Sonia, can you give us some insight into the relationship between Jessica and her boyfriend, Travis Riley? Might she be running away from him?'

The therapist was shaking her head before she'd even finished her question.

'I very much doubt it. And if you're thinking he might have been responsible for those cuts and bruises her mother saw, I doubt that too. Jessica often complained . . . no, that's too strong a word for it, she . . . observed . . . that the relationship was marked by a deficit of passion. I think if Jessica had wanted out of the relationship that badly, it wouldn't have been too difficult to end it.'

Kim tried not to think about Sean and how it had been over the last few months, with his mouth a thin line every time she came home late from work and her feeling more and more like work was the place she went to relax, and home was where everything tensed up again. All the times she'd wanted there to be less passion, fewer intense moods, so she could concentrate on holding together the things she really did feel passionately about, work and kids. Did it show in her face? she wondered. The failure of her marriage?

Sonia Rubenstein kept glancing at the clock above the door in the consulting room where they sat.

'I'm afraid I do have another client arriving soon,' she said eventually. But as Martin and Kim were about to leave, she held on to Kim's sleeve. 'She's tougher than you think, you know. She's one of the toughest people I know.'

Then, abruptly, she turned away. 'Can you show your-selves out?'

I had become institutionalized.

I understood it on the fourth day when I looked out of the huge glass windows at the tiny cars moving across the bridge in the distance, and felt anxiety in place of longing. The outside world still looked beautiful, but also scary.

Go figure, as Travis used to say in a fake American accent when he was trying to be funny.

So how did Dominic and I fill our time together? It's hard to recall. Time does weird things when you're in that situation, winding itself around and around you until you're in a cocoon where you can't tell the difference between a minute and an hour. We watched films. We played Scrabble and I didn't say anything when Dominic used American spellings to win points. We read. There was a large drawer under Dominic's bed crammed with books. At first I was disappointed to find they were all non-fiction and mostly concerned with the Second World War, but after reading a couple I became fascinated by the way it all unfolded. For the first time I saw history is just a succession of consequences, one after the other. Without end. Don't ask me why, but I found that a comfort in my current predicament. Dominic and I and this million-pound prison in Wapping didn't exist in a bubble outside of everything else. We were part of a chain of events, cause and effects, that had led us here, and would continue on long after this had all been resolved.

Occasionally I even forgot the circumstances and would find myself chatting to him almost as if he was a normal person and this a normal social situation. I had a glimpse during those moments of how Dominic might have been in a parallel universe where there was no Mrs Meadowbank, no smothering mother, no plastic stool. Then he'd get up to go to the bathroom and cuff me to the radiator, or I'd look down and see how the skin around my tattoo was pink and raised and decorated with tiny blobs of congealed blood, and reality would come crashing back in. On one occasion we were talking about films and we got on to discussing Heath Ledger, the *Batman* actor. And I was saying he was in *Brokeback Mountain* and Dominic disagreed, and we were almost like a married couple bickering good-naturedly over the Sunday papers. All of a sudden Dominic jumped up and disappeared around the wall of the kitchen, and I heard the sound of a key being turned in the lock, and assumed he was opening the other door, the one that was always locked. Immediately my thoughts raced. My eyes cast wildly around

the room. Could I pick up that floor lamp and swing it at him? What if I jumped up on the kitchen island and smashed a plate down on his head? Before I'd even had a chance to put my thoughts in order, I heard the key turning again in the lock and he was back.

'You're quite right,' he said, and his mouth was smiling, but his eyes weren't. 'He *was* in *Brokeback Mountain*. I just Googled it.'

After that he refused to talk to me for an hour. But that was all right because all I could think was, 'There's Internet here.' The knowledge warmed my cold heart like a flame.

That fourth day, I plucked up courage to ask him about her. Natalie. He was telling me about his first car and he was trying to describe the colour. 'Like that,' he said, getting up to indicate a shade in the hideous half-cat, half-woman painting on the wall facing the sofa.

The conversation was flowing so easily, it just popped out, without me even thinking about it. Maybe it also had something to do with me being so light-headed now due to lack of food.

'What happened to her?'

'Who?'

I gestured towards the painting.

Dominic's voice was dangerously soft when he replied. 'And why would you want to know about her, sweetheart?'

'No reason,' I said. 'No reason at all, I just—'

The slap came from nowhere. One second, I was looking at his blue eyes and willing them to soften, and the next I was flying backwards, clutching my hand to my burning cheek. I crouched down on the floor by the sofa too shocked

to speak. For a long moment we looked at each other, him and me, and then he walked over and leaned down and scooped me up, sitting carefully back on the sofa cushions with me on his lap like a child.

'Poor Jessica Gold,' he whispered in my ear, stroking my cheek that was flaming with pain.

We sat together rocking gently.

'Poor old you,' he said again.

EIGHTEEN

The fourth package was rectangular, quite heavy, and I instinctively knew even before I'd fully unwrapped it that it would be a photograph. The frame was solid silver, old style, and the picture was the kind you have taken in primary school – fixed smiles and grey V-neck pullovers with white shirts and grey and yellow striped ties. The boy looked about nine or ten and his smile was tight, as if he was trying to hide his just visible front teeth which had grown through huge, like pebbles, dwarfing the other baby teeth around them. The girl was much younger – four or five – and her smile was big enough to drive a bus into.

The boy was unmistakably Dominic. The blue eyes were intense, even then, although there was something, a light, in them that was now missing. The girl had light brown hair in two tight short plaits, and huge eyes, the same colour as her brother's but with a navy ring around the iris, and astonishingly thick black lashes, and a matching dimple in her cheek. She looked bursting with life. He had his arm around her in a traditional protective big-brother mode.

'Me, and my sister,' he explained, unnecessarily.

And then I heard her, for the first time. A tinkly voice

that drifted down around my ears like glitter, making me think of the children in the snow globe on the front of my parents' Christmas card.

'I'm cold,' she said. 'I'm so cold.'

'It's a lovely photograph.' I said it to drown her out and because I knew he was waiting for my reaction. But actually it *was* a lovely photograph. They were so obviously siblings, and seemed to be so close.

'Tell me about your schooldays, Jessica. I want to know all about you. So far it's been all me, me, me. Now it's your turn.'

I knew he didn't really want to know about me. Or only inasmuch as what I said might shed more light on himself.

'I was a bit of an odd child,' I began. 'Even at that age' – I indicated the photograph – 'I knew I wasn't the same as the others. I remember spending a lot of time staring at other children, trying to work out how they did it.'

'Did what?'

'How they knew how to talk to each other and play with each other, and what to do in break times and how to act. Everything was difficult for me. Nothing came naturally. Even in primary school I felt like I was playing the part of a normal kid.'

'And why would you want to be like the others, Jessica? Enough sheep in the world, don't you think?'

'I had two brothers at home who kept laughing at me for being weird. All I wanted was to find the magical key that would make me fit in.'

'And did you?'

'Not really. Though I did learn that if you work hard

enough at it, you can fake being normal. Most of the time, anyway.'

'That's fascinating, sweetie.' He had shuffled along the sofa so that he was sitting right next to me, stroking my hair like I was a pet cat.

'What's her name? Your sister?'

His fingers became abruptly still, resting on my head.

'I thought I already told you. Annabel. We called her Bella.'

Immediately I heard her again. Her tinkling voice. 'I'm cold,' she said. 'So cold.'

'It looks like you two were close.' I was still staring down at the photograph, hoping he wouldn't look at my face and guess what I was hearing.

'Does it?' His voice was barely louder than a whisper.

For a moment I thought I'd said the wrong thing and my chest tightened, but then to my relief he started talking again.

'Has there been anyone in your life that you feel so strongly about you just can't tell what those feelings are? Like when you put your hand in water that's so extreme in temperature, for a moment you can't tell if it's boiling or freezing?'

I thought about Travis and how, when he walks into a room, my head says, 'There's Travis,' and my heart says nothing at all. I thought about the cards he used to write me on birthdays and Christmases that he signed off with 'lots of love'. Not 'all my love'. Not even just plain 'love'. As if there was an ever-replenishing pool of love and he'd reached into it quite casually and scooped out a random load and ladled it on my plate before moving on to the next person. I thought about the times he'd called me to say he'd gone out straight from his shift at the hospital, and my reaction was relief that I could watch whatever I wanted on the telly.

'Not really,' I admitted.

'Well, that's how it was with Bella. Right from the word go, these enormous, churning feelings I didn't know how to process. On the one hand, she was so tiny and helpless she made me want to jump in front of trains to save her or pull her out of burning buildings. But on the other hand, I was also eaten away with jealousy. You see, Mummy and Daddy adored Bella. Everyone did. Like I said before, Bella even brought them back together for a while. Mrs Meadowbank kept away, and they slept in the same bedroom, often with Bella, even though she had her own room.'

'Surely that must have been a relief?'

He'd started stroking my hair again and I felt his fingers shake as he laughed.

'Sweet Jessica, you are so touchingly naive. Don't you know that people will do anything for attention from those they love, or think they love, even if that attention hurts them?

'As she grew bigger, those conflicting feelings just intensified. I used to spy on her when she played with her friends, following them around like a shadow. I didn't want her to have friends, you see. I wanted her to need only me. But when it was just us at home with our parents, I did everything I could to put her down and make her look stupid. I wouldn't let up until she cried. Sometimes at night I'd go into her room to watch her sleeping.'

'I'm cold.' Her voice was louder now, more strident. When she spoke I felt tiny bumps of coldness popping up in sympathy all over my skin.

I shut her out.

'So where is she now? Bella?'

Dominic made a claw of his fingers and clamped them down hard on my head.

'Patience, Jessica,' he said, digging them into my scalp.

Kim felt like she had entered an entirely new time/space dimension. A combination of lack of sleep and the guilt that ate away at her whenever she allowed her mind to relax meant she was on constant alert, throwing herself into work in a way she could only have dreamed of when the kids and Sean were at home.

'Sean's taken the kids to his parents' for a visit,' she explained to Martin when he complained, only half joking, that her industriousness was making him look bad. 'I need to make the most of it.'

She didn't tell him that Sean had given her a week to find somewhere else to live. Or how sad his voice had sounded when he said he'd had enough of feeling like him and the kids were getting in the way of her career. She didn't mention how she felt energized at being free to work as long and as late as she liked, or how much that realization made her hate herself, or how Sean had left a space at the end of his speech for her to tell him she'd been a fool and wanted them back, and the silence had stretched on until she'd heard the gentle click of him ending the call.

In her overheated, sleep-deprived state, Kim knew she

was over-obsessing about the Jessica Gold case. There was still nothing to show that she hadn't gone off with a friend or a secret lover. She could be using a pay-as-you-go phone and have another hidden bank account. People did that all the time. When Kim was first starting out she'd worked on a case where a man, by all accounts a loving father and husband, had set off to buy a Lottery ticket and never been seen again. Eventually he'd been tracked down to a bedsit in Eastbourne. 'I've always wanted to live by the sea,' he'd said.

So she knew it happened. But somehow she couldn't believe Jessica Gold had walked out of her own life.

Today Kim's restlessness had led her to Perivale on the fringes of west London. When she'd first heard that Jessica Gold worked for a television company, she'd imagined somewhere cool and bustling, staffed with trendy young things in designer clothes. Instead, she found herself on an industrial estate, in front of a square newish-looking building that, according to the security guard, used to be some kind of factory. When she got inside, the people working there were on the whole scruffily dressed in jeans and jumpers and working at banks of computers scattered through the building.

As it was still that no-man's-land between Christmas and New Year, there was only a skeleton staff on, and Jessica's boss would be on holiday in the Caribbean until the following week, but the boss's deputy, Joe Tunstall, was on hand, an eager-to-please young man with curly red hair and freckles on his forehead that joined together when he frowned, as he was doing now.

'Don't get me wrong, everyone likes Jessica, it's just that

no one is her particular friend, if you know what I mean,' he was saying. 'She likes to keep to herself. We always ask her to join us if we go out for lunch, but she always has some excuse and scurries off before the rest of us have even got our coats on. And she's usually back after us as well. Not that I'm saying she takes the piss or anything. She works bloody hard.'

Kim had met lots of people like Joe in the force – insecure young men who latched gratefully on to the camaraderie of life in an organization, accepting every invitation that came their way, thankful for that sense of belonging to a team, and threatened by anyone who refused that lunchtime sarnie in the cafeteria or that pint after work. She'd seen their faces when she said she was sorry but she had to rush back to bath Katy and Rory before putting them to bed. And she'd hated that treacherous part of her that felt she was missing out.

'Did she strike you as . . . troubled at all?'

Joe wasn't sure what she meant, so Kim clarified it. 'Did she seem preoccupied or depressed?'

He shook his head. 'No. Like I say, she's quite private. She seems to get a lot of texts, if that's any help. She sits next to me and even though her mobile is on silent, it vibrates when a text comes in and I can feel the vibrations through my desk.'

Kim didn't like to think of how many texts she received over the course of a day. From Sean, asking what time she was going to be back, from the childminder who took the kids home from school two days a week, from Sean again, to find out why she still wasn't back when she said she'd be, from Rory, wanting to know where the game she'd confiscated the day before was, from Sean again, informing her in clipped tones that she needed to pick herself up a takeaway on the way home as her dinner was ruined. Oh, and not to rush, because the kids were in bed already.

'How would you describe Jessica?' she asked Joe as he walked her over to reception.

He looked taken aback at the question, as though what she was asking him was somehow improper. 'I'm not really sure,' he said. Then something seemed to occur to him. 'Slippery,' he added. Immediately the freckles were forced together into a dark splodge as he frowned. 'No. Not slippery. Mysterious. Just when you think you've worked her out, something changes and you realize you're still way off the mark.'

'Not a team player then?'

Kim watched his face relax in relief at being on more solid ground.

'No. Not a team player at all.'

NINETEEN

The locked room.

Ever since I'd arrived in that flat I'd been wondering about that closed door leading off the inner hallway. I knew there were three rooms – the bathroom, Dominic's bedroom (I couldn't bring myself to think of it as *our* bedroom) and the mystery room. It could have been a closet, but then, why would a closet be locked?

That night when I lay once more across the foot of the bed unable to sleep, I fantasized about breaking into that room, and what I might find. A telephone, an arsenal of weapons, a trap door leading to the flat below. I already knew there was a computer in there. And broadband. Not to mention the bags of presents I'd bought before Christmas. In my imagination, the room became like a gateway to another world. The world outside.

I'd now passed beyond hunger into a state of constant empty ache but still my mind played tricks on my body, visualizing breaking open the door and finding tables groaning with the kind of food I missed. Pasta, pizza, perfect bananas, still slightly green at the tips, biscuits, baked potatoes oozing with butter and cheese. Comfort food. I knew by now that Dominic had a strange relationship with food, and that night I shared it – picturing dishes that summed up my childhood until my tastebuds wept with the loss of it all.

I wondered if my parents were asleep in the double bed they'd had ever since I can remember. I hoped my mum wasn't using my disappearance as an excuse to go back on to the prescription pills she'd only recently weaned herself off: the codeine, the mirtazapine, the chlorphenamine for when she wanted to 'take the edge off things'. She'd got into them after I left home. After the Buddhism failed. And the meditation. And the Hatha yoga. Sometimes it helped, she said, to be outside of yourself. I didn't blame her. I only wished I had even one sleeping pill that I could take and escape everything for a while. What wouldn't I have given for just a few hours of total oblivion?

I tried to shift position without moving the chain attached to my ankle, but I'd misjudged how close I was to the iron bedframe. The clanking sounded like an explosion in the still of the room.

Instantly I knew Dominic's eyes were open. There was a change in the quality of the air, a tingling.

I pretended to be asleep but he kicked me through the covers. Hard.

'You're not an attractive sleeper, Jessica. Has anyone ever told you that?'

It shouldn't have hurt, but it did.

'You sound like an asthmatic sow. This is the sound you make.'

He made a noise that I won't even attempt to replicate in writing.

'I'm sorry,' I said, and to my complete shame, felt hot tears at the backs of my eyes.

'To tell you the truth, Jessica, you're turning out to be a big disappointment to me. In fact, I'm starting to wonder if I've made a mistake. A lot of preparation went into all this, you know. Now I'm doubting we'll even get to the twelfth present.'

He was growing sick of me.

And I knew that my continued survival here depended on holding Dominic's interest.

At breakfast on that fifth day, Dominic's bad mood clung to him like a needy lover.

'Stop watching me eat,' he commanded. 'It's really off-putting.'

I couldn't help it. My stomach was so desperate to be fed, it hijacked my brain, sending instructions to my eyes to follow every movement of spoon to mouth.

'You want to eat?' he snapped.

I knew it was a trick, but I nodded.

'Fine. You can eat. I'll even make you a smoothie.'

He got to his feet and started throwing anything he could see lying around the kitchen into a blender that he'd retrieved from one of the kitchen cupboards. Cereal, butter, eggs, last night's leftover wine, all went in together and were blitzed on the top speed setting.

'There you are, sweetheart.'

He placed the glass of pinky-beige liquid in front of me.

I was so hungry, I ignored the stringy bits of egg yolk floating on the top and the unmixed lumps of butter and drank the whole glass down in one, gulping it back without stopping to think.

Dominic eyed me with undisguised disgust.

For a few seconds I stared brazenly back, emboldened by the sudden rush of pure joy that came from being momentarily full. Then I felt a now familiar rumbling in my stomach and rushed to the bathroom. Dominic's chuckles echoed around the flat.

For once he didn't follow me. As I knelt on the tiled floor, my eyes scanned the room. Soap, towel, shampoo. I checked behind the toilet for bleach that I could throw into his eyes when he wasn't prepared.

Nothing.

What kind of man doesn't have bleach behind his toilet?

Still Dominic didn't appear.

Alarm bells should have been ringing, but there were a lot of other noises in my head. Maybe I just couldn't make them out.

In the inner hallway, I hesitated. The bedroom door was ajar, and through there was the ensuite bathroom with another unexplored cupboard. But it was the locked room that held me enthralled. What if I turned the handle and, just for once, it opened? What if I walked in, locked the door behind me, and found that portal back to the life I'd become convinced lay inside? As soon as the thought crossed my mind it was instantly real. In my head I saw myself crossing the threshold and right on to the outside where the blue winter sky was shot through with the white imprint of passing aeroplanes and the breeze blowing off the river whipped your hair back in your face and froze the breath in your mouth.

I crossed the hall. I wrapped my hand around the cool, metal orb of the doorknob. Nothing.

'Oh Jessica, you didn't really think, did you . . . ?'

His disembodied voice punched me out of my trance.

'Leave the handle alone, sweetheart. It really is too pitiful to watch.'

I looked around at the empty hallway. And only then did I get it – the tiny red light up in the corner that I'd always assumed to be part of some intricate alarm system. It was a camera. So too the ones in the bedroom and bathroom.

I walked slowly back around the partition wall of the kitchen.

'Where are the screens?'

He frowned. 'Screens?'

'The ones you've been watching me on? Where are they?'

'Oh those. Why they're right here, of course.' He withdrew from his back pocket a Smartphone in a black leather case. 'Don't worry, Jessica, it's not connected to a network. I wouldn't want anything to distract us from one another. I just use some of the apps, like Nannycam. It's supposed to be for anxious parents who want to check up on their kids while they're away, or over-attached dog owners. But it suits my purposes.'

I hoisted myself back up on to the chrome stool at the breakfast bar and gazed down dully at my hands in my lap.

The incident with the webcam seemed to have cheered Dominic up. He hummed as he cleared away in the kitchen.

I was noticing that he responded to me being caught on the back foot. He needed to feel he was the one in charge.

Travis is a bit like that in some ways. If you want him to do something, you have to make him believe the decision is his. The thought that Travis and Dominic might have something in common was not a comforting one.

Edward and Liz Gold looked even smaller than the last time Kim saw them, as if they'd shrunk in the wash overnight.

'How do you mean, happy?'

Edward Gold was looking at her as if she'd used a term he was unfamiliar with.

'I mean, does it seem to you that Jessica and Travis' relationship is solid? Are they close as a couple?'

The Golds exchanged a glance.

'They seem happy enough,' Edward said slowly.

'But Jessica has never really confided in us about things like that,' Liz said. 'She's a private person. She always has been.'

Kim nodded. *Private* seemed to be everyone's favourite word when it came to Jessica. What Kim wanted to know was where the line was between private and secretive.

'So there's a chance things could have been going wrong in the relationship and you wouldn't have necessarily known?'

Liz frowned. She clearly didn't like the inference that hers was the type of family where unhappiness would go unnoticed, sneaking in the back door like someone else's cat.

'What kind of a person is Travis, would you say?'

This time there was no hesitation.

'Oh, he's wonderful. We're all very fond of him.' Liz Gold's wiry curls shook when she talked, as if to underline her vehemence on the subject of Travis Riley's good qualities. 'You must understand, Detective Harper, Jessica is a very unusual girl and there was a time we worried that she might not find anyone who . . . well . . . appreciates her quirkiness. So when she brought Travis home and he was so—'

'Normal,' her husband butted in.

Liz Gold didn't look too pleased about being interrupted. 'I wasn't going to use exactly that word, but yes, I suppose it was a relief that she'd found someone who was nice and engaging and ambitious for the future, and who seemed to accept her for who she was.'

'So as far as you know they weren't arguing about anything?'

'Arguing? No. Look, what exactly are you suggesting? Do you think Travis has something to do with Jessica's disappearance?'

Liz Gold's voice had risen rapidly during this speech and her husband reached out and put a reassuring hand on her arm.

'We're just trying to build up a picture of Jessica's life at the moment,' Kim said. 'We want to make sure we don't miss any clues.'

'Well, I can tell you now you're barking up the wrong tree with that one.'

'So, Jessica is happy with him?'

Edward Gold made a strange noise through his nose. 'Good luck in working that one out. We've been trying for twenty-nine years to find what makes Jessica happy.'

'You bought her sessions with a psychotherapist?'

'That was her mother's idea.'

Liz looked sheepish. 'We just wanted to make sure she was achieving her potential, that she wasn't stressed about anything.'

'And do you think they worked?'

The couple glanced at each other, and then away.

'Not really,' Liz Gold admitted. 'If anything, she's seemed more withdrawn. Certainly the last few months. I think it might have something to do with work.'

'Really? Why do you say that?'

'She's been spending a lot of time there. Working late a lot. Weekends even. And there was that Facebook thing.'

'I really don't think she wants to know about that, Liz.'

Edward was clearly unhappy with the turn the conversation was taking.

Kim smiled in what she hoped was a warm way. 'Tell me anything at all, no matter how trivial you think it is. You never know what could turn out to be important.'

'Her brother James told us about it. Apparently someone made a spoof account for Jessica. Photoshopped her face on to a pretty hardcore image. Pornographic, you know.' Liz Gold mouthed the word 'pornographic' as if Kim might be shocked. 'It got taken down almost immediately and James says it happens all the time, but it must have upset her. She wouldn't talk about it. Just said someone at work had been bullying her a bit but she'd sorted it out. That was months ago though.'

'And Travis was supportive? Is supportive?'

'I'm sure,' said Edward.

'They've had their ups and downs though,' said his wife.

146

'There was that period, wasn't there, about a year or so ago where they seemed to be drifting apart a bit. Remember, we were all a bit worried about it? But they came through that. Travis is worried sick about her. You can see that in his face.'

Kim nodded and smiled, saying nothing.

'Can I ask you something, Detective?' Liz Gold's tortured green eyes were locked on to hers. 'Do you have children of your own?'

The pain was sharp and savage.

'Yes, two.'

'Then you might understand. Your children don't always turn out quite the way you'd expected but all you can do is love them and hope they find other people to love them too.'

TWENTY

Dominic had insisted that I change for dinner. I was wearing a raspberry-pink top cut low at the front and a pair of white jeans which I'd had to roll up several times.

Dinner had been yet two more plastic containers from the fridge, one with salmon en croûte and the other dauphinoise potatoes. I was starving but after almost three days without food, apart from the disastrous smoothie, my digestive system recoiled in disgust. As I shovelled in my food, I could almost feel the fat bubbling up through the pores of my skin.

Afterwards Dominic led the way to two leather armchairs by the door to the balcony in the far corner of the living space.

'It suddenly occurred to me that you might be getting claustrophobic, sweetheart,' he said. 'If we sit here you'll be able to make the most of the view. It's so important, isn't it, to feel part of the world?'

I looked at his face, those blue eyes, and had no idea if he was being ironic.

Tonight he seemed to have completely forgotten his bad mood of earlier. He brought me champagne and told me I was beautiful. I remembered how flattered I'd been when he said that to me in the café. Who was that woman I'd been then?

'We are soulmates, you and I,' he told me. 'Conjoined twins.'

A large boat appeared on the river with coloured lights flashing and music ringing out and the sounds, getting louder and louder, of people enjoying themselves. Could it be New Year's Eve already? I tried to work it out in my head, but already the days were slipping away from me in a blur of empty hours. How many presents had I already had? Four? And still one to come today? That would mean it was the 29th of December, my fifth full day of captivity. There was still time for me to be rescued and out of here before this year turned into the next.

The thought that I might not see the next year flitted briefly across my mind like a sweet wrapper on a breeze. I batted it away.

As the boat passed the flat, the sound of a 1980s disco hit wafted inside, accompanied by screeching laughter. Normally a party boat would be my idea of hell. Stuck in a confined space with crowds of people and thumping music, no way of escape. Once Travis and I went on an overnight ferry from Portsmouth to Santander. The vessel was the size of a small town, yet still I couldn't fight off that fear of being trapped once it pulled away from the harbour, knowing I couldn't get off until we docked again. 'You need professional help,' Travis had snapped at the end of the journey, fed up with my tight-lipped silence. But now I longed to be on that boat with every fibre of my being. I wondered if any of those party-goers might glance up here to the sixth floor. We'd be tiny figures, Dominic and I, but they might just be able to make out that we were sitting at the vast window of an opulent apartment, me in a pink top. They wouldn't be able to see the champagne, but they might guess at it. They might even envy us, in our warehouse-conversion splendour.

How many assumptions do we make each day based on a total travesty of truth? I wonder.

And now it was that time again. The moment that had become the focal point of our day.

'Which one is it today? Have a guess.' Dominic was standing by the Christmas tree with an impish smile, quite as if he was a normal husband or boyfriend playing a flirtatious little game with his beloved. He was wearing black jeans and a blue long-sleeved T-shirt, the exact colour of his eyes.

'That one.' I indicated the largest present under the tree.

'Greedy, Jessica. Try again.'

'The one over there, with the sticking-out bit.'

'Nope. Here it is. This one is today's.'

He brought the present over, carrying it carefully as if it was made of eggshell.

Definitely a book, I thought. Even through the thick wrapping paper, I could feel its sharp corners. I was reminded of when my brothers and I would gather around the tree on Christmas morning, before our parents were up, and carefully feel all the presents, my brothers rounding on me if, during my inspection, the paper was pierced by a plastic doll's limb or the edge of a toy car.

When the paper came off, it was revealed to be a hardback of *Bleak House*. At first I thought the title might be Dominic's idea of a joke. Then I opened it. There was an inscription on the title page.

Congratulations, Dominic Lacey
Winner of the English Prize 1988
Silverton Park School

So Dominic was real then. I know it shouldn't have been a surprise, yet somehow it was. All the stuff he'd told me before about his sister and his parents, I'd been able to convince myself it was fiction, a story he was spinning to freak me out. Somehow this book, with its message in blue ink with big, loopy writing made him real.

'I bet you were a model pupil at school, Jessica.'

His tone was teasing. Gentle. The memory of yesterday's stinging slap to my cheek and this morning's smoothie was fading as if it had happened to someone else. I found I wanted to talk. I remembered a documentary I'd once seen where they interviewed a girl who'd been kidnapped and held for a few days in a huge iron pipe. 'I kept talking about myself. I knew I had to show him I was human,' she said. 'Then it would make it harder for him to kill me.'

'I wouldn't say model. I was too odd for that. I never quite got the hang of class participation. I'd be mute when asked a question and then suddenly start spouting when something occurred to me. The teachers didn't like that. They thought I was being rude.'

Dominic was nodding. Encouraging, desperate to add an anecdote of his own.

151

'My teachers didn't much like me either. *Dominic is a bright boy, but perhaps not as bright as he thinks he is.* All except Miss Fullerton. She was my English teacher in my last year at primary school. I wrote a story about a boy with magical powers. He could make people disappear just by looking at them. She got me to read it out in assembly and gave me this prize.' He held up the book. 'Miss Fullerton had only just graduated as a teacher. She was very small and youthful. One of the parents actually thought she was one of the children. When I told her I'd decided to make my story into a book, she was ecstatic. She gave up a lunchtime every week to help me. I think she thought this was what teaching was all about, unlocking a child's potential.'

'And did you finish your book?'

'What do you think, Jessica? I was eleven years old. I'd only said that thing about the book because I'd decided I was in love with her. I thought we were soulmates. I lived for Thursdays, scribbling stuff down in a big notebook ready to bring in to show her at lunchtime. I would have gone on indefinitely if it wasn't for him.'

'Him?'

'Mr Paphides, the deputy head. One time I saw them kissing in the car park after school. I was so shocked I threw up all over the tarmac. Remember those potato cakes with smiley faces on they used to serve for school lunches? What a mess they make coming back up. The next Thursday she cancelled our writing session, saying she had too much work to do, but when I crept past her classroom window, she was in there with him. Laughing. And the time after that, she had a big flashy engagement ring on her finger.

'After that my book changed direction. Now the boy with the magical powers wasn't using them entirely for good. In fact he became quite violent. Miss Fullerton stopped being quite so encouraging. The boy in the story turned blatantly evil. He pulled the legs off insects and tortured kittens. Clichéd sadism. Miss Fullerton called a halt to the writing sessions.'

I could picture her in my head. The young, newly minted teacher, burning with idealistic zeal, gradually sensing her pet project wasn't quite what she'd thought it was.

'What happened to your Miss Fullerton?'

'Oh, it was a shame. She left teaching.'

I knew I didn't really want to know, but I was sure I was about to find out anyway.

'You see, Miss Fullerton really had unlocked something in me, just as she'd hoped. After the lunchtime sessions stopped, I still had all these stories buzzing around my head. Only they weren't quite the stories she had in mind. She'd always said to me, "By all means, use your imagination, but also observe what goes on around you. If you write what you know, your writing will feel believable and authentic." So I wrote what I knew. Starting with Dad and Mrs Meadowbank and what I'd seen while I sat on my little stool. I didn't name them, of course, I just incorporated it into my stories. And my mother and how I felt about Bella. A lot of quite unpleasant things happened to the boy in my book. And he did lots of quite unpleasant things back.'

'But she'd stopped the sessions.'

'Yes, but I used to leave chapters for her in her classroom, or tucked under the wipers of her car. She didn't like it. The head teacher had to be involved.'

'You got into trouble.'

'A counsellor was called in. There were meetings with my parents. Everybody shook their heads a lot.'

'And then?'

'Then I left school to go to secondary, and the counsellor got to cross my name out of her book, and the head teacher was quietly relieved and everything went back to normal. Except . . .'

Dominic broke off, gazing into the distance.

'Except?'

'You see, Jessica, once the creative process is unleashed, you can't just switch it off like a tap. The words kept coming. The book almost wrote itself, as they say. So I posted chapters to her at my old school and when the head got in touch with my parents, I found out where she lived and started dropping them off at her house. By that time, the storyline had changed in that I'd introduced a new character, a young female teacher.

'Like I say, Miss Fullerton left teaching quite soon after that development. It was probably for the best. She became an estate agent in the end.

'Coincidentally, she showed me round a house a few years later. I'd made the appointment over the phone. You should have seen her face when I turned up.'

I pictured her again, this fresh-faced teacher from my imagination. How she'd have looked when Dominic arrived – the face of her youthful failure.

'You'd have thought, wouldn't you, that estate agencies would be more careful these days about sending lone females out on viewings. I'd given them a whole load of misinformation when I registered, but they never checked it.'

My stomach, still distended from its long stretch without food, contracted painfully, as if it had been punched.

He's playing with you, I told myself. It's another story he's making up. But I couldn't stop staring at that handwritten inscription, with the hopeful, open loopy writing. My head was aching, and the rash on my front seemed to have spread to the backs of my knees and elbows, and was itching like mad. When I looked over at Dominic, my vision was blurred, so he seemed to be shimmering like a mirage in the heat.

The talk of Miss Fullerton had clearly affected Dominic and he spent the next couple of hours reading in complete silence. I tried hard to make out what was keeping him so engrossed and was nonplussed to discover it was a cookery book by a well-known female celebrity chef.

I won't say the name. She doesn't need the publicity.

While he read I gazed out of the window. Whenever a boat passed, I willed someone to turn their heads up this way, but I knew it was futile. Every now and then faint screams from the condemned men wafted in from the site of Execution Dock and pattered against the glass of the window like so much rain, but I ignored them. When it grew late, he finally looked at me as if he'd forgotten I was there. He didn't seem happy to see me.

'I don't know what I expected when I invited you here, Jessica,' he said, his voice varnished hard. 'But it certainly wasn't this. I have to tell you I feel cheated. Must my whole life be about coping with disappointment?'

That night I was once again relegated to the dog kennel. I lay in the dark, rigid with cold, and wondered what had happened to Bella and to Natalie, and what was going to happen to me. In my head I composed messages to the people I loved. The aching in my gut had returned and now there was a new feeling as well, a sharp tingling as if my nerve ends were on fire.

It occurred to me suddenly that I might die there in that flat, not through an act of violence, but through a hundred tiny acts of neglect. Not through the things that were done, but the things that weren't.

Sean was working his way methodically through the wardrobe, pausing every few minutes to assess some item of clothing before tossing it into the suitcase on the bed.

'It doesn't have to be like this,' Kim said for the hundredth time.

'No. It doesn't. You can stop this right now. You just have to prioritize your family, that's all.'

'You mean, give up work.'

'I mean, give up that work. *That job*. Train as a teacher or do a conversion course to become a lawyer. Or stay in the force but accept you're not going to have a meteoric rise through the ranks – or at least not until the kids are older. Do your set hours. No overtime.'

'I can't. All the work I've put into this. How would you like it if I told you to chuck in your job?'

'My job is not destroying our family life.'

Kim watched him moving around the bedroom.

'But I don't want to go.'

Later, she stood at the bottom of the stairs with her case, looking around the hall they'd painted together, running her fingers over the stair banister she'd lovingly sanded by hand. Surely he couldn't really be asking her to leave all this?

'We've been through this, Kim. Either you go, or I'll go. And if I go, who will look after the kids while you're doing your sodding job every minute of every day?'

'But what about us, Sean? You and me?'

He looked at her with a face full of regret.

'There is no you and me any more, Kim. There hasn't been for years.'

Later, she sat on the bed in her best friend Heather's spare room and sobbed into the photo of Rory and Katy that she'd brought from home.

'I don't get it,' said Heather, from the doorway. 'No job is worth losing your family over. Quit. Do something else.'

Heather had never understood what made her join the police in the first place, or the stomach-churning thrill she got from knowing she was good at her job, or the secret ambition to go right to the top that sometimes burned so much it kept her awake. She could never tell Heather that even while her heart was breaking over leaving her children behind at home, her head was already calculating how much more she'd be able to cram into her working day, and how much faster she could advance.

'You can't have it all,' she told Heather. 'You think you can, people tell you you can, but you can't.'

Her voice sounded whiny even to her own ears.

TWENTY-ONE

Shower day again. Our shower in the Wood Green flat is barely functional. The head is blocked with limescale so the water dribbles out of random holes. The one in the Wapping apartment with its blast of pressure and multi-level jets should have been a treat.

As it was I stood curled in on myself while the water pummelled me, hot then cold, until I couldn't tell the difference between the two. Whenever I looked down, I was shocked first by the rash that seemed to have spread now all over my right side, and then by the tattoo with the pink and sore-looking ridged outline.

Then he wanted to wash my hair. He brought the shampoo and beckoned me over to him. I hung my head and he rubbed the white, coconut-smelling stuff brusquely into my hair, keeping the shower running. Then abruptly he stopped, switching off the water.

I opened my eyes to look up at him, blinking the soapy water away.

He was standing by the shower looking down at his hands. I followed his eyes and saw there was black stuff all over his fingers.

I recognized what it was. My hair.

Afterwards, he treated me like a baby. Again wrapping me in a big towel and drying me almost tenderly. He let me stand in front of the mirror and run my fingers through my hair, and made tutting noises when they came away with long dark strands wrapped around them.

As I stood gazing at my reflection where the scalp shone obscenely pink through the hair at my temples, Dominic put his arm around me.

'Sometimes hair loss is stress-related,' he told me. 'Do you think you could be stressed, sweetie?'

I met his eyes in the mirror. There was not a flicker of a smile.

All through that sixth day I obsessed about my hair and what it could mean. I've never been a vain sort of person. But there are some bits of me I like more than others. These are the bits that give me my identity, my sense of being me.

One of those is my hair.

Dark, thick, tending to frizz. My hair has been at or near the centre of my life ever since I can remember. There were the years when I tried in vain to grow it into a thick glossy sheet that hung down across my eyes, to hide me from the world. Long straight dark hair would make me look French and mysterious. But it refused to do what it was told, frizzing out at the bottom into a kind of triangle until my mother would beg me to go to the hairdresser. 'Just a couple of inches,' she'd beseech me. 'Just to give it some shape.' But I wouldn't countenance it. My power was in my hair. Thick and monstrous as it was.

When I grew older, it was my search for the magic

product that would bring my hair under control that took over my life. My hair exerted almost as big an influence over my life as my work and my love life. If my hair was looking good, there was nothing I couldn't do. If it looked shit I dissolved into self-loathing.

And now it was all falling out. I knew that Dominic was right. Hair loss came along with stress. At university I'd known a man whose hair had fallen out overnight after his girlfriend dumped him. Not only on his head, but all over his body – on his face, arms, legs.

Would that be me? I thought about Travis and how he'd liked to grab on to my hair when we had sex, and wondered if anyone would ever want to have sex with me again.

Then I remembered where I was, and that having sex and being bald were the least of my problems.

'And you're sure it was her?'

The girl shot a nervous look at Martin, and Kim briefly closed her eyes, trying to control her annoyance. He had a way of talking to people that came across as aggressive. This girl couldn't be more than eighteen or nineteen and, though her English was pretty good, it was obviously not her first language and she was clearly finding Martin intimidating. It wouldn't be the first time a witness had clammed up entirely under questioning from him.

That was another reason the bosses would be crazy to recommend him over her. He rubbed people up the wrong way.

'You're doing really well, love,' said Kim, cringing at her own sudden switch into TV-policewoman-speak. She never

n her normal life, but stick her in front
s and out it tumbled every time. 'Just
k. To be sure.'

ped her hands on her grey apron and
om her outstretched hands.

s her. She had many bags for the

n't with anyone?'

ad so that her black ponytail

Kim. Another dead end. They'd
ound all the different depart-
now knew Jessica Gold had
e. Checking the timings of her
abled their colleagues to find
nts, but there were too many
r exact movements in between
tograph around the shop. This
was working temporarily in
the first positive identification
ge, it failed to provide any
ed, had done her Christmas
long with thousands of others.

thin air.

tonight's present, Jessica?'
sofa following an unsuccessful
a that Dominic had declared

th S
e, thou
nothin
aterialistic
her when
of a Kurt
don't have
bly won't

my teens.
cause my
nt. It was
int to me
personal
despite all
id care. I
but then
nd then I

as I was
as I went
g to spin
coming, I

nic mug,
star. On

161

inedible and scraped into the bin despite my
stomach.

'What's the best present you ever got?'

I thought about it. Not the sessions wi
Rubenstein, which had been mortifying at the tim
later on I'd come to appreciate them. Certainl
Travis had ever bought me. 'I love how non-ma
you are,' he said to me on my first birthday toge
he presented me with a battered hardback copy
Vonnegut novel he'd found in a charity shop. 'I
to worry about buying you stuff that you proba
ever use.'

Then I remembered a birthday when I was in
Or maybe it was Christmas. It was remarkable be
brothers had clubbed together to buy me a prese
an eyeshadow palette, and it was probably a big h
that I ought to be paying more attention to my
grooming, but it was the first time I realized that
our differences and their constant teasing, they
was about to share this story with Dominic
I remembered that he'd had a little sister too. A
didn't feel like saying anything at all.

Today's present was irregularly shaped. Even
opening it, painstakingly smoothing out the paper
along, feeling along the bumps of the glitter, tryir
out the time before I had to face whatever was
heard her.

'I'm cold,' she said. 'So very cold.'

Inside the layers of wrapping was a glazed cera
pink with yellow and green spots and a bright re

the front was emblazoned the message: *Best Brother*. It was the kind of thing kids made at special ceramics cafés where parties of schoolchildren chose an item of crockery to decorate themselves and then collected it once it had been fired in the kiln. I remembered going to one with my mum and being appalled to find I couldn't take my work home there and then. I'd painted a bowl for my dad's birthday and was desperate to see it all shiny and beautiful.

The inside of the mug was purple with bright blue rings. The whole thing was typically over the top, like you'd expect from a child let loose with a paintbrush and unlimited colours.

'From your sister, I take it.'

'Well, duh.'

The juvenile expression sounded preposterous coming from this grown man with his flick knife, and the metal cuffs he kept attached to the radiator.

'Bella made it for me at one of her friends' parties. She was always going to parties. She had so many friends, you see. Not like me.' Here Dominic made a mock-sad face. 'I was too clever. The other children didn't like it. You weren't supposed to be clever, and if you were, you were supposed to be embarrassed about it. I could never be bothered with all that crap.'

Somehow this didn't surprise me.

'But everyone loved Bella. She was just one of those kids who could get away with being clever, and sporty, and pretty, because she acted like she didn't know it. And if anyone ever pointed it out, she acted like it was the most astonishing thing she'd ever heard.

'At home the honeymoon stage was over, but things had never quite gone back to being as they were before she arrived. Mrs Meadowbank had moved away, but Daddy had other special friends. He and Mummy would argue about them when we were supposed to be in bed. They'd carried on sharing a bedroom, although Mummy still came in to see me in the night sometimes, though she didn't stay. Even through sleep I could feel her presence, hot and heavy.

'She was fat, was Mummy. Did I tell you that? She used to do all these diets. Soup only, no carbohydrates, eating only on alternative days. The worst was the oily-fish diet. She tried to eat salmon or mackerel three times a day until fish oil came out of her pores. The whole house stank of it. Nothing worked though, because she had no self-control. She'd spend all day carefully weighing out cereal and potatoes and then at night she'd go into the garage and gorge herself on chocolate and biscuits from a secret stash she had out there. Sometimes I'd spy on her. She made me sick. Mind you, not as sick as she made herself, if you get my meaning. And she was drinking by this time. She favoured those miniature bottles so she could hide them in her coat pockets, and kid herself they didn't count. She kept the empty bottles in her handbag – every time we went out she headed straight for the nearest bin so she could get rid of them all, pretending she was chucking out a tissue or something. She clinked when she walked.

'Anyway, Mummy and Daddy kept up a pretence of being normal for Bella. That's the kind of effect she had. You wanted to show yourself in the best light when she was around.

'In one way, of course, that was a relief. No more sitting scrunched up on that stool panting like a little dog. No more sharing a bed with Mummy. But in another sense, it made me explode with anger. Why were they making such an effort to put their best selves forward for her, while I'd had to put up with all their twisted shit? Why me?

'Can you imagine how that feels, Jessica?'

The weird thing was he was appealing to me for approval. He wanted to hear he was right to be angry, right to feel the way he'd felt.

'Did your parents have a favourite?' he wanted to know now.

I'd been deliberately trying to push my parents from my thoughts. Thinking about them gave me an exquisite ripple of pleasure followed immediately by a vicious rush of pain. Had they favoured my brothers? Almost certainly, yes. They were so straightforward, so easy. They made friends, played sport, had girlfriends. Theirs were the usual problems my parents' many child-rearing manuals had prepared them for. A predilection for violent video games, an aggressive stage in their teens where they locked horns with my father over curfews and clearing up, a bag of weed in a jacket pocket, a middle-of-the-night phone call from the police when one of them was involved in a fight outside a local pub. Those things my parents could deal with, indeed almost enjoyed dealing with. But with me it was different. They weren't prepared for the singular difficulties I presented. They'd been expecting schoolgirl quarrels and petty jealousies. They'd imagined arguments over boys and make-up and skirt lengths. They'd already decided in advance that they'd be more laid back this time around, would allow me the freedom to make my own mistakes as they hadn't always with the boys. What they hadn't expected was a child who struggled to make friends and who rarely went anywhere except into the dark recesses of her own mind. Who talked about voices in her head.

'If they had a favourite, it wasn't me,' I said eventually.

Instantly his hand was outstretched, fingers gripping my knee like a vice.

'I knew it, Jessica,' he said. 'I knew as soon as I saw you we were kindred spirits. We are both damaged.'

He picked up the mug from my lap and turned it over in his hands like a hallowed object.

'No child should be made to feel second-best. I feel that very strongly. And if parents allow that to happen? Well then, they should be brought to account.'

What I felt very strongly was that I didn't want to know how.

'Dommy, I'm cold,' said the child's voice. 'Please, Dommy. I'm so cold.'

Could he hear it?

'But you loved her too? Your sister? It was obvious from that photo of the two of you.'

I was saying it for her benefit. So she'd know she was loved.

'Oh yes. I loved her. Well, as much as I've ever loved anyone. But you know, Jessica, love is pretty much over-rated. It comes, it goes. It's conditional on so many things and the fact is, most of the time you don't really know what they are. So it's pretty much an artificial construct.'

He thought he was clever, all right.

'When the time came for me to go to secondary school, following all that Miss Fullerton business that my parents refused to talk about, there was much debate about where I should go. There was a decent state secondary down the road, and a couple of well-thought-of private schools. I didn't really care where I went. I knew wherever it was the teachers would dislike me and the other kids distrust me.

'Then one day I overheard my parents talking. Arguing. Well, yawn, yawn. They were always arguing. But then I heard my name mentioned, and started listening more closely. "It'll be good for him to go," my father said. "And for us." "For you, you mean," my mother said. "Admit it, you're frightened of the boy."

'Then they argued about me some more until my father told her it would be better for Bella too. That made Mummy stop and think for a while. And then she said, and I can hear it now, as clearly as if she was right where you are, "I'll only agree to let you send Dominic to boarding school if you promise Bella can stay here."

'That stupid fat cow bartered me like a box of fucking eggs.'

Dominic looked as if he might be about to cry. He looked ugly then and I almost felt sorry for him.

'You must have found it hard not to resent Bella for that,' I said in my best Sonia Rubenstein voice.

'And therein lies the rub.' His smile was back. 'In the end it came down to this. What was worth more, the pain of losing someone I loved, or the pleasure of inflicting pain on the people I hated?'

'I'm cold,' she said.

And suddenly, so was I.

TWENTY-TWO

The next morning there was hair on the floor of the kennel. I picked it up in my fingers and let it play over my face, tickling my skin. When I put my hand up to my head, I was relieved to find there was still hair attached to my scalp, but it felt decidedly thinner, and there were small patches where there was no hair at all.

While I was holding a lock of hair in front of my eyes, inspecting the roots to see if I could see what was causing it to fall out, I noticed something weird about my hand. I was sure the skin of my palm felt thicker than it normally did, like it had grown an extra layer. Worse, the nail of my little finger was completely missing. I prodded the space where it used to be gingerly with my thumb and felt an answering jolt of pain.

Dominic seemed agitated today as if the preceding six long days of incarceration had taken their toll on him as well. He kept pacing the floor at the far end of the apartment, close to the windows, stopping every now and then to gaze out at the river, as if it might hold the answer to his problems.

'We need fresh air,' he announced suddenly, looking out at the grey day. 'Come here.'

At the door, he grabbed my elbow, propelling me roughly out on to the iron balcony.

By now he was in a foul mood, as if it was somehow my fault he'd been kept cooped up all this time. We sat on the wrought-iron bistro chairs and stared in silence at the brown, mud-churning river beneath us.

'Arrogant pricks,' he said.

I was silent.

'Those people who built that,' he continued, gesticulating at the Shard, the much-discussed building that spiked into the skyline in the distance on the far side of the river. 'A building like that, it's basically a great big ego stroke to the architect and developer. A huge giant wank.'

It was the first time I'd sensed just how insecure Dominic's own ego was. It was like there wasn't room for anyone else's. It was too much of a threat.

I was pondering this new revelation when I suddenly found myself being hauled out of my chair.

'Don't go silent on me, Jessica.' He was pressing me up against the balcony railing. Looking down, I could see the river swirling angrily underneath.

'I've seen the way you look at me sometimes, as if I'm some kind of idiot you just need to keep placated. You need to give me some respect.'

He was pressing harder against me from behind so that I was bending ever further forward over the railings.

Now my feet were losing contact with the ground. The river looked suddenly extremely close. I gazed in desperation across to the other bank but there was no one about, and even if there had been, we'd only have been two faint dots on a sixth-floor balcony.

'Do you understand me, Jessica?' His voice was wet in my ear.

'Yes,' I shouted into the wind. My hips were now balancing on the top of the railing – I could feel the metal digging into the sore place where the tattoo was. One more push from behind and I'd topple right over, down into the muddy water below. 'I understand you. I'm sorry.'

And then my feet were back on the ground again, and he'd moved away as if nothing had happened.

'We really should be going in now,' he said in a completely different voice. 'It's freezing out here, sweetheart, you look like you're actually trembling.'

'I'm cold,' said a child's voice in my head.

'Yes,' I said. 'Thank you.'

That's how long it took for him to break me all over again.

When we went inside he told me we were going to play chess.

'I've noticed that your mind is getting flabby, Jessica. You really need to watch that. Don't take this the wrong way, but a girl like you needs to rely on more than just looks.'

Dominic shackled me to the radiator while he went to fetch the chess set. I heard him take the bunch of keys from his pocket as he went around the wall of the kitchen to the inner hallway, and then the sound of a key in a lock was followed by a hiss, as if someone was sucking in their breath.

When he returned, he was carrying an expensive-looking box. Inside was a folding wooden board and a velvet pouch which contained the chess pieces – dark wood and ivory. Dominic took each one out in turn, lining them up side by side on opposite ends of the board. 'I'll let you be white. White always goes first.'

I picked up a pawn from the middle of the board. It was light as air and beautifully carved and so smooth I fought an urge to stroke it against my cheek.

'Exquisite, isn't it?' He was looking on proprietorially.

'Lovely. I bet this didn't come from one of your bankrupt clients.'

His smile broadened like it was being stretched out on a rack. 'There are many different forms of bankruptcy, Jessica. You'd be amazed. And not all of them are to do with money.'

Seeing Rory and Katy again was like being slapped in the face with happiness. Hard enough to hurt. Already, when she walked into the living room, despite the familiarity of the furniture she'd chosen and the rug she'd helped carry back from the house of a neighbour who was moving abroad, she felt like a visitor. When she noticed the dirty teacups on the coffee table, it no longer occurred to her to take them through to the kitchen.

Instead she sat on the sofa, with Katy and Rory clinging to her as if she might blow away.

'Have you come back now, Mummy?' Katy wanted to know. 'Has your sleepover with Heather finished?'

Kim buried her face in her daughter's neck so no one could see the tears that suddenly blurred her vision.

'It's not a sleepover, silly,' said Rory. 'Mummy and Daddy are getting divorced.'

Kim's head shot up. 'That's not true. Who told you that?'

'Daddy.'

Rory was trying to be very tough, but his voice wobbled on the last word and Kim hugged him to her.

'Why did you tell him that?' she demanded when she and Sean were alone in the kitchen.

'Because whether you like it or not, that's the next step, Kim. When are you going to realize the consequences of what you're doing?'

'I'm not doing anything. It's you who made me leave. Why don't we call a truce for tonight – spend New Year's Eve together?'

Sean acted like he hadn't heard. 'Have you pulled out of that promotion application?'

Kim didn't reply.

'Thought not. I bet you've been using this time apart to work even harder and earn even more Brownie points, instead of finding out where your priorities lie. I still love you, Kim, but we are heading for divorce unless you sort yourself out. And there's no one to blame but you and your bloody ambition.'

'I've something very special for you to wear today, Jessica.'

I was chained to the radiator again, while he searched for something in the locked room. Now he reappeared with one of those bags people put over expensive clothes to protect them from the elements. He was wearing a black velvet jacket with a crisp white shirt underneath. For a moment I wondered what the occasion was, then I remembered.

Oh yes. New Year's Eve.

'What were you doing this time last year?' he asked me, laying the bag carefully across the dining table. 'Can you believe we didn't even know each other then? I feel like you've been in my life for ever.'

'I was at a party. With my boyfriend.'

Sometimes Dominic didn't like me to mention Travis at all, going stiff when I said his name. Other times he would go out of his way to get me to talk about him, quizzing me about his likes and dislikes, his quirks and annoying habits.

'I thought you didn't like parties, Jessica.'

'I don't, but Travis wanted to go. It was given by one of his new friends from the hospital. He was still pretty junior, so he was keen to make a good impression and fit in.'

I didn't tell Dominic how I'd sulked about going. I didn't mention all the obstacles I'd raised – the fact that it was right across London ('but the Tubes run all night, Jessica – and they're free'), the fact that it would be full of people I didn't know ('but this is your opportunity to get to know them'), the fact that I'd misguidedly been persuaded into having layers cut in my hair and it looked awful ('it does not look anything like a mullet, just forget about it'). Since Travis had started earning a junior doctor's salary and wasn't financially dependent on me any more, he'd become less tolerant of my anti-social tendencies. 'You stay at home if you like,' he'd snapped in the end. 'I'll go on my own.' I had the distinct impression then that was what he'd wanted all along. But I didn't relish the thought of being alone for New Year's Eve. I knew my parents would ask me the next day what I'd done and they'd exchange one of those looks I dreaded if they found out I'd stayed at home.

'And how was it, this party?'

Dominic's voice was jocular, gently probing, like we were normal people having a normal conversation.

'Hideous. Travis chatted all night to people I didn't know while I stood in a corner of the kitchen and pretended to be reading the postcards and notes stuck on the noticeboard. On the way back we had a big row about me not having made enough of an effort.'

I omitted to mention the woman who'd smirked at me as though I had a big smudge of toothpaste on my cheek and said to him, 'So this is who you rush off to see when we're all waiting for you down the pub,' and how I'd thought that was a bit rich as he hardly ever seemed to be at home any more.

'How about you?' I dared putting a question to Dominic, who had sat himself down at the table and was leaning back, quite relaxed, as if he'd forgotten that I was still crouching naked by the radiator.

'Me? Oh, I was with the missus.' He jerked his head in the direction of the hideous painting. 'We were up a mountain in Switzerland if I remember right. On a skiing holiday. The two of us, holed up together in a chalet surrounded by snow and tomato-faced Austrians in fluorescent Puffa jackets. She was up to her usual tricks, of course. Texting all the time like a teenager, sneaking off to make phone calls when she thought I was asleep.'

'Was that what she was like?'

He wagged a finger in my face. 'All in good time, sweetheart.'

He turned his attention now to the bag on the table,

unzipping it all around to reveal a long white dress. Rather like something one might wear to a wedding.

If one were the bride.

'As it's a special night, I thought we would make a special effort,' he said, holding the dress up.

He unlocked the cuffs and helped me slip the gown over my head. The front gaped unattractively and the hem seemed slightly greying, as if it had got dirty at one time, but Dominic seemed almost touchingly pleased with the results.

'She wore this one on our wedding day,' he said, stepping back to take a proper look. 'We got married on a beach in India. It was very romantic. I'm a big believer in romance. Aren't you, Jessica? Don't you believe the right one is out there for us all?'

I didn't answer as I was trying to reconcile what I knew of Natalie to this image of the barefoot bride getting married with no one but her groom to see her. The Natalie in my imagination would have demanded an audience, a grand entrance.

In honour of New Year's Eve, Dominic had decided to cook a special meal, rather than just warming something up. For nearly an hour, an unpleasantly pungent, gamey smell had been emanating from the kitchen area, and when he summoned me to sit at the table, I had to press my hand down in my lap to stop it from flying up to cover my nose and mouth.

When Dominic lifted the saucepan lid to stir whatever was simmering there, the stench was unbearable, though it didn't seem to bother him. He ladled the contents into a large bowl and placed it in the middle of the table. 'Voilà!'

I gazed down. An obscenely swollen brown globe, its sweating skin stretched so tight as to be almost translucent over the mass of minced flesh it was barely able to contain.

'The secret with Haggis is not to overcook it,' he said. 'Well, go on, Jessica. You do the honours.'

I picked up the metal spoon he was offering me and gingerly prodded the glistening casing that stretched like a latex balloon until it finally burst open, scrambled innards exploding out of the open wound.

'Eat,' he said, grabbing hold of the spoon to deposit on my plate a mound of skin and minced meat that glistened with fat where it hit the light. 'Don't let it get cold.'

I picked up a forkful, but hesitated before bringing it to my mouth.

'Eat,' he said again, and his voice was no longer cajoling.

The casing burst like a blister in my mouth and I'd swallowed a chunk of it before Dominic, laughing, told me you weren't actually supposed to eat it. 'Though it's sheep stomach, so I don't imagine it will do you much harm.'

He brought a loaded forkful to his mouth and ate it with his too-close-together eyes fixed on me as I chewed.

'Don't worry if you find a lump, Jessica. It's far more likely to be a bit of gristle than a whole kidney or lung or spleen.'

He smiled, revealing a shred of flesh caught between his bottom teeth.

I ate it. Every last bit.

Afterwards I almost enjoyed the heavy feeling in my gut.

'Why, I do believe you're getting a taste for flesh, Jessica,' he said. And I could tell that he wasn't happy about it.

We sat down in the leather armchairs to watch the scores of party boats on the river gearing up for the festivities.

After a while Dominic got to his feet. I didn't need to ask him where he was going.

Again he brought me the parcel with a curious, formal ceremony, resting it on the fingers of both hands, and deposited it in my lap.

'Any guesses?'

I ran my hands over the wrapping, feeling how the top of the object inside was soft and yielding. 'I don't know. A cushion of some sort?'

When I opened it, I found the package contained a wooden box, around the length and width of a paperback book and about four inches deep. The lid was padded, and the whole thing was bright pink and decorated with yellow and white fairies and glitter stars. Though I'd tuned out the voice of the child I assumed to be Bella, I could sense her all around me and I dreaded what I might find. But inside there were only shells, the kind children pick up on beaches when they are still shiny and slick and beautiful with the sea, only to get them home and discover they're dull and ordinary after all.

'Bella's collection,' Dominic explained unecessarily. 'She spent whole days on our holidays combing the beach for shells. When she was very little, she used to group them into families and have mummy and daddy shells and little baby shells too. You'd have thought she might have had quite enough of families.

'The last holiday we ever went on was the summer before I was due to start boarding school. We were staying in a villa on the south coast of Spain. One of those that look really good in the brochure but turn out to be in some sort of continental housing estate. Bella loved it, of course, because there were lots of other children around and she soon became part of a little gang. Their parents would take them down to the beach and they'd swim out to the inflatable raft, where all the older kids gathered to take turns going down the twisty slide. There were a few kids my age, but on the whole they were a pretty imbecilic lot and I preferred my own company.

'Mummy and Daddy were fighting quite a lot by this point. Mostly about me, I think. Mummy still wasn't keen on me going away to school. Particularly as I'd threatened to top myself if they actually went through with it.'

I could imagine it very clearly. I was sure Dominic would have been very specific in his threats of what he would do and how he would do it.

'Mind you, Mummy was always drunk by lunchtime so no one really paid much attention to what she said. One day we went to the beach as usual and the red flags were up, meaning swimming was prohibited. They'd been up once before, but people had still been in the water and in the end we'd gone in too, just paddling about near to the shore. "They just put up the flags to cover themselves if they think there's the slightest current," the woman next to us had said. "No one takes any notice." "Jobsworths," was my father's verdict.

'Well, this time too, there were swimmers in the water –

mostly fit young men. When I went to test the water, I could see why the flags were up. Though the surface appeared calm enough, underneath there was a vicious undertow if you went out too far and the wind felt like it was picking up.

'I went back to the sand where Bella was playing bat and ball with her friend and Mummy was lying comatose on a towel like a beached whale. It was mid-afternoon so she was already half-cut. Daddy had made an excuse to stay back at the villa. I knew exactly why. I'd seen the way he looked at the woman in the villa two doors down. Is your father a womanizer, Jessica?'

I almost laughed at the thought of it. 'No. I'd be surprised if he'd even looked at another woman since he got together with my mum.'

'You're lucky then. There's no sight so pathetic as a middle-aged man in Speedos in thrall to his own desires.

'I suggested to Bella that she come into the water with me. I told her it was fine. We could swim out to the raft, I suggested. She was dubious – she was only seven and wasn't at all a confident swimmer – but I pointed out there were a couple of other people there. And anyway, I'd be with her all the way. That decided her – she would have done anything to please me. As we walked down to the water, I heard a shout behind and Mummy appeared, staggering slightly, and blinking as if confused. She'd tied one of those flowery sarongs around her waist to hide her rolls of stomach and she was picking at the knot. "Where are you going?" she wanted to know. I told her we were just going for a dip. "But it's red," she said. "You shouldn't . . ." But we were already in the water by then. I heard a giant splash as she crashed in after us.

'At first, it wasn't so bad, and Bella kept up a stream of commentary as she always did. "I'm swimming really good aren't I, Dommy? Do you want to see my breast stroke? You have to make your fingers into a straight line and then push the water out with your hands." But after a while, she was concentrating too hard to speak. The current was getting stronger now that we'd gone beyond where we could stand up and the surface was rippled with quite sizeable waves. I heard Mummy behind me shouting at us to stop. "Not far now, Bella," I told her, indicating the raft ahead with its bed of blue inflatable buoys. But because of the current, we seemed to be making very little headway. The water in this section was cold, and getting colder. When I looked behind, I saw she was panting, her face tinged with blue. "I'm cold," she said, and her little arms were scrabbling around in the water like a dog's paws. "Want to go back". "We're nearly there now," I said, "no point going back." I was also struggling to keep my head above the waves that were getting bigger now, and to keep the current from dragging me under the freezing water. In calm conditions, the swim out took less than five minutes, but we must have already been in the water at least a quarter of an hour.

'When I looked behind for the last time, her face was the colour of a Smurf. It really was. Her teeth were chattering too much to speak, but I could see her lips moving. She was still saying she was cold. Much further back, I could just make out my mother's head bobbing in the water as she floundered around. Then I turned my head so I was looking ahead and kept my eyes fixed on the raft, using every last drop of strength to keep myself afloat.

'Finally I arrived and hauled myself up, using the rope ladder on the side. Only then, when I was lying across the wooden platform, did I look back.'

'And?' I almost couldn't bring myself to ask but I needed to know.

'There were a lot of people in the water suddenly. The lifeguards had been alerted and two had arrived in a dinghy and were hauling my mother out. You can imagine, that was no mean feat. I couldn't hear much because of the wind, but I could hear her shouting, "My baby, my baby." Nothing about me, of course. Just Bella. Then they brought the dinghy over to the raft. "Are you OK?" they asked me. I told them they had to find my sister, so they got on to the raft and started diving off, searching. When they finally pulled her out, she was limp and heavy like a waterlogged sack. I cried when I saw her. I think that might be the last time I ever cried.' He halted. 'Oh no. There was that other time. But that came later. Much later.'

I'd been staring at him while he told his story, knowing all the time where it was leading and yet convincing myself there was some place else for it to go.

'That's so awful,' I said. 'Your poor, poor mother.'

It was the wrong thing to say, as I'd known it would be.

'Want to know what happened to my *poor, poor mother*? It's quite funny.' His voice was once again dangerously light. 'She was arrested by the Spanish authorities. They were going to charge her with criminal neglect or child neglect or something. They did a blood test and discovered she was slaughtered. They ran columns about her in the papers saying she was the worst kind of mother, taking her kids swimming in those conditions. The police quizzed me, of course, and I was the very picture of a guilt-ridden older brother. "It's all my fault."' He put on a high warbling child's voice. "I should have been able to save her." I even told them it was my idea to go swimming in the first place, although I might have added something about Mummy not saying no, which made me feel "like it was OK". I never could resist embellishing a good anecdote.'

'So what happened?'

'They dropped the charges. Not enough evidence. And besides, she was a complete fruitcake by then. I think they figured they'd spend all this time and effort bringing her to trial, only to have to put her up in a mental institution for the next god knows how many years. Just imagine the paella bill.

'Daddy never forgave her. But then she never forgave herself either, so that made two of them.'

'And did you go off to school?'

'In the traumatized state I was in? No one would be that cruel. Besides, when Mummy was finally released, I was all she had in the world. She didn't want to let me out of her sight.'

I picked up a shell from the box and held it in the palm of my hand, admiring how its smooth inside glittered where it picked up the reflection from the Christmas-tree lights. I could feel Bella's spirit coursing through it and found myself thinking about how once this would have been the home to some underwater sea creature, and here it was in a warehouse apartment in one of the world's major cities. Life didn't always take you where you thought it would. I might have been losing my hair, I might be wearing what would almost certainly turn out to be a dead woman's wedding dress. I might have a nasty rash on my stomach and a septic tattoo on my hip and be eating food that made me sick. But I was alive.

Poor, blue Bella had been fished out of the sea like so much rubbish, but I was still here. I was still breathing.

Yet while I was quietly triumphant at my survival, in another sense I also felt disappointed, let down almost. All these days had been building up to finding out what happened to Bella, and now I knew.

And there were still five presents under the tree.

Dominic saw me looking at them and smiled, guessing some of what was going through my head.

'Don't worry, there's still so much to learn about each other, Jessica. Isn't that exciting? You still don't know the worst.'

Later, Dominic and I stood at the window and watched fireworks exploding across London's skyline to celebrate the New Year. He counted down the seconds to midnight on his watch and then pulled me towards him, pressing his mouth on to mine, his tongue disappearing down my throat like an endoscopy camera.

His mouth tasted of sausage and blood.

TWENTY-THREE

The next morning when I awoke, I lay in the kennel for a long time, stroking the palms of my hands and the soles of my feet with a kind of fascinated curiosity as if I was my own scientific guinea pig, wondering at how thick and hard the skin had become and what it might mean.

Later, we sat on the sofa watching an episode of a popular American TV series. Dominic had the box set and had already watched the whole thing through. He was one of those people who try to manipulate your viewing. 'Oh, you're going to love this bit.' Or, 'You might want to look away for this scene.' My nerves were still tingling and I had very little energy. He was sitting next to me, stroking his finger up and down the blade of his knife.

'I love this series because it's one of the few programmes that tell the truth – that everyone is corruptible.'

I wondered if that was the real message of the show, or just Dominic's own spin on it.

After a while, I couldn't concentrate on the screen. My eyes were mesmerized by his finger on that long, sharp blade. I imagined how it would feel going through my skin. Would it be a sharp, burning pain, or would it be so excruciating I wouldn't feel it at all? How much pressure would he have to put on the hilt for the knife to slice cleanly through? I imagined it like cutting a watermelon – tough on the surface, but like sliding through butter once you got to the flesh.

We watched all the episodes on the first disc of season one. Afterwards Dominic folded up the knife and put it back into his pocket.

'Have you made any resolutions?' he asked out of the blue.

I remembered then about it being New Year's Day and shook my head.

'In that case, I have one for you,' he said. 'To live each day as if it's your last.'

He leaned over and squeezed my knee, as if he'd given me a gift. Then he stood up.

'It's that time again, Jessica. Present time.' He almost sang the last two words. 'Can you believe this is the eighth day already? Doesn't time fly?'

Today's present was long and thin – just like his knife. Again he insisted that I feel it thoroughly before opening it, so I could try to guess what it contained.

'Drumsticks?' I tried. 'One of those hand-held blenders?'

But when I'd untied the ribbons and opened the paper, it was neither of these things. It was a leather-handled whip, deceptively heavy.

There was a sharp intake of breath, like a gasp of shock that I could have sworn didn't come from me.

'Tell me about your first experience of sex, Jessica.' He

was leaning back on the perpendicular bit of the sofa so that he could see me properly.

I was silent.

'Coyness is overrated, Jessica. How old were you?'

'Eighteen. It was at university with a boy called Tom.'

'And?' Dominic wanted to know. 'Did you enjoy it? Was he good? Did it hurt? Tell me everything, Jessica.'

'There isn't really much to tell. It was his first time too, and when it was over I looked at him and said, "Was that right, do you think?" and he said he wasn't completely sure but he thought so.'

'And did you like it?'

I tried to force my mind back to my single bed in my little room at the hall of residence, with the grey sky pressing damp against the window.

'I wouldn't say I liked it. I was just relieved to get it over with.'

Dominic seemed disappointed with my story.

'My first time was noticeably different,' he said. 'Of course I'm not counting what happened in the moist darkness of my mother's bedroom. Those were the fumblings of a very confused boy.

'The first time I had sex I had just turned fourteen. She was forty-something. My parents had given me money for my birthday. They always gave me money – they had no idea what I liked or didn't like, or anything about me. They weren't communicating with each other by this stage, so it wasn't surprising. We didn't go in for celebrations in our house. Not after Bella. Anyway, it was enough money to buy Salome. I found Salome in the back of one of Daddy's magazines. When she first saw me she was a bit under-whelmed, but I showed her the money and told her I was sixteen and that was good enough for her.'

'And was . . . Salome . . . expensive?'

'Extortionate, sweetheart. But that was because of the extras.'

I looked down at the whip in my hands. I was starting to see what the extras might mean.

'After Salome, I was hooked. They say you never forget your first time, don't they? The only thing was, I didn't have the money to pay for it. I tried to persuade a girl I knew at school to try it – I'd grown into my looks by then and was quite in demand – but that ended badly. In my defence, I didn't know then how easily skin splits open.

'Her parents were furious. Mine weren't too happy either. I left that school under a cloud.

'After that I realized I had to be more subtle. By that time I was buying hard-core magazines and I discovered that the truth is, everyone's at it. Everyone you look at on the Tube or walking past your house or drinking fucking skinny lattes in Starbucks. They're all carrying round these great ugly secrets. The things they like to do when no one is watching. The things they like to have done to them. You'd be shocked, Jessica. How filthy most people are under their clothes.

'So I developed this façade. I became everything a girl could want me to be. Groomed, respectful, attentive. I only brought out this' – he indicated the whip with the slightest movement of his hand – 'when it was too late for her to get out. When she was already in too deep.'

My head was aching and I was still feeling weak.

'Are you in too deep, Jessica?' His voice was feather light.

'Did you have any long-term relationships?' I asked him the first thing that came into my head, just to change the subject.

He smiled broadly, dimples opening up in his cheek and chin like mouths. 'Oh yes, I had a few long relationships. A couple of women who turned out to like the same things I did. Trouble is, when you know the other person is enjoying themselves, it kind of negates the whole purpose, if you see what I mean. The pleasure is in the pain. And the pain is only truly pain if there is no pleasure.

'My longest relationship was with my wife. My first wife, I should say.'

Suddenly I was alert. His *first* wife? It was the first indication he'd given that he'd been married before.

'Was she beautiful – like her?' I indicated the painting of Natalie.

Dominic shook his head. 'Francesca was no looker. But she had the lowest threshold for fear and pain of anyone I've ever met, and that excited me. There's nothing as intimate as inflicting and receiving pain, Jessica. Plus she was rich. Cesca's parents own most of a small town in Yorkshire. That excited me too.'

'Where is she now?'

Now his expression turned dark, his mouth a line that sewed his face together. 'In hell, I very much hope.'

'Why? Did she do something to upset you?'

'You might say that, Jessica. She killed our son.'

After that, Dominic clammed up, refusing to speak.

But when in the evening I followed him into the back of the flat to go to bed, he stopped in the kitchen.

'Haven't you forgotten something, Jessica?' he said without turning round.

He meant the whip.

Two hours later, I sat in a shallow bath of warm water, while he knelt beside me and dabbed antiseptic at the weeping welts on my back and breasts and thighs. On some level, I was aware of the antiseptic stinging, but I was too numb for it to fully register. Dully I noted that the rash seemed now to have spread to my upper thighs. There were ugly purple marks on my wrists and ankles where the restraints had been, and I could feel the stripes across my buttocks every time I shifted position. I wrapped my arms around my knees so I couldn't see the angry-red raised lines that crisscrossed my chest.

Now I knew all about my threshold for pain.

TWENTY-FOUR

If Henrietta Belvedere's skiing holiday had been relaxing, the benefits had worn off very quickly. Jessica Gold's boss at the TV archive held one hand to her lightly tanned forehead and was tapping the fingers of the other insistently on her desk as if sending out an SOS message.

'Sorry,' she said when she caught Kim looking. 'Given up fags for New Year. Only Day Two and I'm already gagging.'

'Be worth it in the end, though,' said Martin, who had given up himself the previous year. Kim had lived through a couple of months of hell while he chewed nicotine gum so relentlessly and loudly she dreamed about the sound in her sleep.

She tried to steer the conversation back to the case in point. 'So there was no workplace bullying you were aware of?'

'Absolutely not.' Henrietta Belvedere appeared genuinely appalled at the idea. 'Look around you, does this look like the kind of place where members of staff make fake pornographic webpages on social media sites to persecute other members of staff?'

Kim had to agree it did not. Everyone they'd spoken to

191

had seemed considerate and amiable, just keen to get on with their own jobs.

'So Jessica gave no indication at all that she was unhappy, or that she might be considering a change?'

'None at all. She kept herself to herself, but she was always perfectly friendly and conscientious. There *was* an odd thing that happened, but that was months ago, and she's been fine ever since.'

'Odd?' Kim could tell from the inflection in Martin's voice that his attention had been grabbed.

'Well, one of the preservation team – they're the ones responsible for making sure the recordings and documents and reels we store here are kept in optimum condition and fully digitalized – was concerned that he'd found Jessica in one of the climate-controlled vaults long after she'd usually have gone home.'

'Climate-controlled vaults?' Kim hadn't really been paying attention when they were looking around the archive earlier on.

'You must understand that most of our work here is done on computers. Every single reel and tape is catalogued and kept in a digital format, so there's very little call for us to actually access the physical recordings themselves. Some of these recordings are incredibly valuable, and because of the need to preserve them, we try to handle them as little as possible, keeping them in special vaults, so for Jessica to be there was really quite . . . irregular.'

'And what was her explanation?' Martin wanted to know.

'She came up with some story about needing to double-check something for a research assignment she'd been given, but it was very weak. It was her demeanour that was suspect more than what she was actually doing. Jessica is normally a very calm, very self-contained individual, but she seemed very stressed. I would even say *distressed*.'

'And you never found out why?' asked Kim.

'No. I asked her if she was all right and she assured me she was fine. And that was that. Nothing like that ever happened again, as far as I know.'

As they walked to Martin's car, Kim tried to fit this bit of information into everything else she knew about Jessica Gold, but as always when she tried to build up a picture of the missing woman, the pieces refused to fit together, and when she tried to force them together, the result was something deformed and not quite human.

All night I'd lain awake in the kennel. Dominic, still in Solicitous Mode, had given me an extra blanket to go between my flayed skin and the hard wooden floor, but still pain surged across my back and shoulders where the whip had lashed them. My body seemed to have entered into another dimension where all was magnified – every single follicle, cell, atom inside me burned, and the light-headed feeling was worse than ever.

But the physical discomfort wasn't the only thing keeping me awake. The weaker I was the less able I was to keep the voices at bay. I kept hearing a woman weeping and thinking about what Dominic had said about his wife killing their son, and feeling sick. Bella was back as well. I must have been delirious because when she said she felt cold, I tried to give her a blanket.

That morning passed in a blur of pain. Dominic couldn't do enough for me. He made me breakfast and brought it to me on the sofa as it hurt to sit on the stool. He made so much fuss of me, I found myself feeling grateful to him. And when he stroked me gently on my cheek and said, 'You know, I do love you, Jessica Gold,' actual tears came to my eyes. 'I love you too,' I told him. For once lunch did not contain a single morsel of meat. Butternut-squash risotto with crème brûlée for pudding. I ate it obediently though it tasted of nothing.

I tried to add up the number of days I'd been in that flat by listing all the presents, but my mind kept going blank. At one point I looked down at my hand and noticed that two more fingernails seemed to have fallen out.

'Are you up to a present today?' Dominic asked mid-afternoon, his face a picture of concern.

I knew I was about to find out something I didn't want to know but at the same time I had a compulsion to know what had happened to Cesca – and to their son. I was starting to realize that my destiny was bound up in theirs and Natalie's and Bella's, that we were all part of the same long, twisted path, though where it led, I had no clue.

This present was small and soft to the touch. When I placed it gently against my hot cheek I felt a fluttery vibration deep inside me like a baby's chuckle.

Inside the package was a miniature Arsenal football strip. The back was emblazoned with the message *Sam Lacey 1*. There were tiny knee-length socks and even little soft replica football boots with padded soles.

Dominic took the top from me and held it up in front of him. It was hardly bigger than his face.

'I bought this for him for his first birthday. I can still remember how he looked in it. He had blond hair that his mother refused to cut, so it curled around his face like a girl's, and a dimple in his cheek just like mine. His eyes were huge. He was the most beautiful child. I know all parents think that about their children, but trust me, Jessica, he really was.' He glanced up at me. 'Oh, I forgot, you're barren so you have no idea what a parent thinks. You're just going to have to use your imagination.'

Barren. It shouldn't have hurt but it did.

'The trouble is, of course, that by the time I gave it to him, I had already met Natalie. Oh, I'm jumping ahead. Let me start from the beginning.'

I'd noticed how, when Dominic was about to start telling one of his tales, he settled back into his seat to make himself more comfortable as if it was story time at school and he was the teacher.

'I was never in love with Cesca, but as I told you, I was excited by her ignorance of pain. Her parents had cushioned her from hurt so it came as twice as much of a shock to her. She opened herself right up to it, like a flower. Also, she was rich. And she was head over heels in love with me. She used to stay awake all night watching me sleep. I'd wake up in the morning to find her inches away. It was quite sweet really. At first I made a huge effort to be nice to her, focusing on the money, but then I realized that being unkind actually made her want me more so I stopped bothering.

'Our wedding was a huge fussy affair with a helicopter

and a castle. When she first told me she was pregnant, I wasn't ecstatic. I think I refused to talk to her for a whole week that time. She was a total wreck by the end of it. I wasn't the kindest of husbands though, in my defence, her body disgusted me. The skin of her belly was stretched so tight and thin by the end, like it could tear right open like pizza dough.

'But when Sam was born, everything changed. I never knew you could love someone so completely and un-complicatedly. And you know, I felt such a sense of loss that Bella wasn't there to meet him.'

Even in my groggy state, that one shocked me. It was as if Dominic had no memory of having told me his part in his sister's death.

'I'd hoped having a baby might make Cesca grow up a bit so she was more of an equal to me, but instead she let her-self go completely. Always smelling of sour milk and her skin all yellow and her eyes all sunken in her face. At first she used to complain to her parents. "Oh, I'm so tired, oh, Dominic never helps."' He raised his voice to a falsetto for this imitation. 'But that didn't last long. It's quite common for there to be a rift between in-laws and new parents at that time, I've since discovered.

'I didn't ban them. Nothing like that. I just made it quite uncomfortable for them to come round. Or any of Cesca's old friends. Or her sister. I didn't see why she needed other people now she had Sam. He should have been enough for her. *We* should have been enough for her.'

I pictured Cesca, isolated and cowed, with her yellow face.

'Things were plodding along. We were the very image of domestic bliss. Then along came Natalie and destroyed it all.'

I stayed silent while he continued.

'Natalie knew that I was married but she made a beeline for me. She was a successful stylist – very beautiful, very determined. I was powerless.'

I looked at Dominic and tried to imagine him powerless. It was impossible.

'Ours was a whirlwind romance. I didn't want to leave Sam, but Natalie wore me down. She was like an addiction. I left Cesca and moved in with Natalie. Cesca went to pieces, of course. She was such a sensitive little thing. She rarely left the house and practically mainlined prescription pills so I had no choice but to apply for custody of Sam.

'Of course, Cesca's parents didn't like that one bit. They launched a law suit. Against me. Can you believe that? They wanted Cesca to divorce me – even offered to pay me off if I'd give up my claim to Sam. That's the kind of people they are. They believe money is at the heart of everything.'

What is at the heart of everything? I wondered. Power?

'I kept going back to see Cesca, to persuade her to see sense and to check Sam was being properly cared for. I worried about him so. Then, get this, she took out a restraining order against me. Said I was harassing her. That was her parents' doing all right. Now I could only see Sam in the company of a social worker. *My own son.* This dumpy, nosy old cow in a beige mac was always there watching whenever I picked him up or changed him. It was a total violation.

'So I went to see Cesca again, to explain things from my point of view. And I got threatened with court. For being a concerned father. British justice for you. I went to see her a few more times. She was a complete mess by this stage. She wasn't capable of looking after anyone. She shook all the time. I didn't want to take Sam away from her, but she wasn't capable of looking after him. I had no choice.'

'So what happened?'

'Cesca moved house. Without telling me. I had no idea where they'd gone. I was completely frantic. In the end I hired a private detective to find them and paid her a visit. I was pretty angry, I have to confess, but I think I was justified, don't you?'

He was looking at me as if genuinely seeking validation.

I nodded, which seemed to appease him, so he continued.

'Well, after I left her that time, it seems she completely lost the plot. I blame the quack doctor who prescribed her all those pills. They were messing with her head. She crushed up five sleeping pills and put them in Sam's night-time bottle. And then she smothered him with a pillow.'

After his passionate outburst about the justice system, Dominic delivered this last snippet of information in a flat, indifferent voice, but my own emotions were all over the place. I looked down at the little football kit in my lap and felt again the gentle rumble of a baby's chuckle. 'What happened to her? Did she go to jail?'

Dominic's smile flashed across his face like a blade catching the light. 'No. After killing Sam she downed enough pills from her personal arsenal to fell a fucking elephant and then hung herself from the light fitting on the landing for good measure.'

I had my hand over my mouth now. Cesca dead, Sam dead. Bella too. Death seemed to follow Dominic around like a love-struck fan and yet it never properly touched him.

'Her poor parents,' I said, then immediately regretted it.

To my surprise he threw back his head and laughed. 'They weren't happy, as you can imagine. But not as unhappy as when they realized she'd never changed the will she made when we first got married, leaving all her money to me.'

Was that true? Could someone really drive a person to suicide and infanticide and then walk away with everything?

'Oh, there was an enormous legal challenge,' he said, seeing the disbelief on my face. 'In the end we settled out of court. I could have won. But I thought the parents had suffered enough, even though they'd brought it on themselves. Their daughter killed my son. Any decent people would have felt guilty enough to offer me the shirts off their backs. If they hadn't encouraged her to be so obstructive, none of it would have happened. They and the doctor have got to take equal blame – as well as Cesca, of course. I don't know how they live with themselves.'

He wasn't joking.

'Sam's funeral was the worst day of my life. As I carried that little white coffin I could hardly see for the tears. Thank god Natalie was there or I might have actually stumbled.'

I shouldn't have been shocked that he'd taken his girl-friend to his baby son's funeral, but I was. I imagined how it must have been for the grieving grandparents. And then I thought about my own parents and how their faces might look at my funeral. It was the first time I'd allowed myself to think of how this whole thing would end.

It's a measure of my weakened state that it almost felt like a relief.

TWENTY-FIVE

Natalie. Since the minute I learned of her existence, her presence had hovered on the edge of my vision. In my weaker moments she crawled beneath my skin.

I'd seen there were only three presents remaining and I knew I was getting closer to finding out what had happened to her. But I also knew there was a big part of me that didn't want to know, particularly not when finding out about her brought me closer to finding out what would happen to me.

Sometimes I allowed myself to fantasize that he would let me go once the whole charade of the presents was over. I'd picture myself stumbling out on to an unfamiliar east London road, blinking in the winter sun. But mostly I tried not to think ahead.

By this time it was almost second nature to me to avoid moving the leg with the shackle on. Instead, I lay still and held up my hands in front of my face, checking what new damage the night had wrought on my nails and skin. I saw immediately that the rash had now spread to the backs of my hands, but it was almost as if I was observing this development on someone else. I reached the fingers of my left hand up to my head and felt experimentally along my hairline. Loosened hairs cascaded down my forehead into my eyes and I brushed them absently away.

The tingling in my nerve endings was like a million mini electric shocks, and I was so very, very tired.

'Rise and shine,' carolled Dominic by the archway to the kennel. There seemed to be a curious correlation between his mood and my health – the weaker I became, the more cheerful he was.

Go figure, said Travis' voice in my head.

Breakfast was toast and coffee – almost civilized, apart from the four sugars Dominic insisted on heaping into my drink. I saw that the freezer was stuffed with bread and milk that Dominic defrosted overnight as and when we were running low so there was no need to go to the shops. He'd really thought of everything. I felt a sudden irrational pang of gratitude towards him for how he was looking after me.

'As it's our tenth day together – our anniversary, you could say – I'm giving you a treat.'

Even in the state I was in, I brightened up. A treat. I'd been reduced to the level of a child.

'We're going to go in there today. I know you've been desperate to, ever since you arrived.'

I didn't know what he was talking about, but I smiled so that he would know I was pleased to be going wherever it was he thought I'd wanted to go.

'We might even have present time there. Just to spice things up a bit. We wouldn't want everything to get too samey, would we, sweetheart?'

No, I agreed. We wouldn't.

It was only afterwards, when I was lying back on the sofa

cushions, listening to some classical music that Dominic had kindly put on, that I grasped what he meant.

We were going into the locked room.

Kim couldn't seem to get a handle on Travis Riley.

When they'd first met, she'd found him slightly over-earnest but attractive in a geeky kind of way. But the more she got to know him, the more that seemed to be a front. A couple of times when she'd been talking to the Gold family about Jessica, she'd glanced over and caught an expression of annoyance on his face, in place of his habitual eternal-student gawkiness. Of course most people play a part to an extent, Kim knew that, but this was more than adopting a persona or conforming to type. She couldn't help feeling he was hiding something – not necessarily about Jessica's disappearance, but something about their relation-ship that might throw a different light on the case.

In her own time she'd started researching into Travis' background, trawling through social media sites. He had a Facebook page, but didn't seem to be very active on it. She guessed he didn't have a lot of spare time.

This morning's visit to Travis' boss wasn't exactly secret, it was just that she hadn't got around to mentioning it to Martin yet.

She knew Travis was still off work – on compassionate leave was what she believed – so there was little chance of him spotting her as she entered the brown-brick teaching hospital in east London; still, she couldn't shake off the feel-ing that she was betraying him by checking up on him. Of course, Travis' movements over the day of Jessica's disappearance had already been thoroughly verified and there seemed little chance that between leaving work mid-afternoon and meeting friends for drinks that evening, he'd managed to make his girlfriend disappear so thoroughly that no trace of her had been found. However, Kim still wasn't completely satisfied. She didn't know what she was looking for, but something wasn't falling into place.

After wandering around numerous different blocks and wings, she eventually located the medical school in a building at the back of the hospital site, possibly the furthest point away from the way she'd come in. Travis' supervisor in the paediatrics department was a small, wiry man with those disconcerting frameless glasses that disappear and reappear on a person's face according to the angle you're looking at them. He introduced himself formally as Mr Stevens. Though Kim knew hospital consultants were always misters not doctors, she couldn't stop herself addressing him as 'doctor'. After the third time he stopped correcting her.

'Shall we sit over here?' They'd met in a corridor that smelt like swimming baths and he now led her to a seating area, where they perched side by side on orange plastic chairs as if they'd come to watch a show.

'We're just gathering information at the moment,' she told him. 'It's purely routine.'

'I understand,' he said. Though he was making an effort to be cool, Kim could see by the flush in his cheeks that he was quite enjoying being so close to a crime investigation.

'I'm just looking for a bit of background on Travis Riley—'

Mr Stevens interrupted her quickly. 'I have to tell you, Detective, I haven't known Travis long. He's only been specializing in paediatrics since August. Before that, he was on our foundation training programme, working in different departments around the hospital.'

'OK, but maybe you'd be able to tell me if he's been acting out of character at all recently. Has he taken time off without explanation? Gone home early? Arrived late? Got into arguments with his peers?'

Mr Stevens shook his head with an expression of regret. Kim got the impression he was desperately trying to scrape up some piece of information that would help, to be the hero of the hour. In her last posting they used to call it the *Crimewatch* syndrome – where people are so keen to be part of the investigation they sometimes invent details, or wrongfully identify suspects.

'Before you arrived I checked the notes from his previous supervisors in his file. Apparently there was a period, just over a year ago, where his timekeeping went a bit haywire and he skipped a few sessions without a proper explanation. I think there might have been some concern about his commitment, but that seems to have been a short-lived blip.'

'And that was, what, fourteen or fifteen months ago?'

'Thereabouts.'

So it didn't have anything to do with Jessica's odd behaviour at work which had happened around five or six months ago.

For all her extra work, Kim was right back where she started.

* * *

Time was doing weird things. Now that I existed in this
fevered state I could no longer tell whether a minute had
passed or an hour. I couldn't remember a past before I'd
been in this apartment and the thought of getting out of it
was oddly terrifying. Yet the day after tomorrow the last
present would be opened, and then he'd either have to kill
me or let me go.

I lay on the sofa and gazed at the ceiling high above and
imagined how it would have looked when this place was still
a working warehouse. I thought of how many men would
have laboured in this very room, day in, day out, heaving
crates and packing boxes, hoping, dreaming, living, dying.

Dominic no longer shackled me to the radiator when he
disappeared off to the bathroom. I had no energy to get up,
let alone make an escape. Whenever I attempted to stand
everything ached, and my nerves burned when I moved.
Better to lie still and do nothing. He came and sat behind
me, gently lifting my head on to his lap and stroking it like
it was a cat.

His touch still made my skin crawl and yet it *was* touch.
A reminder that I was human. I could have lain there almost
happily for ever, it seemed to me, but then I felt Dominic
sigh.

'It's time,' he said.

I didn't ask him what it was time for. It no longer mattered.

He helped me to my feet and we set off shuffling across the
wooden floor. The flat seemed to have taken on stadium-size
proportions and progress was agonizing and slow.

At first Dominic was solicitous, matching his steps to

mine and asking if I was all right, but after a while he became impatient.

'You're not even trying,' he snapped. 'Why must you make such a big deal out of everything? You've only got a common cold. Do you know your trouble, Jessica?'

I shook my head, the slightest of movements.

'You're spoilt. All the women I've ever known have been spoilt. Except Mummy, of course.'

'But you hated your mother.'

Wham! The explosion came from nowhere, knocking me across the floor.

I put my hand up to my head and it came away wet with blood, mixed with hair.

'You have to do it, don't you, Jessica? You have to go making your silly ignorant assumptions based on nothing but your own non-existent experience of life. I loved my mother. What, you think you non-dysfunctional types have a monopoly on love? It's time you grew up, Jessica Gold.'

'I'm sorry,' I said.

I couldn't stand that I'd upset him. Not when he was being so nice to me.

'Don't cry, Jessica,' he said. 'You're so ugly when you cry.'

The blow to my head had shaken off my torpor and now I felt everything keenly – the pains in my abdomen, the disturbing tingling in my nerve endings, as if someone was plucking them like the strings of a harp.

I stopped still in the middle of the hallway, eyeing the locked door. Dread lodged in my throat, making it hard to breathe.

'I don't want to go in there.'

'Nonsense, Jessica. I know you've been itching to get in there, ever since you arrived.'

I tried to deny it, but he was already reaching into his pocket for his huge bunch of keys.

'The green one, I think, today,' he said. 'Do come closer, sweetheart. I wouldn't want to leave you behind.'

He put the green-fobbed key in the lock and turned it. The clicking noise was like a gunshot.

'Come on,' he said, turning the handle. He reached out and grabbed my arm as he nudged open the door and he yanked me in front of him and shoved me through.

Kim was leaning against the wall at the side of the station building and wishing she smoked.

All around her, she could see other police officers drawing on cigarettes with that semi-orgasmic expression endemic to smokers. If she could just have a cigarette to distract her, she thought, she might be able to get through this phone call with her mother without falling apart.

'I just don't understand,' her mum was saying, for the millionth time. 'How can any job be worth your family?'

'It's not. That's not the way it is. I just think there must be a way I can have both – a job *and* my kids.'

'Yes, but just not that particular job. At least not at this particular time.'

'But I'm good at my job, Mum. Play to your strengths, that's what you always told us to do.'

'Well, I'm afraid in this case you just have to compromise. Or go part-time until the kids are older. The police force is always bleating on about offering flexible hours for women.

Sean even emailed me a link to a newspaper feature about it.'

So it had come to that. Her husband sending internet links to her mother to win her support.

'We can't afford for me to be part-time. Have you looked at the cost of living in London lately? And anyway, how it looks on paper isn't how it works in reality. Have you seen how few senior policewomen there are? And by the time the kids are independent I'll be too old. Mum, I'm sick of apologizing for wanting to do well.'

'Kim, love, I want you to do well too. I know your job's important to you, but some things are more important. Your marriage. Your children.'

Kim was finding it hard to talk around the bitter lump that had suddenly formed in the back of her mouth.

'So Sean gets to keep his job and his house and his kids because he's a man, but I have to choose.'

'Oh, don't be so simplistic!'

Kim had rarely heard her mum so angry.

'This isn't about men and women, it's about the fact that Sean's job allows him to be home every night and to arrange reliable childcare with regular hours, not be calling around everyone you know to find emergency playdates because you're not going to be back when you said. Those children need you. You're their mother.'

'And I'm just to forget my own dreams.'

'Yes. Frankly, yes.'

The room was pretty much a mirror image in size and shape to the bedroom next door, with the same high, small window giving out on to the brick sidewall of the next building. There was another double bed with crisp white bedding facing the door, while the wall to the left was completely covered by a storage system made up of deep white cube-like shelves on which various things were neatly stacked – books, photograph albums, CDs. I saw the art equipment he'd used a few days before – the paints and brushes. And the beautiful chess set. The opposite wall was raw brick and almost obscured by another huge painting, like the one in the living room. I could recognize Dominic's trade marks – the curiously lumpy texture of the paint, the unsubtle colour palette, the model. Natalie again, this time sprawling completely naked on a bed, with only a crumpled sheet preserving what scraps of modesty remained.

Now we were inside the room, Dominic's high spirits were restored, in fact he bubbled with barely concealed delight, reminding me of my niece and nephew when they'd got me a present and couldn't wait for me to open it.

'Stay here,' he said, steering me on to the bed. I sank back among the pillows, which were instantly stained red from where my head had hit the floor. I listened to his footsteps as he made his way through the hallway to the living area of the flat.

Though there was nothing obviously out of place in that room, still there was something about it that made the sweat prickle on my already clammy skin. Surveying the shelves again to take my mind off my growing fear, I noticed most of the books seemed to be to do with cooking, and remembered seeing Dominic reading a recipe book. My eyes drifted over the rest of the shelves: more books, papers, a pack of tea lights, a laptop.

A laptop.

Something roared into life in my chest and it took me a while to identify it as hope. Here was a link to the world outside this flat. I was too weak now to fantasize about escaping on my own, but perhaps I could bring rescuers here.

All too quickly the door was pushed open again and Dominic came back into the room. He was carrying a smallish cylindrical present.

'Tell me about this boyfriend of yours,' Dominic said, lying down next to me on the red-streaked bedding.

'Travis?'

'How many boyfriends do you have, naughty Jessica Gold?'

His fingers played across my stomach as he spoke and I remembered what he'd said about Cesca's pregnant belly and how easily it would rip open.

'Travis is . . . nice.'

'*Nice?* Sweetheart, nice is for picnics and next-door neighbours and other people's cats. It's not for boyfriends. When I first met Natalie, I wanted to swallow her whole.'

I glanced at the cookery books, and felt a bit queasy.

'Where did you two meet?' I wanted to keep him talking, so I wouldn't have to open the present.

'I went to price up a company that had gone bust. It was in some industrial backwater – all broken windows and dilapidated buildings. There was literally nothing around there, and then suddenly out of nowhere a truckload of stylists and models and photographers turned up to do a fashion shoot. Two-thousand-quid dresses dragging in the dirt. Natalie was the stylist. The second I saw her, I knew. Do you believe in love at first sight, Jessica?'

I nodded my head weakly without lifting it from the pillow. It wasn't true, but it seemed safer to agree. This was clearly the right response.

'So you understand then that I knew instantly I'd have to leave Cesca. It was a shame, but there you are. The heart wants what the heart wants. Isn't that right?'

'So you left straight away?'

'No. There was the obligatory back-and-forth period. Sam was still so little. I couldn't bear not to be around him. But every time I tried to stop the affair with Natalie, I got sucked right back in. She's the only woman I've ever met whose appetite for pain exceeds my own.'

I remembered then how the whip had felt cutting across my skin.

'She's very beautiful.' I was looking at the painting – the long blonde hair, the curves, the cheekbones.

'And she knew exactly how to use it. Natalie was constantly playing games. Picking up men, then dropping them. Playing off one against the other. At first I was so besotted I went along with it. I even got off on it, I admit. She would pick up men all over the place and toy with them for an hour or a night or a week, then come home to tell me all about it.

'Of course, when I finally ripped myself away from Sam and bought this place for her – she chose everything in here, you know, I had it all specially done up – I told her there could be no other men. I even married her, because I thought it would tie her to me. But she couldn't stop. Or wouldn't. We used to have crashing, violent rows and she'd disappear, and then come home and taunt me with stories of the men she'd been with.

'I loved her but it wasn't enough. You see, she brought it all – all of it – on herself.'

I shivered as I remembered him using the same phrase about Cesca's parents.

'And you didn't . . . retaliate?'

Dominic didn't strike me as the sitting-at-home-waiting-by-the-phone type.

'Obviously I retaliated. It became something of a game for a while. We'd each go off and pick up other people, using elaborate aliases we'd invent together at home. But the problem was, I couldn't bear to think of her with other men. In the end it drove me to distraction. Maybe it's hard for someone like you – someone so repressed – to understand, Jessica, how a person can have such an effect on you that you can't think straight any more. Our rows grew more violent, and our making-up more violent still. There were times I really thought we'd both end up dead.'

'In the summer she went AWOL – again. So what's new. Turned out she'd booked herself into a clinic somewhere to have a boob job. We'd had a massive row before she went, and she told me she was leaving me. Said she'd been seeing a Saudi playboy. He was the one who wanted her to get her tits done.

'I didn't hear from her for ages. I was going bloody crazy not knowing where she was. I tracked down the playboy. We had words. I don't imagine he did much playing after that. Not long afterwards, she turned up again, out of the blue. It was late at night and she was in a terrible mood.

'She started straight in, taunting me, and I'm afraid that was it – the red mist descended. I got out the whip. The very one I gave you the day before yesterday in fact. She was goading me constantly, saying it didn't hurt, that I was impotent, flaccid, useless. Well, you can imagine.'

I could imagine only too well.

'I was in a sort of trance and when I came out of it, I was still holding the whip and Natalie was . . . well, let's just say she wasn't modelling material any more.'

Raising myself up on to my elbows, I retched over the blood-streaked pillow, but nothing came out save a dribble of saliva.

'Careful, Jessica. You must take it easy, my sweet. You've got a present to open, don't forget.'

He placed the compact package very carefully on the bed next to me. When I found the strength to pick it up, it was heavier than I'd expected.

I hesitated, my fingers wandering nervously over the paper.

'The present, Jessica.' His voice was sharp and pointed, like the knife I noticed he had taken out of his pocket. It rested on his lap, the blade pointing towards me. I pulled off the wrapping to reveal a candle in a thick glass cylinder. It looked like one of the expensive ones, the wax the rich yellow of cake batter.

Scented candles. It didn't surprise me. I figured Natalie might have been the scented-candle type. I held it up to my nose and inhaled deeply.

A heavy, sour smell like dried sweat. I sniffed again. This time it wasn't quite so bad.

'Well?' He was clearly expecting more of a response.

'It's . . . distinctive. What is it?'

His face erupted with delight. 'It's *her*, sweetheart! It's all her.'

I swear, he clapped his hands together in joy, like a child.

'I don't understand.'

'The candle, the paintbrushes, the chess set. It's all Natalie. Fat, hair, bone. It's amazing how many uses a human body can have. I can't think why that isn't more widely acknowledged.'

I remembered the brushes, with their soft bristles, and the chess set with those beautiful carved white pieces I'd assumed were ivory. I looked at the candle and the room swam in front of my eyes.

'What do you think of the painting, Jessica?'

The question was so unexpected it took me a while to drag my eyes away from the candle to the huge nude figure on the far wall. The crude brushstrokes, the slightly lascivious smile, straight out of a schoolboy's fantasy, the dull-brown flesh tones, so that the body looked bruised, that strange lumpy texture like woodchip.

'Amazing how I've captured the essence of Natalie in that painting and in the one in the living room, wouldn't you say?' His voice could hardly contain his glee.

I looked again – and everything went black.

When I woke up I was in a hot bubble bath.

There was a candle burning.

TWENTY-SIX

The next twenty-four hours came and went like through a camera lens passing in and out of focus. There were dreams that didn't seem like dreams at all. In one, Travis was right next to me on the end of Dominic's bed, dangling Winston's lifeless body from his outstretched hands. 'You wouldn't listen to me, would you?' he was saying. 'And now look what's happened.' In another, I saw my parents standing at a grave surrounded by mourners. 'I can't wear black,' my mum sobbed. 'It drains me.' In a third, Natalie was stretched out naked on a bed. 'I'm cold,' she was saying in Bella's childish voice. 'I'm so cold.'

Consciousness was like a blanket I pulled on and kicked off. I couldn't tell what was real: Natalie in her vulgar nudity, or Dominic who at some point had carried me in from the bathroom and dressed me in a silk nightdress (one of hers, I supposed) and laid me in the heavy-framed bed right next to him this time. Once I awoke panicking that my head wound had bled on to his crisp white pillowcases and I scrubbed at them with the side of my fist.

I knew by now there was something seriously wrong with me. In addition to the still painful sores from the whip, the

216

rash had spread until it covered almost my entire body, even around the hip bone where the festering tattoo had turned septic and was oozing pus. Every few minutes, my stomach would cramp up with crippling pains, I'd lost all but one of my nails and could feel bald patches the diameter of golf balls on the sides of my head. Though Dominic had cuffed me to the bed frame, there was little need. I didn't have the strength to hit him.

For the first stretch of the strange dreamlike day that followed that restless night, Dominic appeared by my side at intervals like a concerned nurse, laying a cool hand across my forehead, or cupping the back of my head in his palm to raise it up so I could sip from the glass of water he brought me. In my fevered state, I forgot about the whip and the tattoo and the blow that had sent me crashing to the floor the day before. Instead I focused on how his skin felt on mine. Desperate again for human contact, I craved his touch, curling into it like a cat.

But gradually his demeanour changed. On a couple of occasions I opened my eyes to find him glaring at me from the doorway. Once he came in and prodded my stomach as if I was a cut of beef on a supermarket shelf. When I groaned, he turned on me with narrowed, mean eyes.

'I've been as patient as I can,' he said. 'But I do have limits. We were supposed to be enjoying this time together. How enjoyable do you think this is for me – watching you lying there, yellow and sweating like a lump of cheese in the sun? We have so little time left and you're wasting it.'

I mumbled an apology and tried to sit up.

'That's better. Good girl.'

He propped another pillow under my head so I was semi-upright.

'Now wait here while I go to fetch today's present. I've been so worried we might have to ditch the whole plan.'

After he'd gone, I tried to stay awake, but my eyelids were made of lead, closing like shop shutters over my vision. After that I was vaguely aware of being shaken, but the shaking merged into my dream where I was on a boat being tossed around by a violent storm. 'We have to save her,' I said, leaning over the side of the bucking vessel. 'We have to save Bella.' In my dream I could hear her crying, a pitiful sound like a kitten's mew. But when I finally forced my eyes open, it wasn't Bella crying at all, but Dominic.

He was sitting on the floor next to the bed with his back to the wall and his head in his hands, his shoulders shaking.

'It's all ruined,' he said, as if he somehow knew I was watching him. 'All that planning. You've spoiled everything.'

I tried to battle through the cotton wool in my head to reply. 'But I'm awake now. We can do presents now.'

He flung his head back then to glare at me through reddened eyes.

'You don't get it, do you? Even after everything you still don't get it. It's after midnight. You've missed the whole of Day Eleven. It's too late now. Everything's too late.'

'But I'm ready to . . .'

'I threw it in the river, Jessica!' His voice was shrill, breaking like a dry twig on the last word. 'You know you're just like her. Just like Mummy. You pretend to care, but really it's all about you. Everything is about poor, weak Jessica and how she's feeling. Well, what about how I feel? What about *me*? What a prize bitch you've turned out to be, Jessica.'

Tears pricked at the back of my eyes, but I hadn't the strength to shed them. So this was it? The end? I'd ruined his plans and now it was all over. In a way the knowledge felt like a release. When the shop shutters came down again, I welcomed the blackness like a friend.

TWENTY-SEVEN

'It's been twelve days, Detective Harper. Kim. And the police seem no nearer to finding my daughter than when she first disappeared.'

Kim sighed. She felt for Liz Gold, of course she did. But did she really think they needed reminding that despite all their investigations, they'd drawn a complete blank?

'We're still following a number of lines of inquiry, Mrs Gold,' said Martin.

Kim was well aware of what his own personal line of inquiry was – finding out how quickly they would discover the body. Ever since the Golds first mentioned Jessica's 'voices' Martin had remained convinced she'd taken herself off to a dark forest with a length of rope and a copy of *The Bell Jar*, and nothing they'd learned since had changed his mind.

He'd been openly patronizing when he heard about Kim's fruitless trip to see Travis Riley's supervisor. 'We're going to be judged on our results, Kim,' he'd said, referring to the promotion they were both hoping for, but had mostly avoided talking about. 'Not on how much extra time we spend chasing up blind alleys. You don't get Brownie points for wasting time.'

The Liz Gold that had greeted them at the front door early in the morning on 5th January was a very different woman to the one they'd met on Christmas Day. She was still well dressed – in a knee-length tartan wool skirt and long brown flat boots – but the whites of her green eyes were tinged with pink, and her skin was wrapped too tightly over her cheekbones. Her husband kept a protective arm around her shoulder, as if to stop her toppling right over, and Kim found her eyes fixed on how his hand, with his broad, black-haired fingers, gripped on to his wife tightly.

'We heard you've been asking about Travis. Is he a suspect?' It was one of the brothers speaking. Kim had been surprised when she and Martin had turned up and found both of the junior Golds at home on a weekday morning. They were a close family, she realized now. She found herself praying that Martin was wrong and Jessica would be found alive. Her loss would rip this family apart.

'No,' Kim was quick to reply. 'We have to check up on everyone in a case like this. I'm sure you understand.'

'I just hope you appreciate how hard this is for my parents, Detective. My daughter, Grace, is only thirteen, but if anything happened to her . . .'

'We are doing everything we can,' Kim said, aware of how inadequate that sounded.

On the way out, Liz Gold tugged her arm.

'You're a mother,' she said. 'You know how impossible it is to function unless you know your children are safe. Please bring her home.'

Kim nodded, unable to speak, and spent an unnecessary

time doing up the zip of her coat so no one would be able to see her tear-blurred eyes.

I hadn't expected to wake up at all.

I certainly hadn't expected to wake up lying in the bed next to Dominic with my whole body aching, but my mind clearer than it had been in days.

I wondered if I'd dreamed that scene with Dominic sitting on the floor crying, his face scrunched up like a paper bag. Would he really have thrown away one of his carefully planned presents just because I'd missed a day? If so, how would he make me pay?

I've no idea how long I lay awake listening to the soft sigh of Dominic's breathing while images of my parents and brothers and nephews and niece and Travis fluttered like flags just out of reach. With my newly clear vision, I started adding up the days I'd been in that apartment and the tally of presents. If he had been telling the truth about yesterday and the unopened present he'd hurled into the Thames, it meant that today was the twelfth day of Christmas and there was just one present left.

And then I'd be dead.

At the same time the thought occurred to me, I sensed I'd always known it. Dominic had brought me here, to play out this Twelve Presents charade, because he couldn't face being alone and because directly or indirectly, he'd already killed the only people he cared about. But he could not let me live.

'What are you thinking about, Jessica?'

He had propped himself up on his elbow and was running his free hand up and down my arm. My nerve endings felt so exposed his finger might as well have been the blade of his knife. At least he didn't look angry any more. In fact the tearful scene of last night seemed completely forgotten.

'About what's going to happen after today is over.'

His mouth turned down in a mock-sad expression. 'Jessica, Jessica. Why are you wishing away what's left of our time together? You know your trouble, sweetheart? You don't allow yourself to live in the moment.'

'What will you do with my body?'

I needed to know if my parents would have something to grieve over or if they'd always be left wondering.

Dominic screwed up his face, as if I'd said something distasteful. 'I don't really want to talk about that, Jessica, if you don't mind. Not on our last day.'

But I couldn't leave it alone.

'You obviously disposed of Natalie's body here, piece by piece. What about her family? Do they have any idea what happened to her? What about the police? Didn't they search here?'

Now he gave the dismissive scathing look I'd come to dread.

'Of course they searched here, Jessica. And my offices in Vauxhall. Where they didn't search – at least, not until it was too late – is the overspill warehouse in Kent I sub-let from another company to store all the stuff I buy and then can't shift – pallet after pallet of it, all stacked up to the rafters. By the time they did get round to searching it I'd brought her back here – the choice bits of her anyway.

'They had their suspicions, of course, but there was

nothing they could do, particularly not after a woman vaguely matching Natalie's description turned up in a jeweller's in Edinburgh trying to flog a diamond necklace that belonged to me, or rather to Cesca, which I'd reported had gone missing the same time she disappeared from the clinic. They'd been looking out for it.'

'A friend of yours, was she, that woman?'

'Hardly a friend. Someone who owed me a favour, put it like that.'

'But CCTV . . .'

Dominic looked bored now.

'Haven't you ever seen how grainy that footage is? All you need is a hat and sunglasses and it could be anyone.'

He really did think of every angle.

When Dominic pulled up the blind in the bedroom, we could see it was one of those rare, crisp winter days in London where aeroplanes rip sharp white lines across a clear blue sky. After more than twenty-four hours in the half-darkness, the sudden brightness hurt my eyes.

'Breakfast outside on the balcony today,' he decided, and carried me through the apartment like we were newlyweds, depositing me on the sofa while he dug around in his pocket for the key to open the glass door.

When he eventually got me outside, the cold literally snatched the breath from my lungs, but I also felt an exhilaration I hadn't felt for a long time. I looked at the sun reflecting gold and silver off the river, and the glittering Shard, soaring up into the sky. I watched the distant cars on the bridge, and noticed how every now and then one of them would explode like a fire cracker when a ray of sunlight bounced off its bonnet. It was all so beautiful. Even the voices calling from Execution Dock didn't seem so desperate. If I tuned them out, just a little, they joined with the noises from the building site across the river and the cries of the seagulls overhead, to form an almost pleasant background drone.

I lay back in one of the chairs, wrapped in the blanket Dominic had brought from the bedroom, while he went inside to make breakfast. He left the door open, even though I wasn't shackled. As I sat back, letting the sun soak in through my ravaged skin, sending jets of warmth shooting through arteries and veins, into tissue and muscle and liver and heart, I started to return to myself. And bit by bit, as I returned, I had second thoughts. No, I wasn't going to die. Not today. Not while the river was sparkling like that diamond necklace Dominic had claimed was stolen. He *would* let me go. He'd give me the last present and then I'd walk out of there and back into my life as if none of this had ever happened.

He emerged through the glass door carrying a tray which he deposited carefully on the metal table in front of me. There was a plate of croissants piled high, a pot of coffee, jam, butter. And, there in the centre, was the last present.

This one was around a foot high and half as wide. I swallowed. Hard.

'Are you frightened, Jessica?' he asked.

I picked up the package and began slowly to open it, lingering over every stage. He watched without hurrying me. I should have smelled a rat.

'It's lovely, isn't it, that paper,' he said, as I made a meal of feeling around for the edge of the Sellotape, trying to put off the moment I'd have to confront what was inside. I nodded, and ran a hand over the white, glitter-encrusted surface.

Finally, when I could delay it no longer, I peeled the paper back to reveal a ceramic vase with a lid.

'Turn it round,' commanded Dominic. 'You're looking at the back.'

Leaning forward, I edged the vase round to reveal a plaque on the front with a message inscribed in curly gold writing.

RIP Jessica Gold
Born 17th September 1985
Died 5th January 2015

Not a vase then. An urn.

My brain was swamped with confusing thoughts. Had he sent away for that plaque since we'd been in the flat? Or could he have engraved it himself, somehow without me noticing?

A scream sounded all around me, high-pitched and terrible to listen to. Only as I tried in vain to tune it out did I understand that the one screaming was me. Dominic's hand reached out and clamped itself over my mouth. I could feel something hard and sharp jabbing into my ribs.

'If you don't stop making that noise,' he hissed, 'I will slice you clean in half.'

I stopped.

'Pick up the urn, Jessica, so we can get rid of the wrapping underneath it.'

As I held the paper in my hand, he smiled. That dimple – a black hole you could get sucked into and never return.

'It's interesting, you know, that glitter' – he gestured to the silver-snowflake pattern and I ran my hand over it, almost without thinking – 'isn't really glitter at all but granules of thallium. Are you familiar with thallium, Jessica?'

I shook my head. Now, looking back, I can see what an idiot I was, but at the time, I didn't have a clue what he was getting at. Was it a special kind of decoration? Was it edible?

'It's poison, sweetheart. It can be absorbed through the skin and the effects of repeated exposure are cumulative. And, sadly, it's fatal. It's not an exact science, obviously, but by my calculations it should just about be getting to the end. Of course I've been adding the odd spoonful to your drinks too, just to be on the safe side. I've even sprinkled some on your food.'

Poison. I let the paper fall and inspected my fingers. There was a trace of powder on them.

Dominic watched as the information sank in, his smile growing broader. By now I could tell when he was excited: a muscle spasmed in his jaw.

'Of course, I could have put the whole lot into your drinks. That might have made the dosage more accurate, but this felt so much more festive somehow. More fun. Oh, don't look so sad, sweetheart, there is an antidote. Jessica, you didn't happen to bring any Prussian blue along with you, did you?'

'I just think you're wrong, that's all.'

Kim knew she wasn't explaining herself well, and was

frustrated by her own inarticulateness, especially in front of DSI Paul Robertson whom she was so desperate to impress, but Martin had put her on the back foot by implying she was allowing sentimentality to overrule the facts. Kim wondered if he'd found out she was living apart from her children and was somehow going to use that against her.

'Her boss, her counsellor, both of them said we shouldn't underestimate her, that she's tougher than she appears. That's all I was saying.'

'And what about Travis Riley? Is he in the clear?'

'Yes, sir,' said Martin.

'Kim?'

'Yes, except I still think there's something he's not saying.'

Robertson frowned, causing a deep furrow to appear between his eyebrows. He was sitting behind his desk in a black padded chair while she and Martin perched on hard seats opposite him like schoolchildren called in to see the head.

'He feels guilty, that's all,' said Martin. 'Maybe they weren't getting on well. Maybe he hasn't been so nice to her. She's got all these voices in her head and he hasn't got time for it. Ignores her cries for help. Course he's going to feel guilty if she goes off and tops herself.'

'So why would she buy all those presents then?' Kim wanted to know. 'If she was about to kill herself. Why go to the bother of trailing around Oxford Street on Christmas Eve if you know you're never going to see Christmas Day?'

Martin turned to face her with such a patronizing look on his face that Kim had a sudden urge to slap him.

'People who are mentally ill don't always do things according to a logical plan. Christmas is very stressful for some people. Anything could have set her off when she was out.'

'There's no evidence that Jessica Gold is mentally ill.' Kim could hear how her voice had crept up a few notes, and knew that would make her sound even more like she was allowing emotion to influence her judgement. 'I just think if Jessica had done something to hurt herself, we'd have found the body by now. And until we do I'm keeping an open mind.'

Was she imagining the look that passed between the two men just before she and Martin left the Super's office?

There's nothing like a shot of sheer terror for revitalizing you. Now I knew my body was closing down I began resisting it, clenching my muscles against the pain, trying to use the calming techniques Sonia Rubenstein had taught me, breathing from my stomach and repeating in my head, 'You will be all right, you're not going to die.'

Dominic seemed more animated than he had in days. Probably the prospect of getting out of this apartment was as welcome to him as it would have been to me.

'I want to paint you again,' he declared. 'Just as you are now.'

It didn't surprise me that he would want to document his handiwork. I wondered if bits of me would also end up on his walls.

'I'm going to fetch the paints. Don't go away now.'

He almost skipped out through the glass door. Once

again he hadn't bothered to leave me tethered, so convinced was he of my frailty. I was alone. Uncuffed.

I grabbed the urn that was still on the table in front of me. It was a risk that he would notice its absence, but I had to take it. I concentrated all my efforts on standing up. Pulling the glass door almost closed to muffle the noise, I slammed the urn against the railing of the balcony. Nothing. Gathering all my strength, I did it again. This time there was a smash I felt sure could be heard as far as the Shard itself. My stomach knotted itself together as I turned and glanced through the window, expecting to see Dominic racing across the floor. Nothing.

I selected the sharpest sliver of china and kicked the remaining fragments into the corner of the balcony behind my chair. Then I sat back down, trying to slow my racing heart.

'Wake up, Jessica.' I'd closed my eyes pretending to be asleep. 'Wake up.'

My hand was resting on my belly and I controlled my breathing from in there just as Sonia had taught me. I heard the sound of Dominic putting the paints down.

'Not yet, Jessica. I still have plans for you. It's not time yet. Wake up!'

I kept my eyes shut.

'Shit,' I heard him mutter.

I felt his breath a split second before he put his hands on my shoulders, then his hair brushing my lips as he put his head to my chest to listen. The shard of china was in my left hand and I channelled all my energy and adrenalin into my forearm as I brought my fist high above my head and plunged the sharp tip deep into the back of his neck. For a moment we were both silent and still. Then Dominic let out a cry that was more like a bellow and slumped forward. I wriggled out from underneath him, calling on strength I hadn't known I still had in me. Sure he would be right on my heels, I flung open the glass door and stumbled inside, propelling myself across the wooden floor, only turning to look once I'd reached the far end of the room. Incredibly, there was no sign of him. Sobbing, I threw myself on the handle of the huge, metal front door and turned it.

Nothing.

Then I remembered how Dominic had taken out the purple-fobbed key that first night and locked us in. He always kept the bunch of keys in his pocket. What about the laptop in the other room? Would he have bothered to lock that door again after fetching the art stuff?

I made my way back through the kitchen and around the half wall to the back part of the flat and lunged forward to open that door.

Locked.

I was still sobbing – horrible gulping sobs that ripped painfully from my throat – but I forced myself to retrace my steps across the huge apartment. Before I reached the glass door to the balcony, I stopped. 'You *will* carry on breathing. You're *not* going to die,' I told myself. But everything around seemed to be lurching as if I was on a boat. I made myself look outside but the table and chairs where I'd been sitting were to the left of the door and out of view.

Taking a deep breath, I stepped outside.

He wasn't there.

He'd managed to crawl to the railing in the far corner of the balcony, leaving a trail of blood like snail slime in his wake. He was half standing, half crouching where the balustrade met the wall, with his back to the river so he was facing me.

'Forgotten something, Jessica?' he asked in a voice that sounded stretched on a rack.

And now I saw that he had brought the huge bunch of keys out from his pocket and was holding them in his right hand – the hand that wasn't clutching on to the railing. With the multicoloured fobs they looked like a posy of flowers in the bright light and for a wild second, I thought he was about to toss them to me. I raised my hands to catch them and Dominic smiled straight at me as if we were sharing the hugest joke. Then he lifted his right arm in an arc and the keys flew over the balustrade and through the crisp winter day, swooping like a dazzling parakeet before entering the river with a splash.

I watched as Dominic slumped to the ground, his strength too depleted by this final, drastic act. Pain was again clouding my head. It was surely over. There were no keys, no way out. Desperate, my eyes scanned the balcony, alighting on the paints.

A message. I could paint an SOS message and hang it from the railing.

The flare of hope that lit inside me at that thought lasted only as long as it took for me to size up the tiny tubes of paint, most of them already rolled up at one end to force the last dregs out. There wasn't a sufficient quantity to create a message big enough to read from all the way down there.

I staggered back inside and dropped down on to the sofa and rested my head back. Then it came to me.

I knew what I had to do.

Everyone else had gone out for lunch. It was strange being in the empty office. Creepy. It occurred to Kim that when they came back they might think she'd been going through their things, and immediately she was cross with herself for the ridiculous notion. She tried to concentrate on the notepad in front of her where she was writing out a list of all the troubling aspects of the Jessica Gold case. She wondered what it was about lists that always made her feel instantly more in control.

- *Self-harming*
- *Voices in head (Luton airport incident?)*
- *Travis Riley acting weird at work (14/15 months ago)*
- *Jessica Gold acting weird at work (5/6 months ago)*

Her phone rang. Sean. He'd be at work, wanting to talk about them – him and her. About what she'd decided. About whether she'd come to her senses. He'd probably tell her which one of the children had cried themselves to sleep last night, although like as not, they'd have been right as rain in the morning.

She let it go to voicemail.

I tugged the bottom sheet off the bed, then dragged it to the kitchen and went through the cupboards. Luckily the one that housed the mop bucket wasn't locked. Even better, there was a serrated knife by the sink. I felt a surge of triumph as I pictured him preparing breakfast and lazily leaving it out, convinced I was too weak to present any kind of threat.

I dropped the sheet in the middle of the floor of the living area, and then carefully spread it out across the wooden boards. Each movement was an effort. Then I put the knife in between my teeth, picked up the bucket and headed towards the balcony, pausing before I went outside to check that Dominic hadn't moved. He was still slumped where he'd been before. The sun was now quite low, dissolving into a low wall of yellowy-grey haze before it reached the river. I didn't have long. My heart plummeted when I saw his shoulders moving. He was still alive, then. That would make what I had to do so much harder.

The more she stared at the list in front of her, the more despondent Kim became. Maybe Martin was right. Jessica would be fished out of a canal somewhere, or washed up on a beach. Everyone always went on about this being a nanny state with CCTV cameras everywhere, but Kim knew very well that there were hundreds of places a body could get lost. She'd once worked on the case of a twenty-one-year-old man who'd just wandered out of his life one day and never come back. The family had done everything to find him – posters, appeals, the works – and had clung to the fact that there was no body as proof that he was still alive somewhere. New York, his younger brother reckoned. Brighton, thought his parents. Then five months later, a couple of weekend fishermen on a motorboat had noticed what they assumed to be a pile of rags tucked into a ledge at the bottom of a cliff a hundred miles away.

'Why didn't he tell us he was unhappy,' his mother kept saying at the funeral.

The thing was, you just never knew.

Yet still, as she looked down at the piece of paper, she couldn't bring herself to believe that Jessica Gold was dead. There was something there, some clue that would unlock the mystery of her disappearance, if only Kim could find it.

When I went out on to the balcony, Dominic was facing away from me and was making a strange noise. Like a gurgle, but it didn't seem to be coming out of his mouth, rather from some other, deeper part of him. The shard of china had come out of his neck and there was a thick channel of blood snaking out from under his hair.

Transferring the knife to my left hand, and holding the bucket with the other, I approached slowly. Even slumped over and gravely wounded, I didn't trust Dominic.

When I put the bucket down, he turned his head slightly and opened his eyes. The whites were almost totally blood-shot, so that the irises appeared like blue ping-pong balls floating in a sea of red.

I grasped the knife. I could do this. Yet already I could feel my strength seeping away in the glare of those piercing eyes.

Grabbing hold of his hair I pulled his head back. The blue ping-pong balls fixed on to my eyes and wouldn't let go.

I forced myself to remember all the things he'd done to

me. But it was no use. I let my hand drop, and as I did, he reached into his pocket and before I had time to react, withdrew his flick knife. Without stopping to think, I plunged the kitchen knife twice into his chest.

The 5th of January. Didn't that date mean something in some countries? Kim had once spent a New Year's holiday in Spain with her parents and been delighted when she found out Spanish children receive presents in January, not at Christmas. Her parents couldn't allow Kim and her brother to feel left out. Cue another last-minute Christmas gift. She couldn't now recall what it was, just that it had felt deliciously decadent – an unexpected extra that none of her friends back home were having. She remembered a nighttime procession through the streets. Idly she fired up her computer and Googled it. Yes, the evening of the 5th was when the Three Wise Men or Three Kings paraded through the streets and threw sweets to the crowd. And the morning of the 6th was when the children received their presents.

Epiphany. The end of the Twelve Days of Christmas.

Kim smiled for the first time that day. So tomorrow was Epiphany.

Whenever I looked at the handle of the knife sticking out of Dominic's chest, I felt like I was about to vomit. At least he'd stopped making those gurgling noises. I didn't check to see if he was still alive. He was doing a very good impression of someone dead.

I grabbed hold of his hand. His fingers were still curled

around his knife and I had to prise them off one by one. Finally I was able to flick it open. When I saw the length of that blade, I remembered how it had felt resting against my skin and I hardened my resolve.

It's him or me, I kept reminding myself, once more grabbing hold of his hair and yanking his head back. I have no choice.

Still I wavered while holding the blade against his throat. His skin was milk-white in the fading light and vulnerable, like the delicate membrane over the yolk of a poached egg. I thought about the little boy he'd once been, sitting on that plastic stool.

Then I felt again a fluttering vibration inside me like a baby's chuckle and remembered little Sam who'd had no chance.

I squeezed my eyes shut and slid the knife across his throat.

Adrenalin was pumping through me as strongly as the blood oozing from Dominic's neck. I grabbed the bucket and held it under the red viscous stream, watching impatiently. It wasn't shooting out like I'd thought it would, so I knew I hadn't hit an artery, but there was a steady trickle. Come on, I urged. Hurry up.

The sky was already darkening. There wasn't much time.

As soon as the bottom of the bucket was covered by blood I made my way back inside the flat, grabbing a brush from the table as I went. The sheet was still spread out on the floor and I set the bucket down and dropped on to my knees. Dipping the brush into the blood, I began to write.

A few moments later, I sat back to survey the sheet.

The letters weren't regular and the red was fast turning brown, but the 'HELP' was clearly legible. It would have to do. I heaved myself upright and stumbled back outside. I could feel my strength failing as I tied the top two corners of the sheet to opposite ends of the railing so that the huge message hung down over the side of the balcony.

Then I collapsed on to one of the chairs. My breath still fast and uneven. In a moment it would be completely dark. There would be very little river traffic overnight – not this early in January with London collectively sobering up and counting the cost of its hangover, and I knew the chances of my message being seen before tomorrow were low.

By the time help arrived, I'd probably be dead. The thought registered as a fact, without actually sinking in. Dominic's A3 sketchpad was still on the table outside, along with the paints and brushes. There was also a small flat box which turned out to contain drawing pencils of varying degrees of hardness. I took the box and the sketchpad and went back inside the apartment, closing the glass door behind me. I hadn't realized until I got inside how cold I was, but now I found myself shivering, uncontrollably.

When I dropped down on to the sofa, the last of the adrenalin that had been keeping me going drained away, leaving me hollowed out inside. I wanted to close my eyes, but I knew if I did, I'd never wake up. And there needs to be a record. People need to know what has gone on here. My family need to know.

I picked up the hardest-looking pencil, opened up the thick pad and, in tiny letters on the top of the page, I wrote:

Three interesting things about me. Well, I'm twenty-nine years old, I'm phobic about buttons. Oh yes, and I'm dying. Not as in I've got two years to live, but hey, here's a list of things I want to cram into the time I have left. No, I'm dying right here and now. Chances are, by the time you finish reading this, I'll already be dead.

In a sense, you are reading a snuff book.

Well, you know the rest.

PART TWO

TWENTY-EIGHT

If I'm ever tempted to have another tattoo, which is hardly likely, I'm going to have the words *Don't Trust Natalie* tattooed right across my forehead.

That's what's going through my head when Mum asks me, 'What's going through your head?'

It's been three days since I was brought to the hospital. I don't remember anything about my arrival and very little about the first forty-eight hours. There are odd images – a young doctor with very bad skin who leaned so close to me I could see where an ingrown hair on his upper lip had become inflamed; a snatch of conversation between two women where one was complaining that the weather forecast hadn't mentioned rain and she'd come out in suede shoes. I have no idea who they were, or if the voices were all in my head.

I've spent the time since I regained consciousness pretending to be more ill than I am in order to ward off the moment where I'll be formally questioned by the police. No one is telling me anything. Instead I lie here obsessing about what happened and her role in it all.

Her.

Natalie.

Of him, I try not to think at all.

My parents have been here the whole time. My mum has done a lot of crying. My brothers drift in and out, operating a shift system. There are conversations in muffled voices that I'm not supposed to hear. At one point James clearly says, 'That twisted piece of shit,' and my mum hushes him. Jonathan covers my hand with his, which is strange because we're not touchy-feely in our family and it feels all wrong.

I am weak and emptied out and my stomach hurts. Hospital staff bustle around, lifting parts of me up, moving me on to my side. I allow myself to be arranged and rearranged like a prized ornament. I want this part never to be over because I don't want to face what I know is coming next.

'What's going through your head?' asks my mother again, her chair pulled right up to the hospital bed, her head bent towards mine as if she could absorb its contents by osmosis.

Even if I could speak, I wouldn't be able to tell her.

Safer to focus on her.

Don't Trust Natalie.

I should get a T-shirt made.

TWENTY-NINE

I'm in the bathroom in the hospital. I have a private room with its own ensuite. The door is wide enough for a wheelchair and there are plastic handles everywhere and a button to press marked *Alarm*. I'm examining the contents of the toilet and am tempted to press that button. Because the thing that's just come out of my body is blue.

'Don't you be worrying about that at *all*,' says the Irish nurse with the moon face and nose so snub that in profile it's completely hidden by the round of her cheek. 'It's that stuff they've given you to counteract the poison. Prussian blue, it's called. It has that effect on some.'

The police arrive. They ask me questions gently – 'a preliminary chat' is how they phrase it – and I tell them exactly what's in the account I wrote down in Dominic's sketchbook. I don't deviate. They're very polite when they are here – two men and a woman. One of the men stands against the wall because there aren't enough chairs. The Irish nurse offers to bring him one but he says no, he's been sitting all day and his leg muscles will seize up if he's not careful.

The older police guy, the one in charge, explains that

they've been to the apartment and seen what was in there –
the kennel, the whip, the shackles. The blood. They all
make shocked faces and shake their heads. They know
about my injuries – the septic tattoo, the welts from the
whip, the bruising around ankles and wrists from the metal
cuffs. And of course, the cumulative effects of exposure
to thallium poison. I was lucky, the main guy says.
Considering how many days it had been building in my
system, my symptoms have been mercifully mild. They've
inspected all the presents, and the paintbrushes and the
chess set and the candle.

The woman sits slightly behind him and nods when
required. She has a brown bob and a long fringe beneath
which her grey eyes gaze at me intently as if she is studying
me for a test. She was introduced as Detective Constable
Kim Something. I recall my parents talking about someone
called Kim and realize this must be her.

It's the first day I've been compos mentis enough for my
parents to have a proper conversation with me, but they've
been cagey about what's been going on. 'The police will fill
you in,' my mother keeps saying. My mum has never had
any dealings with the authorities. I think she is worried
about what she is and isn't allowed to say.

'Am I being charged with anything?' I ask the main police
guy – what was his name, Robinson? And then, because I
can't put it off any longer, I add, 'Am I being charged with
murder?'

The main guy looks surprised. He has a broad red face
that sits squarely on his shoulders and matching red-
rimmed eyes that widen at my question. 'Dominic Lacey

isn't dead,' he says. 'He's in a critical condition in a different hospital but he's still alive.'

When I lean over the side of the bed to vomit, I expect they believe it's from relief.

She's not what Kim was expecting. Less ethereal. The fact of her physical presence is rammed home by the drip in her arm, the sluicing of fluids, the stream of yellow vomit that comes out at the end when they tell her about Dominic Lacey.

She's terrified of him. Kim can see that straight away. She spent two years attached to the Domestic Violence Unit early on in her career and she recognizes the signs. And yet there is something here that is not fitting together. Something Jessica is not saying. Kim is sure of it.

'Doesn't bear thinking about, does it,' says Martin, as they make their way back out into the pale winter sunshine as washed out as if a painter had spilled water across the sky. 'What he put that girl through.'

'Allegedly,' she corrects him.

Martin looks at her in surprise, at the pointedness of her tone.

'There's still so much that doesn't make sense,' Kim says. 'Like how did she manage, in the state she was in, to stay up all night writing that detailed account?'

Martin is dismissive. 'People draw on superhuman sources of strength when they really think they're about to die. It's the survival reflex. Adrenalin. Whatever you want to call it.'

'That's another thing. How *did* she survive? Nearly two

weeks of daily exposure to thallium. That doctor we spoke to was amazed she's recovered so quickly and with seemingly so few long-term effects.'

Paul Robertson shrugs. 'Poisoning people isn't an exact science.' He allows himself a small smile. 'That's why it's gone out of fashion.'

'Yes, so why would he choose that way then, sir? Why not use a method he knows will do the job?'

Martin jumps in before the Super can reply. 'There's no point second-guessing this guy. He's a psycho. You know what was in that flat. You've read the file about his first wife and son, about what he was like as a kid. Did you read the deposition from that teacher? She was terrified of him, and he was only eleven, twelve years old. People like that don't think the same as you and me. It's all about game-playing.'

'Whatever the case, the CPS will obviously be considering the evidence very carefully – against both of them.' Robertson is looking thoughtful. 'Whatever the provocation, Jessica Gold committed a very serious assault on Dominic Lacey. We're not talking a single defence wound here, there were three separate stab wounds on his body – neck, throat and chest. That's going to take some explaining. We'll be interviewing her formally at the station as soon as she's out of the hospital.'

'Yeah, but you have to say the circumstances are pretty mitigating, wouldn't you agree, sir? If CPS do charge her, it'll be for something minor. No?'

Afterwards Kim wonders whether the usually taciturn Martin was being so opinionated because Robertson just happens to be the one whose recommendation will count with the promotions board. Maybe she should stop being so contrary and throw herself behind Jessica Gold as Martin seems to be doing. Lacey is clearly a deeply warped individual, a sociopath if not a psychopath, with a trail of destruction in his wake, a danger to women. Jessica Gold is a normal, unremarkable young woman – or at least she was until Christmas Eve – who had the misfortune to be in the wrong place at the wrong time.

Except that Kim doesn't believe Jessica is either normal or unremarkable.

And she knows she's hiding something.

THIRTY

From: ddc115@hotmail.co.uk
To: nowalkinthepark@hotmail.com
Subject: what the fuck
What the fuck. WHAT THE ACTUAL FUCK.

From: nowalkinthepark@hotmail.com
To: ddc115@hotmail.co.uk
Subject: re: what the fuck
I've been worried about you. I knew you
wouldn't be able to get in touch straight away,
but still . . . (BTW, there's no chance they could
be logging this, is there? Hope you're being
careful.) Are you OK? Did we work out the doses
properly? I know you're upset about what
happened, but you have to see it was the only
way. If I hadn't done what I did, it would have
been his word against yours. It still might be if
he recovers but I don't think there's much chance
of that, do you? Can you believe the fucker
survived that? I always said he wasn't human.
You've done brilliantly. I'm so impressed. Now

all you have to do is stick to the story and
everything will be fine. Trust me.

Nx

PS: Remember to delete this as soon as you've
read it.

From: ddc115@hotmail.co.uk

To: nowalkinthepark@hotmail.com

Subject: re: re: what the fuck

Trust you? Really? Do you have any idea what I've
just been through? I spent twelve days locked up
with that psycho. You of all people know what
that means. Funny how it slipped your mind to
mention the dog kennel when you were persuading
me into this. A fucking dog kennel! And what
about the whip, and the handcuffs? How did I ever
agree to the tattoo? Every time I catch sight of
it I feel physically sick. You took advantage.
That's the bottom line. I was practically at
death's door and you took advantage. And now I've
got to go to the station for a formal interview.
Can you even begin to imagine how terrifying that
is? We've had to hire a solicitor — some guy my
dad shared a house with at uni. Great reunion
phone call, that was — 'Yes, my sons are doing
very well, thank you. Three grandchildren, and a
daughter who might be up for murder.' Why did you
come back? Which bit about sticking to the plan
did you not understand?

TAMMY COHEN

From: nowalkinthepark@hotmail.com
To: ddc115@hotmail.co.uk
Subject: re: re: re: what the fuck
They won't charge you. Look at the papers. You're
a hero. Have you seen all the innuendo about me
and crazy Cesca? Legally they're not allowed to
go into details, but the media have basically
hung, drawn and quartered him already. Everyone
knows he's a scumbag. If it ever went to court
(which it won't), there'd be queues of women to
testify that he's a sick fuck who gets his kicks
out of hurting people. All you have to do is sit
tight. Everything you did was in self-defence.
The press love you. You're the Christmas Kidnap
Miracle Girl. Remember why you had to do it —
think of the tape. Think of your gorgeous little
niece, Grace. And as for why I did what I did,
wait until the heat is off a bit, and I'll
explain it all. Until then I think we'd better
hold off contact for a bit. Don't worry. Dominic
was hit by the Karma Bus, that's all.
Nx
PS: Delete? Remember?

I log out of my email and delete the history. It's second
nature to me now even though the laptop is a new one. I am
almost too angry to breathe. Sometimes I'm so scared of
what I've done, I feel my insides shrivelling up like newspaper in the blaze of my own fear. What if Dominic recovers
and claims I've made it all up, and it was all consensual?

What if they believe him? I could go to prison for years. I'd be older than my parents by the time I came out. The thought makes me clammy and I struggle to get myself under control, putting a hand on my belly and forcing myself to take deep regular breaths.

It still feels weird to be back at my parents' house, in the room that used to be James's but is now a generic spare room with a black and beige duvet cover that matches the curtains and a framed Degas ballerina print on the wall. I think Travis was relieved when my parents insisted on me coming back to theirs to recuperate. It puts off the moment when we have to talk about the things we don't want to talk about.

My family treat me like I am made from ancient parchment that will crumble to dust if touched or exposed to light. My father hovers in the doorway and tries to be jolly. My mum brings endless cups of tea and leaves them on the bedside table where they mostly grow cold until they are taken away again. Sometimes there's a little plate with a couple of gingernuts and custard creams laid out like jewels. I think they've agreed a list of safe subjects to talk to me about. Sport, my nephews and niece, the flooding in the South-West. There's a telly in here and every now and again they come up to see if I've watched the same show as them so we can discuss it. There's a pile of books next to my bed for when I get my concentration back.

We don't talk about the cluster of reporters camped out in front of the house.

We don't talk about Dominic Lacey or about what happened in that apartment.

We don't mention the lingering red marks around my wrists or the tattoo on my hip.

I'm glad of their tact because I'm struggling with what's real and what's not. I'm struggling with the story Natalie and I so carefully concocted, and she so completely derailed at the end. I think they all believe me so far. Why wouldn't they when the evidence is staring them in the face? Dominic's apartment was packed with props to support his own particular brand of sadism. He'd call it consensual, if he were able to speak, but who'd believe that anyone would willingly allow themselves to be chained and manacled, whipped till they bled? Branded even? Besides, there's all that history: the harassment of Cesca that led to her death and Sam's, the unexplained disappearance of his second wife, bits of whom turn up all over his flat.

Natalie had been so pleased with herself about that one – her assiduous harvesting of her own DNA. Prior to going into the clinic to have her boobs done, she'd already had a couple of other clandestine procedures – two of her ribs removed to cinch in her waist, liposuction to suck out excess fat. And during her most recent stay, it wasn't just her boobs she'd had done, but her nose too – a small bump removed to give her a startling new profile. Amazing how much of a human body you can take away and still be able to walk and talk and breathe. I don't know who she bribed to keep hold of all the bits. Maybe she didn't need to. One of my old bosses who had a six-month stay in a cancer ward used to collect cysts in a jar. The porters used to sneak them to him. People are weird like that. Just look at Dominic and his baby teeth.

The presents. Another of Natalie's brainwaves. The stories behind them are all true – they're the beads that, threaded together, make up Dominic's twisted life. He related them to Natalie over the course of their marriage, showed her the mementos. That's when it started to sink in that she'd married a madman. The candle she made herself with instructions off the internet. And she sent off to somewhere in America for the engraving for the urn. Utah, I think. She thought engravers in Utah were unlikely to read the English papers.

I try to remember this as I lie in bed in my parents' spare room with the spherical white paper lampshade, staring at the three vases on the chest of drawers bearing the last of the flowers we brought home from the hospital. It's all true. All the things he did during his life or had done to him. All the things I wrote. And though he didn't kidnap me or force me to do the things we did, neither would I say it was exactly consensual. So that bit is sort of true as well, when you look at it like that.

You'd have to be some kind of sick fuck, as Natalie says, to make it up.

THIRTY-ONE

'How did someone like you get mixed up with someone like him?'

That's what Natalie asked me the first time we met. I don't think 'someone like you' was intended to be flattering, but even so, she had a point. People like me don't know people like Dominic Lacey.

The funny thing is, we did meet in a department-store café more or less as I wrote in my account. Not exactly on Christmas Eve but thereabouts. And not the Christmas just gone but the one before. I had a lot of shopping. He came and sat down. We got talking. I was flattered. Travis and I weren't getting on. He was distant and cold, and had been hanging out with the medics from the hospital instead of coming home. I'd had the abortion a few weeks before and Travis had taken two days off but on the second day he'd asked if I minded if he went in after all. There was something important he had to do. More important than me. He went back to his parents' that Christmas for once – they'd cut short their usual five-month sojourn in Florida on account of his dad's prostate operation – and I really thought it might be over. I wanted out of my life for a bit.

I didn't just take the bait, I bit the hand that hooked it on.

Dominic drove me from Oxford Street to a hotel near Luton airport. I was so embarrassed I stayed in the car till he got the room key and then slipped into the lift when no one was about. I felt people would be able to tell what I was about to do just by looking at me.

He didn't get out his box of tricks, not that night, but there were things I did, things he somehow got me to do, that when I thought about them afterwards, I couldn't believe it had been me. Later, I found it helped to think of the woman in that bed as someone separate, not me at all. It meant that when I went back to my normal life I could put that night in a box, bringing it out only rarely when I was alone, handling it gingerly like a dangerous animal.

If he'd just left it at that, how differently would things have turned out? I'd never have met Natalie. This last night-marish year would never have happened. Dominic wouldn't be in a coma in intensive care. I wouldn't be the Christmas Kidnap Miracle Girl. I would still have a passport.

I want it all to go away. I want to go back to how it was. If I just find the right combination in my mind, surely I can unlock the door in time and space that'll lead me back to the life I had before.

I lie on the spare-room bed and look up at the paper lightshade and spot a smattering of dust on the top that has escaped my father's notice. Since he retired, my father likes to go around the house with the hoover brush attachment, reaching up to top shelves and high corners. I suspect it makes him feel in control.

I lean back against the pillows and try to think myself backwards in time.

She is wearing out Heather's patience. Kim can tell. When Heather first invited her to stay for as long as she needed, she probably imagined nights sitting up far too late while Kim bared her soul over a bottle of wine, like they used to do when they shared a flat as twenty-somethings, and Sunday-afternoon trips to the cinema, maybe the odd dinner party even. Instead she has a flatmate who, on the rare occasions she isn't at work or visiting her kids, is too depressed to speak. They bump into each other when Kim is in the kitchen waiting for the kettle to boil, or dashing to the bathroom, hugging her towel to her chest, eager for the oblivion of a hot bath. And Heather puts her head to one side and makes that face people make when they want to commiserate but don't know what to say, or she says, 'How are you bearing up?' And Kim says, 'Oh, you know.' Not because Kim doesn't want to talk but because there's a great big boulder lodged in her throat that makes it impossible for the words to come out. And she worries that if that boulder ever moved, there'd be such a tsunami of words and feelings, they'd never ever stop.

She goes home to see the kids every day – tense occasions where she paints on a layer of jollity like varnish before she steps inside – but it doesn't stop the constant ache she feels whenever she thinks about them.

Yet still work consumes her. She knows she is over-involved in this Jessica Gold investigation. There is something about the younger woman that is weirdly familiar – a stubborn streak of 'otherness' that reminds her of herself as she was before marriage and motherhood homogenized her into someone else. It's no longer just a case, it's the case that will decide the next stage of her career, and the case that might cost her her family.

At night she revisits it in her dreams.

THIRTY-TWO

The solicitor has a pouched face with pockets of sallow, sagging flesh and brown eyes which look to have seen altogether too much. My dad introduces us in a café near the police station and there's a surreal ten minutes while they reminisce about someone called Tucker who once fell asleep on the last bus home and spent the night locked up in a bus garage. The solicitor, whose name is David Gallant ('by name if not by nature,' says my dad, with a poor attempt at a joke), thinks Tucker spent a couple of years in Australia but then came back and went to work for the Civil Service. 'Good pension then, lucky sod,' says my dad. Only now do they feel that sufficient preliminaries have been exchanged to broach the subject that brings them both here. The subject that is sipping a tasteless white coffee while her nerves prick and fizzle like a short-circuited plug. Me.

David talks me through what will happen at the police station. He checks I've brought my passport and when he tells me I'll be interviewed under caution, I say 'Oh' so loudly the couple on the next table turn round to look. 'It's just procedure,' he assures me. 'Nothing to worry about.'

My father presses my leg under the table, but doesn't speak, and when we leave him there a few minutes later I have a horrible feeling he's about to cry.

In the waiting area at the police station there's a man playing a drum. He has three children with him. David starts to explain about saying 'No comment' but it's impossible to concentrate on what he's saying over the noise of the drum. 'Please,' he says eventually, turning to the man. 'We're trying to have a conversation here.'

'Sorry, bro.' The man doesn't stop drumming, but he does indeed look sorry. 'This here is a peaceful protest. My nephew, these kids' brother, is being abused in foster care, but no one is doing nothing about it, so this is the only power I have to try to make them take notice. I been here all day, and yesterday and the day before, and I'm going to be here every day until they listen to me.'

David glances over at the duty officer behind the glass at the reception counter, who raises his eyebrows in a 'What can you do?' gesture.

I lock eyes with the girl sitting to the man's left. She is about eleven or twelve. Her hair is set in masses of braids, each knotted at the end with a different coloured bead, and she has a resigned expression on her face as if she's heard all this before. As she gazes at me impassively, I hear a woman singing a pop song that was a mega-hit for a boy band a couple of years ago, but she's slowed it right down like a sad lullaby. She is singing so close to my ear that my eardrum vibrates, but I don't turn around because I know she's not there, and when the little girl looks away, the singing stops and only the sadness remains.

A new policeman comes out to fetch us. He's wearing a dark jacket with a shiny, greasy strip at the back of the neck and pointy shoes that click along the corridor. We follow him into an interview room with a blue carpet, a laminated table, four chairs and a CCTV camera on the wall that I try to ignore. I'm both relieved and disappointed that there's no sign of a two-way mirror. A few minutes later, the older police guy, who introduces himself again as DSI Robertson, comes in and explains that the interview will be taped. I swallow hard and try not to think of the implications. It was one thing writing those lies down in the sketchbook account when I could still kid myself no one would read them. Even that 'chat' in the hospital could have been explained away as the result of trauma and heavy medication. But this is different. There is no going back from this.

'Do you understand, Jessica?' DSI Robertson asks me after he finishes reading me my rights. I nod, but the truth is I don't understand. None of it. I don't understand how I ended up here, or how my life went so badly wrong. I don't understand how they can't see I don't belong here.

They each have a transcript of the sketchbook account and they ask me questions and I don't deviate from what I wrote, grateful for all those role-play sessions with Natalie during those long hours in the cottage in Scotland. Only when it gets to the end, to the bits we didn't plan, does my voice start to falter. They break off the interview to fetch me water in a plastic cup. When I raise it to my lips, my fingers are shaking.

'My client is still very weak,' David Gallant says. 'She's

been through a major trauma and has only just been released from hospital. How long are you intending to keep her here?'

'We can break off for today, if you like, and resume tomorrow.' DSI Robertson is a picture of amenability, but the prospect of coming back again is like a tight band around my chest and I shake my head.

Somehow we get through to the end, though I play up my physical weakness, putting my hand to my forehead often as if massaging an aching head or blinking when asked a question as if trying to unscramble the words in my mind. After it's over, and they've shown me the typed statement and I've signed it in writing so spidery it looks more like an illustration than a signature, I am released on police bail. Even though David warned me this could be the outcome, I'm still shocked by it, and experience an acute sense of loss when I hand over my passport.

'It's just a formality,' David shouts over the top of the drumming as we make our way back out through the waiting room. 'It's security while they carry out their investigations and wait to see if the CPS decides to charge you with anything.' He catches sight of my face. 'Don't worry. In view of the circumstances, I'm sure they'll be lenient.'

But still I make him tell me the worst-case scenarios. As my dad comes rushing over to meet us at the bottom of the station steps, his features twisted into a question mark, I repeat the possible charges to myself in my head like a chant: *Attempted Murder, Actual Bodily Harm, Unlawful Wounding, Grievous Bodily Harm.*

Walking to the car, I watch the faces of the people we pass

and it's as if they're separated from me by a wall of glass, as if I'm already in the dock waiting to be sentenced.

'I did wonder a few times whether she was all there.'

Lennie Fraser taps the side of his head meaningfully. He is describing the interview he's just carried out with Jessica Gold, and Kim is trying to hide her resentment that Robertson picked him and not her. Still, at least it wasn't Martin. That really would have grated.

'Shouldn't you have terminated the interview? If she was obviously struggling?'

'Nah. The Guv'ner gave her the chance of coming back again, but she wanted to get it over with. Anyway she had a brief with her.'

'So she didn't contradict herself?'

Lennie shakes his head. 'She was vague on a few things, particularly towards the end, but that's not surprising given she was being poisoned at the time.'

'And what did you make of her?'

Lennie shrugs. 'She's an odd one, isn't she? Other-worldly. Nearly passed out when we told her we'd need to take her passport. You can't quite imagine how she ever came into the same orbit as someone like Lacey.'

Kim doodles a sun in her notebook with a tiny planet circling round it, then she crosses it out and writes herself a reminder to call Jessica later that day. It's become a pattern now, that daily phone call. She tells Jessica it's part of her duty of care as an FLO. But really it's because she's convinced that, sooner or later, Jessica Gold will crack.

THIRTY-THREE

'I still don't see why you had to put in all that crap about the voices in your head. You were supposed to be making it as convincing as possible, not showing yourself as a total whacko.'

Natalie is in a shitty mood. She keeps tugging at her long, newly red hair and glaring at the ends with animosity. And she's pacing around in front of her laptop so she keeps going in and out of shot which is quite disconcerting.

'It's not crap. It happens to be true. That's how my family and Travis will know that it's authentic – because they know it's something that's always happened to me.'

It occurs to me now how strange it is that we never discuss it, my family and I, those voices that creep into my head when I'm too tired to stop them. But then, I suppose, to talk about it would be to acknowledge it – this thing that sets me apart. Besides, it can be useful on occasion – a get-out-of-jail-free card to cover all sorts of behavioural quirks. Like sexual encounters with strange men in hotels near Luton airport.

'And I don't know why you put in that bit about him never having sex. You could have totally gone to town on his creepy sexual perversions. No jury would ever acquit him if they knew what turns that sick fuck on.'

'I knew my family might read it. I couldn't.'

'For fuck's sake, Jessica. What's more important, sparing your parents' blushes or getting rid of that man once and for all?'

When Natalie gets angry, her cheeks glow pink, clashing with her newly scarlet hair. I'm still not completely used to Natalie's new hair colour either. Sometimes it's hard to believe that the snub-nosed, blue-eyed redhead is the same tall blonde who scared me shitless when I first met her all those months ago.

She still scares me, only not quite in the same way.

At first Kim can't place the photograph at all, but by a process of deduction she dates it to a holiday in Brittany very early on in their marriage. She is in the early stages of her pregnancy with Rory and she can just make out the soft swell of her belly beneath the white sundress she has on. Both she and Sean have that broiled look of British holidaymakers who have overdone it on the beach after a sun-starved winter. She can't remember who took the photograph but she can see why Sean has sent it to her. They are happy, the two of them. It shows in the way her head dips towards his, and the gentle cupping of his big hand around her bare shoulder. It shows in their matching smiles which are angled towards each other rather than towards the camera lens. Looking at the picture hurts in the same way that looking at a photo of her dad who died two years ago hurts. *We are still the same people if you'd just give us a chance*, Sean has written in the message that accompanied the photo. But they are not the same people. The day-to-day disappointments and resentments of the last years have broken them down, making them less than the sum of their parts. Kim deletes the message, feeling angry and manipulated and sad.

But most of all sad.

In the hour and a half since I Skyped Natalie, I've been thinking a lot about her transformation and everything she went through at that clinic, and everything we both did to help her disappear afterwards. And how she wrecked the whole thing. It has made me furious all over again. She's like a child who can't understand why she can't do whatever she wants whenever she wants. So I call her back. This time I use Facetime as I'm on my phone, pacing around the garden while my parents are out.

She doesn't seem thrilled to hear from me again so soon. 'You know, Jess, I'm worried you're developing dependency issues.'

'I just don't get it,' I say. 'All you had to do was disappear, right after your surgery. There were enough grounds for suspicion after what happened with Cesca and Sam. And once I'd planted all your DNA, he wouldn't have stood a chance. But you had to get greedy. A diamond necklace, for fuck's sake.'

She is defiant. 'He'd got it from Cesca, so it wasn't his to start with. I didn't think he'd even notice it was gone. Anyway, we covered that one, didn't we? You wrote about it in your story – about him persuading someone to put on a hat and go into a jeweller's pretending to be me? They'll buy that. And apart from that, there's been no sighting of me since the clinic. Well, apart from all those bits and pieces of me they've found at his apartment. It's enough to get him on a murder charge. If he ever wakes up. Which he won't.'

But now I've been reminded of what she did, I feel myself getting worked up all over again. It's not good for me to get emotional. I'm still supposed to be taking it easy. I try Sonia Rubenstein's breathing trick with one hand on my stomach, hoping it will calm me down.

'You know I can't forgive you for that,' I say, and I try to stare her out, through the phone screen, all the way through the miles of ether that separate us, and through her laptop screen to wherever she is now.

'How many times did we go over it? How many times? We were so nearly at the end. It was so nearly over, and then you have to show up there and try to kill him. That was never agreed. I *never* would have said yes to that.'

She rolls her eyes and I find myself hoping those stupid blue contact lenses get stuck on the inside of her eyelids.

'Jess, if we'd stuck to the original plan and you'd walked out of there claiming to have escaped and it was your word against his, you'd have buckled by now. It's better this way.'

'But you botched it. He didn't die! So now I've got to sit here and try to be calm while the police decide if they want to charge me with attempted murder. And if he wakes up and starts telling them what really happened, that's exactly what they'll do. I'm shitting myself. I'm on *bail*. They made me feel like a criminal.'

'Well, hon, technically you *are* a criminal, I suppose.'

'They've even taken my passport!'

Natalie smirks. 'No Club Med for you this year.'

'Do you think this is a joke?' I ask her.

Sometimes I'm convinced that's exactly what she thinks – that this will become another amusing anecdote to add to the string of amusing anecdotes that people like Natalie have instead of lives. I imagine her telling it to the Saudi prince or whoever comes after him. But then I remind myself I've seen her scars. In the places no one looks.

Suddenly I'm furious at the injustice of it all – the way she's got off scot-free.

'Do you know how many reporters there are outside my parents' house at this minute? They constantly ring the doorbell and post things through the letterbox. And you're hidden safely away wherever it is you are.'

Natalie makes a funny noise then like she's blowing out air through her nose. 'My life's not so great either, you know. I'm going stir-crazy here. I don't know why you're so adamant I've got to stay hidden. It's not like anyone would recognize me like this.' She's got that infuriating sulky-child expression on again.

'We can't take any more chances. Where exactly are you anyway?'

I'm looking at the fragment of cushion cover I can see just behind her on the screen. The pattern looks strangely familiar although I haven't a clue where from.

'It's better if you don't know where I am. Safer.'

Safer for you, you mean.

I think it, but I don't say it.

* * *

Kim is back in Perivale. Funny how a few weeks ago she'd never even heard of the place and now it's all starting to look so familiar. This time Henrietta Belvedere is in full work mode, all trace of holiday zen completely eradicated.

'Back-to-back meetings today,' she says, bustling out to meet Kim in reception in dark trousers and a dark jacket with a plum-coloured silk shirt that exactly matches the frames of her glasses. 'You're lucky you caught me. Such shocking news about what happened to Jessica. Thank god she's going to be OK. It just goes to show, doesn't it, that none of us are completely safe.'

'Quite.'

Kim is a bit disappointed to find Henrietta available. She was hoping for a word with her deputy, Joe, the guy she and Martin met the first time they were here.

'Remember we spoke about that fake Facebook account someone set up with Jessica's face photoshopped on to a pornographic image?'

Henrietta nods, but she's frowning. This is a conversation she clearly feels they exhausted the last time they met.

'Yes, and I did explain that had nothing to do with anyone at work.'

'Of course. I was just wondering if I could speak to someone she worked more directly alongside, to see if she'd mentioned it at all. Joe Tunstall maybe.'

'Joe?' Henrietta doesn't much like that suggestion. 'I can't think what he'd know. He and Jessica aren't particularly close. Well, I wouldn't say Jessica is particularly close to anyone. Still, I'll ask him to come out and talk to you if you like, just to set your mind at rest. Just bear in mind we're incredibly busy.'

Joe Tunstall looks self-important when he steps out through the reception doors wearing a blue crew-necked jumper, corduroy jeans and a concerned expression.

'Detective, so nice to see you again. Thank goodness with better news. Not, of course, that Jessica's kidnap is good news, but at least she's home safe and sound. That's what matters, isn't it?'

Kim finds herself nodding, even though there's a feeling like an elastic band pinging against her heart when he says that phrase 'home safe and sound'.

'I was just wondering,' she says, 'if Jessica had ever mentioned anything about someone setting up a fake Facebook account in her name?'

Joe frowns, the freckles on his forehead again knitting into a uniform brown splodge.

'You know, I think she might have mentioned something – months ago. She seemed upset and I asked her why, and she told me there'd been this account set up. Didn't say what it was. I advised her to contact Facebook and to take a screen grab of the page just in case it turned out to be the start of a campaign of harassment. I even looked over her shoulder while she did it, although she put a hand over the photograph so I couldn't see it. She was still embarrassed, even though it wasn't even her. That's what Jessica was like.'

'A screen grab? Might that be on her computer here then? Could I take a look?'

Half an hour later, Kim is into Jessica's account on the work computer she used. She isn't very comfortable with technology and baulks at all the icons on the desktop, but the IT person who helped her log in shows her where the documents folder is.

'Look for something with *photo* in the title, or *Facebook*, or *FB*,' he suggests and Kim finds herself briefly transfixed by the Adam's apple moving in his throat like the lottery balls down the chute on the telly.

'Aha.' He points to a file where the mouse cursor is bobbing insistently. '*Fbacct.doc*. I'd try that one if I was you.'

At first she can't really make out the photograph and it looks like just another Facebook page. Then she double-clicks on the profile picture which reveals itself to be that of a naked woman on all fours on a cheap hotel-room bed. Instantly Kim realizes two things:

1) The face is definitely Jessica Gold's.

2) The picture has definitely not been photoshopped.

THIRTY-FOUR

It was James who'd first seen the Facebook page. His wife's sister brought it to his attention in that way people do when they're trying to act all helpful, but really they can't wait to see your reaction. 'I just thought you'd want to know . . .'

'Your face has obviously been photoshopped but they've done it very well,' he told me when he rang, and I could imagine how his ears would be turning pink with embarrassment. 'You've got to get straight on to them to take it down. I wouldn't look at it though, if I were you. It'll just freak you out.'

I put my name straight into the search box. When the page came up with that photo my heart stopped dead. What had I been thinking of? I hadn't *been* thinking. I'd looked up and there he was with his phone. 'It's only for me,' he said. 'So I'll always remember this night.'

The Facebook thing came in April, three months after he'd first got back in touch suggesting a reprise of the night in the hotel. The original message had come through on my work email and even though it was innocuous I erased it immediately. Then I'd set up a separate Hotmail account using random letters and characters instead of a name and told him to use that. Even so, I knew I wasn't going to meet him again. Something about the way he'd been during that first night had scared me. But he wouldn't be put off. 'Didn't we have fun?' he said in his emails. 'I thought we had a connection.'

I stopped replying. By then Travis and I were getting on a bit better and, while thinking about that night with the stranger in the hotel thrilled me (the idea that I was capable of *that*), it terrified me as well (the idea that I was capable of *that*).

Dominic's messages took on a sour, curdled tone before, to my relief, stopping altogether.

There was a gap of a couple of weeks. And then came James's call.

'There's something you need to know . . .'

'I don't see what this has to do with anything.'

Martin is angry. Kim sees a red flush crawling around the side of his neck.

They are crowded around her computer screen – she, Martin and Paul Robertson – looking at the photograph of Jessica Gold on the hotel-room bed. Despite her stint on Vice, Kim feels oddly embarrassed and protective of Jessica and wishes they didn't all have to see this.

'So a bitter ex posts a private photograph online as a revenge tactic. It happens all the time.'

'Yes, but as far as we know, Jessica didn't have any bitter exes. She's been with Travis Riley since university.'

'Well, maybe she had an affair. Or maybe Travis did it himself. Stranger things happen in relationships.'

Kim knows Martin is fed up that she went to the TV archive without telling him.

The Super moves away from the computer screen, gesturing for Kim to close the file. He has a daughter around Jessica's age, Kim remembers now. Perhaps this is making him feel uncomfortable.

'It's certainly a different side to Jessica that we haven't seen before,' he says. 'Worth following up with her.'

'The fake Facebook account was set up back in April.' Martin is sulky, unwilling to concede anything. 'That's eight months before Jessica Gold was kidnapped. I really don't see how this is going to be relevant.'

'I'm inclined to agree,' says Robertson. 'But I still think it warrants checking out.'

THIRTY-FIVE

I wonder if they can smell the fear wafting off me.

When she first handed me the photo, my heart started beating so fast I thought I would have a heart attack there and then in the living room of my parents' house. How did they find that picture? Then I remembered the screen grab on my computer at work. That's the thing about computers. You think you're cleverer than them. You think you can bury things in them, but they bring them right back up to the surface, like the Thames giving up its dead. That got me thinking about the flat in Wapping and Execution Dock and the voices that blew in the wind over the river, and since then I've been too terrified to think of anything at all.

But they're waiting – the policewoman with the brown bob and the younger male officer with the black pores on his nose like poppy seeds.

I put my hands over my face and my horror isn't faked. I'm ashamed that they've looked at this picture, these police people with their polite smiles and their pink glowing winter skin. I'm ashamed they've seen who I am when I'm not being me.

'We know it isn't photoshopped, Jessica.' She sounds kind but tired.

'I'm so embarrassed! Please, please don't tell my family, or Travis. It was three years ago, when Travis was in his final year at Manchester and I was already working in London. I didn't hear from this bloke for ages. Then he rang a few months ago, out of the blue, wanting to meet, and I refused and things got a bit nasty, and the next thing I knew there was that Facebook account.'

'What was his name?'

She has her notebook out and is waiting with a pencil held between her fingers.

'I never knew his surname. He said his name was Ben and he was a civil engineer. We got talking to each other on the Tube. It was stuck in a tunnel. I get claustrophobic. He calmed me down. We got off at the next station and went to the pub for a drink. And then another. We ended up in a hotel in King's Cross.'

Poppy-Seed Face doesn't think much of this.

'First him and then Dominic Lacey. You really need to think more carefully about going home with strange men.'

'I know. I'm an idiot. Please tell me you're not going to tell Travis! This has absolutely nothing to do with the case. I never heard from him again after the account got taken down.'

I imagine how I must look to them. I've lost a lot of weight since Christmas Eve. Though my hair has started growing back, it's still patchy. My skin is red and flaky. I'm pathetic.

'You're all right,' says the man, and he looks pleased with

his own largesse. 'We all make mistakes from time to time. We see more and more of this kind of thing. Revenge porn, it's called. It's a criminal offence.'

The woman, Kim, is less quick to absolve me. 'Of course, everything depends on what happens legally from here. Whether this ends up in court. There are cases where defence lawyers have jumped on this kind of thing to discredit a witness – or prosecutors to discredit a defendant.'

I stop listening when she says that word 'court'. For 90 per cent of the time, I'm able to forget about Dominic being kept alive by machines in a hospital somewhere. But every so often I'll be reminded, and this huge mass of dread forms like a tumour inside me. The thought of facing him again, feeling those blue eyes burning holes in the tissue of lies Natalie and I have spun makes me weak with fear.

For a wild moment, I imagine telling these two police officers everything. Surely they'll understand if I explain that I never meant Dominic to be killed, or even attacked. That was all Natalie's doing. I imagine shrugging off my guilt like a heavy rucksack. And then I snap back into the real world. I am in this too deep to go back.

'Happens all the time,' Martin is saying as he drives back through the stop-start traffic.

This part of London is lined with Turkish restaurants. Kim makes a mental note of them, wondering if she and Sean should come here one night, before remembering there is no she and Sean.

'Girls let themselves be photographed like that thinking it's romantic, and before they know it they're on some porn site being wanked over by millions of strangers. Remember that case last year, Tara Flanagan?'

'*Flannery*,' Kim corrects him. A beautiful fifteen-year-old girl whose boyfriend filmed her on his phone giving him a blowjob and then sent the footage to his friends who all forwarded it, until it was everywhere. The police had got involved after the girl's father went round to the boyfriend's and beat the shit out of him. 'She's only a kid. She still wears braces, for god's sake,' the man said.

So Martin is right. It does happen all the time. But still there is something about Jessica Gold's reaction that isn't ringing true. Something she can't quite put her finger on.

For half an hour after the police visit, I sat on the sofa rocking, but now the adrenalin is starting to subside. I go over what I said to them, looking for holes, but can't find any. They seemed to believe me, particularly the man. Probably because it wasn't a million miles from the truth. The photograph *was* the result of an ill-judged one-night stand, and the Facebook account *was* payback for me refusing a repeat encounter. But everything else was a lie. The man who took the photo was Dominic Lacey. And Dominic Lacey never gives up.

After the account was taken down, he sent me another message at work sounding totally contrite. He said I probably wanted the photograph back, and of course he'd give it to me. In return for just one more date. (He actually did call it a date – like what we did on that hotel bed had anything to do with romance.)

Of course, sitting here on the oatmeal sofa my parents

bought in 1992, which used to be cream but was re-covered in 1995 after an incident involving me and a set of Sharpie pens, I can see what an idiot I was to even consider it. But he sounded so sorry. He said he'd set up the account when he was drunk and felt like a total shit about it. He really liked me, he said, that's why he'd taken rejection so badly. Just one date, he pleaded. He'd give me back the photograph. I could personally delete it from his phone.

And even though I should have known better, I found myself listening to his charming voice, and remembering the dimple in his cheek and the delicious thrill of discovering that, like a Russian doll, I contained within me another self, capable of acting in ways I'd never imagined. I met him in a hotel on an industrial estate off the M1. All the way there I asked myself what I was doing, and when I arrived I rang him from the car park to say I'd changed my mind. But he was so very sorry, so full of promises, his voice so sexy. I went in the side entrance so that no one would see me. When I got to the room, he was already waiting. It was an hour or two later – after a bottle of champagne that left me feeling divorced from my own body, drowsy but compliant, that he got out his Pleasure Chest.

I was so naive I had no idea of the things people like Dominic did in the comfort of their own homes. The restraints, the harnesses, the whips, the clamps.

'I'll go to the police,' I said when I realized my drink had been drugged.

'And have to explain all this to your family and your boyfriend and all those people at work? And anyway, I'll just say it was consensual. I already have the photograph to prove it's not the first time. It'll be your word against mine.

'And let me tell you, sweetheart, I can be very persuasive.'

So afterwards I went away and I didn't tell anyone, and I convinced myself it was something I dreamed up after eating too much cheese late at night. I didn't let myself call it what it was. I didn't think of myself as a victim. I didn't think to wonder what that light was, blinking red on the hotel-room dressing table.

'So when it comes to picking up men, Miss Gold doesn't seem to have the best possible taste.'

'You could say that, sir. Seems this was some slimeball geek who has problems with women.'

Martin is talking as if he himself is some kind of babe magnet, but Kim is pretty sure he hasn't had a proper girl-friend in the three years she's known him.

'OK, let's sit on that photograph then, for the time being anyway. The girl's been through enough without dragging up indiscretions from her past as well. Something like that would just muddy the waters and we can do without that when we're building such a convincing case against Lacey.'

'Have you found out anything more, sir?'

Kim knows there's a whole team working on digging through Dominic Lacey's past. Martin is itching to join them, sure that's where the glory lies, but Robertson thinks they should stick with the Jessica Gold side of things, especially in view of Kim being Family Liaison for the Golds.

The Super looks quietly pleased. 'Plenty. I'm just amazed he's been getting away with things for as long as he has. His school reports make for interesting reading – bullying, aggressive behaviour, a particularly nasty episode involving a young female teacher who ended up leaving the profession because of him. Suggestion of abuse at home, though that was never proven. A history of violence with girlfriends starting from when he was a teenager. Then the first marriage which ends with the wife taking out a restraining order, and then killing herself and their baby son. And then the second marriage with the wife who disappeared earlier this year.'

Martin is shaking his head, even though they've heard most of this before, some in official briefings, some through office tittle-tattle.

'Some people are just born scum, aren't they, sir?'

The Super isn't so sure. 'Sometimes people become scum. Nature versus nurture.'

As she makes her way back to Heather's, Kim can't stop thinking about that comment. *Nature versus nurture.* Was Dominic Lacey born bad, or made bad? Might her own children be so affected by her being away from them that it changes them in some way, hardens them, warps them, even?

The thought makes her chest hurt.

THIRTY-SIX

When Travis walks into the bedroom, it's like he's someone I don't know. Someone else's boyfriend. His hair has grown and his face seems older. I have seen him every day since I left hospital, but each time he seems more and more like a stranger. Did his bottom teeth always cross over like that? Was he always so slow to respond to my jokes, considering them carefully before chancing a smile?

'I feel like David Beckham whenever I arrive here,' he says. 'All those reporters shouting out my name, taking my photograph.'

'Perhaps you could bring out a range of underpants,' I suggest. 'Or have my name tattooed across your chest in Chinese.'

He hesitates for a moment before allowing himself to smile.

'I'm thinking about moving back home.'

Until I say it, I have no idea I've been thinking about it, but now I find it makes sense. I'm bored here at my parents' house. I need to get back to normality. Travis, it's fair to say, doesn't jump at the chance of having me home.

'I'm working really long shifts at the hospital so you'd be

on your own a lot, and you're still not properly recovered. And what about the police?'

'What about the police?'

'Well, don't they want you to stay put while they're investigating what happened? You still can't be sure they're not going to charge you with anything.'

'Thanks for reminding me that I could be up for attempted murder.'

'Or murder, if he dies.' He sits down in the chair by the window, giving nothing away. 'How are you feeling?' he asks.

His face, when he turns it to me, sags with concern, and I feel bad for doubting him just now. But Travis and I still haven't discussed the elephant in the room. He has read the account I spent the night writing in the apartment while I waited for someone to read the SOS banner and tried to forget there was a bleeding man outside on the balcony. Though come to think of it I'd already written most of that account before I set foot in Dominic's apartment that time. See what I mean about not being able to tell the difference between fact and fiction any more?

That account tells how I allowed myself to be picked up by a charming stranger and went with him willingly to his apartment. It's not the kind of thing you want to read about your girlfriend.

Particularly not now it's come to light Lacey is being treated in the same hospital where Travis works. It's a huge building and Travis' department, Paediatrics, is in a completely separate block to the rest of the hospital, but still, knowing that he's nearby must add salt to the wounds.

'I'm sorry,' I say now, making a nervous gesture with my arms that lifts the cuff of my sweatshirt slightly so that he can see the marks on my wrists. 'I know I should never have gone to his apartment. I hate myself for being so easily flattered. It's just that you and I were . . . not getting on so well. First the abortion, then Winston . . . and you've seemed so distant lately.'

Sometimes when I lie awake in the dead hours of the night, forcing my eyes open so I don't have to listen to Cesca in my head sobbing or Sam or Bella, I wonder what possessed me to write all that stuff about our relationship for all the world to read – the stuff about the lack of passion and our mutual ambivalence. Was I deliberately trying to provoke a reaction from Travis to catapult us out of the rut we seemed to be in? Or was I just using it as a forum to say the things I was unable to say to his face?

He gazes at me through his black-rimmed specs and suddenly I want more than anything to win back his favour. My Travis. We've been through so much together. After twelve days with Dominic I appreciate everything Travis has to offer – his steadiness, his kindness, the way he doesn't switch moods for no reason at all, his lack of vanity, his integrity.

'Please come and sit next to me,' I say. 'It was an error of judgement, a moment of madness. I just wanted to be someone else for a while.'

Travis sighs heavily, but he does come over and drop down next to me on the bed, allowing me to nestle under his arm just as we've done a million and one times before.

'This feels right, doesn't it?' I ask him.

And it does. For the first time since it all began, I feel relaxed.

Only later, after he's gone, does it occur to me that Travis never replied.

THIRTY-SEVEN

From: ddc115@hotmail.co.uk
To: nowalkinthepark@hotmail.com
Subject: he woke up!
I am hyperventilating. Oh fuck oh fuck. Dominic
woke up. They just told me. He was conscious
for about ten minutes or so. He didn't say
anything. Maybe that's because you severed his
vocal cords. But they're going to get a pen
and notepad ready for the next time. THE
NEXT TIME. Did you get that? Dominic is
going to come round and tell them
everything.

From: nowalkinthepark@hotmail.com
To: ddc115@hotmail.co.uk
Subject: CHILL THE FUCK OUT!
And breathe. This is just how we planned it,
remember? Plan A? You would escape while Dominic
was out of the flat and it would be his word
against yours. They won't believe him. This last
week while he's been unconscious has bought us a

head start on the public image stuff. You should
be grateful.

Nx

From: ddc115@hotmail.co.uk
To: nowalkinthepark@hotmail.com
Subject: not grateful — shitting it!
You know perfectly well the minute the press get
wind that Dominic might pull through, they'll
have to back right off. If there's a court case
in the offing, everything becomes *sub judice*. Why
did I ever, EVER, let you talk me into this? You
have ruined my life.

From: nowalkinthepark@hotmail.com
To: ddc115@hotmail.co.uk
Subject: GET OVER YOURSELF!
Firstly, I haven't ruined your life. You did that
all by yourself by sleeping with Dominic in the
first place. If you'd just been satisfied with
your nice, sweet boyfriend none of this would
have happened. Secondly, you know very well why
you went into this. You had no choice. Think
about the film. Think about your gorgeous niece.
And thirdly, I'm about to start eating my own
arm off with boredom sat in here all day watching
Jeremy fucking *Kyle*, and you don't catch me
moaning about it all the time.

N

She's right.

I slam down the lid on my laptop and push it off my knees on to the sofa next to me, and stare at the wall ahead. Even after a couple of days it still feels weird to be back here in Wood Green.

I'm still fuming – but I know she's right. I did this to myself.

It wasn't long after my second encounter with Dominic that the emails started again. He knew deep down I'd enjoyed it, he said. I needed to explore that side of my personality. He had no shortage of willing partners, he assured me. But there was something special about me. Something restrained and hidden and repressed that turned him on. A boil waiting to be lanced.

I ignored the emails and deleted them. I didn't want to be reminded of that second night in a hotel room with him. Then one Wednesday evening in June as I lay on the sofa while Travis studied at the table, I heard the ping of a message arriving in the Hotmail account. There was a knot of sickness in my throat when I went to my inbox and saw he'd sent an email with a movie attachment. As I watched the footage, I had to clamp my hand over my mouth to stop myself from screaming out loud. Edited highlights of our night together, every nauseating moment.

There was a message: *One more night and I'll delete the footage.*

I won't fall for your blackmail a second time, I emailed back. There followed a couple of weeks of silence from him and I dared to hope he'd gone away. Sitting back against the sofa cushions staring up at the ceiling in our flat, I allow myself a smile at the preposterousness of it – me imagining Dominic would give up like that.

The next time he emailed, there was another attachment. It was a photograph of one of our vaults at work. I couldn't tell which one, as they all look very alike. Nestling on the shelf amid the hundreds of silver reels was a DVD case. There was a close-up of the spine: *Jessica & Dominic*, it read.

Of course I tried to find it. I quizzed the security guards on reception. I even stayed late and went down to the vaults, but there are dozens of them, and I hadn't even got a quarter of the way through before someone came in and I had to come up with an excuse for being there. After that I couldn't risk it again.

I'm going to the police, I emailed him.

That's a shame, he replied. *If you watch the film carefully – which believe me, I have done, many, many times – there's no sign of you putting up much resistance. I wonder what your parents will think, when they watch it. And your brothers. And your boss . . .*

That night I didn't sleep.

The following day I emailed him again: *One more night and you'll delete that film?*

I wasn't going to go along with it. I just wanted to keep the dialogue open, so he wouldn't post the footage anywhere else.

No, silly Jessica Gold, that was the Early Bird rate. Now you've taken so long, I'm afraid the price has to go up.

And then . . . Nothing.

Every morning I logged into the secret Hotmail account

with my mouth dusty with dread. And after the initial relief of not seeing his name in my inbox would come the inevitable slump when I understood the agonizing wait would continue. I realized by now that he wasn't going to just disappear. He was biding his time.

And then one day there was a message. Only it wasn't from him, it was from her.

Natalie.

Jessica Gold is hiding something. Kim was watching her carefully when Robertson told her about Dominic Lacey waking up. There was something in her eyes, a particular kind of fear.

'Obviously she's going to be afraid. The bastard practically killed her, and now it looks like he's going to pull through. She's going to be shitting herself.'

Martin is right. Of course Jessica is going to be petrified thinking that the man who put her through such un-imaginable horror is awake. But Kim saw something else in her reaction, something other than the primal sweat-fear she's seen in victims of domestic violence. Jessica Gold was scared on a whole other level – a rational, knowing level. It was the fear of someone who has a lot to lose. Kim recognized it from her own face in the mirror.

THIRTY-EIGHT

Travis is sleeping on the sofa. I try not to mind. He says it's because I'm still so fragile, still recuperating, but I think it's because of the tattoo on my hip and the lash marks on my body, faded now but still visible, a pattern of pale pink lace on my skin. I lie on his side of the bed, and imagine things are different.

Now I've started thinking about her, Natalie, I find I can't stop. Her face, with that expression of entitlement beautiful women so often wear, crowds my memory and even here in our bedroom, I can almost smell a trace of the perfume she always wears.

When she first sent that email, I thought it was Dominic playing more mind games. It hadn't occurred to me he could be married. She'd found my messages on his computer, she said. She watched the film of our night together. She thought I'd probably worked out by now that Dominic was dangerous.

She wanted to meet up.

We met in a crowded bar in Charing Cross. I'd asked her how we'd recognize each other and she reminded me that she'd already seen me. Every bit of me.

In the event I knew it was her, even before she saw me. I expected that Dominic's wife would have to be striking. And she was. Long tawny hair and green eyes. She was wearing a tight jacket of soft, butter-coloured suede that zipped up snugly over her chest. I felt like a frump in my work outfit – plain black top and trousers.

'You're not his usual type,' is what she said.

As we got talking, I quickly realized we had nothing in common, except that we were both scared to death of the same man.

I'd told Travis I was going for a quick drink with some colleagues, and he seemed pleased, relieved even that I was finally making some friends at work. I didn't think I'd be long but I ended up talking to Natalie for over three hours.

She told me the whole story. The stool, the teacher, Bella, Cesca, Sam. She told me what Dominic was capable of and what he'd done – the trail of deaths he left behind. She told me what life was like for her being married to him, how she kept trying to get away, and he kept reeling her back in. He had various holds on her, she said. She didn't elaborate, but after my own experience, I could guess. She told me I'd never get rid of him, but when I asked her why she'd married him, she looked at me as if I was crazy. 'Love,' she said. 'Why else?'

'How come you have access to his computer?'

She looked smug. 'I installed a keylogger. I've done that with all the boyfriends I've had. I like to know what they're up to.'

I was appalled. 'What about trust?' I asked.

She rolled her eyes. 'Is that what that video I watched was about?' she asked. '*Trust?* Bet your boyfriend would be chuffed to death with that one.'

'I made a mistake,' I said. 'He'd understand.'

She laughed out loud.

She had an idea, she told me. That would set both of us free. She would disappear. Make it look like she was dead, so suspicion would fall on him. The police were itching to get something on him after the deaths of his ex-wife and child. It wouldn't take much. She knew it sounded extreme, but Dominic was a very extreme man.

She needed my help, she told me. She didn't have many friends – not ones she could trust not to blab to Dominic. She wasn't a woman's woman. You don't say, I thought.

In return, she'd delete the film. Anyway, she said, once she'd disappeared I'd be free of him. Under suspicion for murder, he'd have to drop everything else.

My part in her plan was minimal, she assured me. She'd already kick-started the process by booking herself into the cosmetic surgery clinic. All I had to do was rent a cottage far away, Scotland perhaps, then collect her from the clinic and drive her up there, and stock up the kitchen before I left, so that she could recuperate from her various operations undisturbed. She had funds stashed away – money she'd got from someone she'd been sleeping with. A Saudi, I think. Plus a couple of styling jobs she'd done cash-in-hand. Enough to keep her going while she recovered. After that, she knew people who knew people who could get you false passports. And she knew people who owed her favours. She knew a *lot* of people. She'd go abroad for a while, she said. It was worth it to get away from him.

When she told me all this, my first reaction was to laugh. My second was to refuse to have anything to do with it. But by the end of the night, I'd changed my mind. Three jugs of margarita will do that. But it was more than the alcohol. This was the only option I'd been offered. The only way out of the mess I was in. Even so, when I told her I'd help her, I honestly believed I'd call it off the next day.

Somehow I never did.

When Kim was starting out in CID, she worked on the case of a woman who'd drowned her four-month-old son in the bath while in the grip of undiagnosed post-natal depression. After she'd killed him, she looked after the body as carefully as if he was still alive – wrapping him up in his favourite blanket and putting him down for a nap, taking him out for a walk in a sling close to her chest – until her husband came home from a five-day business trip and found her bathing a corpse. Afterwards, and this is what Kim had struggled with most, she explained she'd killed her baby to protect him – from herself. She knew that she was capable of doing him harm and so she held him under the water to save him from what she might do. In her muddled head, that had made a kind of sense. The case had affected everyone who dealt with it, but Kim had been totally rocked by it. She'd thought she understood by then how nothing is ever really just black or white, but this had made her rethink everything she believed she knew about responsibility and blame and love. By the time the case was reported in the papers some months later, Kim was already pregnant with Rory. The first time she read about the woman described as the 'Baby Killer' she felt like she'd been punched. The point is, she reflects as she drives into work through still-darkened streets, the truth has as many layers as an onion. Whatever she thinks she knows about Jessica Gold and Dominic Lacey, the reality is likely to lie somewhere in between.

I have collected all the pillows and built myself a nest in our double bed in which I am cocooned against the discoloured patch on the ceiling where the water tank once leaked and the broken plastic blind cord that flaps uselessly against the window.

Somehow it feels safer here to think about all the stuff that happened. Sonia Rubenstein is always trying to get me to take responsibility for my own actions. 'Own your shit,' she tells me, so from the security of my nest I force myself to think back to what happened after my meeting with Natalie, when there was still time to stop.

It was easy enough to come up with an excuse to tell Travis why I needed to be away for a couple of days. I told him I was going on a team-bonding weekend with work. Two days in a hotel in Norfolk.

The initial stages of Natalie's plan went fairly smoothly. It wasn't hard to make it look like she had left the clinic under duress. I phoned her at an agreed time when she was having lunch with a couple of other 'guests'. Later, they would describe in great, overblown detail how she shook as she spoke to her husband, before reluctantly agreeing to meet him outside the clinic gates as long as he promised to leave her alone after that. She didn't take her phone or her bank cards or her passport or her clothes. She had no intention of going anywhere, they insisted.

She must have put on a bloody good act. The papers later reported that the two women, who declined to give their names or details of the procedures they'd undergone, told police they'd begged her not to meet him.

I was waiting for her in the hire car as planned. When we drove off up the M1 there was a moment where we felt euphoric, like we were in some kind of feel-good female-bonding road movie. We put on Radio 2 and danced in our seats. But by the time we arrived in Scotland, the novelty had worn off and we were both anxious and crotchety. Natalie accused me of driving like an old woman, and I said, 'Well you'd know all about that,' which I knew would get to her. She's only seven years older than me, but she's one of those women who really mind about that sort of thing. We were both relieved when, after a fretful night, I got in the car again and came home.

Incredibly, the plan worked. Natalie had disappeared off the face of the earth and every finger pointed at Dominic. The papers were full of it for a while: *Search Intensifies for Missing Stylist.* The story had everything – jealous husband, gorgeous woman, a history of extra-marital affairs, boob job. It even made the television news on one occasion. Travis and I were watching together and I jolted so violently, I made him jolt too. I think he was embarrassed, because neither of us mentioned my odd reaction.

For a couple of weeks following our road trip to Scotland, I heard nothing from Natalie or Dominic and was starting to believe it was all really over. Lying on the sofa in our Wood Green flat I stroke one of the bald patches where the hair has started to grow through, soft like suede. (I'm lucky, apparently, some people never regain their hair.) It's a new habit I've developed and it drives Travis mad. 'You're just going to rub all the new hair away,' he said yesterday. 'Do you want to end up bald?'

Sometime in September, one of the papers ran a story on a jeweller in Edinburgh who'd come forward with CCTV footage of a woman trying to sell a diamond necklace that had been reported stolen. It turned out Dominic Lacey was the person who'd reported it stolen, at the same time he learned his wife was missing from the clinic. The woman in the film was wearing a baseball cap and glasses and the footage was grainy, but there was enough of a resemblance to Natalie Lacey to plant a seed of doubt. In the absence of a body or any evidence of foul play, Dominic Lacey was off the hook.

By the time I read through to the end of the news story, I could hardly make out the words through the red mist that had descended over my eyes. I knew immediately, and beyond any doubt, that it was Natalie. I should have known it wouldn't be enough for her to get away from her abusive husband. She had to steal from him as well. Natalie's greed had wrecked everything.

I was back to square one.

* * *

Kim tells herself she is just doing her job. She is still Family Liaison for the Golds, and that extends to Travis Riley. So what could be more natural than to be sitting in a coffee shop round the corner from the hospital where he works, sipping from a cappuccino cup as large as a goldfish bowl and observing the look of total incomprehension on the young medic's face.

'What photograph?'

Kim likes Travis. Or at least she thinks she does, though she still can't quite shake off the niggling feeling that he has secrets. But now his pale eyes are looking at her blankly through those black-rimmed glasses and he is leaning forward and twiddling a piece of hair around a long, elegant finger. And she knows she is about to tell him something he won't want to hear. When she explains about the pornographic Facebook photo, she says Jessica's family believes it to have been photoshopped. She doesn't say that she knows this to be false, but leaves Travis to decide for himself.

'They think it's a work colleague with a grudge,' she says.

Travis makes all those gestures people make when they're miming disbelief, knitting his brows together and turning down the corners of his mouth while moving his head back slightly and his shoulders up.

'I don't understand. Jessica gets on well with the people at work. She even went on a team-building weekend with them in the summer.'

It's the first Kim has heard of the team-building weekend. She stores the information away.

'And how is Jessica coping?'

She spoke to her only recently but she wants to hear it from Travis. She is curious about these two. There is affection there, but she doesn't sense much passion.

Travis shrugs. His shoulders are narrow, even in the hooded sweatshirt he is wearing over a grey T-shirt.

'She's been through a lot,' he says. 'She's bound to be a bit . . . weird.'

'More weird than usual,' Kim says, smiling to show it's a joke.

He has a way of laughing that sounds more like a sigh, softening out into thin air. 'You know, she seems to be getting more stressed rather than less. More scared. That's what I mean. Obviously not knowing if she'll be charged, and what with, is getting to her. And it doesn't help that Lacey has regained consciousness. She's now convinced herself he'll insist it was all consensual. She thinks she'll have to face him in court and go through all the grubby details of what he did to her. She thinks he'll get off on that. It's what men like Lacey do.'

Kim doesn't demur. It's what men like Lacey do – they violate their victim over and over again. First with the original assault, then in court and then again in prison. Sex offenders exchange copies of their own official court papers like pornography.

'And how are you coping, Travis? It must be tough knowing the man responsible for Jessica's ordeal is just a few hundred feet away, on another ward.'

Superintendent Robertson had studied the layout of the hospital and spoken to Travis' supervisor and been assured there was no chance of him accidentally coming into contact with Lacey. Also, Lacey was being held under guard.

Travis shrugs. 'Just knowing he exists is bad enough – it doesn't make any difference whether he's five minutes away or five hours.'

On her way back to Heather's flat, Kim puts in a call to Henrietta Belvedere, Jessica's boss.

'You're lucky you caught me,' the other woman says, making it obvious she feels the luck to be one-sided. 'I'm completely frantic today.' ·

'Jessica Gold mentioned she attended a team-bonding event back in August sometime. A weekend in Norfolk?'

There's a brief silence, during which Kim pictures the other woman drumming her restless, cigarette-free fingers insistently on her desk.

'I'm afraid that doesn't ring any bells. We don't go in for that sort of thing here. Grown-up people pretending to be trees and goodness knows what else. Better to take everyone down to the pub and get rip-roaring drunk, I think.'

Quite, Kim agrees.

First the photograph, now the lie about the weekend. Clearly Jessica Gold also has things she'd rather keep hidden. The obvious conclusion is that she has been having an affair. Was someone with her when she said she was off on a team-building weekend in Norfolk? Perhaps the mysterious Ben she claimed was responsible for the compromising Facebook photo. Having met the Gold family, Kim isn't surprised Jessica wants to keep that episode under wraps, but she needs to realize she is in a very serious situation. Whatever charges she and Dominic Lacey end up facing, there is no doubt there will be a court case, if not two, and every detail of her life will be picked over.

People in Jessica Gold's position aren't allowed the luxury of secrets.

THIRTY-NINE

When Travis comes home from the hospital he's in a foul mood. He goes straight into the kitchen and gets himself a beer from the fridge. Sourness seeps out of him and snakes its way along the hallway and into the living room where I am watching a programme on Catch Up in which ordinary people are filmed watching television in their own homes and commenting on what they see.

'Is this it?' says Travis, coming in from the kitchen brandishing the bottle of beer in his hand like a weapon. 'Is this your life from now on? No more working, just slobbing around watching TV all day?'

The unfairness of this stings. Surely I'm allowed to wallow for a bit after what I've been through. Then I remember I haven't actually been through what he thinks I've been through. It's getting harder and harder to remember what is and isn't real. I see I've started to think of myself as a victim, which of course I am, only not quite in the way I mean.

Travis sits down in the one armchair we own, rather than next to me on the sofa. We never sit in that chair on account of the lumpiness of the bottom cushion so I know something's up.

'What's wrong with you anyway?'

The voice in my head is strong and confrontational, however the one that comes out of my mouth is whiny and self-pitying.

Travis takes a swig from his beer and glares at me. I can see the lower lid of his left eye twitching as it does when he is tired. I've been so focused on myself that I haven't even thought about what effect all this has had on him, but now I'm reminded that he hasn't been sleeping well either. When I wake up in the night – which is every hour or so, if I'm lucky enough to sleep at all – I sometimes tiptoe into the living room and find Travis also awake, on the sofa, his eyes, curiously vulnerable without the glasses, gazing myopically into the darkness.

'It's like I don't even know you,' he says now, as if we are carrying on an earlier conversation only he has been privy to. 'All this time we've been together and we might as well be strangers.'

'Where did all this come from?' I say.

He opens his mouth, with that extravagantly curved upper lip, as if he's about to speak, and then thinks better of it.

I go back to watching the telly where a middle-aged couple who look half-cut are sitting side by side on a velvet sofa holding hands and chatting about the reality TV show they're watching. I try to picture Travis and me in thirty years' time.

My mind goes blank.

* * *

Kim isn't prepared for how she reacts when seeing Dominic Lacey for the first time. The feeling is deep within her like someone is taking hold of her intestines and squeezing hard. The inside of her mouth is suddenly dry and she hopes Martin can't hear her struggling to swallow. There is a strange smell in the room. In addition to the usual hospital stench of antiseptic and bleach with an acrid undercurrent of bedpans and dried blood, there's an unpleasant musky scent she can't place.

She hangs back by the door behind Robertson and Martin. The room is on the second floor of the hospital, and the windows running along the opposite wall give out on to the grey concrete of a different wing behind which lurks an equally grey sky. Dominic Lacey lies propped up on pillows. His eyes are open but so far he has yet to speak or make use of the notebook and pen laid out carefully on his bedside table. Medical staff are still not sure whether his brain function has been affected by the disruption to the oxygen supply during the hours he spent bleeding on the balcony while Jessica Gold waited inside for help to arrive. They are calling his survival a miracle. Though the cut to his throat was more superficial than first appeared, certainly than Jessica indicated in her account, he had to keep up a constant pressure on it to stop himself bleeding to death. If he'd allowed himself to slip into unconsciousness, chances are he wouldn't have survived the night.

His will to live overrode his own body's limitations. Kim finds that chilling.

There is a bandage around his throat through which the tracheostomy tube extrudes. His chest too is bandaged where the knife wounds are. One of the stab wounds collapsed a lung. Amazingly, both missed his heart. However, the fragment of china in the back of his neck did damage his spinal cord. If he lives it's doubtful he will walk again.

Detective Superintendent Robertson is talking to one of the doctors.

'As I say, you can talk to him for a few minutes, but at present we've no way of knowing how much he understands.'

The doctor – tall with long grey hair pulled back from a surprisingly youthful face, and jaunty blue suede kitten-heel shoes – appears unfazed by the infamy of her charge, unmoved by the knot of reporters still camped outside the main gate to the hospital. There is none of that bustling self-importance Kim has observed in people who find themselves in proximity to an international news story.

The Super moves closer to the bed and starts addressing the prone body, telling Lacey that the police need to question him urgently about events in an apartment in Wapping.

There is no response. Lacey remains staring straight ahead. He is staring at Kim, blue eyes like lasers boring into her.

FORTY

Travis is still sleeping on the sofa.

I don't bother asking him why. In the context of all the inexplicable things that have happened to me in the last few weeks, his new darkness of mood hardly registers. I imagine that now the initial relief at my rescue has died away, he's gone back to questioning just what I was doing going home with a man I've only just met. I'm waiting for him to quiz me about it, but he doesn't. There is a sense in which my 'ordeal', as it has euphemistically become known, has moved me into a different dimension to everyone else.

So Travis contents himself with angry glances and sleeping on the sofa every night, but doesn't confront me.

Which leaves me free to lie awake in our bed with the white waffle-pattern duvet, trying to drown out the voices of Dominic's dead by thinking about all the things that have gone wrong.

After Natalie made her reappearance on the Edinburgh jeweller's grainy CCTV, and the pressure on Dominic lessened, I knew it was only a matter of time before he crawled back out of the woodwork. Every time my phone rang with a number I didn't recognize, or my computer pinged to tell me an email had come through, my chest tightened like it had been bound with wet bandages that were slowly drying and shrinking.

The whole reason I got involved in the first place was so that Natalie would find the video of me and him and delete it, but there was a hard nugget of doubt inside me that wouldn't go away. When I finally managed to get hold of her, she was non-committal.

'I was in a very dangerous position,' she said. 'You. don't know what that man is capable of. I was in fear of my life.'

'Not so much fear that it stopped you blowing your cover just to cash in a bloody necklace.'

'I was broke. Don't forget, I haven't got access to my bank account. My friends can't be expected to support me for ever.'

By friends I'd now realized she meant one friend – that very rich Arab friend.

And he – it turned out – wasn't really a friend.

'Anyway,' she said. 'That photo of the vault shelves probably isn't even real. Didn't it occur to you that he might have photoshopped it? Superimposed the image of a DVD on to a picture of the vault?'

Despite my brothers' theory about the Facebook-account photo, somehow the thought that Dominic might have doctored the photograph of the vaults had never crossed my mind. Too late I saw I'd allowed him to take on almost superhuman powers in my head, able to stroll into heavily secured buildings without being seen.

'So I did all that to help you, and only now it occurs to you to tell me that the photograph wasn't even real? You tricked me.'

She was unconcerned, brushing off my anger like a speck of dust on her jacket.

After that I tried to convince myself that Dominic would move on. He was attractive, rich and now free. He could jump into bed with whomever he chose. Why would he bother with me? Looked at objectively, I should have felt safe. But I didn't. What I'd learned of Dominic Lacey was that he was driven by a lust for power rather than sexual desire. Power and possession. Now he was no longer under the shadow of suspicion, Dominic was free to turn his attention back to me. Which he eventually did.

'I'm willing to remove the film from the vaults, Jessica, but I'm afraid it will cost you a bit more now that you've been so obstructive. I want you again for a night. No interruptions.'

He'd called while I was on one of my daily lunchtime walks. Whenever the rest of my colleagues made for the nearest café, it was my habit to pull out my old trainers from the bottom drawer of my desk, head in the opposite direction and walk randomly for an hour, trying to clear my head.

When the display came up as *no caller ID*, even though I hadn't given him my number, I guessed who it was. I was determined to face him down, to call his bluff.

Now, when I think back to that terrified but defiant Jessica, standing in the car park of a Perivale industrial estate in her work skirt and grubby trainers, I'm embarrassed for myself.

'I know the photo is a hoax, Dominic,' I said, hoping that the fuzzy quality of the line might just disguise the wobble in my voice. 'You photoshopped it. I'm not playing your games any more. Leave me alone or I *will* go to the police.'

When I ended the call, I was shaking but euphoric. I really thought I'd got rid of him. I felt lighter than I had done in months. I even ran back to work, savouring my own power and energy, arriving at my desk flushed and smiling, and full of magnanimity towards the workmates I usually avoided. I blocked Dominic from my Hotmail account. I felt free.

Kim has tilted her chair back so that she can't see the photograph on Lennie Fraser's desk. It shows her colleague and his wife on their most recent wedding anniversary, arms around each other, flanked by their four children, and whenever she catches sight of it unprepared, her grief is like barbed wire around her heart. No one ever asks Lennie how he manages to juggle the long hours at work with having young kids. No one ever glances pointedly at the clock when he comes in late, assuming he got held up on the school run, which is somehow less acceptable an excuse than oversleeping after a heavy night down the pub.

She has to stop thinking like this or it will drive her mad.

She calls up the screen grab of the fake Facebook page

they'd found on Jessica Gold's work computer. Even though she's now seen the image several times it still shocks her all over again. Jessica is so exposed, naked there on the bed. Her expression is a mixture of so many things – clearly there's sexual excitement there, but also a kind of shy appeal, as if she knows how much trust she is placing in the photographer and is hoping he won't let her down. When she told them about the guy she'd stupidly slept with, her shame and embarrassment were palpable. But where was the anger? She should have been full of rage that someone had done that to her and got away with it, and yet Kim hadn't detected any of that. Either Jessica Gold is keeping her emotions on a very tight leash, or she has found some way of exorcizing that anger. She opens her notebook and makes a note to call Sonia Rubenstein.

I am so enamoured of my new Nest in a Bed that I eat my dinner in there, cursing when a solitary baked bean drops with an orange splatter on to the white sheet. It's so womb-like in here surrounded by pillows. I find I am able to think about hurtful stuff without it actually touching me. Stuff like what happened after I called Dominic's bluff over the photograph of our sex tape in the television company's vaults.

For a few blissful weeks, I heard nothing. I threw myself into making it up to Travis. I cooked him complicated meals from the cookbooks people were always giving us for Christmas but sat largely unused on a special shelf in the kitchen. I took an interest in his job, quizzing him about his patients and taking the time to learn the names and domestic set-ups of the other junior doctors so I could comment on the workplace gossip he brought home. I even steeled myself to go into a sex shop in town, walking past its entrance four or five times before working up the courage to go in, emerging some time later with scratchy, ill-fitting underwear and various pink plastic 'toys'. It almost made me laugh, perusing the shelves, at the innocence of it all. After the things Dominic had done, his stash of leather and chains and harnesses and buckles, the pink feathers and fake fur seemed like a child's idea of a bedroom fantasy.

Travis was startled by this sudden change in me. 'But what exactly does it *do*?' he wanted to know, sitting up in bed, mystified, turning a purple plastic nipple clamp over in his hand.

Then in November my Hotmail account once again pinged with an email that changed everything.

It was from an address I didn't recognize. The subject line said *selfie surprise* and there was a paperclip to indicate a photo attachment. I don't know why I didn't just move it straight to the trash, but maybe because it was in my regular inbox rather than my spam folder, or because the name looked genuine, I double-clicked and instantly a photograph came up in the main body of the message.

I remember I was sitting cross-legged on our sofa at home with my laptop resting on my knees. It was a Saturday morning, around eleven thirty, which is the one time of day when the sun manages to infiltrate our north-facing flat, falling in slants of light across the laminate flooring near the television. As the meaning of the photograph registered there was a split second when the whole world stopped.

The photo was taken in a park, from above and from arm's length, in usual selfie style. It was of Dominic. He was dressed in black jeans and a dark blue Levi's jacket with a crisp white T-shirt underneath. His brown hair was slightly messy, his eyes appeared particularly blue against the white cotton of his T-shirt and he was gazing up into the lens with a half-smile. But my attention wasn't on him, it was on a couple of girls sitting on a park bench a few metres behind him. One of them was plump and blonde and unfamiliar. The other was my thirteen-year-old niece, Grace.

The girls, both wearing school-uniform black blazers and short black skirts rolled up around their waists as they all seem to, were deep in conversation. The blonde one was gesturing with her hands and Grace was listening intently and smiling, her thick brown hair tumbling over one shoulder. She has reached that age girls get to where they might be anything from twelve to twenty-five. She has huge brown eyes with thick – and when she can get away with it, mascaraed – lashes, a long thin nose and beautifully shaped dark brows, and she is the kind of skinny you take for granted at that age.

The girls didn't seem to be aware of the man standing in front of them taking a picture on his phone, and even if they had noticed, they probably wouldn't have thought it remarkable. In Teenage Girl World chronicling your every movement photographically is as natural as breathing.

I don't know how long I stared at the image on the screen, but after a while I became aware that I was rocking backwards and forwards, with my hand over my mouth.

He was sending me a message. That much was clear. Telling me how easy it was to get access to the people I loved. How easy it would be to do them harm.

But *Grace*. Funny, smart, silly, lovely Grace on the cusp of her life.

My first instinct was to call her, warning her to look out for a handsome stranger with blue eyes, but I knew it would just pique her curiosity. Plus, I didn't want my brother James getting involved, demanding to know what it was all about.

Anyway, I knew that any warnings would be too little, too late. Now Dominic knew how to find her there was nothing to stop him doing so again. I thought of the long black sports bag he'd brought to the second hotel and the things that were inside. Things with studs and clamps and heavy chains. I thought of the candles he'd used to drip hot wax on to my skin and the metal cuffs that left my wrists red and bruised, and how I'd had to tell Travis I'd been carrying heavy shopping with the plastic bag handles wrapped around my wrists so that they cut into my skin, and how he'd looked at me as if he didn't believe me, but said nothing.

I thought of all these things. And then I thought about my niece who I first held when she was only five hours old and who I'd read stories to and taken swimming and cooked fishfingers for and tucked into bed.

For a few minutes, I thought again about going to the police. But there was nothing to link Dominic to the fake Facebook account, and if the vault photograph turned out to be a fake also, there'd been no crime committed there.

And there was certainly nothing illegal about taking your own photograph in a public park. Would I really risk everything only to be disbelieved anyway?

That night I didn't sleep. The next morning I got up and rang the number I had for Natalie, and kept ringing every five minutes until finally she answered.

'You owe me,' I told her.

That didn't sway her. Who was I kidding to think she might feel some kind of loyalty to me for helping her run away from her husband. Dominic had already started looking for her. Now he knew she'd been in Edinburgh trying to sell on the diamond necklace, he was coming to find her, closing in on the trail she'd left behind. The woman who owned the cottage I'd rented for her had emailed me telling me there was someone who wanted to get in touch with her, a friend from the past. Dominic wouldn't leave her alone, just as he wouldn't leave me alone. We would never ever be free of him.

Unless we fought back.

In Heather's spare room, Kim hears her phone vibrating on the bedside table. The screen lights up with a text from Sean. *Been to talk to a lawyer about a divorce.* She lies back on the single bed and tries to go back to sleep, but every time she closes her eyes she sees Dominic Lacey staring at her from the hospital bed. It's like his face is glued to the inside of her eyelids. Next to him, Sean appears reassuringly safe, normal, decent. She reaches out for her phone once more and clicks on to the wallpaper image – a photograph of Rory and Katy, arms wrapped around each other on a beach in Cornwall just four months ago. They are dripping with water and shining with excitement and cold. Kim tries to memorize their smiles as a talisman against the man in the hospital bed.

FORTY-ONE

Sunday lunch around the big table at my parents' house. It's the first time since I went missing that all of us have been in the same place at the same time – brothers, sisters-in-law, niece, nephews, Travis. I'm dreading an inquisition but at the same time I'm relieved to be spared another awkward meal at home in our flat with both of us determinedly steering clear of the things we most need to say.

'Earth to Jessica.'

I blink as Travis clicks his fingers in front of my face, and am disconcerted to find the whole table looking at me – apart from my brother Jonathan, who is rolling his eyes at James.

'You were completely away with the fairies there. I was asking about the roast beef,' says James's wife Sarah, who used to be important in advertising and still can't quite shake off her demeanour of authority even though it's been six years since she went off on maternity leave and never returned to work. 'Since when do you eat meat?'

My vegetarianism is another casualty of my sojourn in Dominic's flat. That much of the account is true. Dominic did fill the fridge with meat and meat-based ready-meals that he commanded me to eat. It was all part of his power game. And since then I've developed a taste for it.

'Well, I for one am very glad,' says my mother. 'Humans are biologically evolved to eat meat. It's a fact.'

She's never really got on with Sarah who once said she believed James's stubborn concentration on details at the expense of the bigger picture to be an inherited genetic trait.

Grace is sitting opposite me and I glance at her as we eat. Her long brown hair is pulled up into a ponytail which makes her look younger than usual and her soft cheeks are flushed pink from the game she was playing with her younger cousin. For a moment, all my doubts disappear. This is why I did what I did. This is what makes this whole ordeal worthwhile. I feel momentarily vindicated. More than vindicated, elated.

'I did think about inviting Kim,' my mother says suddenly.

'Kim?' Jonathan's brows are knitted together so they form one unified black line across his forehead. 'Policewoman Kim?'

My mother ignores the note of incredulity in his voice. 'Yes. I like her. And I sense a real sadness there. She and her husband are living separately, you know. And with two small children too.'

I'm astonished, thinking of the quiet policewoman with her neat brown bob and grey eyes.

'How do you know all that?'

'Oh, you're not the only one with dramas in your life, you know.' Mum doesn't look up as she carries on eating, methodically moving her fork between her plate and her mouth.

'She's not a friend, Lizzie.' My dad has put down his cutlery and is peering down the table at his wife, his frown echoing his younger son's. 'I've told you before, you mustn't let the lines get blurred. Kim is doing a job. That's all. In the same way that David Gallant is just doing a job. Yes, she's been supporting us, but she's also been finding out information about us and reporting back. That's what she's there for.'

I go cold when he says that, about finding out information and reporting back. It's a reminder that I'm still under suspicion, still vulnerable. For a second I feel a jolt of pure hatred for the policewoman whose job it is to find the snags in my story and pull on them until gaping holes appear. Those daily phone calls she makes: 'Just checking in', 'Any more thoughts?' Then I look at Grace again and I calm down.

No one would blame me if they knew the circumstances.

I am not the one who's done wrong.

On a Sunday afternoon the station is a weird place to be. Not empty exactly but a sense of normal life suspended. Robertson is off visiting his married daughter with his wife and their two teenage boys. He always comes back from these weekends ruddier than ever, as if he's spent the time outdoors. Kim imagines him helping her in the garden. It's the sort of thing he might do.

Martin is in though. They are matching each other hour for hour, neither wanting to be seen as less committed. Between them they are going through the reports into Natalie Lacey's disappearance. Another team has been investigating that case, following up leads from the time she was first reported missing, but has drawn a blank. Now Martin and Kim are having a look to see if they can find any connection to Jessica Gold. Any connection other than Dominic Lacey, that is.

Kim gazes at the photo of Natalie Lacey, née Paepke. It shows a blonde woman wearing a black tailored trouser suit with a sequinned top underneath and high silver heels. It was taken from Natalie's own website where she show-cased her skills as an 'international stylist'. The site has endless .pdfs of magazine fashion shoots Natalie has worked on, and links to many pop videos she's helped to style.

As a freelancer, it seems Natalie was much in demand – always flying off to Florida or South Africa at a moment's notice. People who knew her said she always kept a bag packed, ready for the airport if a rush job came up. Kim can't even begin to imagine such freedom.

Not that Natalie had many close friends from the sound of it. Just hundreds of acquaintances. And those who did profess to know her well said they had hardly seen her since her marriage to Dominic.

'She changed,' Mel Newton, who occasionally assisted Natalie on big-budget shoots, said in one of several written statements given by those close to the missing woman. 'Before, she used to like to go out for a few drinks with the crew after filming was over, but once she got married she was different. If she went out, her phone would be constantly buzzing with texts and calls and sometimes she'd go off into a different room and you'd hear her having a row. After a while it got so she hardly went out at all.'

That figures. From her work in the Domestic Violence Unit, Kim knows that people like Lacey operate by isolating their victims from their support network. She studies the photograph carefully.

'There's something I don't understand,' she says to Martin. 'Look at the photo of Natalie Lacey. How would you describe her? You're a red-blooded male.'

She can tell Martin is pleased by this.

'Well. She's a trophy woman, isn't she?' he says. 'She's A list.'

'And how about Jessica Gold? How would you describe her?'

Martin glances up sharply as if this might be some sort of trick. 'She seems like a nice woman. Interesting.'

'But not trophy?'

Again he glances over, before shaking his head.

'So why her? Clearly Natalie is his type. His level, if you like. So why would he go for Jessica Gold? He didn't know whether she was interesting or nice before he sat down at that table and chatted her up.'

'He's a pervert. He was just after anyone he could exercise some power over. He'd set everything up at home – the meals, the presents, the bloody dog kennel. All he was interested in was finding someone who'd come back with him. She was just in the wrong place at the wrong time.'

'But it doesn't fit any kind of pattern,' Kim persists. 'Lacey is a manipulator. He does things that bring about other people's deaths but he doesn't kill them himself. Why change now? Abduction? Murder? Why take those risks?'

'Because he's upping the ante – making it more exciting for himself.'

Kim is looking at the photograph of Natalie Lacey again. The woman is certainly striking – the kind of looks you don't forget.

'I still don't think it makes sense. If he was going out prowling for victims, why do it there in a busy department store where everyone is rushing about with a purpose? Why not go to a bar?'

Martin shrugs. 'Jessica Gold was in a department store, on a mission to get her Christmas shopping done, and she still ended up going home with him. He just took a chance. Maybe he's done it before. Or maybe he'd already been to loads of other places and hadn't had any luck so he decided to try there.'

It was as plausible as anything else, Kim supposes. Yet still when Martin has gone, she puts the picture of Natalie Lacey on her desk alongside the missing-persons photo of Jessica Gold, and she gazes at them for a long time.

FORTY-TWO

'What's he waiting for? I don't get it.'

I'm sitting on the sofa at home trying to avoid looking at the little square in the bottom corner of my laptop screen that shows what Natalie can see from her end – namely my own face gazing out pastily from under my unwashed hair. I tell myself it's the angle of the computer webcam that makes me look so awful, but I know that's not true. I look awful because I've given up. I no longer go out of the flat except to my parents' house. I rarely get dressed. Luckily, Skype can't transmit smells as well. I smell like something that has crawled under the floorboards and died.

'Jess, you're such a pessimist. Maybe he's not waiting for anything. Maybe he's just a vegetable in a bed, incapable of intelligent thought. Hasn't that occurred to you?'

That's the kind of thing Natalie says: 'vegetable in a bed'. How do I even know someone like this? I try to imagine Dominic so brain-damaged he can't write or even respond, but I can't.

'I've just got this feeling it's all closing in on us. Did I tell you the police are waiting on one of those CSI reports, though they call it something else. SOCO, I think. Yes, that's it. They've been collecting all the forensic evidence – looking for fingerprints, measuring blood spatters or whatever else they do.'

'Relax. It's fine. I wore gloves, and everything else happened just the way you said it did.'

'Yes, but that police liaison woman, Kim, has been asking loads of questions. She calls me every day. To "check in", she says, but really it's to catch me tripping myself up. It doesn't help that my mother has now decided she's her best friend and tells her everything. She's probably talking her through my baby pictures as we speak. And now even Travis is being weird. He keeps looking at me like he doesn't believe me.

'Or maybe he's looking at you like a man might look at his girlfriend who went to a hotel with a strange guy, a *married* strange guy, and shagged his brains out.'

For a moment my brain freezes with shock. Travis *knows* about the hotel and the shagging? Then I remember what's real and my insides are washed by a tsunami of relief.

'You know very well Travis doesn't have a clue about that bit. All he knows is I went home with Dominic Lacey for a drink after a random meeting with him on Christmas Eve. And as you also know I had no idea he was married. And if we're finding fault here, which we clearly are, at least I realized my mistake straight away. At least I didn't *marry* him.'

Natalie glares at me with her blue contact lenses. Who knows why she wears them when she's at home in her supposed 'safe house', as she insists on calling it. It's not as if anyone else can see her. In fact, now I think about it,

Natalie looks very dressed up today for someone marooned in a house on her own. She never looks exactly slobby, but today she has on a clingy emerald-green dress and, when she stands up to move around, yes, tights. Who wears tights when no one is going to see them?

'You *are* on your own, aren't you?'

My voice thrums with accusation and Natalie makes one of her rolling-eye faces.

She flicks back her red hair and drops down into the chair, flinging herself back against the cushion. I have another fleeting twinge of recognition when I see the pattern on the fabric, but it's gone almost as soon as it arrives.

For a few seconds we stare at each other through our respective screens with an animosity we don't bother to hide. If Natalie and I had met in other circumstances we'd have had nothing to say to each other. Correction: Natalie and I would never have met. Full stop.

Even when we were putting together the Christmas Plan (that's what we called it, as if it was a party we were planning), I had major misgivings. She'd left the cottage I'd found her by that time and was moving around the country, trying to keep ahead of Dominic. The friend of a friend who was supposed to be getting her a fake passport proved to be elusive. This is something I quickly came to learn about Natalie. All the friends and contacts she used to boast of didn't actually exist. Or else they existed, but they weren't her friends.

We formulated the plan over Skype sessions like this one, while Travis was at work or off with his new hospital friends.

It started as Natalie's idea. My first reaction was derision. The whole idea was preposterous. That I would willingly give in to Dominic's demands, knowing what he was capable of, was ridiculous. By this stage he was insisting that I spend Christmas with him, cut off from the outside world, just me and him. I think he liked the symbolism of Christmas, the idea that he would be dividing me from my family. It played to his sense of power. Plus, of course, he had no one else to spend Christmas with. That much of my account was true. He was lonely, in his own twisted way. And he wanted me to be lonely too.

When Natalie first suggested I play along with it, or at least pretend to play along with it, I dismissed it out of hand. And not just because the idea of voluntarily spending time with him, pretending to enjoy it, was so abhorrent. There was also the little question of how I'd explain my change of heart so he wouldn't be suspicious.

'He'll know it's a trick. Why on earth would he believe I'd suddenly give way like that, after he'd drugged me and threatened my family?'

'Because he's a narcissist. Remember, he truly believes he can manipulate anyone. He knows you're shit-scared of what might happen to your niece. Plus he has no problem believing you secretly enjoyed what he did to you in that hotel room and can't resist coming back for more.'

Still I held out. There would be another way. There had to be. Dominic's emails grew more threatening. After the message with the photo of Grace I didn't dare block him for fear of missing some vital clue that my niece was in danger.

Then the second photograph arrived. It was the same

selfie idea, only this time he was on a bus and Grace was sitting two rows behind. This time she was on her own, still wearing the school blazer, iPhone ear pieces plugged in. Dominic was wearing a grey suit jacket and a black shirt.

You're running out of time, Jessica Gold, read the message. *I might have to start looking for companionship elsewhere. Hmmm . . . where should I start?*

I was at work when I read that, peering at it on my iPhone screen on my lap under my desk. I slumped forward with my head in my hands.

'Are you OK, Jessica?' Joe Tunstall's freckly face was wearing a freckly expression of concern.

Then I went to the women's toilets and locked myself in a cubicle and leaned against the thin partition wall and closed my eyes.

And then I clicked my phone on and sent Natalie a message.

Which is how come I've ended up here in my pyjama bottoms, Skyping with this woman. I can't wait until this is all over and she is out of my life.

But first of all I've got to get *him* out of my life. And for that I need her.

We're looking at each other in silence through our little screens when I hear a noise in the background. It sounds like glasses clinking.

'There's someone there. I heard them. You've got someone with you.'

She denies it.

She's lying.

* * *

At first glance Francesca Dunbar's parents do not give the appearance of people staggering under the weight of a huge sadness, but as they speak, the evidence of the double tragedy they've endured comes through in small ways. Catherine Dunbar's smoothly sculpted face, when not animated with a polite smile, caves in on itself, the skin pleating into folds of grief. Her husband, Andrew, can't quite keep still, his fingers constantly moving, running through his hair or else turning his mobile phone over and over on the meeting room table, until his wife suddenly shoots out a hand and places it over his, trapping it there.

'Thank you for seeing us, Detective Superintendent.'

Catherine's voice is soft but steady, in contrast to the rushed, almost breathless way her husband introduced them. Robertson doesn't tell them he's cut short a fund-raising lunch to be there.

'I hope you didn't have to travel too far. I know you don't live . . .'

'Don't worry about that,' Andrew interrupts. 'We were in town anyway. Our older daughter, Cesca's sister, Anna, lives in London with her family.'

'We just want to know what's happening with him. Dominic Lacey.' When she says his name, Catherine's mouth puckers as if she is sucking on a lemon. 'Is he going to survive?'

'And if so, will you charge him?' Andrew breaks in. 'And what are you going to charge him with?'

His wife closes her eyes momentarily as if well used to him leaping ahead of himself.

'I'm afraid we can't give out very much information at this

point.' Robertson's wide, honest face wears an expression of sincere apology. 'All I can tell you is that Dominic Lacey is alive but he has not yet spoken. As yet no charges have been brought, but obviously we are considering the options very carefully.'

While he is speaking, Catherine Dunbar starts rooting around in her smart leather handbag. When she straightens up, her pale face is flushed pink as if she's been running. Her hair is a perfect blend of ash blonde and silver highlights, so her rosy cheeks appear garish by contrast.

She lays a photograph down on the table in front of them. They are in the small meeting room on the first floor. There's a blue institutional-type carpet and magnolia walls and even a small kettle on the windowsill, although everyone brings their coffee or tea from the kitchen along the corridor. The Dunbars are on the opposite side of the table from where Robertson sits, flanked by Kim and Martin, so Catherine turns the photo round as she pushes it across.

The picture shows a young woman with dull, straight, shoulder-length brown hair parted on the side and wide-set brown eyes. She has her arms wrapped around a little boy, hardly more than a baby, with a mass of fine blond curls, the type that will darken as he gets older, and distinctive blue eyes. They are both smiling into the camera and if it wasn't for the deep purple smudges under the woman's eyes and the sharp angles of her cheekbones, you might think they were a perfectly happy mother and son.

'Our daughter and grandson,' Andrew explains. 'Dominic Lacey murdered them just as surely as if he'd taken out a gun and shot them.'

Kim is finding it hard to look at the photograph. She sees how forcefully the woman is gripping the child, sees the tightness of the smile. She senses her desperation, although how much of her reaction is based on what she knows about the woman's fate, she can't be sure. Cesca Lacey, née Dunbar, loved her son so much she was willing to kill him to save him from danger and to kill herself to be with him.

Kim has moved out of her house and left her children behind. What kind of mother does that make her? She tries not to think about that other case of the mother who killed her baby to save it from herself. She thinks she might not be able to bear it.

'Have you ever met anyone evil, Detective?' Catherine Dunbar's pale, sad eyes are fixed on Kim.

'In the police, we meet a lot of people who've done things that might not exactly win them a badge from the Boy Scouts.' Kim is attempting a light, humorous tone but she is aware of it falling flat. In her mind, she sees Dominic Lacey staring at her from the hospital bed, his eyes two pinpricks of blue.

Catherine looks away and Kim can see she is disappointed. All of a sudden she wishes she could take the flippant answer back and give a different one. But it is too late.

'Dominic Lacey is evil,' says Andrew Dunbar, running his hands through his sandy hair. It is starting to recede on top, and Kim wants to tell him to stop playing with it, but of course she doesn't. 'There's no other word for it.'

The Super looks uncomfortable with the turn the

conversation is taking. He doesn't want to be debating moral absolutes with the Dunbars, Kim suspects.

'Why do you say he killed them?' he asks now, trying to take control. 'As I understand it, he was a couple of hundred miles away when it happened.'

By 'it' he is referring to Cesca Lacey sedating her baby son with sleeping pills and then smothering him with a pillow before hanging herself from the light fitting on the upstairs landing of a borrowed house. Every time Kim remembers this, her chest tightens painfully. She looks again at Catherine Dunbar. Would she be able to keep on going if something like that happened to Rory or Katy?

'I have another photograph here, Detective Superintendent.'

Catherine has withdrawn a different picture from her bag which she now places in front of them, side by side with the other one. It shows a much younger Cesca standing on a beach, steeped in sunshine, her hair bleached with strands of blonde, her skin the colour of honey. She is wearing a bright pink sarong wrapped around under her arms and tied loosely at the neck and is striking a deliberate pose with her hands on her hips. Her smile cracks her face wide open. She isn't beautiful, not like Natalie, but she has something about her. Life.

Next to it, the Cesca in the other photograph looks ten, twenty years older, as if all the exuberance and vitality of the earlier woman has been sucked right out.

'This photograph was taken the summer before she met Dominic Lacey. Just three years before the first one I showed you,' says Catherine. 'Does that surprise you? Cesca had a difficult adolescence. She was terribly shy and found friendships hard to negotiate, but when she went to university all that changed and by the time she was in her early twenties she was starting to come into her own. She had started a job working for a friend of ours who runs a publishing company. Cesca was an assistant in the publicity department. She loved it. I can't tell you what a relief it was to see her happy at last. You don't have children, do you, Detective?'

For one sickening moment, Kim thinks she is addressing her but it is Martin she is talking to.

'No,' he says. 'Not yet.'

Kim is surprised. As far as she knows Martin has never had a relationship that lasted longer than a few weeks. 'I don't do commitment,' he'd once boasted to her. But he sounds almost wistful now with that 'not yet', as if it's something he's aspiring to.

'I thought not,' Mrs Dunbar resumes. 'You won't understand then how heart-wrenching it is to see your children suffer. But as I say, she'd turned a corner.'

'And then she met *him*.' Andrew Dunbar can't resist jumping in, moving the conversation back to Lacey.

'How did they meet, Mr Dunbar?' asks Robertson.

'He was clearing out an office on a different floor of the building where the publishing company is based. You know that's what he does — buying up stuff from businesses that have gone bankrupt. Vulture. She was standing outside with a couple of girls from work who smoke. She was keeping them company. He came up and chatted to them and then Cesca went inside. We believe one of the other girls must have let slip that she had money, because after that he pursued her relentlessly. She wasn't used to that kind of attention. She was completely bowled over.'

'Please understand' – Catherine reaches out across the table and rests her hand briefly on Kim's – 'it's not that we're underselling our daughter. To us she was the most beautiful girl in the world. But a man like that, who is interested only in appearances – in making everyone else envy him – wouldn't have looked at Cesca twice if she hadn't been wealthy.'

'What did you think of him, when you first met him?' Kim asks her.

'I thought he was incredibly charming, incredibly good-looking. But there was a sense in which he was almost *too* charming, do you know what I mean? It was like it was all on the surface of him – something he wore, not something he was.'

Andrew grunts. 'I didn't like him from the start.'

Kim wonders if it is a male trait, this insistence that he wasn't taken in, even if in the end that might mean shouldering more blame for not preventing what happened.

'How quickly did you realize he was a . . . something was amiss?' Martin ventures. Robertson's presence is tempering his usual bullishness.

'For the first six months or so, everything was fine. I've never seen Cesca so happy,' says Catherine. 'But as soon as they got engaged, things began to change. He took control over planning the wedding. Whatever Cesca suggested, he'd very subtly criticize it and if she tried to insist, he'd withdraw until she gave in. She forgave him everything. She said it was just because he wanted the wedding to be so perfect for her. That's what men like that do, they make their failings into someone else's responsibility.'

'And after the wedding?'

Kim is aware of the Super, sitting to her left, glancing fleetingly at the clock on the wall of the room as he moves the conversation on.

'Everything changed. Cesca became even quieter, more reserved.'

'And she kept cancelling arrangements,' Andrew says. 'We'd invite them up for the weekend and either she was always too busy, or they'd accept and then at the last minute there'd be some reason they couldn't come.'

'We bought them a sweet little cottage in Kentish Town as a wedding present,' his wife continues. 'They chose it themselves but apparently as soon as they moved in Dominic wasn't happy with it. He said the proportions were all wrong. The rooms were too small apparently. They made him depressed.'

Kim knows that sweet little cottages in Kentish Town go for well over a million quid.

'When Cesca got pregnant with Sammy, things improved for a while. She came up to stay on her own a couple of times and seemed almost like her old self. And after Sammy was born she just glowed. She loved that little boy so much. We all did.' Catherine Dunbar's voice cracks on that last sentence.

Even with Robertson between them, Kim senses Martin's discomfort. He doesn't deal well with women's emotions.

'But things rapidly deteriorated again. There was always

an excuse for why we couldn't come to stay, and even if we stayed with Cesca's sister, Anna, Cesca mostly wouldn't let us come round. Sammy was sleeping, Sammy had a bug. Then one night, Anna rang us, very upset. She'd been so worried because Cesca kept putting her off, so she'd called round unexpectedly. Cesca didn't want to let her in, but relented in the end. She had a cut over one of her eyes. She said she'd walked into the corner of a kitchen cupboard. Anna says she was so quiet she was practically a zombie.'

'Didn't your older daughter confront Cesca about what was going on?' Martin asked.

'Of course. But the fact is, she was besotted by him. A couple of times she left him and came up to us to stay with Sammy but all he had to do was call her and say he was sorry and tell her she was the love of his life and she'd go back to him.'

'When he started the affair with that *other woman*, Cesca was beside herself.'

Kim suspects Andrew can't bring himself to say Natalie's name. 'She knew it was going on, then?' she asks.

'Oh yes. He used to rub her nose in it. It was part of his way of controlling her. He made her think it was her fault for not being interesting enough. He accused her of letting herself go after Sammy was born.'

Robertson glances up at the clock, again. 'It must have been a relief for you all when Dominic finally walked out,' he says.

'At first it was bloody awful.' Andrew Dunbar again. 'Cesca was in bits. But gradually she came back to us. Bits of her old self began to reappear. But every time *he* came up to see Sammy, it set her back for days.'

'Why did she take out a restraining order?' Martin wants the facts.

'He started turning up out of the blue and following Cesca if she went out. He didn't want her, but he didn't want her to have a life of her own either. He also started taking Sammy off and not bringing him back on time. Once he took him for two nights without telling Cesca where they were going. She was completely beside herself. It was more of his mind games. We consulted our solicitor and he got a court order to restrict Lacey's access to Sammy to supervised contact at a contact centre. He turned up at our home threatening all sorts. We called the police and Cesca took out a restraining order.'

'Did that improve things?' Even as she is asking, Kim knows it's a stupid question. They all know the answer.

To her relief, Catherine Dunbar doesn't remonstrate. 'For a while Dominic stayed away, but even so, something had broken inside Cesca. She was fearful, withdrawn. She jumped at the slightest sound. She was loaded up with anti-depressants and sleeping pills. A doctor advised a fresh start and she and Sammy moved into a house belonging to a friend of ours in a village about half an hour away from us. She hadn't been there a week before she walked past the village pub and saw Dominic Lacey sitting at the bar having a drink.'

'That's what he does, you see?' Her husband can't hold back any longer. 'He fucks with people's heads. She was a nervous wreck. She couldn't focus on anything. He'd made her feel like she was worthless. When she heard he'd applied for full custody of Sam, she just cracked. You know my wife hasn't been able to go upstairs since it happened? Not any stairs. Not in three years.'

Martin is leafing through a pile of notes in front of him on the table. 'But you weren't the one who found them, Mrs Dunbar? I thought—'

'I was at the inquest, Detective. I'm the mother. I'm the grandmother. I listened to the evidence the cleaning lady gave. I saw it all in my head just as clearly as if I'd been there myself. I see it still. Going up the stairs. Seeing Cesca's feet. I even know what shoes she was wearing. The beat-up blue Converses I was always trying to get her to throw out.'

'He drove her to that, and then he got half her money, did you know that?' Andrew Dunbar is glaring at the Superintendent as if he is personally to blame. 'I can't tell you how many times I'd asked Cesca to get her bloody will changed but she was in such a pit of depression by the end she didn't have the energy for anything. Everything was left to him – the London house, the trust she'd inherited when she was twenty-one. The lot. Of course we said we'd challenge it but we ended up having to settle out of court. We could have lost everything. We didn't want to give him that satisfaction. But he murdered our daughter and our grandson, just like he murdered the second one, and was planning to murder Jessica Gold too. I bet there are more as well. Have you searched his computer? What about his photographs?'

'I'm afraid I can't give you that information.'

Like the other two officers, Kim is well aware that the computer-forensics guys have combed through Lacey's hard drive looking for photographs of other potential victims he might have hidden away or even deleted completely. Among the hundreds of largely innocuous images on Lacey's computer, they'd found photographs of three different women all involved in a variety of sexually sadistic practices but they'd all been traced and had admitted that, despite the violence, the sex was consensual – or at least it had started off that way, and even if it had turned nastier than they'd envisaged, they certainly weren't about to press any charges. So what made Jessica Gold the exception? Why suddenly did Lacey decide to kill someone himself?

After the Dunbars finally leave, the atmosphere in the meeting room is heavy.

'Amazing he's been getting away with it all his life.' Two spots of righteous anger colour Martin's cheeks. 'His little sister, his first wife, his second wife. His bloody budgie, for fuck's sake! At least now we can get him on something.'

'But he didn't kill his sister or Cesca or Sam, and there's only circumstantial evidence that says he killed Natalie.' Kim doesn't know how much she is arguing because she believes it, and how much because she wants to disagree with Martin.

'DNA. Fingerprints. How much evidence do you need?' Martin insists.

'Of course there are Natalie's fingerprints in the apartment. She lived there, didn't she? And the DNA doesn't prove she's dead. What about the woman in the Edinburgh jeweller's?'

'And the kidnapping of Jessica Gold? The wounds she suffered? The poison in her system? Will that also turn out somehow not to be his fault?'

By this time the Super has gathered up his things and is standing by the door, clearly impatient to be gone. 'If you have any theories, Detective Harper, I'd be happy to hear them. Lacey is awake now. If he's compos mentis as his doctors seem to believe he is, we're going to have to go back and interview him formally so the CPS can start to form some idea how to charge him. The last thing we want is him out and walking around.'

'I don't think he'll be doing much walking, sir,' Martin says as they leave the room, and Kim is shocked by how much she resents him.

FORTY-THREE

Sonia Rubenstein has pushed the boat out today with a wildly patterned scarf in purples and pinks. Above it her head appears like it is floating on a bed of pansies. She is looking at me in that way she has, with her head cocked slightly to one side, as if she's not entirely sure what to make of me.

'I feel guilty,' I've just told her. 'Even though it wasn't my fault. And Travis isn't supporting me. I shouldn't have gone home with Dominic Lacey, I know that, but it was a lapse in judgement.'

'Another lapse,' she says.

I study her face looking for clues as to her meaning, but it is blank. 'What do you mean?'

'I mean it's not the first time you've done this, is it? Remember how you spent the night with that man you'd just met – the one you met in a café over a year ago? Perhaps when all this has died down a bit we can explore why you've made such poor choices twice now.'

I gaze at her, pretending to be deep in thought, hoping she can't hear the thud of my heart slamming itself against my ribcage.

'The two situations are completely different,' I say. 'You can't compare them. Incidentally' – *slam, slam, slam* – 'I'm assuming you didn't mention that other incident to the police when they talked to you. I did tell you in complete confidence. Isn't there some kind of Omertà code among therapists in cases like this?'

It had been one of those rash, spur-of-the-moment confessions. I hadn't told Sonia about Dominic at first. I actually felt I'd outgrown her. Then when the blackmail first started, I got so stressed I ended up on the couch in Sonia's consulting room, learning visualization techniques for coping with Tube journeys, and I had to come clean. I was too embarrassed to tell her the sordid details of what happened in that hotel room, which I guess makes as little sense as going to see your GP and refusing to get undressed. But I did tell her I'd had a one-night stand with a stranger and was still having to deal with the fallout.

She shakes her head. 'One of the police officers – the woman – did call me to ask about a compromising photograph but a confidence is a confidence. I take the client—therapist privilege very seriously. And besides, I never knew any details about that man so what could I have said? Why is that so important to you, Jessica?'

She has a way of saying my name that makes me feel about five years old.

'I just want to keep some things private. Especially now I've become some kind of public freak show.'

I am courting her sympathy, I realize. I want her to feel sorry for me like everyone else does and talk to me in a soothing voice and tell me how brave I'm being. I want her to recognize what I've been through.

Even if what I've been through is a lie.

In her own living room, on her own sofa, Kim feels out of place. Her mind is still full of work. The Jessica Gold case has got into her bloodstream so it pumps constantly around her brain and she finds it difficult to concentrate on anything else. Not even her own children.

Katy has started doing a new thing every time Kim goes round, sticking to her mother like a plaster, trying to match her little five-year-old's hands to Kim's big adult ones, pressing her cheek to her mother's like she is trying to wear her. Rory shadows her every movement but keeps his distance. He'd make a good undercover cop, it occurs to her.

'When are you coming home? I want you to come home.'

Katy's refrain started approximately thirty seconds after Kim came through the door.

'I just need to finish the case I'm on,' says Kim.

There's a small part of her that actually believes this. Now that she's able to devote so much time to the Gold case, she'll be key to resolving it. Then, once she has the promotion, with the extra money that will mean, Sean will change his mind. She'll move back in. The promotion will make her more confident, happier. The kids will understand.

'I don't know if I'm in love with him any more,' she told Heather last night.

Heather, twice divorced and about to turn forty, gazed at her with something approaching incredulity. 'Grow up,' was all she said.

'Daddy wants you to come home,' says Katy now, shooting Kim a crafty look from lowered eyes. 'He cries at night-time. Like this—' She breaks off to do a helpful imitation of someone crying, deep sobs that sound more like groans.

'Dumbo,' hisses Rory from behind the armchair.

Kim feels her heart bending against its will like metal in a flame.

My visit to Sonia Rubenstein has ruffled me. I'm pretty sure she didn't say anything to the police, but the fact that she could have done just reminds me how precarious this whole edifice is that I've created. My story only works if there is no previous connection between me and Dominic Lacey. I never told anyone at the time and I thought I'd destroyed every possible link – got rid of emails and photographs, and even my laptop, spilling coffee over it so it had to be sold for parts on eBay and another purchased in its place. Yet still I keep being caught out – the screen grab of the Facebook page that Joe made me do and now Sonia remembering what I'd told her about the one-night stand with its ongoing consequences. How I met him in a café, not on the Tube as I told the police. I didn't mention it again, not after that one time, but Sonia never forgets anything.

Though Travis said he probably wouldn't be home, I still get the taxi to drop me off a few streets away and walk, just in case. It's getting dark and I'm wearing one of those lightweight down jackets that is no match for the cold wind that seems to have come out of nowhere. I have that antsy, pins-and-needles feeling that makes it impossible to relax. I call

David Gallant, who soulds like he's in the middle of eating, and absurdly I find myself resenting this, wanting him to be concentrating solely on me to the exclusion of all else. I'm after reassurance that Dominic waking up doesn't change anything, but in the event, reassurance isn't forthcoming.

'I have to prepare you for the possibility that you will face charges, Jessica. And if that happens I can recommend some excellent barristers. But I'm confident that despite this new . . . development . . . any charges would be relatively minor and, taking the circumstances into account, you're unlikely to be looking at a custodial sentence.'

I don't like these words he's using. *Possibility. Unlikely.* I crave certainty. As long as certainty is in my favour. As I come off the phone to David, the need to speak to someone about it all is overwhelming but there is only one person I can talk to.

It's at least nine or ten rings before Natalie finally answers and she sounds out of breath and cross. 'I thought we'd agreed we wouldn't be in touch unless it was necessary. We don't want to take any risks.'

'Yes, I know, but I've got to talk to someone. I'm going crazy. You don't know what it's like being questioned the whole time, having the threat of prison hanging over your head. Why are you breathing like that anyway? Have you been running?'

I start to tell Natalie about the policewoman and how she looks at me as if she doesn't believe a word I'm saying; the daily phone calls I've come to dread. Then, as always, I move the subject back to Dominic, awake now in his hospital bed, biding his time.

'Why did you have to change the plan?' I ask her again. 'After everything we'd agreed? I should have known after the necklace fiasco that you weren't to be trusted.'

'That worked out fine in the end, didn't it?'

'Only because I came up with that stupid story about Dominic getting a friend of a friend to pretend to be you so the police would drop their murder investigation. As if Dominic has friends!'

'And you came up with another perfectly good story when I changed the Christmas Plan, as I knew you would. I have faith in you, Jessica. I just wish you'd do me the same courtesy.'

Unbelievable. She's actually making out she's the wounded party.

'But we had it all worked out,' I remind her. 'We even role-played the phone call. How hard could it be?'

In the original plan, I was supposed to escape while Dominic was out of the flat. The idea was that Natalie would call him on the last day of our twelve-day festive love-in, claiming to work for an upmarket design company that had gone bust and giving him eight hours to price up its stock and clear it out. Dominic and I were supposed to have switched off our phones as part of his 'immersing ourselves in each other' vision. But Natalie insisted his need for control meant he would cheat, and she was right. Whenever I sneaked into the spare room where he'd stashed both our phones, his was on silent. And he checked it every hour or so when he thought I wasn't watching.

Natalie's brief was to make this offer too good to turn down. All the staff of this mythical design company had state-of-the-art Apple Macs, she was to tell him. There was lots of original artwork on the walls. The snob in Dominic would have leapt at the offer. Natalie was a good actress but even so, I made her try out on me her phone voice with a flat Lancashire accent so I could reassure myself he wouldn't recognize her.

Then while he was out of the flat, tearing up the motorway, she would sweep in with all the props we needed for the story. There were the presents she'd carefully wrapped using the thallium she'd ordered off the Internet ('Thank god for the Silk Road,' she said, and it took her ages to convince me there actually was a site where you could buy drugs and illegal chemicals and have them delivered to your door like a pizza). Then there were the brushes she'd painstakingly made from her own hair, and the candle from the fat that had been liposuctioned from her stomach and thighs. Then there was the wash she insisted on slapping over the paintings in the flat. God knows what that was made of (I couldn't even *look* at those lumps). I was convinced it would never dry out in time, though in the event it was a few days before the police ran a check on the artwork. She never told me who she'd got to make the chess pieces from the bits of bone she'd sneaked out of the clinic. Perhaps she really did know some very dodgy people.

I knew Natalie was genuinely terrified of Dominic but I couldn't help feeling part of her was getting off on the melodrama of it all.

The point is, Natalie had very strict instructions. We hadn't left anything to chance. She was supposed to bring with her the presents for my family I'd bought on Christmas

Eve and left in her car after she drove me from Oxford Street to Dominic's flat. And the sketchbook containing the hand-written fictional account of what happened that I'd laboured over for days (and ultimately ended up having to hastily add to when the ending suddenly changed). She was to bring the DIY tattoo kit we'd also bought off the net (she told me she'd done it before. She lied). And of course, the extra thallium.

I'd smuggled a tiny bit in with me in the pocket of the jeans I was wearing when I arrived on Dominic's doorstep on Christmas Eve and I'd started taking it on the tenth day, rubbing it into my skin, and especially my scalp. It was almost funny watching Dominic freak out when he grabbed my hair and a great big hank came off in his hand. 'It's stressful being blackmailed,' I told him. 'It's a wonder I'm not completely bald.' But I needed to take a serious amount more to give credence to our story of being slowly poisoned over twelve days. 'You're sure it's not going to kill me?' I kept asking her as we planned it, but we'd both done the research, so we would be equally to blame if I died a horrible, lingering death. I even ended up adding it to my drinks as well, just to make doubly sure it had an effect.

In the event, Natalie did bring all this stuff just as agreed. Except she never first made the call that was to take him out of the flat and allow for my escape.

'What possessed you?' I say again now, reliving the moment when, lying awake in that dog kennel, with the metal cuff around my ankle tethering me to the bed frame, listening to Dominic's rhythmic breathing, I froze, hearing the sound of a key turning in the front-door lock.

'Will you stop going on about it?' she says. 'There were too many things that didn't add up. Like his phone. Remember?'

She means that he would still have had his mobile on him when he came back to the flat to find it swarming with police after I'd managed to raise the alarm. While he was showering I'd managed to delete his call history and any messages between him and me, but we had no idea what else was on that phone. It was a gamble. As it was, we'd ended up tossing both phones – his and mine – into the Thames, another bit that had to be added into the written account at the last minute.

I don't believe Natalie's excuses. She didn't let herself into the flat while Dominic was still there, on Epiphany Eve, as I've now learned it's called, just because she was worried about us being caught. She did it for revenge. I understand now she'd always meant to do it. Dominic Lacey had abused and degraded her, just as he did me, but instead of lying down and taking it as I had done, she wanted her pound of flesh.

'You're lying,' I insist. 'You enjoyed it. I was there, remember? You enjoyed hurting him.' Saying it out loud, even in the empty street as I walk home, it sounds preposterous.

'Yes, well, I didn't see you holding back either, Jessica Good as Gold.'

Instantly I feel cold. My body temperature plummets. This is what I've blocked out until now. This, more than anything else, is what I cannot face – what happened after Natalie arrived.

In my memory I see Dominic's face, ghostly white in the

moonlight. After unshackling me, she'd picked up his flick knife and forced him from his bed and out on to the balcony where we would leave, she explained to me afterwards, less forensic evidence to worry about. During her enforced exile in Scotland she was addicted to a television programme called *CSI*, she told me. She'd picked up a thing or two, including wearing latex gloves. He'd been at first shocked, then angry when she'd drawn the first blood and he realized she meant it – finally he'd been scared. Natalie liked that. She'd liked seeing him fearful and cowed. We'd both enjoyed seeing him that way. By this stage I'd been locked away with him for eleven days. My body was covered in bruises and cuts that wept when I moved.

He'd called it fun. 'I know you secretly get off on this, Jessica,' he said.

'You have to help,' she told me. 'Get a knife from the kitchen.' By the time I came back with the other knife, she was cutting his throat. I stood in the doorway, frozen.

For the long days I'd allowed myself to be incarcerated with him as his sexual plaything, I'd subliminated my feelings, knowing I could only get through by scrunching them up into a hard, compact ball and making my body into a detachable shell that was completely separate to me. But watching Natalie run her blade across his neck like she was slitting open a banana brought me erupting back to life.

'Now you,' she said, gesturing towards the kitchen knife. 'We both have to be in this together.'

When I remember how it felt plunging it into his chest, the momentary euphoria followed by the wave of revulsion, my brain freezes with the horror of it. And as for what happened next, after Natalie smashed the urn and selected a shard as matter-of-factly as if she was choosing a cut of meat at the butcher's, my mind only allows me to see it in snatches, as if viewing the past through my own fingers.

'It makes more sense in terms of your narrative arc,' she said, gazing down at the jagged piece of china sticking out from her husband's neck. 'For when you write up your account.' *Narrative arc,* I kid you not.

Reminded of all this, my voice on the phone is petulant. 'I never would have done it if you had just stuck to what we agreed.'

I hear a noise in the background, like a door shutting.

'Hang on, don't—' Natalie yells.

'Who's there with you?' I demand.

But Natalie has gone.

FORTY-FOUR

In the doorway of the hospital room, Kim hesitates. It's almost physical, this revulsion she feels, a barrier holding her back from entering. Her lips are dry and she licks them at the same moment she glances over and catches him staring at her with those intense, close-together eyes. Instantly she regrets the gesture, instinctively aware Lacey will assume it is for his benefit.

As she approaches the bed, her heart is thudding so wildly in her chest it is as if it has come loose from its moorings. She keeps reminding herself that he is just another man, a weak man who has something missing in his head, a gap where his sense of right and wrong should be. Labelling him a monster like the commentators on Twitter and other online forums have done gives him too much power. He is just a human being whose psyche was deformed early on. Still, when she forces herself to meet his eyes she has to hold back a shudder.

When the Super called her into his office to tell her that Dominic Lacey had started to speak – or at least write – and had asked for 'the policewoman with the pretty eyes', causing much confusion until the grey-haired doctor worked out he meant Kim, at first she was flattered. Who doesn't like being singled out as special? But in the intervening two hours, she's become increasingly nervous. Martin is with her, and Robertson too. But when the figure in the bed holds up his hand to stop them coming further, they remain just inside the doorway and Kim alone moves forward. As she comes close to him, he opens his mouth and a sound emerges such as she has never heard before – a croaking, gravelly noise that she struggles to understand. He reaches for the notepad on the bed next to him and writes, his fingers moving the pen laboriously over the paper. She wonders how much his brain injury is holding him back.

After what seems like for ever, he finishes and pushes the notebook towards her. She picks it up. At first the writing is hard to decipher, the letters misshapen and badly formed, but when she gets used to them she is able to read what it says: *pink was better.* Instantly she feels her face burning. When she came to the hospital the time before, she was wearing a pink jumper and black trousers. Today she has on the same trousers but with a grey shirt and black jacket. Dominic Lacey watches her face carefully, soaking up her reaction. Even here in the hospital, surrounded by police and medical equipment, with his neck still bandaged and a drip attached to his arm, he is still playing power games. The doctors have told them he is heavily dosed up with morphine and his movements have that sluggish quality. He gestures vaguely towards the chair next to his bed, and she reluctantly sits.

First she reads him his rights and explains that, despite

the circumstances, this is being treated as a formal interview and will be recorded.

He keeps his eyes trained on her as she speaks and she starts to feel flustered, regretting the grey shirt.

'I need to ask you some questions, Dominic,' she says then, following the script she and Robertson have already agreed. 'I need to ask you about what happened in your apartment with Jessica Gold. She has alleged you kept her prisoner in that flat against her will and subjected her to various forms of abuse, including a slow form of poisoning, until she attacked you with a knife in self-defence to save her own life. Does that conform to your own version of events, Dominic?'

His eyes never move from her face as she speaks and she presses her fingernails into her palms to force herself not to look away. The tall doctor with the grey hair and nice shoes is standing over the other side of the room by the window, discreetly keeping watch over her patient. She looks tired today. Kim wonders what she thinks of the man in the bed. Doctors are trained to be objective but surely there must be some people who get under their skin?

'Nah!'

When the noise comes – the rasping croak from the back of Lacey's damaged throat – it takes her by surprise.

She glances at the doctor to see if she can translate. The doctor shrugs almost imperceptibly.

'Can you try again, Dominic?'

'Na–ah!'

She can see he is struggling, the muscles of his face straining.

'I'm afraid I can't understand you. Can you write it down?'

He picks up the pen once more, but this time his movements are slow and he winces when he tries to press the nib down on the paper. Kim waits for him to make his laborious marks on the notepad.

Lacey stops writing and drops the notebook on to the mattress before falling back against the pillows.

She stares at the writing, trying to make sense of the jagged black markings that start off large and get smaller as they cross the page before tailing off into almost nothing. At first she fails to notice it, seeing only a ridge of mountain peaks. Then, magically, they reassemble themselves into a word:

Natalie.

'What does this mean, Dominic?' she asks him. 'You want to see your wife, is that it? Do you know where she is?'

He stares at her, impassive. And then he closes his eyes.

'I think that's enough for now,' says the grey-haired doctor, coming over to check a reading on a monitor.

'But we haven't started properly.' Robertson is by her side, his face dusky with annoyance.

'I'm sorry,' the doctor says. 'His concentration span is very limited. We'll try again tomorrow. Hopefully he'll feel more like talking.'

Kim finds herself at the same time relieved and disappointed.

Outside in the car park, Martin is keen to place his interpretation on the cryptic one-word message. 'I think he was about to confess. He knows the game is up. He's going to try to make some sort of deal. He'll tell us what he's done with Natalie in return for a lesser charge on Jessica Gold.'

Robertson looks at Kim. 'What's your opinion?'

'I don't know, sir. But knowing what we do about Dominic Lacey I'd be very surprised if he was about to admit to anything. Maybe he was trying to tell us something about where Natalie is.' Now another explanation occurs to her. 'Or maybe he was even saying there's a connection between her and Jessica. Why else would he reply "Natalie" when the question was expressly about Jessica?'

'But Natalie Lacey and Jessica Gold have never crossed paths.'

'No, sir, but I still have this feeling that Jessica isn't being completely transparent.'

Kim is aware that without any evidence she sounds as clueless as Martin, tossing theories around like confetti.

After the Super has driven off in his car, she and Martin make their way to hers.

'Do you think it's a woman thing?' he asks her as he buckles up his seatbelt.

'What?'

'Your refusal to see Jessica Gold as a victim, despite the fact she had wounds all over her body and could have died? Do you think you're just not a woman's woman?'

Kim thinks about reaching over the hand-brake and grabbing hold of his hair and slamming his head down hard on to the dashboard.

For a split second it actually makes her feel better.

From: nowalkinthepark@hotmail.com
To: ddc115@hotmail.co.uk
Subject: WTF
Just listened to your message from last night.
There's no need to make such a big fuss just
because I didn't pick up. I'm confused though.
Why did Dominic ask to see your Family Liaison
woman? How does he even know who she is? And what
did he tell her?

From: ddc115@hotmail.co.uk
To: nowalkinthepark@hotmail.com
Subject: re: WTF
I called you five times. I have no idea why he
asked for Kim. All Kim told us is he still isn't
speaking properly but he wrote down one word.
Natalie. He's going to pull through. And then
he's going to tell them everything and we're
going to prison for a very long time. Why did I
ever let you talk me into this?

From: nowalkinthepark@hotmail.com
To: ddc115@hotmail.co.uk
Subject: re: re: WTF
Let's just think. You let me talk you into this
because you wanted to save your thirteen-year-old
niece from a blackmailing, sadistic psychopath.
And save yourself while you were at it, so Mummy
and Daddy wouldn't have to turn on the telly and
see a film of their darling daughter trussed up

like a side of beef and being sodomized by my
husband.

From: ddc115@hotmail.co.uk
To: nowalkinthepark@hotmail.com
Subject: re: re: re: WTF
So what do we do? Kim's going in to see him
again tomorrow evening. He'll tell her
everything.

From: nowalkinthepark@hotmail.com
To: ddc115@hotmail.co.uk
Subject: re: re: re: re: WTF
Then it will be his word against yours. Don't
forget that as well as your written statement and
the fact that you were almost dead, there's also
the case for my murder. With all my DNA around
the apartment there's no way he can convince them
I just disappeared of my own accord. You just
have to hold your nerve.

FORTY-FIVE

Kim can't remember the last time she was so nervous before an interview with a suspect. Back at Heather's flat, she'd put the pink jumper on and stood in front of the bathroom mirror for a long time before swapping it for a blue top and the black jacket. She took extra care with her make-up, and then felt disgusted with herself.

Now in the station, she's scrolling through all the police reports without really seeing them, checking the time every minute or so. When her mobile rings she sees Sean's name on her screen and feels a pang of irritation, and then guilt.

'Rory's not good,' he tells her, as if it's her doing.

Kim's stomach cramps with anxiety as she asks him why.

'A bad tackle at after-school football. I always said that Connor kid was a nutter. Rory fell on his arm. We've just arrived at A&E. He's asking for you. How soon can you get here?'

The hospital in North London is in the opposite direction from the hospital in the East End where Dominic Lacey is being treated. Her poor boy. But why now, when she is on the point of one of the biggest moments of her career? Why not an hour ago or two hours later? Of course she knows the answer. There will always be domestic crises, and there will always be career crunch points, and they will always coincide, pulling her in opposite directions.

'I'll come just as soon as I finish questioning the suspect in the Jessica Gold case.'

There's a silence, followed by an explosion. 'What? Please tell me you're not serious. Your eight-year-old son has broken his arm and you're going to fit him in after you've finished work?'

'Tell Rory I'll be there just as quickly as I can. It's just that I have to do this.'

Walking alone through the main hospital entrance, she feels oddly vulnerable and wishes for the first time that Martin was with her. When Robertson first told her Martin wouldn't be accompanying them to the interview, she'd been quietly thrilled. Though there was a reason given – a lead on a potential witness that needed checking out – Kim can't help feeling it's a vote of no confidence in her partner. She wonders if it means the Super has made up his mind about his recommendation and immediately slaps herself down for tempting fate.

She steps out of the lift on the second floor and through the double doors on the left, expecting to find Robertson waiting for her. Instead she is greeted by a scene of complete chaos. Uniformed police officers and white-coated doctors block the corridor, and when she pushes through to the doorway of Lacey's room, it is a blur of activity and noise, with medical staff and police crowded around Lacey's bed, and everyone shouting over everyone else. Kim spots her superior in a corner of the room and goes to find him, flashing her badge at a uniform on the door who tries to stop her going in.

As she crosses to her boss, she tries not to look at the inert figure in the bed, but she senses immediately – from the absence of that peculiar intensity Dominic Lacey generated – that their suspect is dead.

'A nurse raised the alarm half an hour ago,' the Super explains, as they make their way out of the over-crowded room. 'The last time Lacey was checked he was OK. Weak, but stable, as he was when we saw him yesterday. Then less than an hour later he's dead. Looks like he just stopped breathing. I really thought we were on the verge of getting somewhere. What a fucking cock-up!'

The boss is known for his calm, almost plodding manner. It's the first time she's seen him lose his composure. The corridor outside has emptied since she first arrived and they sink down on to the chairs recently occupied by uniformed police guards. She feels numb. Since yesterday she has been building herself up to another encounter with Dominic Lacey and now it has come to nothing.

She feels her phone vibrate in her handbag with an in-coming call.

She lets it ring on.

'I don't believe it.'

My voice in my own ears sounds strangely flat and unconvincing.

It will be all over the news shortly, Kim says, so she wants to give me the heads-up. I think fleetingly about that term 'heads-up' and wonder what on earth it means.

I don't know how to feel.

I ought to be either elated that the bastard is gone, or else terrified because it means I could be charged with murder. But instead I am detached, as if it is someone I hardly know, a friend of a friend I once met at a party and have difficulty recalling their face.

'What's the matter?' Mum is watching me anxiously. 'What did Kim want?'

I wish I was back at my flat where I could turn this news over in my head to find out how I feel, but my parents are both looking at me across the dinner table which is still strewn with our finished plates, and I have to say something.

'Dominic Lacey is dead,' I say out loud, and then I start laughing as if it's the most tremendous joke.

My mother clamps her hand to her mouth and stares at me in horror, while my father knits his brows together. Neither knows what to make of me. So what's new?

I am desperate to call Natalie. There's a childish side of me that wants to be the one to break the momentous news.

I excuse myself, push back from the table and run upstairs with my phone.

In the bathroom I try Natalie's number again and again, but she doesn't pick up.

In between failed attempts I lean back against the tiles and think about Dominic. I think about the small boy forced to sit on that plastic stool and watch his father having violent sex with a woman who wasn't his mother, and about his mother literally smothering him with a love that was more like obsession. I think of his little sister Bella, who shouldn't have died, and the teacher who'd only wanted to make a difference. I think of poor Cesca and baby Sam in his mini football kit. I think of Natalie and me and all the other people whose lives will never be the same because of him.

After a while I go back downstairs where my parents have clearly been discussing the best way to behave around me.

'You mustn't blame yourself for—' my father starts the minute I step into the hallway.

'Can't talk now,' I call, pulling on my scarf and coat. 'I've got to go.'

'Jessica!' my mother has hurried out and has her hand on my arm. 'Come on. We need to talk about this.'

'No, Mum,' I say, gently removing her hand. '*We* don't need to talk about anything.'

All the way home in the taxi I keep trying Natalie's number, frustration growing exponentially with the number of unanswered rings. My earlier detachment has given way to a churning biliousness and images of Dominic pass through my head on a continuous loop. The way he looked when he first introduced himself at that department-store café, his stiff, scarcely held-in excitement when he inflicted pain, his tenderness when he washed the wounds he'd caused, his look of betrayal when Natalie let herself into his flat and he grasped he'd been set up, the utter incomprehension on his face when she slid the knife across his throat.

I need to talk to her. I need to ask her why I feel like something in me has died with him.

But she's not answering.

Bursting into our flat, I search out Travis. He was still at work when I left to have dinner at my parents' but he should be back by now, yet as soon as I let myself in I can tell the flat is empty. Switching on the television, I turn straight to the twenty-four-hour news channel. The first thing that appears on the screen is a photograph of Dominic and this confirmation of his death hits me like a punch to the stomach. On screen the police officer with a ruddy face is saying that at this time it appears Dominic died from injuries sustained during the incarceration of Jessica Gold, although a full autopsy will be carried out.

They flash up a photograph of me taken on graduation day at Manchester with the wind blowing my hair up in a dark cloud behind me and making my dress billow. I am smiling and holding on to the mortar board on my head to stop it blowing away.

Alone on the sofa in my flat, I find myself weeping for the girl I won't ever be again.

FORTY-SIX

Kim knows she looks appalling. She has not slept all night and her grey eyes are ringed with shadows. Sean would not look at her when she walked through the front door last night after pushing her way out of the hospital past a throng of television crews from all over the world. When she'd rung him from the car, he told her only that they were back home, adding only, 'Suit yourself,' when she told him she was on her way.

Rory looked so pale and small on the sofa with a blanket over his legs and his purple cast resting on his chest. Kim felt a rush of love so powerful she almost couldn't breathe.

She flung herself across the room and wrapped her arms around him, planting kisses on his forehead and cheeks.

'Ow, Mum. Careful.'

She pulled back to look at him properly. He was holding his arm with a kind of awed pride, but she could see shock and pain still etched on his hollow, delicately featured face. When he went to bed just after eleven, she insisted on going up with him and sleeping in a sleeping bag on the floor next to his bed in case he needed her in the night.

When Katy woke up in the morning and found her mother in the house she was so excited Kim felt her heart breaking all over again.

Now, back in the office, she feels like something that has been dug up. Something less than human.

'Kim. Come with me, please.'

Robertson has come bursting out of his glass-walled office, shrugging on his jacket, and is already waiting for her by the door. Kim has a brief glimpse of Martin's hurt expression before she rushes to join him.

'Where are we going, sir?'

'Savile Row,' says Robertson, naming a police station in the West End. 'Natalie Lacey has reappeared.'

I've hardly slept – and when I did I dreamed of that baby I never had except it wasn't my baby, it was poor little smothered Sam with a blue face just like Bella's. 'It's not my fault,' I kept saying. 'I didn't kill him. It's not my fault.' Except I knew it was.

At some point in the night, I tried Natalie's phone again and instead of ringing, it went dead as if it had been cut off. Travis still hasn't come home. Sometimes it happens that the hospital is short-staffed and he has to cover for someone at the last minute, so he'll grab a few hours' sleep in one of the overnight rooms before starting another shift, but he usually calls. I wonder what the chances are that he hasn't yet heard about Dominic Lacey's death and decide they're quite low. Hospitals are renowned for being insular places where news from the outside world rarely penetrates, but in this case Lacey was in the same building. Word would have spread.

I'm sure of it. Besides, by now half the world's media must be camped outside the main doors.

I'm back on the sofa, watching the television. The news is showing the same clips over and over. Me walking out of the hospital on the day I was released. Photos of Dominic and of Natalie and of the apartment in Wapping. When they start showing footage from the balcony of the flat below his with the view of the river and the Shard in the distance, I feel sick and change the channel fast.

Sometimes when you meet people in the flesh after only having seen them in photographs, it's hard to recognize them, but in Natalie Lacey's case it's like the two-dimensional image on the page has burst into life. Everything from her blonde-streaked hair to her startling green eyes is just as Kim would have expected from pictures she's seen, and from the painting on Lacey's wall. Only her nose seems different. Smaller somehow.

'I was terrified of my husband,' she is telling the two detectives in the interview room with her. Kim and Robertson are watching from a neighbouring room, through a two-way mirror. 'As soon as I heard he was dead, it was like a massive weight lifting off me. Finally I can pick up my life again.'

Natalie has already talked them through what life was like married to Dominic Lacey. She has shown them scars on her wrists and legs, and was about to take her top off to show the ones on her back, but the detectives told her it wasn't necessary.

'What do you make of her?'

Kim tries to analyse her own reactions before replying to her superior's question. 'Well, on one hand I can't help feeling this is all a bit of a show. She's like an actress, don't you think, sir? Have you noticed how she keeps looking up here? She knows she's being observed and she's playing to it.'

'And on the other?'

'I would say she seems genuinely to have been afraid of her husband. Her voice changes when she talks about him, it gets smaller and kind of harder.'

Robertson nods, not giving much away. 'She didn't waste much time before making her reappearance,' he says.

'Well, I guess she's been waiting for the chance to step back into her old life, and now that he's gone . . .'

The Super nods and turns back to the window. 'I'm sure that's true,' he says. 'Nevertheless, I think it's worth checking whether Dominic Lacey left a will. Nothing like an inheritance for bringing grieving widows back to life.'

FORTY-SEVEN

When Kim says it the first time, I think I've misheard. I ask her to repeat it.

'Natalie Lacey turned up in a central-London police station early this morning. She isn't dead.'

The room starts spinning and I have to close my eyes until it stops.

I say how wonderful I think the news is.

'Of course, now there's no possibility that Dominic Lacey murdered his wife, or in fact anyone, it slightly changes the complexion of the case,' Kim goes on.

After I come off the phone, I am hit by a wave of panic as I work out what she means. Now there's no evidence of a pattern of murder, now that murder isn't part of his MO – I think that's the right term – it's even more of a mystery why he kidnapped me, intending to kill me. It doesn't fit his pattern.

I pick up my phone to try Travis' number but get put through to his voicemail. I leave yet another message to add to all the others.

Now Natalie has come out, I am totally alone and I can't bear it. Turning the television back on, I flick through the channels restlessly, trying to calm my racing thoughts. I pause on a soap opera, my eye caught by something in the scene. At first I can't work out what it is that attracted my attention but then I realize it's the curtains. They're made from the same fabric as the cushions in Travis' parents' living room.

And now I'm running for the bathroom, feeling the bile rising up into my mouth.

That's why I recognized the cushion when I was Skyping Natalie.

Her safe house is Travis' parents' home.

Since this morning's visit to Savile Row, adrenalin has replaced tiredness and Kim's mind is jumping around from place to place like a flea on a dog's coat. Martin was sniffy when she returned, and didn't seem to think there was much to be read into the timing of Natalie Lacey's reappearance.

'Why wouldn't she come back now? She was petrified of her husband and now he's dead. Simples.'

It is simples, as Martin says, and yet there's something else buzzing at the edges of Kim's consciousness that she can't quite crystallize into thought.

At lunchtime she calls home and speaks to Rory. His voice sounds small and tearful and when she asks to speak to Sean he says Dad was called into work so Teri is there. The babysitter comes to the phone and assures her she doesn't mind at all and tells her how brave Rory is being.

Kim hangs up and puts her head in her hands. It's still there when Robertson calls her and Martin in to his office.

'There's been a development,' he says.

'Don't tell me, Cesca Dunbar has just strolled into a police station.' Kim suspects Martin is attempting to be funny to show he's not bothered about being left out of this morning's trip to Savile Row.

'I had a call an hour ago from the medical examiner. Unofficially, preliminary investigations indicate Dominic Lacey didn't die of his existing injuries. Signs are he died of an overdose of insulin. I checked with the hospital, and they've just come back to me to say they believe his saline drip was tampered with.

'It's very likely Dominic Lacey was murdered.'

When Travis lets himself into the flat, I'm so taken aback that there's a delay before I recognize him. Already in my mind he's gone from boyfriend to stranger and his sudden presence in the living room feels like a shocking intrusion.

He drops his keys on the table without speaking and sinks down into the lumpy-cushioned armchair.

Taking off his glasses, he rubs the lenses with the hem of his T-shirt. His eyes are red-ringed, the whites threaded through with tiny pink veins, and there's at least two days' growth on his top lip and chin. I am reminded suddenly of the time he tried to grow a goatee, and his outrage when he saw his beard was coming through ginger.

He replaces his glasses and then at last he speaks. 'I could say I'm sorry, but what would be the point?'

If passive-aggressive hadn't already existed, Travis would have just invented it.

'She's just using you,' I point out. 'Women like Natalie Lacey don't go for speccy junior doctors.'

He shrugs, not bothering to argue.

'How long has it been going on?'

He glances at me with his pink lab-mice eyes and then looks away again.

'Come on. I deserve to know that at least. Did she contact you during those twelve days that I was away? Before?'

It's that one point in the day where the sun is at the right angle to penetrate our living room, and a shimmer of dust hovers in the patch of pale light in between us.

'*When*, Travis?'

I need to hear I'm wrong. I need to hear that despite all the other parts of my life that have turned out to be lies, this one truth at least remains.

'I met her in November.'

I relax. This I can cope with.

'November the year before last.'

There's a sickening lurch as the world shifts from one reality to another. November the year before last was one month before Dominic Lacey came up to me in the department-store café, before our first encounter in the Luton airport hotel.

And now I understand.

It wasn't chance. It wasn't random. Dominic Lacey targeted me because of Travis.

Rage is a lump in my throat too big to swallow.

'It was a one-night stand.' Travis isn't looking at me. 'I'd treated her at A&E a couple of times before, injuries she said she'd sustained kickboxing. Of course I knew what was really going on. We're trained to look for that sort of thing. What can I say? She just got to me.'

'So a victim of domestic abuse comes to you for help and you shag her? Classy.'

'The next day I felt awful. As a doctor it was unforgivable.'

'And as a boyfriend? What about that?' My voice has risen until it is a shrill note reverberating in the air.

Travis shakes his head in disbelief. 'Don't play the moral-outrage card, Jessica. Not after you did exactly the same thing a month later.'

He means by sleeping with Dominic. I open my mouth to tell him how it is different. Then close it again.

'After that I didn't hear from her again for months. I felt guilty. I tried to make it up to you. Of course I didn't realize you had guilty secrets of your own.'

Now it's my turn to look away.

'Then last September, out of the blue, she called me up. She said she'd left him. She said she wanted to see me. I was flattered. You'd been acting so distant and so weird with those episodes where you blanked out and couldn't remember anything, or came home with bruises you couldn't explain. Course I didn't know then you were just covering up for your little bondage sessions.'

I ignore the childish barb. September. That would be when Natalie was holed up in Edinburgh, going stir-crazy with boredom. I can just imagine her scrolling through her list of past conquests wondering who to ˜contact next.

'You're not the Saudi playboy by any chance, are you?' I ask him.

He gives me a blank look. 'I travelled up to Scotland overnight to meet her.'

'That would be when you told me you were on secondment to the teaching hospital in Newcastle?'

He nods. 'I fell in love with her.'

I'm amazed how much it hurts, hearing him say it.

'I told her she could stay at my parents' house while they were away in Florida. I wanted to protect her.'

The idea of Natalie needing protecting is laughable.

'I became obsessed with her. I went to see her whenever I could get away.'

'So why didn't you just leave me?'

Travis shrugs. 'Because you seemed so lost. Because I wasn't completely sure that this thing with Natalie would ever amount to anything. Because I was weak.'

'Because you're a knob.'

He raises a tight smile. 'That too.'

The silence that follows reverberates with what Travis didn't say. *Because I love you.*

'So when did you realize there was a connection to me?'

'I was jealous, convinced she was seeing other men behind my back. Whatever you think, I'm not a complete idiot. I know she's out of my league and it made me paranoid. We hardly saw each other and then when we were together she'd go off to make phone calls or send texts. We had a huge row about it one night and I grabbed hold of her phone and went to her call list to find the last number she'd called. And it was yours.'

I allow myself a smile at this. It is funny, after all.

'So she had no idea either, that you and I were together?'

'No. She thought you were just some woman he'd randomly picked up. Of course, once she realized you were my girlfriend, she guessed immediately that he'd deliberately targeted you in a tit-for-tat act of revenge. She said that's exactly how his mind would work. Natalie reckoned that's partly what this Christmas lock-in thing was about – he liked the idea you'd be with him instead of me. He'd probably present me with some sort of souvenir video afterwards, she thought.'

Now something else is occurring to me. 'Did you know the whole time that I was planning to spend Christmas with him? And you didn't try to stop me?'

He shakes his head. 'Don't be stupid. I'd never have let you go through with it.'

'Not even to help the new love of your life?'

Sarcasm drips off my tongue but Travis doesn't rise to it.

'I rang her the night you disappeared to find out if she knew what was going on, and she told me then what you'd planned. I was absolutely livid. I tried to force her to tell me the address – I'd treated her in the hospital, don't forget. I knew what that animal was capable of. But then she told me about Grace being in danger and convinced me that Lacey wasn't going to hurt you – not unless he felt under attack. She told me if I told anyone, she'd disappear and I'd never see her, or probably you, again. She never told me where he'd taken you – or that anyone was going to get killed.'

I decided to believe him because the alternative was too awful to contemplate. Something else occurs to me. 'That's another thing. The police went through your phone records when they were investigating you. How come they didn't find any record of all these touching little chats?'

He makes a face at me – the kind of face that says, '*Really?*'

'A second pay-as-you-go mobile phone. The cheater's best friend. I'm surprised you never thought about getting one, too.'

We glare at each other, and then each look away.

'If you must know, Christmas was horrible. I was going out of my head with worry about you. I hated lying to your family. But Natalie convinced me this was the one way you were both going to be able to get rid of that bastard. And she has a hold over me, I can't even explain it.'

'She's just using you,' I say again. 'She needed somewhere to stay. She was bored. Do you really think she's going to look at you twice now she's staged her triumphant comeback?'

Now it's Travis' turn to be shocked. His face, already pale, turns chalky white.

'What do you mean?'

'You didn't know, did you? Now Dominic Lacey is dead, Natalie has taken out those contact lenses, dyed her hair back, donned some widow's weeds and come back from the dead.'

'Bitch,' Travis whispers to himself and I can see that though he's upset, this development isn't entirely un-expected. 'She's after his money,' he says, flatly. 'That's what she's been after all along. Now he's dead, as his wife she stands to inherit everything.'

Of course. It's so obvious. Why didn't it occur to me before? That's why she turned up at the flat and tried to kill him. It was never about just getting him out of the way. She wanted him dead.

'What the fuck did you see in her?' I can't stop myself. 'You must have known you were just a distraction, a means to an end?'

'I could ask you the same thing,' he says. 'You and Dominic Lacey. What possessed you?'

We exchange glances, two tired, angry people just starting to grasp that the great drama of their lives is nothing but a side show in someone else's.

He groans, letting his head fall into his hands. 'I can't believe I've been so stupid.'

I don't reply. I'm too busy thinking what a coincidence it is that Natalie wanted Dominic dead, and now he is dead, even though everyone expected him to pull through. And now I'm looking at Travis' bent head and his shoulders shaking through his T-shirt and I'm thinking, no.

No, no, *no*.

FORTY-EIGHT

Kim, Martin and the Super are clustered around the computer screen in Robertson's office, so close together Kim can smell the fried bacon Martin had for breakfast. They are watching CCTV footage taken from the camera in Dominic Lacey's hospital room.

'Six different staff members adjusted Lacey's intravenous equipment in the timeframe the medical examiner has indicated,' Robertson is explaining. 'Five of them have been traced and questioned. This one remains a mystery.'

The footage shows a bearded, white-coated doctor with a security pass around his neck and short, thick dark hair. He has his back to the camera and is fiddling with the saline bag feeding into the intravenous tube. Lacey himself has his eyes closed and appears to be asleep.

'Did the guards get a good look at him?' Martin wants to know.

'Well, that's the interesting thing.' Robertson seems to be quite enjoying this. 'Take a look at the footage from the corridor outside Lacey's room in the minutes just before our mystery doctor pays his bedside visit.'

This time the footage is much grainier. As Kim squints,

she can make out the two uniforms sitting on plastic chairs. One of them is looking at his phone, the other appears to be in the middle of recounting a story. Then there is some sort of commotion at the double doors to the lifts and one of the guards gets up to investigate. Because of the camera angle, it's hard at first to see what's going on, then a woman with short dark curly hair appears briefly in the corridor, waving her arms around. She seems drunk or upset and the second officer gets up to help his colleague deal with her. While they are engaged in animated conversation with the woman, the bearded doctor appears, flashes his security pass and is waved through. By the time he reappears, just moments later, the guards are bundling the woman through the doors and he is able to slip past, almost unnoticed. The whole thing doesn't last two minutes.

'And the morons didn't get any descriptions at all?' Martin is disgusted.

'The woman apparently has blue eyes, the man brown, although one of the guards described them as more hazel. But that's about it.'

The three detectives straighten up and Kim hears her back creaking like an old woman's. Heather's spare bed is proving not very comfortable.

'So the woman couldn't be Natalie Lacey, sir,' she asks.

Robertson shrugs. 'It would be neat if it was, but the description doesn't match. Besides, the man had a hospital security pass.'

Martin folds his arms across his white shirt, and Kim notices that the cotton is straining. His is the type of physique that will run to fat if he doesn't work at staying in shape.

'A man like Lacey will have made loads of enemies. I'm sure those women in the photos we got from Lacey's hard drive wouldn't be too happy about their bondage sessions being made public. We need to start re-interviewing them,' he suggests

'Good idea,' says the Super, and Kim is annoyed by her own childish jealousy at hearing her colleague praised.

Only after she's left Robertson's office and is sinking back into her seat does it occur to her that Natalie Lacey is a professional stylist who makes her living from knowing how to transform a person's appearance.

After so long being the victim, it feels something of a relief to be looking after someone else for a change. Travis is like someone who's been in a traumatic accident. All his reactions are delayed and when I say something to him he looks confused as if he's having to translate it in his head.

Part of me thinks, 'Serves you right.' But a bigger part of me has had enough of seeing people hurt and in pain. He is a survivor too. And we survivors must support each other.

We both know this is the end for the two of us. Not so much because of what we've done with other people, but because of who we've been. With Natalie, Travis was a man in love, and even though she turned out to be a fake, it's too late now to stuff all that love back into whatever bag he's been hiding it in. And he can't get past all the things I never told him.

It's the secrets he can't accept, he says. Not the betrayal itself. But that's not entirely true. He can't stand the things I've done with Dominic Lacey that I've never done with him. In the end, it's what's lacking in our relationship that will be the end of it – the things we haven't done, rather than the things we have.

I'll move back to my parents' house, I suppose. It'll be weird to move back home at nearly thirty. My mum and dad will pretend not to mind but I know they'll miss that veneer of normality that Travis lends me. Though, after all the publicity, I'm not sure how normal my life will ever be again.

'At least my notoriety will ensure a capacity turn-out at Mum's next book-group meeting.

After Travis has gone to bed, I start thinking about Natalie and all the things she's done, the people she's used. Dominic broke her in the end, I don't doubt that. She earned her payoff from him. But not at my expense, or Travis' either. I haven't asked him whether it's a coincidence that Dominic Lacey died at the same hospital where he works. I don't want to know. Travis is a doctor – he's been trained to preserve life, not to end it. A thing like that would mark a person. A thing like that would change a person's view of themselves.

I should know.

The more I think about Natalie, the angrier I get. I met people like her at university. Careless people who'd toss out an invite to a night out and then forget to call, leaving you sitting at home with newly washed hair, watching *Casualty* in your best clothes. That they don't mean to be cruel is what hurts the most. It's not because they don't like you. It's because they don't think about you. You don't feature.

I remember now how it felt to be Natalie, if only briefly.

Dressed up in her expensive clothes – the bright pink top with the deep neckline, the overlong skin-tight leggings, the wedding dress.

A little seed of excitement starts to grow. I picture the long white strappy dress, cut on the bias, with the slightly damaged hem where it had dragged on the sand. I remember how surprised I was that Natalie had settled for a low-key private wedding on a beach rather than a big showy production with her at the centre of it. It didn't make sense at the time. Dominic had described it as a romantic gesture, but now a different explanation is suggesting itself.

If he was still married to Francesca Dunbar, stalling on a divorce that would cut him off from all that money, he and Natalie would have had to settle for a token ceremony, probably on a beach somewhere.

I take out my laptop and spend an hour or so Googling 'beach weddings India illegal'.

Then I Google 'Andrew and Catherine Dunbar contact details'.

Then I write a very long email.

FORTY-NINE

Kim wasn't planning on coming into work today. It's Saturday and she woke up sickened by the whole Jessica Gold case which has smeared itself across her consciousness like a grubby stain. She'd arranged to go to the house this morning and found she couldn't wait to spend time with her children, breathing in their innocence. But when she called Sean to let him know she was on her way, he told her, in the new brusque voice he reserves for her, that both children were out – Rory at a friend's and Katy at a Saturday-morning dance class. One of the other mothers had taken a group of them.

So now Kim is in the office and feeling bereft. It occurs to her that this is how things will be if she and Sean separate. Yes, there will be times when she will relish being free to immerse herself in work, but there will also be times where her life seems empty enough to lift up and blow clean away. She wants the promotion, the recognition, but without the children, who is she doing it all for?

Sometimes she misses them so much she can't breathe.

She logs into her emails and is surprised to find a message from Catherine Dunbar. She opens it and reads how the Dunbars have just discovered Dominic's 'wedding' to Natalie took place while he was still very much married to Cesca, rendering that second marriage little more than a sham. Natalie, it seems, will not automatically inherit Lacey's fortune. In fact, with the Dunbars preparing a legal challenge, it seems very likely that the money he got after his first wife's death will now revert back to her family.

Kim allows herself a smile as she pictures the expression on Natalie Lacey's face when she hears that news.

Before long, though, the black mood returns and she is plunged back into gloom thinking about Katy and Rory and how they are growing up, getting independent lives. Whoever worked life out got the design all wrong, it seems to her. There's such a narrow window of opportunity when your children need you – why does that window have to overlap with the very years when you're expected to be building up your career, feeling most creative? Why couldn't your kids' needs coincide with the retirement years, say, when you'd have so much more time to give them? And so much more willingly?

She forces herself to focus on work. After Martin's bright idea that they should get back in touch with the women in Dominic Lacey's picture library, IT have sent her a disc of photos. There's a covering note attached warning that though most of the photos are perfectly innocuous, the ones featuring women are pretty hardcore. Kim sighs. She once spent eighteen months working on Vice and has never managed to come to terms with how people can derive pleasure from watching women or, worse, children in pain and distress.

The photographs, all recovered from Lacey's hard drive, are in no particular order. She scrolls through and winces when the hardcore images come up, somehow more shocking in the mundane context of the semi-deserted station. Women hooked up to various contraptions, close-ups of flayed skin and what looks to be burn marks on arms and buttocks.

Other images are clearly related to his work. There's a series of photographs of individual items in a furniture warehouse he was obviously pricing up – picture after picture of Italian leather sofas in cream or red and elaborate glass dining tables. It doesn't surprise Kim to find that Lacey has also taken many photographs of himself. As a narcissist, it makes perfect sense he'd be his own favourite model.

There are moody black and white shots of him on the balcony of his flat, with Tower Bridge in the distance and the Shard looming up behind it. There are photographs of him on a beach somewhere, his shoulders tanned and well defined. Even though he's dead, Kim can't look into those eyes without a shiver, the hypnotic pull of them wrenching her out of her world and into his. He's even taken a photograph of himself on the top deck of a bus. Alone in the office, Kim snorts with derision at the sheer vanity of it. Then, abruptly, she stops laughing.

'Oh my god,' she says out loud, to no one.

Her mouth is dry and her heart slams painfully against her ribcage.

Two rows behind Lacey sits a schoolgirl in a blazer with long brown hair and headphones in her ears. If you were glancing through the photographs you wouldn't even notice her, a young girl lost in her own thoughts, gazing out through the window. But Kim notices her because she recognizes her.

It's Grace Gold.

Discovering that Natalie won't, after all, be getting rich, puts me in the best mood I've been in since before this whole thing started. She thought she could use me to get what she wanted, just like her husband. And now it's all been for nothing. I pour myself a large glass of wine, even though it's not yet midday and, feeling buoyant, I decide to be productive for a change and open some of the mail that's been stacking up on our dining table. The reporters and news crews have largely disappeared now, but Travis and my parents have diligently collected all the envelopes they stuffed through the letterbox during the giddy days following my release, and still the odd letter arrives, plopping into our communal hall along with the flyers from pizza outlets and cab companies and charity bags for unwanted clothes.

After looking in on Travis, who is curled up on his side in bed facing away from the door so I can't tell if he's awake or not, I take the pile of post to the sofa and rip open the envelope on the top.

All this time Kim has been convinced Jessica Gold was hiding something and now she has the evidence. This photograph of Dominic Lacey, with Jessica Gold's niece in the background, can't be a coincidence and it proves there's a link between them that predates Christmas Eve. She goes back through the photos, paying special attention to the backgrounds. Finally she finds it, another selfie in a park somewhere. Dominic is in the foreground and there in the background on a bench are two girls in school ties and short skirts with the waistbands rolled up in that way they all wear them. The one on the left is Grace Gold.

Now there can be no doubting that there was absolutely nothing random about Jessica Gold being in Dominic Lacey's apartment. In both images the girl seems completely unaware of Lacey's presence, as if he's a total stranger, which leads Kim to believe the pictures must be a warning. She takes a deep breath in, trying to calm her racing nerves. And then she gets a piece of printer paper and writes down everything she now knows about Jessica Gold.

Dear Jessica

I hope you're recovering after your traumatic ordeal.

You might be aware that the Chronicle *newspaper has been a constant champion of yours over the days of your imprisonment. We have kept the story in the public eye and canvassed tirelessly for information that might lead to your release.*

Now that you're thankfully free, we'd love to build our relationship further by inviting you to collaborate with a series of exclusives telling your story in your own words. I don't need to tell you that our newspaper has a readership of millions throughout the world and this would be your chance to share your experience with a wide global audience. It goes without saying that we would handle the whole story with our trademark sensitivity and tact.

*I understand that after what you've been through you might
be reluctant to trust anyone, but, having worked with other
victims in similar situations to yours, I would strongly advise you
not to bottle up your feelings. Many of the victims I have
worked with in the past have said they felt a tremendous release
through sharing what happened to them and have ended up
grateful for the opportunity.*

*I should point out that there is a tremendous amount of
public interest in your story, Jessica, so the press will be focusing
on it whether or not you give your cooperation. How much
better then to have your story told accurately and in a way that
you can control? Though I completely understand that no
amount of money can mitigate for the nightmare you've endured,
we would of course recompense you for your time. In return for a
series of exclusive interviews with photographs plus global
syndication rights we would be prepared to offer you £175,000.
For that we would expect you to sign an immediate and
exclusive contract and commit to spending at least three days
with me at a secret location.*

*I know this might sound extreme, but we have a lot of
experience of dealing with cases like yours and this is the only
way to guarantee that your story is told fully and without
factual errors that might add to your distress.*

*Please reply at your earliest convenience and be assured of our
continuing good wishes.*

The letters all have different wording, and different
numbers after the pound sign, but they are all essentially
saying the same thing. My story, or my 'ordeal', as most of
them prefer to call it, is a valuable commodity. I sit back

against the sofa cushions, surrounded by paper. I've been offered serializations in the biggest newspapers in the country. Someone wants me to write a book. A Hollywood A-lister wants to play me in a film. She's very beautiful and at least a foot taller than me, but that doesn't seem to matter. All in all the various letters on the cushions around me add up to millions of pounds. Even just one of the bigger offers would mean I could quit my job in the archive and move out of my flat.

It means Dominic and Natalie, even Travis, won't have won.

It means I can pay to get rid of that tattoo Natalie did on my hip.

It means I can start to live.

Now that Kim is calmer, the full importance of what she has found is starting to sink in. The photographs linking Dominic to Jessica mean she is vindicated in believing Jessica didn't fit his pattern. There's no doubt he was a very dangerous man, Kim is sure of that. Sometimes at night in Heather's uncomfortable spare bed, she imagines a pair of blue eyes burning at her through the darkness and she has to switch the reading light on. Without question he has caused people to die – his sister, Cesca, Sam. But kidnap? Murder? That wasn't his style.

The two photographs will change the whole direction of the case. The photographs of him with Jessica's niece must be part of some kind of blackmail. Instinctively she thinks of the other photograph on the fake Facebook page, and how she'd been shocked at Jessica's lack of anger against the man

who'd taken advantage of her in this way. Now an explanation is occurring to her. What if that man was Dominic
Lacey? What if that's why she wasn't more outraged –
because she'd already dealt with him? What if that was why
Lacey picked her in the first place, despite her being about
as far from 'his type' as possible – because they already
knew each other?

Later, after she's had time to assimilate the facts, her
conviction grows. She believes Jessica Gold was involved
with Lacey – perhaps only briefly – but long enough for him
to take photographs which he could then use to blackmail
her into coming back for more. A private person like
Jessica, coming from a protective family, would have gone to
extreme lengths to keep those kinds of photographs from
being exposed.

And when the blackmail stopped working, perhaps he
threatened to attack her niece. Kim tries to think herself
into Jessica Gold's shoes, backed into a corner by a
depraved psychopath and now finding out that her niece, to
whom she is clearly very close, is in danger too. By this stage
she might have learned what had happened to his first wife
and would have known that once he had you, he would
never, ever let you go.

So she came up with this elaborate kidnap story to get
rid of him once and for all. Maybe she even had help. Natalie
Lacey also had a lot to gain from seeing Dominic dead. Kim
can't help wondering at the coincidence of her miraculous
return to life at this particular point in time.

And someone finished Lacey off in the hospital. Could
Jessica have been behind that too?

Kim knows this is largely conjecture, but she's convinced she is on to something. The photograph of Dominic Lacey with Jessica Gold's niece is the jigsaw piece that will start slotting everything together.

This is the kind of discovery that doesn't come along often in a detective's life. She will get that promotion. She is sure of it. For a moment she allows herself to imagine the sweet moment of triumph as she's called into the boss's office to be told the news.

Then she forces herself to imagine going home at the end of that day to an empty house. No one to celebrate with. Sean will fight her for custody, she knows it, just as she knows that the erratic hours she'd be working would mean he'd have a good chance of success. And even if he didn't and she had the children half the time or even full-time, would it be fair to leave them with a nanny or an au pair when they could be with a father who loved them? For the first time, Kim allows herself to acknowledge the truth she's been trying to ignore – that being part of a family again means taking a step back, renouncing her ambition.

She takes another look at the two photographs on the screen in front of her. None of the other officers would have spotted Grace Gold. Only she and Martin have ever come across her and she very much doubts Martin even registered the girl's presence. He certainly wouldn't be able to pick her out in a crowd. It's only by fluke that Kim herself noticed her. She scrolls down the contacts list in her phone until she finds Robertson's home number and writes it down on the paper in front of her.

Jessica will be arrested, Kim supposes. And charged either

with murder or attempted murder. Either way she will go to prison.

An image of Liz and Edward Gold pops into Kim's mind. That close-knit family will be torn apart. She imagines them visiting Jessica in prison, shocked at the change in their daughter. Kim knows how tough it is in there for people who are different, for those who don't understand how to fit in.

It goes round and round in her head – the kids, the promotion, Jessica Gold, Grace Gold, Dominic Lacey and the trail of devastation he's left in his wake – until she feels like she's going to explode with it all. She wishes she could speak to Sean. He has a way of calming her down when cases are getting on top of her. Impulsively she brings up his name on her phone, only to remember just in time that she can't call him up for a chat, not unless she's willing to do what he's asked.

She sits at her desk with her head in her hands and her eyes flick between the paper in front of her where Robertson's number is scrawled in blue biro and to her phone where the screen reads simply *My Sean* (to differentiate him from Sean the Plumber a few entries down).

Robertson, Sean, Robertson, Sean. Back and forth until her eyes can no longer focus.

Then she picks up her phone and dials.

EPILOGUE

The new studio is everything the Wood Green flat wasn't. Generous proportions, floor-to-ceiling windows looking out on to a peaceful, leafy Hampstead street. Just one room but full of light and space. Everything in the studio is white – walls, sofa, wide wooden floorboards, rug. Everything is pure and uncontaminated.

It's mid-December and outside, even in this smart area of London, reminders of Christmas are everywhere, from the silver fairy lights threaded through the trees in the front gardens to the heavy wreaths, studded with dried fruit, hanging from wide stained-glass-panelled doors. But here in my flat, there is no trace of the festive season. No cards lined up on the mantelpiece of the white marble fireplace, no pervasive smell of Norwegian spruce. I don't even own a television through which to be bombarded by advertisements for perfume and gold-wrapped chocolates.

I lie back against the sofa cushions and lift my face to the direct winter sunlight that pours through the huge windows. Taking a deep breath in, I close my eyes, giving myself permission to relax completely. And that's when I hear it.

'Hello, sweetheart,' he says, before I can stop him, his voice smooth like treacle. 'You didn't think I'd leave you on your own for Christmas, did you? After everything we went through together?

'*Silly* old Jessica Gold.'